Tye

Dye

Voodoo

To Shannon,
All the best,
Monique Jacob

Monique Jacob

Second Edition, U.S. paperback

Published by Lulu.com

Henrietta, NY, USA

ISBN 978-1-300-03192-5

First Edition, Hard cover

Published by Filidh Publishing, a division of

Lesley Innovations Business Cooperative

Victoria, British Columbia, Canada

ISBN 978-0-9813065-2-0

www.filidhbooks.com

Cover Art by Kimberley Zutz.

Acknowledgements:

It takes a lot of reading to wade through early, muddy drafts and to fine tune the endless re-writes. I'm grateful to those who read Tye Dye Voodoo for pure entertainment, and to the eagle-eyes with their sharp pencils: Edd, Graeme, Irene, Mitch, Gord, Miranda, Sarah, Jenn, Evel, Michelle, Jason, Lucy, Joan, Tara and Diane.

A special thanks to Zoe Duff at Filidh Publishing for taking me on.

this is for chilly bear

PROLOGUE

Winter Solstice, British Columbia

Phineas Marshal swiped his sleeve across his forehead and peeked over his shoulder at the dim windows of the cabin.

Yeah, they were still watching. He swung the hatchet once more and the wood split with a satisfying crack. The two slivers fell to the ground and he huffed out a misty breath, dropping the hatchet to the frosty ground.

Enough stalling.

He gathered an armload of kindling and glanced at the sky as he trudged to the cabin. Dark clouds were thickening and crowding out what was left of the light; there was more snow on the way, and soon. Phin wished he'd thought to double-check the forecast before coming out.

Not that it would have changed their timetable. They'd been packed and waiting when he'd arrived, and eager to be on the road before dark. It had taken the four of them most of the short winter afternoon to find the cabin. He'd had no idea so many roads could be carved into such dense forest.

The cabin door opened as he climbed the rickety steps, and he went in to stack the wood in a pile beside the sooty fireplace. The three women stood in a tight cluster nearby, shivering in the cold room as he built the fire.

"You can just light it and go, dear," said the one called Dora. Or maybe it was Doris, or Norma; he couldn't seem to get them straight. They all had those old lady names. They looked alike with their wrinkly faces and short white hair.

"Does he have to go so soon, Cora?" one asked in a shaky voice. She was shivering the most, and slumped over her cane as if it hurt just to stand. "It really is very cold outside. He could at least warm himself at the fire before he leaves, couldn't he?"

"It will be dark in less than an hour and he's got a long drive ahead of him, Fran," Cora said, gently taking her friend's hand, careful of her swollen knuckles. "We all agreed. Let the boy go. The snow's going to be heavy tonight. We don't want him to have an accident." She led Fran to a rough wooden bench facing the fireplace and helped her to sit. "We'll be okay dear, we always have been."

"I'm just a little nervous, that's all. Cold too. But then I'm always cold these days." Fran rubbed her gnarled fingers together and held them out to the fire that crackled and snapped as it devoured the dry slivers of wood Phin added to it.

The third woman hung back near the door, watching quietly as she clutched her overnight bag tightly to her chest. She hadn't said a single word the entire two-hour trip. Just stared out the car window with a vague smile on her face while her two friends chattered in the back seat and argued about the route they were taking. Phin thought she might be younger than the other two but it was hard to tell. Anyone older than his parents got lumped together as simply old.

He took his time feeding the fire, building it up slowly, allowing it to nearly consume an entire piece of kindling before adding another. It was true that he was anxious to get going before a storm moved in. Even clear of snow he'd barely find his way back through the winding roads that had brought them to the cabin.

But.

Could he just leave these three old ladies out here alone? They'd assured him that they'd be all right and that others would be up to join them soon; they did this sort of thing all the time.

Phin shook his head to clear it and carefully set two split logs onto the grasping flames, watching the wood turn black at the edges. Why should he care anyway? Adults knew what they were doing, right? It was none of his business. He'd promised not to ask any questions, just drive these ladies to their cabin and then leave.

"His mother will be worried if he's late getting back from Cricket Lake. She knows how bad the snow can get this time of

8

year," Cora said to Fran, who was peering nervously into the cabin's shadowy corners. Fran sighed with relief as the fire surged and the light spread, reaching toward the edges of the room.

"I know, Cora, I know. I'm just cold and tired. And maybe a little hungry too. Did Delia bring those sandwiches in from the car?"

"I have them, Fran," Delia said, finally leaving the doorway and stepping closer to the fire. Her nose was red with cold. Her stiff fingers were clumsy as she rummaged through her bag for the packet. She sat next to Fran, setting the sandwiches on the bench beside her. Neither woman made a move to unwrap one. Phin watched them as they stared at the fire, their eyes reflecting sparks from the flickering flames, and he wondered if they'd forgotten he was there.

He was excited about the drive home, even in a snowstorm. Christmas was in four days and he wished he could make the drive last longer than the day or so it would take to get back to Vancouver. He patted his pocket for the tenth time in so many minutes, assuring himself that the keys to the Buick were still there. He realized, as he felt the hard metal edges and heard a muffled jingle, that this simple act of checking for keys, one he'd seen his father do every day, was for him the very essence of being grown up.

He could hardly believe he now owned the Buick. He'd never really owned anything, just his books, model cars and clothes. Now that he and his mother lived in such a cramped apartment, there was no room for anything except the basics. He'd probably have to park the car down the block where he couldn't see it from their windows, but he'd be checking on it constantly.

His Aunt Riva – actually his mom's old school friend – had kept him busy all last summer, fixing the sagging porch on her house, sorting through endless boxes of old magazines and broken bits of dishes, and a dozen other odd jobs around the place. He'd been grateful to be away from home where his parents were tearing his life apart with their messy divorce. By the time he'd come home at the end of August, their house had been sold, his mom was mostly settled into a small two-bedroom apartment and his dad was nowhere to be found. He was glad he'd missed the whole ordeal.

The only drawback to being out of the city for the summer was that there hadn't been many other people his age. Just a bunch of old ladies, drinking tea and whispering as they huddled with Riva, playing with weird cards. There'd been a couple of teenage girls around, but they hardly counted, being only twelve or thirteen. They'd giggled more than they'd spoken and Phin had dismissed them as silly children. They were certainly nothing like the curvy girls at his school.

The cabin was warming up fast and Phin was getting uncomfortable in his heavy jacket and scarf. He walked over to the window to check the light, not surprised to see thick flakes of snow sifting past the glass. He was glad he'd managed to wrestle the heavy chains onto the car's tires before leaving Cricket Lake. He'd need them to get safely back to the highway through the unplowed rural roads.

When Riva had called last week to tell him she wanted him to have her old Buick Special, he couldn't even pretend to politely refuse it. The car was a classic – though not much older than he was – and his hand had trembled when he hung up the phone.

His mom had tried to forbid the trip, but Phin had stood his ground, arguing that he'd need a car next year when he went to college. She had made him promise to stay with friends in Chilliwack overnight, leaving the trip back to Vancouver for daylight hours, but he planned to keep driving as long as the highway was clear.

"I imagine the snow's going to be heavy tonight," Delia said, as she peeled the plastic wrapping from a sandwich. "Should be lovely and quiet. It'll be nice to sleep soundly for a change."

"So who else is coming?" Phin blurted out, unable to resist asking any longer. He may only be a kid to these women, but it seemed crazy to just leave them here. They barely had enough wood cut to keep the fire going a couple of hours. What if the storm got really bad and their friends didn't show up?

"Oh, I imagine someone will appear," Delia said, then looked at Fran in confusion. "Is someone else coming?"

"It's all right dear, we've talked about this before. Everyone who needs to be here will come." Fran frowned at Phin, who looked away and busied himself with the fire.

"But the boy is leaving, right?"

"Don't worry, he isn't staying. He isn't part of this."

Delia smiled at Phin in relief. "That's good then. You'd better go now."

Phin hesitated. None of this seemed right, but he wasn't sure what to do about it. He could leave and go back to Riva, tell her about the storm and the bad roads, but she'd been very clear about going straight home and keeping this a secret. Was it worth losing the car, just to find out that there really was a solstice ritual planned? He'd learned to be wary of rituals, discovering that he was better off not knowing what women did when they gathered in groups.

He'd been wandering through the woods one evening last summer, having left Riva and two of her friends drinking tea and talking in code so he couldn't follow their conversation. The sun had just set. The full moon cast an eerie blue glow onto every leaf in front of Phin as he walked. He'd heard in the village that there were two baby owls living in an old tree stump that were just learning to hunt. He'd been to the clearing only once before, but it was just beyond the oak stand, past the three boulders that looked as if someone had stacked them on purpose.

He'd heard the voices before he saw the women. He hoped they hadn't disturbed the owls. Their voices were barely above a whisper, chanting something in another language. He peered through some low branches; he didn't want to just burst into the clearing and startle them.

His breath caught and he nearly choked, stupefied at the sight of six naked women standing around a small fire, holding hands. He was surprised he hadn't smelled the smoke but that thought dissipated as he realized he could see everything. They were truly naked! His face got warm as he stared. He'd seen nude pictures before but the real thing was unbelievable.

And then he noticed their faces. Each one of the women was at least as old as his mother. He squeezed his eyes shut, but it was too late. His mother's face was now superimposed on all six women. He sputtered out a weak giggle, then turned and ran, hoping they hadn't heard him.

He hadn't recognized any of the women, since his mother's face had so quickly covered theirs, but for weeks afterward he couldn't help blushing whenever any of Riva's friends were around. After that day he'd vowed to avoid women in packs.

Cora walked with him to the door and patted him on the shoulder. "Don't you mind her, young man," she said quietly. "Delia just gets things mixed up sometimes. You go on. We'll take care of her."

"You're sure you'll be all right?" Phin whispered to her. He didn't feel quite right about leaving them, but the Buick beckoned and he let Cora push him gently out the door.

He swiped his arm over the front and back windows of the blue hardtop and dropped into the driver's seat, kicking sticky snow from his boots before he slammed the door. He rolled his window down partway so his breath wouldn't cloud the windshield. He couldn't help grinning at how eagerly the car roared to life. He loved the deep rumble of its powerful eight cylinders. He had to navigate the rutted driveway in reverse and even with the chains on the tires the car kept slewing towards the ditch. He went slowly. Those old ladies wouldn't be much help if he got stuck and needed a push.

The snow was falling more heavily. It would be very dark soon, probably in less than an hour. He hoped to get to the main highway before then. That meant he had to fully concentrate on the trip ahead which, thankfully, would distract him from listening to the frantic voice at the back of his mind demanding he not leave the women behind. Phin paused for a last glimpse of the cabin, squinting past the wipers that barely kept up with the snow. He could just make out three shadowy figures watching him through the cabin's dirty window. Moments before he rounded a curve and lost sight of them, one raised a hand in farewell.

PART ONE

Twenty-five years later

ONE

Late Spring, Cricket Lake, British Columbia

Phin ducked into the narrow lane that led to the back of the house. He was nervous about going in the front door. The kitchen entrance would be less conspicuous. He hoped. Stiff branches from an overgrown cedar hedge forked into the laneway, forcing him to press up against the house as he eased by. The house was smaller than he expected, more like a run-down cottage than the tidy bungalow he remembered. It had once been dark blue with white trim but had faded over many years to shades of watery grey.

Phin hitched up his pack, settling it more comfortably on his back. The padding had leaked out of the frayed straps and the rough fabric chafed his shoulders, more so this time since he'd stuffed everything he owned into the thin canvas sack. There hadn't been much to take – a couple of changes of clothes, his few books and his carving tools. He'd left the rest in the damp basement room he'd been renting by the week. Let the manager deal with it. Phin was sure he'd soon find someone else desperate enough to take the overpriced room with the leaky plumbing.

He stopped at the house's sagging porch and watched a pair of sparrows stuff bits of fluff into a crack in the eaves before squeezing themselves into their home for the night. There were many such cracks, probably with an assortment of critters living in various parts of the house, he thought as he climbed the creaking steps.

A real fixer-upper. Phin hated fixer-uppers unless they were the next contract. He wouldn't know if this one would pay off until after he'd put a lot of work into it. The paint was peeling, the roof dipped in one corner and several windows were cracked. Riva had really let the place fall apart. He ran his hand along the railing. It wobbled and creaked, offering no support whatsoever. He leaned his weight on it and the nails pulled out of the wall, shrieking in protest. Phin gave it a hard yank, and let it drop to the rotted floor.

He tried the door. It was locked. The lawyer who had finally managed to track him down two weeks ago hadn't given him a key. In fact, the man had been in a big hurry to get the papers signed and out of his sight. Phin figured the lawyer hadn't been paid much to start with, and hadn't appreciated the time spent tracing the whereabouts of his client's heir.

It had been a wet spring so far, the winter rains dragging on far into April. The house would probably be damp and cold. It was likely that the power would be off as well, so no lights or heat. He looked back the way he'd come. The lane was empty and rapidly filling with shadows as night crept in. He could just see the edge of another house where lights glowed in the window facing him. Phin wondered if the same family still lived there – mostly women from what he remembered.

There was a bed and breakfast across from the bus stop, just off the highway where it crossed Main Street. It might be better to go back and stay there for the night, come back tomorrow. At least he'd get a warm bed and food in the morning.

No, he'd come this far, might as well get it over with. The window in the door was made up of four smaller panes of glass and two were cracked. Phin jabbed his walking stick at one, clearing out the shards. He was going to have to replace the window anyway. He reached through the gap and turned the deadbolt.

The door was stuck and the wood squealed when Phin put his shoulder against it and shoved. He stumbled into the kitchen, boots crunching on the broken glass. He ran a hand along the wall until he found a switch. The room filled with light immediately and he heaved a sigh of relief. He hadn't realized until that moment how exhausted he was. He eased his pack off his shoulders, groaning as his stiff muscles protested. A long hot shower would take care of most of those aches.

The kitchen was pretty much as he remembered it. All the cupboard doors were missing, exposing stacks of dishes, boxes and jars of dried goods. It was one of the jobs that Riva had given to Phin the summer he'd spent here when he was seventeen. He'd thought then that it was a stupid thing to do, that everything would always get dusty and have to be cleaned more often. But she'd insisted, saying that most kitchens are full of closed doors, as if they have something to hide. He had just done as he was asked.

He opened the fridge on the off chance that there might at least be a jug of juice. To his surprise, the fridge was almost full. At least three casserole dishes vied for shelf space with several plastic containers holding what looked like potato salad and something bright orange that might turn out to be dessert. He pulled out three containers at random and set them on the table.

Phin wondered who could have known he was coming, feeling self-conscious as he peered out the kitchen window. Had a neighbour noticed the lights had come on in Riva's house? A caretaker with the key to the back door he'd just busted into? The gloom outside had deepened and a thin drizzle now beaded the glass. He shivered, glad he'd made it before dark.

He pried the lid off one of the containers. It looked like potato salad, though it seemed more yellow than he thought it should be. His mother had sometimes put a bit of mustard in hers for zing so it was probably alright. He scooped up a big forkful and shoved it in his mouth. He hadn't eaten since lunch and his stomach growled in anticipation just as his taste buds detected something not quite right. His half-starved momentum kept him chewing a couple more times before swallowing quickly.

"What the hell?" he muttered. He sniffed at the bright yellow salad, then drew his head back sharply. "Curry? I hate curry.

16

Who puts curry in potato salad?" He slapped the lid back onto the dish, and opened another plastic tub.

Cold chicken. As he sank his teeth into a drumstick, he realized he'd been fooled again. The drumstick not only had a funny taste, it had a funny shape. Rabbit, maybe? He'd only had it once before. He didn't mind the taste, just seemed weird when you expected chicken. He shrugged, then froze mid-bite at a sudden noise from another room.

Was there someone else in the house? What if he'd made a mistake? Could the place have been sold? He quietly set down the food, picked up the walking stick he'd left leaning against the wall and crept toward the living room. Maybe the lawyer had been wrong or worse yet, lying. It hadn't made sense that Riva had left the house to him, someone she hadn't seen in over two decades and not even a relative. So now he'd not only broken into a stranger's house, but also helped himself to their food. Why else would the fridge be full?

That would be just his kind of luck. He was always on the edge of disaster, at dead-end jobs and in seedy apartments. He'd never managed to feel like he fit anywhere, though he had to admit he hadn't tried very hard. He'd just always preferred his own company and shied away from forming ties. He had no siblings and his mother had died when he was a teenager. He hadn't seen his father in more than ten years, had no idea if the creep was still alive. Didn't care.

Phin held the stick close to his side, ready to raise it if necessary, but not wanting to appear dangerous if he turned out to be the one trespassing in someone else's house. The feel of the smooth wood calmed him, the gnarled root at the top fitting comfortably in his palm. The wood was carved, the rough designs merging in a jumbled geometrical pattern that completely covered its length. It was the third one he'd made.

He'd grown tired of whittling tiny dogs and horses, something he'd done most of his life, ever since his father had given him his first knife when he was a boy. He'd always been able to sell his tiny creatures for extra cash, but lately had been longing for something bigger, something more substantial. His hands had tingled when he'd run them along the rough bark of the four-foot long alder branch he'd brought home from a walk in the forest last fall. His knife had etched deeply into the wood, the broader strokes and cuts much more satisfying than the small nicks and scratches he'd ventured before.

He inched along the hallway, listening intently for another sound. He'd made enough noise coming in that anyone already there would have heard him.

There was a shelf running the full length of the hall, just about eye level. A thin layer of carpeting had been glued to the wood. As he came to the end of the hall and into the living room he flicked a light switch. Two floor lamps at opposite ends of the room showed him that the shelf continued along the length of the wall to his right. Several gaps were cut into it and connected with diagonal ramps leading to other, lower shelves.

They were bare, so not for books. Phin tried to picture what sort of use they might have but could only think of rolling a ball along one shelf and down a ramp to another. It would be tricky to get the ball rolling straight enough so it wouldn't fall off after picking up speed on the ramp. Riva hadn't seemed the sort to make a game so elaborate but the entire living room had had a makeover.

Twenty-five years before, the room had been filled with comfortable overstuffed furniture, dozens of plants and Riva's clunky, floor model television. Now the room looked like some sort of fortune-telling den. Every lamp was draped with a colourful scarf, every available surface cluttered with assorted candles, books and spun glass figurines. There was even a crystal ball sitting on a velvet-covered table. He noted that the windows had been hung with heavy drapes that looked as if they could easily conceal someone. He poked at the cloth with the staff, raising a cloud of dust. He pulled all the scarves off the lamps to brighten the room but saw no one hiding behind any of the delicate furniture that had replaced the comfy sofas he remembered.

He pushed aside a beaded curtain that covered the doorway to the tiny room he had slept in that teenaged summer. It had been converted into a study, with three walls covered in books from floor to ceiling. A tiny desk held a phone and a laptop computer with a scratched cover.

Phin backed out of the cramped room. He turned around abruptly at a low rumbling sound and nearly poked his eye on the corner of the carpeted shelf. The rumble rose to a snarl as he came face to face with a huge orange cat lying on the shelf. He yelped and stumbled backwards, bumping his staff against a small table covered in miniature glass animals.

The table tipped over and the glass figures shattered as they hit the floor in a jumbled heap, their tinkles mingling with the startled hiss of the cat. It turned and disappeared around the corner. When had Riva gotten a cat? There hadn't been one when he was here last. Phin hated cats. It would have to go. No wonder his eyes felt itchy, he thought, as he rubbed them fiercely. At least the noise he'd heard had only been a cat, not someone coming home to find a prowler eating his leftovers.

He kept an eye out for the cat while he pushed the broken bits of glass against the wall with the toe of his boot. He'd sweep it up when he found a broom. He'd only been in the house half an hour and had made two piles of broken glass already. Feeling wearier than ever, he dragged himself back into the kitchen to finish the container of cold rabbit, wishing whoever had left it had thought to stock the fridge with beer as well.

TWO

Phin climbed out of the shower stall, mindful of the shifting tiles under his bare feet. Mildewed grouting made a blackened frame around each stained ceramic square. The entire stall would have to be ripped out and re-tiled. He made a mental note to add the chore to his list, which had grown long in the twelve hours or so since he'd arrived. There was hardly any part of the house that did not need mending, replacing or painting. There were water stains on nearly every ceiling and most of the carpeting was worn thin.

At least there was plenty of hot water, he thought, as he swiped his hand across the misted mirror over the sink. He scowled at his watery image while he towelled himself dry. His black hair and beard – shot through with more silver than he cared to see – were both long-past needing a trim. Phin wondered if Riva had any sharp scissors in the huge sewing chest that hulked in the corner of the bedroom.

He'd wandered the house all night, reluctant to climb into a dead woman's bed. So he'd snooped and poked around, getting used to the idea that he now owned all this junk. He was sure that Riva had never thrown away anything in her life. Every closet in the house was crammed to the ceiling with unlabelled boxes and bags of old clothing. He'd groaned when he realized what a job it was going to be to prepare the house for selling. He'd have to rent a truck to haul away countless loads of junk then spend the rest of the summer making the place presentable.

He had found a stack of flattened cardboard boxes under the bed and had already filled two of them with candleholders and incense burners. He'd also collected the several dozen glass figurines she'd had on display all over the house and covered the kitchen table in a glitter of miniature animals. He'd carefully wrapped each one in a tissue and nestled them all into a third box.

Phin raked his fingers through his hair and tied it back with a short length of leather. It hung down to the middle of his back, dripping on the floor as he padded to the kitchen.

He rummaged through the kitchen cupboards, hoping to find some coffee, but came up with only herbal tea or roasted coffee substitutes that smelled like roots. Grocery shopping was going to need its own list. Maybe the hardware store would let him run a tab for supplies while he fixed the place up. There'd be more than enough from the sale of the house to pay off the bill later.

He set the kettle on the stove and threw two pouches of black tea into a mug. It would be bitter, but at least he'd get some sort of caffeine jolt. As he waited for the water to boil, he stared out the window into the yard.

The greenhouse he'd helped Riva build twenty-five years ago was still standing at the back of the property, though several of its glass panes were cracked. He could see plants inside, leaves plastered against the glass and bright blotches of color. He wondered who had been watering them since Riva died. Probably some neighbour, maybe the same one who had put food in the fridge.

Phin's stomach growled at the thought of food and he opened the refrigerator door and peered inside hopefully. He pulled out another plastic container. Some sort of meatloaf. Dumping the congealed mass onto the counter, he found a sharp knife and cut off several thick slices.

Sliding them into a cast iron frying pan, he lit a second gas burner and set the pan onto the blue flame. Soon, a gentle sizzling and a tantalizing meaty odour filled the small kitchen. Phin poured boiling water over his two teabags and set the table for one. There were plenty of dishes, most of them delicate, all of them covered in dainty flower patterns.

He flipped over his meat slices, took a sip of his tea. It was scalding, very strong. He hadn't found any sugar, only honey and molasses, so he up-ended the honey bottle over the mug and squeezed a generous dollop into his tea. He stirred it and took a tentative sip. Still too bitter, now too sweet. He'd never liked honey, but he was eager to get at least some sort of caffeine trickling through his veins, so he steeled himself and drained the mug in several burning gulps.

The meatloaf smelled wonderful, so he cut a huge bite and crammed it into his mouth. He chewed twice and stopped. It was crumbly and tasteless, but he choked it down as he reached for his mug before remembering that it was empty. He filled it with tepid water from the tap and washed down the dry lump of meat sticking in his throat. He dug through the fridge until he found a small bottle of hot sauce. He doused the rest of the meat on his plate with the red sauce, and salted it heavily before taking another bite. Didn't help. Now it tasted like salty spicy cardboard.

Phin was scraping the rest of it into the garbage can when he noticed the orange cat sitting in the corner. It watched him with narrowed eyes and flattened ears.

"I should feed it to you," Phin told the cat. "This stuff is so bad it would even scare you off." The thought of feeding the hot-sauce-laced meat to the cat struck him as funny. He snickered as he put the empty plate into the sink. "You don't look like you've been starving, but if no one shows up to feed you by dinner time I guess I'll have to toss you something." The cat twitched its ears as another cat sauntered into the room. It was larger than the orange cat, its long jet-black fur making it seem bigger than it probably was. They rubbed their faces against each other then sat side by side glaring at Phin. He eyed them warily as they stared at him, unblinking. Two cats. The lawyer hadn't mentioned one cat, let alone two.

He'd have to discourage these two from staying. The shelves and ramps that they used for running throughout the house would have to go too, though it would take days to tear it all out and repair the damaged walls. Giving the animals their own raised highway had probably kept them from being underfoot all the time but he'd tolerate them even less at eye level.

The black cat sauntered toward Phin, its velvet nose delicately sniffing the air and its claws clicking on the linoleum. Phin balled up a towel and threw it at the cat. It scampered off with a hiss, the orange cat following close behind. Stupid cats. He'd call them Stupid One and Stupid Two, though he couldn't think of any reason why he'd ever need to call them at all.

Phineas heated up the kettle again for more tea. It hadn't satisfied his craving for caffeine the way a strong cup of coffee would have, but it would have to do for now. He was still hungry, so he took a package labeled lasagna out of the freezer and put it into the microwave to thaw. He paced through the house while he waited, assessing how much work had to be done. He'd need at least four more large boxes just for the junk in the living room.

The microwave dinged to let him know breakfast was ready. His mouth watered at the thought of lasagna, dripping with cheese and tangy with tomato sauce. But when he peeled off the lid, he smelled bacon. And eggs. He picked through the layers with a fork. Cheese, noodles and tomato sauce, just as he'd expected, but underneath the noodles were fluffy scrambled eggs. Under the eggs were slices of bacon layered over more noodles.

It might look strange, he thought, but it smells great, so he carried it into the living room and cleared a space on the scarred coffee table. He sat on the sofa he'd dragged up from the basement, put his feet up, and ate breakfast as he tried to make sense of the woman he'd known only briefly, so long ago. Riva's house had seemed normal then, as far as he could tell, anyway. There may have been candles but nothing like what confronted him now. A quick count had given him at least three dozen candles in holders and half as many incense burners, though some were disguised as ornaments.

Phin got up for another look at a trio of colourful dragons. The three ceramic bodies twined sinuously around each other, their wings folded back and their snouts pointed upwards. They howled at the sky like a pack of wolves. An incense stick poked out of each snout. When lit, the three dragons would appear to breathe smoke.

Cool. He'd keep it, though it felt strange to think of the dragons as already his, like everything else in the house.

He'd never really owned anything of great value. Now he had a whole house. It was like finding a treasure chest, something he'd dreamed of as a child. He picked up a photograph in a tarnished silver frame. It was of a much younger Riva than he remembered, many years before he'd met her. She smiled radiantly at the camera, her plump cheeks surrounded by blond curls, holding tightly to a striped cat that hung from her arms with a look of resignation on its whiskered face.

Phin frowned at the photo, reminded again of the two cats roaming the house. He could feel them watching him. He set the photo down with a clatter and went to inspect the aquarium against the far wall. He'd heard its pump grumbling all night but now a buzzing fluorescent tube had joined in, tinting the water pink. It sat on a tall wrought iron stand that brought it up to nearly eye level. Phin peered through the glass at the plants waving in the current of the pump. He didn't see any fish; nothing moved but the greenery.

A locked cabinet sat next to the fishless tank, tall and narrow with chipped filigreed edges. The lock was flimsy and snapped open easily when he jammed his pocketknife into it and twisted. Two shelves held several dozen leather-bound books which, when he flipped through a few, turned out to be journals. Each was dated and signed inside the front cover in Riva's tiny, cramped script. She'd evidently started writing them in her teens and the last entry was only a few months old. He put them back for later.

Phin carried the rest of the bacon-and-egg lasagna back through the kitchen and out onto the porch. The sun was high and warm on his face as he surveyed the neglected yard. Sparrows flitted through apple trees that showed signs of insect damage. They probably hadn't been pruned for years and the stunted leaves and sparse blooms had lost the battle with the local caterpillars. At least the birds would be fed. He wondered if the cats hunted the birds. The trees fed the caterpillars, which fed the birds that the cats then killed and ate. Fair enough.

The greenhouse at the back corner of the yard drew Phin's attention again. The glass panes were misted with condensation that blurred the splashes of yellow, pink and purple peeking out among the greenery.

He left the empty dish and headed for the tiny potting shed that sat against the leaning fence, halfway between the porch and the greenhouse. Its latch was broken and rusted, with the door gaping open. Dirt-encrusted clay pots cluttered most of the available floor space and a variety of rusted garden tools hung from hooks on the unpainted walls.

Next door, the greenhouse door swung open easily and he stepped into warm, moist air, pungent with damp earth and a tantalizing jumble of flowery scents. Planters and pots of all sizes jostled with plastic yogurt tubs and an assortment of chipped crockery. They all brimmed with vegetation; Phin recognized tomato, squash and several tangled pea vines among the colourful clusters of flowers.

Long twisted rags sprouted from each pot like aerial roots. They hung over the sides and drooped into one of many pails of water sitting under the benches and tables. He prodded one of the hanging bits of cloth and found it sodden. The pails would only have to be topped up every few days, probably by the same caretaker who had fed the cats and left provisions.

The greenhouse was even more rundown than it had looked from the outside. Nearly half the glass panes were damaged, their wooden supports starting to crumble, spongy where he chipped at them with a fingernail. One good windstorm and the whole thing would probably come crashing to the ground.

Phin was deciding whether the greenhouse was worth salvaging when he spotted a leaf at the back of the greenhouse that looked familiar. He battled his way to the back, squeezing past damp leaves that smacked him in the face.

A smile slowly spread as he gazed at the two marijuana plants sitting side by side on a narrow shelf. Their leaves drooped in the humid environment and they looked half dead. They were not going to thrive in eight-inch pots. They needed space for a good root system if they were going to get big enough to grow buds.

He picked up the two pots and cradled them to his chest as he fought his way back through the greenery and out the door. He scanned the yard, looking for a likely place to perform a transplant.

On the other side of the yard, facing the shed, was a rectangular patch of weeds. It was surrounded by identical weeds, but was set apart from the rest by being slightly elevated and enclosed by planks of wood set on edge, like a low box. Phin set the two plants down, and went back to the potting shed for a shovel. Rusted or not, it would still turn soil. He also rolled out the wheelbarrow, its wheels squeaking loudly enough to silence the birds for several minutes.

The day was growing even warmer, and he took off his shirt before starting to pull out the knee-high weeds. Some of them came up easily, their shallow roots barely keeping them upright in the first place. Others were more resistant, but it felt good to be working outdoors instead of organizing a house full of old-lady-fortune-teller junk.

When he'd cleared the patch of the biggest weeds, Phin wiped sweat off his forehead with the back of his hand, smearing dirt on his face and in his hair. He moved the overflowing wheelbarrow off to the side, picked up the shovel and began to dig.

THREE

Dee Berkeley walked along the dusty sidewalk leading up to her best friend's house. Make that her late best friend. In the month since Riva had died, Dee had dropped by daily to feed the cats but now her steps slowed as she chided herself for still thinking of the little house as Riva's.

She shifted the plastic bag she carried from one hand to the other so that she could wipe her damp palms on her work pants. The bag bumped her legs as she walked, radiating warmth from the dozen freshly baked rolls inside. They'd come out of the oven not twenty minutes ago and she'd taken her break early to deliver them while they were still warm.

Mabel had been certain that Phineas had arrived last night and had suggested the rolls. Dee couldn't decide if she wanted Mabel to be right or wrong. When she'd heard that Phin had inherited Riva's house, she'd waited for days for him to show up. Then the weeks had dragged by with no sign of his arrival and everyone had gone about their business again. The lawyer had appointed Dee caretaker of the house until the appearance of its new owner. She'd heard nothing until last week, when the lawyer called to let them know he'd finally found the heir to Riva's estate.

Some estate, she thought, as she picked up her pace again. The roof leaked when it rained, none of the doors closed properly and the furnace only worked on cold and dry days, not cold and wet. Riva had also been certain that termites had begun to eat her house from the inside out. Riva's house was no prize, but it was familiar and Dee missed the cats.

For the past week she'd been a wreck, waiting for Phin to show up. And now her heart was racing and her palms were slick with perspiration again. She took several calming breaths. She'd been wavering between giddy joy and terror at the thought of seeing Phineas Marshal again. She had to keep reminding herself that they were now mostly strangers. That she was a grown woman still obsessed with a teenage crush from twenty-five years ago.

"Get a grip, girl," she murmured. She brushed a loose strand of hair off her forehead, wishing she had at least taken the time to go home and change before marching out here. Her clothes were stained and floured from her morning's work. The ovens had been going full force for hours before the sun came up. Their relentless heat had wilted her hair and left a deep flush in her cheeks that she was sure was still a bright glowing pink.

A breeze came up and she lifted her chin and fanned her neck with her free hand. The wind rustled the new leaves and excited the birds in the branches into a frenzied chatter. Dee wondered if Phineas would change the house or the yard much. Would he cut down Riva's trees?

She was close enough now to see the front edge of the house, with its roof missing an entire corner of shingles. They'd blown off three weeks ago, when a freakish windstorm had torn up shingles from half the neighbouring houses. She would point it out to him so he could have it repaired. She wasn't used to talking to men, especially a man she'd been having dreams about since she was practically a girl.

Dee wished, as she had every day for the past several weeks, that Riva was still alive and that she would be waiting for her in the little house. Though Riva had been more than twenty years Dee's senior they had always been close friends, more like sisters than neighbours. Everyone had been amazed that the house hadn't been left to Dee, but Dee was the only one who hadn't been surprised. She'd realized, with more than a little embarrassment, that Riva had ensured the return of the only man who'd ever meant anything to Dee.

The last time she'd seen Riva they'd been sitting in her kitchen, drinking tea and talking about the future. It was an ordinary visit, one of hundreds just like it, until they'd finished drinking their tea and looked into each other's cups at the moist leaves left on the bottom. They'd laughed hysterically as they both insisted they saw a tall, dark stranger. They'd joked about dark strangers before. In fact, any blob of wet tea leaves that vaguely resembled a man was fair game.

Riva had taken out her tarot cards and shuffled the deck. She'd read the cards for both of them, again seeing the dark stranger in Dee's cards. Her own reading had been murky and confused, showing only dark, with no strangers. Two days later she was dead.

Dee could hear a rhythmic thumping now, coming from the other side of the house. She peeked around the corner just as the thump became a ringing clang followed by a string of muffled curses.

He was wearing cut-off jeans and scuffed work boots. Perspiration ran in rivulets down his broad back, carving channels through the dust he'd raised while digging in the garden. His long black hair was tied back, but most of it had come loose and was either waving around his head in the breeze, or clinging to his damp shoulders in sweaty clumps. He squatted over the garden with both hands deep in a hole he'd dug, prying out a rock. He finally wrenched it out with a grunt and stood to set in on the pile, turning in her direction.

She pulled back quickly, but he hadn't noticed her. His face, above an unkempt beard, was streaked with dirt. A scrape over his left eyebrow had stopped bleeding but had left crusted blood mixed with the dirt.

Was this Phineas? She tried to compare him to the boy she'd known so many summers ago, but her mind couldn't link this dirty caveman to the handsome, bashful boy she remembered.

Phin pressed his hands to the small of his back and stretched, feeling the strain in every muscle. He inspected his hands, wincing as he gently poked the swollen, red blisters forming on his palms. Black dirt was deeply lodged under his fingernails and his knuckles were scraped from wrestling large rocks out of the soil. He rubbed the back of his neck with one hand, turning his head left and right to ease the tension. He ached all over, feeling old and out of shape. He was thirsty, too, but knew that if he stopped now to go inside for a drink, the pull of a hot shower would be too alluring and he'd abandon the project for another day.

He'd cleared the entire plot of weeds and had turned over the soil, breaking up the biggest chunks of dirt and hauling out an enormous pile of rocks. More than enough space. Time to plant.

He glanced at the two little plants sitting patiently in their pots. He imagined their relief at finally getting to spread their roots in a real garden. It would be worth every blister and strained muscle to watch them grow into mature marijuana plants. They were surrounded by the many pots and flats of vegetable and flower plants that he'd hauled out of the greenhouse. He stretched again, feeling several joints crackle in protest.

Phin had no idea if Riva's friends had known about the illicit plants she'd kept at the back of the greenhouse, so he planned to surround them with the tomato plants and flowers to disguise their distinctive leaves.

He'd seen several bags of soil conditioners and fertilizers in the greenhouse and wondered if he should mix them in before planting. His mother had kept a big garden out behind their house when he was growing up. Every autumn they'd loaded several large buckets into the truck and driven to the beach, where the tide had deposited huge mounds of sludgy seaweed on the shore. They'd used rakes to transfer it from the sand into the buckets, and Phin had had to fight the nausea that threatened to overcome him each time he'd accidentally touched the slimy, green-black leaves. His mother had revelled in the scents of the sea, deeply inhaling the reek and rot of the coast, claiming that it invigorated her innards. This had always made him laugh, as she knew it would, and took his mind off his stomach.

At home, they'd spread the seaweed thickly on the flowerbeds and the huge vegetable patch that would, at that time of year, have been harvested down to bare earth. His father had complained for weeks that the truck and the yard stank of rotted fish and brine. He threatened every year to pave over the entire property. Phin's mother would simply blow him a kiss and prepare him another fabulous dinner made from food she'd grown that summer.

She had been stunned the day Phin's father had come home from work early to declare that he wanted a divorce. He'd already made arrangements for a realtor to come appraise the house for sale.

It was early spring and her mail order seed packets had arrived the week before. She'd spent an entire afternoon packing soil into tiny pots. Phin's job had been to press a tiny seed into the moist dirt of each pot.

His mother had inspected each one daily, checking the moisture of the soil, watching for mould. This had always been a magical time for Phin when he was younger as she named and described each one for him, drawing a little picture of the plant and taping it to the front of its pot. She'd kept up the habit even though Phin was seventeen that year and had protested that he knew the difference between a tomato plant and a zucchini.

None of the seeds had sprouted yet when Phin's dad made his announcement. They were still days from surfacing. After his father had gone upstairs to pack a bag, Phin had watched his mother sadly drop each little pot into the garbage.

Phin scowled at the jumble of plants. Too many plants. He would never fit them all into this plot. Everything about Riva's house took so much effort. She'd collected and hoarded as much junk outdoors as she had inside.

Deciding that nobody needed twelve tomato plants, he put half of them beside the house, along with all the big gangly plants that he knew would run riot if given the slightest room. Phin hated all squash-type vegetables and wasn't taking the risk they would take over the garden. He carefully set the two marijuana plants in holes near the front of the garden so he could watch them from the kitchen window. He planted a tomato on either side of them with a couple more behind. Anyone looking closely would spot the deception, but it would do for basic camouflage at a distance.

He jammed an old trellis he found in the shed into the centre of the plot. He'd transplant all the bean and pea vines around it and then fan out from there, alternating vegetable plants with yellow and purple flowers. He wasn't certain how much room each plant needed but could always pull out a few later if they got too big.

And then he spotted the cat.

It was a different cat again from the two he had seen indoors, a scruffy grey tom with pale grey eyes. It boldly marched right up to the opposite corner of the garden patch and dug its own little hole. It kept Phin in its sights while it dug, not even looking away when it squatted awkwardly.

Another stupid cat. Phin's field of vision narrowed to the spot where the mangy beast was digging up his hard work. Without taking his eyes off the cat he bent down, scooped up a pebble and let fly with the accuracy of a childhood spent pitching for little league. As the pebble bounced hard off its forehead the cat gave an ear-searing screech, staggered a bit and sped away. Phin picked up another pebble to throw at its retreating back but a shout from behind stopped him short.

Damn! Someone had caught him throwing rocks at their cat. Not a good way to meet the neighbours. He dropped the pebble at his feet and sheepishly turned toward where the shout had come from.

She must have come from the front of the house just in time to catch him with the rock in his hand. Oh well, he thought, good thing I'll be selling this place and moving on soon.

He watched her approach, swinging a plastic bag that she held tightly in her fist. The other hand was fisted too, with a finger raised and pointing at him. She was dressed all in white, blouse, pants and shoes, as if it were a uniform. She could have been a nurse, or maybe she'd been cleaning one of the nearby houses.

The woman surged towards him, backlit by the afternoon sun, her face hidden in shadow, light brown hair highlighted and sparkling as it flew behind her in the sunlight.

"What kind of person throws rocks at defenseless animals?" she shouted as she neared. "Would you react the same way if you'd seen a child digging in your yard?"

"Whoa, lady," Phin said, throwing his hands up as her pointing finger came close enough to jab him in the chest. He backed up a few steps, mindful of the plants behind him. "I'm really sorry," he tried again, bringing his hands down when he saw she had stopped her advance. "It just seems there are cats everywhere, in the house, in the garden, and I can't seem to shake them."

"So that gives you the right to throw rocks at their heads, is that it?"

"Yes. I mean no! I'm sorry if I hurt your cat, but can you try to keep it in its own yard?"

"This *is* its own yard."

"But that would mean three cats living here. Who the hell keeps three cats?"

"Well, there are actually five cats here." She put down the bag she'd been carrying. Phin couldn't ignore the delicious aroma of fresh-baked bread wafting from the bag. His stomach growled loudly, but she didn't seem to notice as she kept her sights on the tree behind which the cat had disappeared.

"What do you mean five cats living here? In this house? My house?"

"There were nine that hung around the house all last winter, but four of them went feral as soon as the snow melted and we hardly see them anymore." She narrowed her eyes at him. "I've left a bunch of notes on the fridge about the cats' feeding schedule and all the phone numbers to call to put the house bills in your name."

"I'm supposed to feed them? Not a chance. I'm allergic to cats. I hate cats."

She faced him squarely with her fists pressed to her hips, as if barely keeping herself from using them on him. Her chest heaved as she breathed deeply, either from her walk or because of her anger. Phin couldn't take his eyes off her blouse buttons as they stretched to their limit with each breath, offering a view of white lace and creamy skin. He realized he was staring but his brain was still trying to register the reality of five cats. Then his stomach growled again and he was able to tear his gaze away, grateful for the distraction. He shook his head and smiled as he thought of the bread distracting him from the breasts that were distracting him from the cats. All this and he still didn't know the woman's name.

"I'm glad someone thinks this is funny," she said. "Some of these cats are delicate creatures. If they get sick, you'll be responsible." She brushed past him and walked towards the back of the yard. "Hercules, come on out sweetie," she called as she approached.

"Hercules?" Phin asked, still eyeing the bag on the ground. He wondered if she had brought it for him and whether it would be rude to peek inside.

"That's his name. Riva named all the cats after constellations. The others are Pegasus, Orion, Castor and Pollux. They're all males, except Peg."

"It was easier just to call them all Stupid," Phin muttered.

"Didn't that damn lawyer tell you about the cats? They're attached to the house. They live here. He assured us that you'd be told about them and that you'd look after them." Her eyes were pale blue marbles as she faced him, their pupils mere pinpoints in the bright light. Her skin glowed a moist pink in the heat.

"The lawyer told me there'd be a caretaker. Is that you? I'm Phineas Marshal." He held out his hand for her to shake, but immediately drew it back when he realized how dirty it was.

"I know who you are," she said tartly, eyeing his dirty hand. "I'm Dee Berkeley. We met when we were kids, teenagers I guess. You were here that summer. I think your parents were divorcing?"

Phin tilted his head and studied her, trying to see her as she would have been twenty-five years ago. He didn't remember anyone his own age when he was here, but there was a small clutch of younger girls that had giggled and squealed every time he'd passed anywhere near them. The neighbourhood had been predominantly female back then, though none his age had shown themselves, if they'd existed. "You'd have been about twelve or thirteen then, right?"

"Definitely thirteen," Dee said with a wry smile. "I'll never forget that year. You probably never heard about it, but that winter three older women just disappeared from the area. My grandmother was one of them."

Phin's heartbeat lurched and he pressed a hand to his chest. Three older women. Disappeared in the winter. Never seen again. He hadn't realized he was staring until Dee looked at him curiously.

"Are you all right?"

He sucked in a deep breath, trying to appear calm. "It must have happened almost exactly when my mother died. She was hit by a bus the winter after I was here, just after Christmas."

"Omigosh! I had no idea. Riva never mentioned it. We never heard about you again after that summer."

"Yeah, it was pretty crazy. My parents had divorced that summer. That's why I'd been shipped off here while they figured themselves out. They sold the house before I got back then I went to live with my mother in an apartment downtown." Phin started to relax as he realized she didn't know he'd come back to Cricket Lake that winter. The three women had lied to everyone. They'd known that he'd be eager to believe their story. That he'd be happy to take his new car and go home and forget about them.

And he *had* forgotten, at least for a while.

The morning his mother was killed – less than two weeks after he came home with the car – he'd been shovelling the walkway around their apartment building. The owner was an aging man who had been happy to give them a break on the rent in exchange for work around the place. He'd given Phin a key to the tool room along with a list of ongoing chores to keep up, only asking him to keep a log of the hours worked. It was easy work and didn't interfere with his other job at the corner convenience mart where he worked Saturdays for an actual paycheque.

It had stormed all night and the snow lay in soft, shin-deep drifts, with a slick layer of ice underneath. Cars had been sliding into one another since the sun had come up. Phin had stopped noticing the scream of police and ambulance sirens as they threaded their way through the bogged-down traffic.

He'd called his father that evening, two hours past the time his mother had been due home. He'd been reluctant to contact him as they hadn't spoken since summer but he had been desperate and didn't know what to do. His father had been drunk, as usual, but had made several calls and found her at the Merciful

Sisters Hospital. She'd had no identification on her when the ambulance had arrived, so there'd been no one to call. Her purse was found later, buried in a snow bank at the scene of the accident.

"What did the police think happened to your grandmother and her friends?" Part of him was curious to know more about the disappearance. A smarter part wished he would just shut up.

"Who knows? There were stories about kidnappings, but who'd kidnap three old ladies? No one contacted us for a ransom, anyway. And my grandmother wasn't really all that old, the youngest of the bunch, really. She was only sixty-eight, but the other two were in their eighties at least." Dee squinted at the sun, checked her watch. "Oh no, I've got to get back to the bakery. I've already been gone too long. Brent will have a fit." She strode to where she'd left the plastic bag and thrust it at Phin.

"Ah, thanks," he said, smiling as his stomach clenched and growled again. He peered into the bag, closing his eyes as he inhaled the warm, rich scent of bread. "Did you bake these?"

"Yeah, I've worked at the bakery in town most of my life. It's a dump and a fire trap but the only one we've got." She cupped her hand over her eyes and looked back at the house. "That reminds me, we had a bad storm a few weeks back. You might want to check the roof for leaks."

"Uh, sure," he said. "Why haven't you left town for a better job?"

"When my grandmother disappeared, my mother took it really hard. She kind of went around the bend so they put her in the hospital for a while. My Aunt Mabel stayed with me. When mom came back, she was different. She got very clingy, never wanting me out of her sight." Dee sighed and tucked her hair behind her ears. "So I stayed after I graduated from high school, kept working at the bakery. Look, I really have to go. Enjoy the bread. There's strawberry jam in there too. Mabel made it."

"Thanks. Um, is the grocery store still in town? I need coffee, badly," he said, laughing.

"Yeah, still there," she said, turning to go. "I'll bring your spare key tomorrow."

Phin didn't mention that it was likely the only key, or that the first thing he'd done when he arrived was break in. He watched her stride toward the house, heading for the lane. Her hips swayed as she walked, mesmerizing him as he stood there clutching the plastic bag full of fresh rolls.

"Oh, almost forgot," she said, turning back suddenly, "the cats always use this patch as their toilet. They just chose it long ago, and Riva didn't bother to stop them. You might want to find another place for those plants. Bye." She waved and disappeared behind the house.

Phin reached into the bag and pulled out a warm roll. He bit deeply into it, rolling his eyes as he chewed. It was heavenly, probably the best bread he'd ever tasted, though his empty stomach hardly made him impartial. He'd keep most of them for later when he could slather them with the jam. He swallowed and surveyed the stretch of dirt he'd turned over.

According to Dee, the cats had been shitting in it for years. That would explain some of those smaller rocks. Well, so what? Manure was supposed to be good for plants, wasn't it?

FOUR

The old woman held her cup out for a refill. Phin smiled tightly and picked up the teapot for the fourth time. As he poured, he watched her mouth open and close repeatedly, talking about nothing – inane observations about the lovely curtains fluttering at the window, her grown grandchildren, the weather, where she'd bought her dress. Her lips were withered and deeply creased. Her lipstick had run into the crevices, giving her a cartoon-like face, as if a child had drawn her and used a heavy hand with the red crayon. Those lips stretched open and puckered shut, over and over again until he wanted to scream at her to shut up.

And then there really was screaming, but it wasn't coming from him. The old woman's mouth distended hideously to reveal tea-stained dentures that rattled in the blast of her shrieking.

Only when hot tea splashed onto his bare feet did he realize her cup had overflowed. He'd scalded her hand and her lap. His mind hardly had time to react and tip the teapot back when her other hand came up and blindsided him with a cast iron frying pan.

Phin's eyes opened, the echoes of screams and the gong of the frying pan fading as he pressed a hand to his left temple. No pain. The last wisps of the dream dissipated as he rolled over and reached for the clock on the bedside table.

Then he saw the blood. Smelled it too. He sat up abruptly, wondering if he'd reopened the cut over his eye while he was in the throes of his nightmare. He gingerly probed his left eyebrow, inspected his fingers for blood. Clean. He threw back the blankets and uncovered a mangled bird, its head crushed and its belly torn open, bloodied black feathers broken and pointing in every direction. Phin groaned in revulsion as he fell off the bed onto the carpet in his haste to put some distance between himself and the carnage.

He pushed himself to his feet and pulled open the curtains. Nightmares and blood were less threatening in broad daylight. He turned back to the bed to inspect the damage, squinting in the early light.

Bloody paw prints matted the pillow next to where he'd slept, splotches of crimson just starting to brown at the edges. The bird – perhaps a crow – lay on the sheet amid a spattering of bloody droplets, its shattered beak pointing to the far corner where the long-haired black cat preened, calmly cleaning its whiskers.

Phin jammed his arms through the sleeves of the too-small housecoat he'd found in the closet. His muscles protested, the ache in his shoulders and back reminding him of the many hours he'd spent digging yesterday. He'd been determined to finish transplanting the entire garden and had managed to get most of the work done before dark.

Then his aching body had convinced him to sleep in a real bed. Too tired to be squeamish, he had climbed into Riva's bed. A bed now streaked with blood and gore.

He knew that cats sometimes brought their owners the animals they killed as an offering. But he wasn't this cat's owner. Was the offering a gift or a threat? Maybe the cat was warning him away from Riva's bed. Or maybe it was just being a smartass. He glared at the cat as it groomed itself, taking its time, clearly pleased with its work.

Phin massaged and rotated his shoulders in an effort to loosen the stiffness as he stared at the cat, wondering how he was going to deal with this new feline assault. He forgot his aching muscles for a moment and threw the bloody pillow at its head. The cat easily avoided the missile. The pillow struck the wall and slid to the floor, leaving a red streak on the rose patterned paper.

Phin bundled up the bloody sheet and dead crow along with the rest of the bedding. He'd have to throw most of it away but he'd seen a hoard of sheets in a hall closet. He wondered if this sort of thing happened regularly.

Out in the kitchen, he found a large garbage bag underneath the sink and stuffed his armload into it. He tossed the bag outside to deal with later and trudged into the bathroom to the shower. He hunched under the hottest water he could stand, letting the spray massage and loosen his neck and shoulder muscles. After towelling off, he opened the cabinet above the sink, hoping that Riva had also kept a stock of painkillers or muscle relaxants on hand.

The inside of the cabinet was a bewildering mess, an assortment of prescription and over-the-counter drugs vying for space with dozens of small brown bottles sporting pictures of flowers and plants on their labels. Were they medicine? He opened one called "Valerian" and took a cautious sniff. He drew his head back sharply at the scent of dirty socks and quickly capped it again.

"What's a medicine cabinet without aspirin?" he muttered, as he shoved aside bottles marked "Goldenseal," "Feverfew," and "Willow Bark." He picked through the more familiar plastic bottles until he found one marked with a familiar brand of painkiller. He shook four pills into his palm and swallowed them, wrenching his head sideways to drink from the cold water tap, wincing at the sharp pain in his neck as he did so.

He inspected the blisters on his palms before rummaging through Riva's sewing kit for a sharp needle. He carefully slid the needle under the edges of the raised bumps, hissing in pain when he probed too deeply, and squeezed out the clear fluid.

Phin pulled on jeans and a tee shirt. Maybe he could get some carving done and finally finish the walking stick, though he should probably just start on a new one. He'd spent too much time on this one already, had overdone it and lost the original design. He'd only meant to carve a few basic shapes, then had felt compelled to fill in nearly every space. Now it just looked clumsy and crude and he wished he could erase most of it and start over again. That was the problem with wood, once you cut into it there was no going back. He was itching to hold his carving tools again, to feel them bite into yielding wood and smell its resinous scent as it fell to the ground in curls. He flexed his fingers and winced; his blistered hands told him to wait.

He turned on the radio when he came into the kitchen and found a local classic rock station. The Guess Who were in the middle of "American Woman," and he turned up the volume, singing along hoarsely. He filled the kettle and set it on the stove to boil then stared morosely at the nearly empty jar of coffee. He hated instant coffee, but he'd found the tiny jar at the back of the fridge yesterday and had saved some for morning. The spoon rattled against the glass as he chased the last of the stale grains, finally giving up and upending the jar over his mug. It would be a weak brew, but fragrant enough to at least scour away the scent of blood that still lingered in his nostrils.

While he waited for the water to boil, he hummed along with an old Beatles tune and gazed out the kitchen's small window into the garden. His new transplants were still standing, but they weren't alone. Dozens of prickly stems poked their heads up among the marijuana and vegetable plants. He probably hadn't dug down far enough to eradicate the weeds' root systems. As he puzzled over the speed with which the weeds had reappeared, the grey tom crept up to the garden and started scratching at the dirt. Phin rapped sharply on the window, startling the cat, which hissed in his general direction and ran off.

Scowling at the retreating cat, he didn't see the woman climb the steps and make her way to the back door. Her knock came just as the kettle began to whistle and spit.

"It's open," he shouted over the noise, as he simultaneously turned off the radio and the flame under the kettle. The door opened and a woman with frizzy auburn hair bustled in, struggling with a cardboard box and two large paper bags. Phin rushed over, took the box from her and set it on the table.

"Hi, I'm Tammy Goldman," she said, dropping the bags next to the box and holding out her hand. "I live three houses over from Dee and Lydia with my husband Fritz and our dogs." She spoke in a fast staccato that left no room for comment. Her movements mimicked her speech as she hurriedly unpacked the box and bags. "You should get that glass replaced before it rains." She waved at the sheet of cardboard taped over one corner of the window.

Tammy was tall, nearly eye to eye with Phin. He poured boiling water into his mug, watching the instant coffee dissolve as she chattered without pause. Phin wondered if poor Fritz ever got a word in edgewise. He was reminded of his early morning dream and became uneasy with her one-sided monologue.

"Um, how long have you lived around here, Tammy?" Phin set his mug on the counter and reached for a bag, trying to help, but she shot him an impatient look and he pulled his hand back.

"My husband Fritz and I moved out here about five years ago. He retired early at fifty-five. We're probably the only ones in town – in our group, that is – that didn't meet you when you were here the last time." She pulled out several photos from her bag and shook them at Phin. He caught a glimpse of white puff balls with beady eyes and pointy snouts. "Fritz and I raise dogs now, a new breed. A cross between a poodle and a pomeranian. We call them poopoms. They're very cute."

Phin disliked small dogs almost as much as cats. He picked up his mug again and drained the rest of his pseudo-coffee so he wouldn't be tempted to make a sarcastic comment about how handy little dogs could be for practicing field goal kicks.

The bags contained several books, which Tammy stacked in a pile and then shoved across the table at Phin. "I borrowed these from Riva months ago, completely forgot about them until today. I guess they're yours now." She folded the paper bags and tucked them between two tin canisters on the counter.

"Go ahead and put those books away. I see you've got hot water ready. I'll make the tea," she said, dismissing him with a wave and reaching for a teapot. Phin stood a moment, a bemused smile on his face as he watched her. She was completely familiar with his kitchen, more so than he was. She took a glass jar down from a shelf and threw several large pinches of dried leaves into the teapot.

Phin left her to make tea and headed for the living room, giving the cat shelf a wide berth as he rounded the corner. The fat orange cat was in its usual place and stretched languidly as Phin passed. It didn't bother to hiss, just yawned and licked its long silky fur to show him how little he mattered in its life.

"Stupid, lazy cat," he muttered, dropping the books on the coffee table. He rolled his eyes at the title of the topmost book, *Auric Sightings*. What he was going to do with an entire library of flaky, new-age books? Maybe donate them to a library – if they would even take them, that is. Riva's many shelves were packed with books. Books were also stacked on the floor of her office; in fact, nearly every available surface in the house that wasn't cluttered with candles and knick-knacks held books, pamphlets and papers. It was going to take a lot of boxes to cart it all away.

Phin hoped Tammy wasn't expecting him to drink tea with her. He had no idea what she had tossed into that teapot. He'd managed to avoid it yesterday when two other neighbours had shown up after Dee left. He had just found the nearly empty jar of instant coffee and had made himself a bitter cup to drink while they sipped their pale red brew. They had brought him a pan of "Rice Surprise" and a huge pot of "Varmint Stew." He'd politely tasted both dishes, nodding his thanks at their proud grins. The rice had been full of hard bits that tasted suspiciously like cloves and peppercorns. Too weird to actually taste good, but not bad either. They'd been vague about what kind of meat was in the stew, gesturing towards the forest and pressing him to finish the bowl. It smelled delicious but, like the rice, was a bit odd to his city palate. He hadn't managed to get to town yet for some shopping. He'd soon be reduced to eating the canned fish and stale crackers he'd found in the pantry.

Mabel and Fiona. That had been their names. The two old girls had been funny and had teased Phin mercilessly. They remembered him from his visit with Riva when he was a teenager and treated him like a long-lost friend. He'd eventually dared to ask why all the food that the neighbours brought him wasn't quite right. They'd laughed and told him about the cooking contest the town held during their summer festival. Nearly everyone in town participated, vying for the prize for the most outrageous twist on an old favourite. Fiona had mentioned that Mabel had won last summer's prize with her bacon and egg lasagna.

Phin watched Tammy make room in the refrigerator for the four square containers she'd taken out of the box. A fifth sat on the table, next to a large oval ceramic platter with a turkey painted on it.

"I brought enough to last at least two weeks," she said, pulling the top off the container and scooping out a hunk of familiar brown meatloaf, which she broke up into smaller chunks and spread out on the platter.

"Um, thanks, but I'm not really hungry right now," he said, glancing longingly into his empty coffee mug. Couldn't anyone around here just make plain old shepherd's pie? Maybe some chicken soup?

Tammy gave him a curious look. She reached for a tiny brass bell that was sitting on the windowsill. It tinkled shrilly and a chorus of meows and trills answered, followed by several furry bodies that arrived at a run. They came from the living room and through a little swinging panel cut into the kitchen door that Phin had not noticed until now. They gathered around Tammy, rubbing their sides and heads against her shins in greeting, tails curving up. She cooed to them as she set the turkey platter on the floor and stepped back. They crowded around, wolfing down the food in silence, jostling each other for space.

Phin could feel his eyes beginning to itch again. He recognized the cat that had left the bloody crow in his bed. It kept glancing at the two humans. Phin wondered if this was Orion, the hunter. And there were not one, but two identical fluffy orange cats. Were they Castor and Pollux? That left the huge mangy tom that kept crapping in the garden and a smaller grey cat that balanced on only three legs. He scowled at the beasts, reminding himself that he had named them all Stupid. They didn't need any other names, as far as he was concerned.

"I'm surprised that Peg's come out at all," Tammy said, petting the cats in turn. "She's usually the shy one."

"What happened to its leg?"

"Peg jumped off the roof when she was only a kitten and shattered her shoulder," Tammy said. "The vet couldn't save it. Riva couldn't bear to put the little thing down, so she became a tripod. Riva named her Pegasus, since she'd tried to fly like her namesake."

"They look a bit nervous," she continued, as she watched the cats devour their meal. "Did you feed them yesterday?"

"They're not starving," he said evasively, "but I, uh well, I met the big grey one in the yard yesterday and I, well, kind of threw a rock at it."

"You threw a rock at Hercules?" she said, glaring at Phin, her eyes sparking in anger. "You're responsible for them now, you know. Riva trusted you enough to leave you her house so there'd be someone here to take care of them. These cats came to mean a lot to her in the last few years."

"It was digging in the garden," he said lamely. He rinsed out his mug and tossed in two orange pekoe tea bags. At least that would give him an excuse not to drink whatever she'd brewed up in the teapot.

"It's their garden to dig in. Would you rather have several stinky litter boxes in the house to clean all the time?"

Tammy searched through the cupboards until she found a bottle of honey, pouring a large glob of the thick amber liquid into a teacup. "Let me know when you run out of cat food again, though I'm sure Riva had the recipe stashed somewhere around here."

"Um, yeah, funny thing about that," he said with a hoarse laugh. "You see, I thought it was meatloaf, you know, like casseroles and other stuff left in the fridge. So I fried it up, with hot sauce and salt, but it tasted like cardboard..." He faltered in her icy glare.

"You mean it tasted like cat food," she said and poured tea into her cup. She stirred it with quick, jerky movements, lips pressed tightly together.

The lingering effects of Phin's dream still floated at the back of his mind. He felt a deep relief that she wasn't wearing red lipstick.

FIVE

Phin cursed at the bicycle. He'd only been in the grocery store for ten minutes and the back tire was even flatter than before he'd pumped it up. Good thing he lived only a few blocks away.

He shrugged off his backpack and transferred the contents of several plastic bags to the pack. He'd bought ground coffee, cream and an assortment of frozen dinners and snack foods. He'd been in Riva's house for nearly a week and continued to receive a steady stream of visitors bearing strange casseroles, sludgy dips, and odd-smelling salads. He appreciated their generosity and didn't really mind experimenting with new foods, but missed the basics: coffee, potato chips, and microwaveable dinners.

He'd have to leave the bicycle locked up in front of the small grocery store and pick it up later. He told himself that walking would give him more time to really get to know the town, though he could see most of Main Street from where he stood.

Phin was surprised at how many people were walking around, considering the town's small size and the general scruffiness of the shops. Cricket Lake had changed drastically in the many years since he'd been here last. The building next to the grocery store was closed up, with faded, yellowed newspapers covering the windows. A chipped barber's pole hanging in front was the only clue as to its past. He would never forget the old barber who had cut his hair so short that Phin had vowed never to cut it again, and except for one short stint as an office temp, he had kept it long ever since.

Directly across from the grocery, next to a beer and wine store, was a tiny shop whose sign declared it to be a veterinary office, animal shelter and pet store all rolled into one. A handwritten sign proclaimed a sale on goldfish. A dozen for a loonie. He still had most of his last two paycheques to hold him over for a while. A dollar for some goldfish wouldn't break the bank.

The bell above the door tinkled as he went in and two very small, extra-fluffy dogs lunged at him, yapping ferociously. He skipped sideways and they ran out of leash before their teeth could reach his ankles. One of them had a bulging stomach, very obviously full of puppies.

"Stop that! Get back here, you two! Bad dogs!" Tammy yanked on the leashes and dragged the dogs back to her chair. She picked them up and set them onto her lap, where they continued to growl, quivering and showing their miniscule teeth. "Hi, Phineas. Sorry about that. Poopoms aren't usually this nasty, but Lola is about to give birth any day now and Prince is very protective of her. Makes them cranky. Are you here to get some food for your cats? You really should keep them on the homemade food, at least until they adjust to their new situation. They've been very traumatized by Riva's death. It may take a while before they accept you, then you can gradually introduce them to something new. They're very sensitive creatures, you know."

Phin stayed against the wall as he edged farther into the store. "Um, no. There's still plenty in the fridge. I was looking for some goldfish for the aquarium in Riva's, um, my living room."

"I don't think I've ever seen fish in that tank," Tammy said, frowning. She wrapped her forearm around the dogs' chests as they tried to launch themselves off her lap again. "I thought it was just for plants. But it's your place now, and if you prefer fish," she whipped her head around as a door opened and an enormous man in a long white coat ducked through the doorway. The dogs immediately stopped barking and cowered against Tammy's chest, trying to burrow into her shirt.

"Come on in, Tammy," he said, beaming at the terrified dogs as Tammy clamped one under each arm and followed him through the door. The veterinarian threw a curious glance at Phin, who nodded his head with a half-smile.

Phin turned to the counter, where a surly woman held a clear plastic bag out to him. Several orange fish swam listlessly in a pint of cloudy water.

"Just the one dozen? I've got more if you want them, but I'll have to put them in another bag," she said, shaking the bag at him.

"No, that should do it." Phin dug out his wallet and paid her. "Are they healthy? They're not moving around much."

"That's twelve fish crammed into a few inches of water. What do you want them to do for a buck, a ballet?" she muttered, and handed him his change. The corners of her mouth almost lifted in a smile until she thought better of it and scowled at him instead. "They'll need food too," she added, snatching a bill back from his hand and thrusting a small tin at him. He crammed the tin into a pocket and grabbed his wallet off the counter before she could get her hands on that too.

It had been a strange week, beer would help. The day was already hot, and it wasn't yet noon. Phin stood on the cracked sidewalk with a six-pack in one hand, his bag of fish in the other, and looked despondently at the bicycle. Its other tire was now flat as well, exactly as it had been when he found it in the basement. The inner tubes definitely needed replacing. The hardware store might carry them, but there was no way he'd be able to carry anything else if he had to walk back.

Phin set his backpack onto a bench and pulled off his jacket, knotting the sleeves around his waist. He emptied the pack again, laying the box of beer in the bottom, with his grocery items on top, until the pack was nearly bursting. He squatted in front of the bench and slid his arms into the straps, groaning at the weight as he pushed himself upright. Not everything had fit, but it would be more comfortable to carry a paper sack holding two bags of potato chips than the six-pack of beer.

When he picked up the bag of fish, he was alarmed to see that one of them was now floating upside down, and the others were nibbling at its orange flesh. He shook the bag, sending all the fish into a swirl, but they quickly all settled back to their same positions, though now a second fish was starting to tilt.

"That's a strange way to kill fish," a voice said near his elbow, startling him so he nearly dropped the bag. A huge pair of gray eyes, magnified by thick lenses, was peering at the agitated fish as they attacked their second dying mate.

Phin recognized her as one of the older women that had recently visited him. The seven or eight faces that he'd met in the last week were all starting to blur together, but he remembered this tiny woman because she'd introduced herself as Dee's Aunt Mabel.

"They shouldn't be out in the sun, you know," she said, squinting up at him.

"I-I didn't think they'd be so sensitive," Phin stammered. "I just bought them not ten minutes ago."

Mabel glared at the pet shop window where a scowling figure watched them. "That old bitch probably knew these were about to keel over. What do you need a bag of goldfish for anyway?" she asked, grabbing his sleeve and pulling him along the sidewalk.

"I just wanted to put some fish into that aquarium in the living room," he mumbled, as he allowed himself to be towed by Mabel.

"I don't think I've ever seen fish in that tank," she muttered. She pushed her way past several people coming out of a door, and dragged him into a shop that was far too warm, but smelled like heaven.

****

Dee wiped her apron across her forehead, catching the bead of sweat that threatened to drip from her eyebrow into her bread dough. She hated the ancient air conditioner that rattled and clanked at the far end of the kitchen and wondered why she even bothered to turn it on every morning. The tepid air it managed to churn out hardly got past the ovens and was no match for the stifling heat that rolled from them all day. Since last summer, with its cruel heat waves, she'd mentioned to the owner several times how it would be nice to fix it before the hot weather returned. Brent had put her off each time, grumbling about unnecessary repairs out of season. Dee suspected that his precious boat got all the repairs it needed, whatever the season.

She punched down the bread dough again and blew a sharp breath up through her bangs. White flour dislodged from her hair and drifted down onto her nose. She could hear customers talking to Brent out front, and hoped he was in a better mood now that he'd had his third cup of coffee. He tended to regard his customers as bothersome, a nuisance he barely tolerated as a part of doing business. He didn't seem to care that they were the only reason he was in business and acted as if he were the one doing them a favour. Most days Dee tried to shield them from his crankiness, rushing out of the back room to sell them bread, pan rolls, or pies before Brent could interfere and scare them off.

He'd inherited the bakery from his brother Sam, whom he'd detested, and seemed to delight in letting the place go to seed. He hadn't put a single penny into repairs or renovations since he'd walked into the bakery two years before. At this rate, the bakery would be worthless in another two, its equipment outdated or broken down and all its clientele making the trip to Chilliwack for their bread and pastries.

Sam had had big plans to renovate the bakery, especially since the huge tract of land that bordered the lake was likely going to be developed, a move that could only help the tourist trade. The land had been willed to the town when its former owner had died, with a stipulation that it not be changed or sold for fifty years. That time was nearly up and Cricket Lake's town council was worried about losing access to the lake, since the town's residents had been swimming and fishing in it for generations. On the other hand, the town needed the revenue they might get from new businesses that would spring up.

Dee missed Sam, who'd taken great pride in his business and had worked very hard to please his clients. She had worked for him for nearly ten years, part-time during the long winter months when only the locals came by regularly, but from dawn to mid-afternoon all through the busy summer season when tourists and commuters swarmed Cricket Lake.

Sam had helped out in summer but had taken it easy in winter, especially in the last couple of years when he got huge and slow. Dee had rarely seen him eating anything but pastries and bread. In fact she'd never seen so much as a carrot pass his pudgy lips and one day found him slumped over his account books, growing cold, his fingers sticky with the glaze from her latest batch of cinnamon buns.

Dee glanced at the big oven in the corner, wondering why she hadn't heard the timer go off yet.

The light was out.

"Cripes, not again!" she muttered, wiping her hands on her apron and opening the oven door. Six trays of biscuits sat, half-baked, their centres slumped inward. The oven was barely warm. She slapped the side of the cantankerous machine. The pilot light flickered a few times and then stayed on. She kicked it for good measure, wondering if it was worth cooking the biscuits at all. They'd be as hard as hockey pucks. Maybe if she brushed them with bacon fat, dredged them in flour and baked them again, she could sell them cheap to the pet shop as dog biscuits. Sam would have loved the idea of baking for dogs and would have welcomed every stray dog in the area that showed up for breakfast.

She sighed as she scanned the kitchen, with its four scuffed work tables covered in rising loaves, knowing full well that she didn't have time for a biscuit rescue mission. She'd barely get the bread done in time for the after-work rush crowd, small as it would be.

Dee hated to waste food, but pulled all six pans of biscuits out of the oven and dumped them in the industrial sized garbage can out the back door. She then tossed in a large bundle of old newspapers to hide the evidence. She'd barely turned her back on them when a pang of guilt had her fishing the newspapers out of the garbage bin. She stacked the papers by the door for the Tuesday recycling pick-up.

Brent-be-damned, she thought, let him find the spoiled biscuits. He'd shout, they'd argue about the ovens again, and Dee would go home upset and vowing to quit and find another job, as usual.

Another job, what a joke. Baking was all she'd ever done; it was all she'd ever wanted to do. The only other jobs in town were cashier positions at either the small grocery or the hardware store. She'd die of boredom, though she probably wouldn't spend each working day sweating through her clothes.

Dee dreamed of moving to a larger city that had modern bakeries with the latest, up-to-date equipment. The last time she'd been in Vancouver, she'd toured every bakery she'd found listed in the phone book. A couple had been fairly new, and catered to young college students and business types. She didn't understand why they called themselves bakeries. The majority had a shiny espresso machine behind the counter, and they sold expensive pastries and oversized cookies. Their loaves of bread were chunky, full of cracked grains, nuts, and seeds, with not a single plain white loaf to be found.

She'd compared their prices with Brent's, and realized that he was selling a whole cake for what these bakeries charged for two thin slices. No wonder there wasn't any money for a new oven.

Dee checked the oven again, satisfied that it was up to temperature. Good thing, since the bread was ready to go. She slid the pans in and closed the door, crossing her fingers as she set the timer once again. She decided it was time for a break, and left the kitchen to wash her hands and shake the flour out of her hair.

Brent was reading a newspaper and ignoring the woman and two young boys that were perusing the display case. The woman cleared her throat, hoping he'd notice them and take their order, but her effort was half-hearted, as if to insist might incite an actual fit of rudeness.

Dee smiled an apology as she squeezed past Brent's chair. He ignored her too but noisily folded his paper before getting up and leaving.

"Sorry about that, Josie; what can I get you?" she asked, as she wiped down the counter. It was greasy and covered in crumbs and something gummy that might once have been jam. The front of the shop almost always smelled faintly of cigarette smoke. It permeated Brent's clothing and was a habit that Dee had been trying to convince him to give up. A bakery should smell like bread, and cake, and cookies, not like an ashtray full of old cigarette butts, she'd argued.

Brent also routinely read his paper with his feet up on the glass display case, handled the food without washing his hands first, and didn't consider a day successful unless he'd offended at least one person to the point of threats or tears.

She didn't understand why he hadn't been shut down yet. She was sure someone must have called the health department at least once, but in the two years since Brent had taken over ownership, no one had come in to investigate a single complaint, or to inspect the kitchen. He and Sam had come from a huge family, with several members working in obscure government positions. He had the smug confidence of someone who would never be found in the wrong.

Dee put two loaves of bread and a dozen pan rolls in a bag, feeling guilty for taking Josie's money, even though she'd thrown in a couple of cookies for the children. As they turned to leave, the door opened and Mabel barged in, towing Phineas by the sleeve.

"Dee, honey, look who I found across the street," she exclaimed. She nearly knocked over the children in her haste. "Nice to see you out and about, Josie. And boy are those kids of yours getting big!" she hollered over her shoulder as the door closed.

"Um, hello again," Phin said, almost crushing the bag of goldfish between himself and the glass. "I was just getting some supplies, you know, coffee and stuff."

"And potato chips and a few dead goldfish," Mabel piped up, squinting up at her niece and smiling widely.

"How long have you had them in that bag? They don't look so good." Dee felt her face flushing. All she seemed to do was blush when Phineas was around. He'd cleaned up since she'd seen him last. His hair was freshly washed and tied into a fluffy tail. Streaks of silver ran through it, glinting from the sun that glared through the window. He'd brushed his beard as well. He was wearing a tye-dyed tee shirt that might have been a riot of psychedelic colors once upon a time, but had faded into a muted pastel swirl.

Dee wished she'd had time to check herself in the bathroom mirror. She probably had flour and various other smudges on her face, judging by the condition of her hands and clothes. "What are you going to do with goldfish?"

"There's an aquarium full of plants at, um, home, in the living room. I thought it could use some fish, since that's what's usually kept in an aquarium. I've never had fish, well, not live ones anyway. Just to eat," he finished lamely. Dee didn't look at all pleased to see him, and he wasn't sure what Mabel was smiling about, but it was making him nervous. He looked around the dingy shop front, anything to keep from staring at that straining top button on Dee's shirt.

The walls needed painting, and many of the stained linoleum floor tiles were cracked or missing. The glass fronting the display cases was so old and scuffed that it looked permanently dirty. Even all the display signs were stained and faded. He wondered how they managed to keep any loyal customers, but then remembered the bag of deliciously warm rolls that Dee had given him.

"Riva originally planned to keep fish in it. I'm not sure if she ever tried, but it's had plants in it forever," Mabel said, glancing back and forth between them. "Phineas has a flat tire. Remember that old bicycle of Riva's? Those tires never stayed pumped up. Not that she ever rode it, I suppose."

"I think I'm having a problem with one of the cats," Phin blurted, grateful to finally have thought of something to say.

"Which one? Is it hurt?"

"No, none of them is hurt, as far as I know. I'm not sure I could tell, unless there was blood involved. Actually there was blood," he said, then quickly added, "but not on a cat. I woke up yesterday next to a dead crow. It was on the bed beside me and it was badly mangled. There was blood everywhere." He frowned as both Dee and Mabel smiled and exchanged a knowing look.

"Not funny, ladies. I woke up to a nightmare. It was right next to me. And this cat just sat across the room, cleaning its whiskers, like it had done a good job or something."

"Well, of course it did. It was probably quite proud of itself and wanted to share it with you," Dee said, trying not to laugh at the stricken look on his face. "Which cat was it? No, don't tell me. I'll bet it was Orion." She looked at Mabel and raised an eyebrow questioningly.

"Maybe it was Hercules," Mabel ventured. "He likes crows."

"But Hercules would have eaten most of it first and only given him a wing, or part of the head. Only Orion would give him the whole bird."

"How should I know?" Phin said, scowling. "It's a cat. It had long black fur, if that helps."

"Ha! I knew it! Orion the great hunter, as usual. He used to bring Riva all sorts of birds, and sometimes mice. He's quite partial to rodents. Birds are just for sport, apparently not good eating." Dee gave him an appraising look, noting that he'd cleaned the dirt out from under his nails. "Orion must like you, though he never left his gifts in Riva's bed. He tended to leave his catch on the porch for her to see, just to show off. Maybe he's trying to make a statement."

"It made a statement all right. The crow's neck was broken, and its guts were spread all over the place. I had to throw everything out, blankets and all."

"Too bad you didn't read those innards before throwing them out," Mabel said, poking Phin in the chest. "Lots you can find out from a crow."

"What?"

"Mabel, stop teasing him. You'll have him thinking we practice black magic around here." She turned to Phin. "I'm guessing you didn't just come in here to say hello?"

He scanned the prices on the wall behind her head and had decided on a dozen butter rolls and an apple pie when Mabel slapped her hand on the scuffed glass counter top. Dee and Phin jumped at the noise and both stared at the diminutive woman.

"Say, Dee, maybe you could give Phineas a drive home in the delivery truck. He's got so much to carry, plus I doubt Vinnie'd want that bicycle left outside his store for too long anyway. You could toss it in the back. I'll come along for the ride." She grinned again, and grabbed the bag of goldfish from Phin. "I'll carry these, so you'll have an extra hand to carry something yummy from here," she said, as she swept out the door, clearly expecting to be followed.

Phin looked at Dee, and wondered if driving him home was the last thing she wanted to do or just way down on the list. But she leaned through the door to the back room.

"Brent, I have a last minute delivery to make," she shouted, "I'll need the truck for about half an hour. Keep an eye on the bread, will you? Take them out when the timer goes off. You can leave them in the pans until I get back."

She grabbed a plastic bag and raised her eyes questioningly at Phin. He pointed to the rolls and pie. She shoved them into the bag, and handed it to him. He pulled out a handful of change, but she shook her head and pointed with her chin to the door. She took a key ring off a hook and joined him on the other side of the counter.

Brent's harsh voice chased them out the door. "Make sure you're back in a half. Every extra minute comes off your pay!"

SIX

Phin opened another journal and squinted at the spiky handwriting that filled the page. More notes on some sort of tea-leaf reading Riva had done years ago for someone or other. Phin had come across a Violet, a Rose and a Jasmine before he realized everyone was named after some sort of flower; Riva had used code names for everyone she wrote about. The lives of all these disguised women intersected in a complex pattern that baffled him.

He bit into a roll slathered with the jam Dee had given him on the first day she'd come by. He'd been reluctant to try it, suspicious of the hand-drawn picture of a strawberry and a garlic bulb nestled together on the jar's lid. They must get bored out here in the boonies, he thought, chewing carefully.

The jam tasted about as weird as he'd expected: a delicate strawberry sweetness to fool the palate, followed by intense garlic fumes that were released as he chewed. He washed down the lump of garlicky-strawberry bun with a huge gulp of strong black coffee.

Phin was near the end of his third cup and already thinking of a fourth. He hadn't had a decent cup of coffee in over a week and could feel his hands starting their familiar jitter from the caffeine.

I'll probably be up all night, he thought, as he twisted the lid back onto the jar of jam and pushed it aside.

He reached for the next journal in the pile. He opened it randomly, marvelling at the unwavering neatness of Riva's handwriting. His own careless scrawl had no style or consistency and could have been made by several different people.

He'd counted fifty-six journals, the first ones dating from before he was born. Those earlier entries were filled with the voice of a much younger woman than he'd known and he'd been embarrassed to find dozens of badly written poems about her romantic yearnings. They were hesitant, naïve rhymes about love, about flowers and trees and clouds. There were gaps between entries, a few months, sometimes years, but she'd obviously had a relentless drive to record her thoughts, along with some of the events in her life.

He'd narrowed his reading to the last ten years or so, hoping to discover something useful or interesting. He wasn't sure what he was looking for and part of him felt guilty for snooping, but he didn't feel right simply throwing away the journals unread.

Most of what she had written about in the past few years had to do with the lives of the women in town – assuming that Tulip and Forsythia were her neighbours. Tulip had asked about her children's futures and whether any of them might accomplish more than she'd been able to in her life. Riva predicted the boys would grow up to make her proud and her daughters would marry well and give her many grandchildren. She'd added a later note to remind herself where she'd exaggerated, as the card reading had shown a possible suicide and at least one incarceration. At least their mother would have the pleasure of being oblivious until all hell broke loose.

Phin brewed a fourth cup of coffee and gazed out the window as he sipped it, wondering if maybe Dee and Tammy had been right about the garden being used as a litter box. The marijuana plants were not growing thick and green as he'd expected. They were spindly, and their leaves were yellowing and curling. They didn't look healthy at all and should probably have stayed in the greenhouse. Small plants would have been better than no plants at all. Most of the flowers in the raised garden plot had dropped their petals and were wilting. They didn't look happy either.

So maybe all manure wasn't alike. The thistles weren't complaining. They had almost completely engulfed his two precious plants, crowding them and blocking out the sunlight. Phin had weeded several times but it didn't matter, the thistles thrived while his pot plants withered.

The squash and zukes had exploded into a riot of giant leaves and garish yellow flowers, spreading out along the side of the house. He wanted to stomp on them every time he walked by, but having doomed most of Riva's garden by planting it in a weed-infested litter box he was loath to destroy the rest.

Phin turned back to the kitchen. No time for wallowing, there was work to do. He took the stack of journals to the living room and put them back in the cabinet. Orange Stupid was lounging on a chair, watching him through slitted eyes. Phin could see its needle-sharp claws going in and out of its front paws as it kneaded the frayed cushion. There was cat hair on every surface, just waiting for him to breathe it in and die of asthmatic asphyxiation. He'd seen an ancient vacuum cleaner in a closet but no spare bags. Maybe he could trade some yard work for one of the local ladies to come in and give the place a good cleaning.

The living room was looking a lot more, well, livable now. Most of the junk was gone, though he'd kept a few candles and the dragon trio incense burner.

He'd taken down a half dozen stained-glass angels hanging in the big window that had been hidden by drapes. The drapes could stay, since he'd found a way to tie them back during the day. He might have kept the beaded curtain that filled the doorway of the small office if it hadn't been made of pink and lavender plastic beads, so into a box it went. He'd also packed up several throw rugs that he'd kept tripping on, along with the crocheted doilies and fancy pillows that had covered every chair in the room. The furniture was old and mostly threadbare, but he preferred the sparer look he'd achieved.

Stupid took a half-hearted swipe at Phin's leg as he passed on the way out of the room. When Phin got back to the kitchen, the cat ran past him and sat down on the exact spot where the feeding platter had appeared the day before.

"You'd like a little meatloaf, eh?" he muttered. The cat meowed and rubbed against his leg. Phin drew back, scowling. He might as well feed it, he thought, opening up the fridge and taking out one of the containers that Tammy had left, otherwise it would probably follow him around for the rest of the day. As soon as Phin pulled off the lid, the cat recognized the smell and yowled. Within seconds, the room was full of furry bodies, all trying to rub up against Phin and meowing piteously. He quickly dumped the contents onto the platter, set it on the floor and stepped back, watching bemusedly. The cats ignored him all day, but as soon as he provided dinner he was their best friend.

Tammy had used the little bell on the windowsill to call them, but Phin hadn't needed it. He'd only had to think of feeding them and a cat had appeared and called the rest of the herd.

"What am I going to do with all of you?" he said. Five pairs of ears flicked in his direction, but not one cat looked his way. "Maybe I could hold a raffle and sell you all, raise some money for a good cause or something." He sneezed explosively and both orange Stupids bolted from the room.

Phin turned away from the cats, needing something constructive to do to take his mind off his itchy eyes. A wooden cabinet stood underneath the window that overlooked the yard. It was made of pine, old and weathered. He didn't know much about antiques, but figured it had to be at least a hundred years old, though the hinges on the door looked new and made no sound as he opened it. The cabinet was filled with glass jars of all sizes, some coloured, but mostly clear. He pulled out a few to have a look. They were filled with dried leaves, twigs, or flowers. Few were labelled.

He switched on the radio and was pleased to hear an American rock station coming in clear and strong. He couldn't always get a good signal but he'd discovered it played hits from the sixties every afternoon. Phin had always felt he'd been born a generation too late. In high school, while his friends raved about The Guess Who and Supertramp, he'd doggedly listened to The Beatles, The Doors and Cream. And when his buddies had begun to haunt the new discotheque, wearing tight clothes and lots of shiny jewelry, Phin had stubbornly kept his frayed jean jacket and ponytail. He still wore the same post-hippy haircut. He'd eventually broadened his musical tastes, but even now preferred earlier rock and roll.

Phin hummed along to the radio as he put a large bowl on the table and began opening jars. He sniffed the contents of each, making a game of trying to identify what they were and dumping out what he didn't recognize. Some were almost familiar, reminding him of lasagna or spaghetti sauce spices; maybe basil or oregano. But he really had no idea what was what and soon it all started to smell the same anyway. There were lots of dried flowers, some smelling sweet, others decayed. He recognized rose petals, but tossed them into the bowl as well, since he couldn't think of any reason why he'd ever use them. It would all go into the compost pile so he didn't bother sorting flowers from leaves or twigs.

Out of thirty or so jars, he'd managed to identify only the rose petals and was contemplating taking the heaped bowl out to the yard to dump, when a sharp rap came at the door.

It opened just as he was reaching for the doorknob and Mabel bustled in. "Phineas dear, I'm sorry to barge in like this," she began, going straight to the table and dropping into a chair. "I just realized this morning that it's exactly halfway between the new and full moon. Time for my reading. It's been months since, well, you know, since Riva left us, and she used to read for me at this time each month."

While Mabel prattled on about the phases of the moon and how it was safe to peek into the cosmic workings at precisely this time, he carried the kettle to the sink to fill it with water. Did she really expect him to tell her fortune?

"Do you want to read tea leaves or cards? Either one would be okay for me today," Mabel said, jumping up to fetch her favourite teapot and two matching cups and saucers. She brought them back to the table, shoving aside several jars to make room. "Riva always said that it depended on what it was I wanted to know. It's been so long, who knows what sort of goodies you'll come up with?" She sniffed at the bowl of leaves and flowers, and held up several of the unopened jars to the window, assessing their contents.

"I don't really have time to get involved, Mabel. There's just too much to get done."

"I guess Riva left you a lot to sort through," she said. "If you want, I can help you pack up some of her stuff. I could get some of the other gals to come over too. I heard about closure on Oprah a few weeks ago. It's supposed to help when someone dies, I guess." Mabel tossed several large pinches of mixed herbs into the teapot and Phin filled it with steaming water from the kettle.

"I'm thinking of just boxing up most of it. You and your friends can look through the boxes before I donate it all to charity." Phin didn't think he could cope with a bunch of women prowling through the place. He was just getting used to the idea that this was now his house.

"Maybe you could take the cats?" he asked hopefully.

"Not a chance. I live in a tiny place above the bakery where Dee works. Pets aren't allowed in the building. Don't worry, you'll get used to them soon enough." She sniffed at the steam rising from the teapot and smiled in satisfaction. "This will take a while to steep. I'll get the cards."

"It's not really my thing," he tried again. "I don't have a psychic bone in my body, Mabel."

"Humour me, sonny. You just sit tight and prepare yourself or whatever it is you need to do." Mabel scurried over to a narrow table that stood in the hallway and pulled out the drawer she'd seen Riva open countless times. She was surprised to find four packs of Tarot cards, each wrapped in a different-coloured piece of velvet. It had never occurred to her that Riva had more than one. She lightly touched each velvet oblong before picking up the green-velvet wrapped pack. It was the only one she had ever seen Riva use.

Mabel slapped the Tarot deck onto the kitchen table and eased into the chair across from Phin. She watched him pour two cups of fragrant tea, thinking that the teenage boy she remembered had become a very odd man. Odd, but interesting. Mabel was happy that Phin was here. He provided a welcome distraction from thoughts about her lost friend.

Riva had been acting strangely in the last weeks before Dee found her lying unconscious on her living room floor. The paramedics hadn't been able to revive her and she'd died before reaching the hospital. Dee and Tammy had later gone through the house, looking through Riva's papers. They'd found her will, dated only three months before, and the search for Phineas Marshal had begun.

"I usually like a bit of milk in my tea but not if we're reading leaves," Mabel said. "But I don't think it makes a difference if you do."

"Uh, black's fine by me," Phin answered, carefully picking up the tiny cup. He sniffed at the steam, and then drank it down in one fast gulp, wincing at the musty bitterness. Bits of twigs and leaves stuck to his tongue, and he tried to spit them back into the teacup.

"I can't imagine you'd want to read my fortune off my false teeth," Mabel said with a smirk. "So I'll just let my message settle to the bottom of the cup on its own, if that's ok with you. Besides, I can't drink it that hot."

Phin refilled his cup, but as the first drops of the reddish brew splashed against the china, he felt a burst of heat in his chest that coursed through his body in a jolting rush. It was gone so fast that it left his ears ringing and sparks daggering his eyes. His tongue felt thick, and it seemed to take an awfully long time to get his mouth to make the sounds his brain wanted him to.

"What kind of tea is this?" The teapot was getting heavier, and he lowered it carefully. It juddered as it settled on the table.

"Well, I'm not exactly sure, but Riva made me tea from these jars all the time. I thought I remembered this little blue one." She peered at his face closely. "Are you feeling okay?"

"Yeah, but this tea tastes mouldy. I'll make a fresh pot." Phin snatched Mabel's cup before she could take a sip, and stood quickly, lurching towards the sink. He nearly fell over when he thought he was about to bang his head on the ceiling and grabbed the edge of the counter for balance. Everything in the kitchen was either much closer or farther than it was supposed to be. He moved slowly and deliberately as he poured the contents of the teapot and two cups down the drain, and turned the flame on under the kettle again.

"Here, maybe Riva's special tea is in this other blue jar. Try this one," Mabel said, holding out another jar.

"No!" Phin spun around and the kitchen swirled, coming to a stop seconds after he did. "Isn't there any ordinary tea in this house?" he asked with his eyes squeezed shut. He wondered if he'd been poisoned, if Riva had collected toxic herbs as well as medicinal.

"Well, sure. There's some plain old orange pekoe, but you can't read your fortune in a teabag, Phineas."

"Let's just stick to those cards for now." He grasped the back of his chair securely before letting go of the counter, and dropped back into his seat.

He'd dump it all in the garbage tomorrow, along with all the mysterious brown bottles in the medicine cabinet. No telling what was in those, either.

"So what do I do with them?" Phin asked, gesturing towards the cards. His arm felt like a rubber band, and he pulled it back to himself with some effort before it could stretch out and smack against the far wall.

"Well, Riva used to just lay out three cards and tell me what the images said to her." Mabel unwrapped the deck of cards, smoothed out the green velvet cloth, and then carefully centred the stack of cards in the middle of it. When Phin made no move to pick them up, she did, and shuffled them awkwardly. The large cards didn't fit well in her small hands, so she gave up and shoved them at Phin, forcing his numb fingers to take them.

He stared at the cards that fanned out in his hands, mesmerized by the coloured pattern printed on the back of each one. Silver crescent moons and stars studded a midnight blue background that stretched across both hands. Color bled out over the edge of each card, expanding until Phin felt he would fall into the blue depths. The stars twinkled and flickered in and out, and the crescent moons left their places to revolve around the largest and brightest stars. Their orbits pulled at other, smaller stars and forced them to follow their paths, the patterns shifting and changing until Phin realized that at least three spiral galaxies were forming. He'd spotted a fourth beginning its life cycle when Mabel squealed.

Phin was so startled that he dropped the cards on the table, scattering them as they slid over their own slippery surfaces. Mabel was bent over, staring at something on the floor. He leaned toward her, but she was so far away he felt he would never quite reach her.

"Look, Phineas, Hercules has brought me a gift," she said excitedly as she sat up. She held out her hand to Phin, displaying a large, hairy, and much mangled spider. "Kind of like when Orion brought you the crow so you could read your future in its innards," she continued.

"Um, spider innards are kind of small," Phin mumbled, pulling his head back as she thrust the spider under his nose for inspection.

"No, no, you don't read spider innards," she said, frowning at him. "Didn't Riva teach you anything?"

"No. All I did when I was here that summer was fix things and remodel the kitchen." He wanted to add that he didn't remember Riva using crow intestines or half-chewed spiders to tell the future but his tongue was too numb to enunciate all of that.

"No wonder you didn't do anything with the crow. What a waste of a good omen." Mabel placed the maimed spider in her cup and poured fresh boiling water over it. She reached down and petted Hercules on the head, thanking him for the gift. He accepted the caress and left the room with his tail swishing proudly.

Mabel set the cup on the table and they bent over it, watching the spider legs unfolding in the hot water. Phin stared, nauseated and horrified, as three of the spider's legs separated from the body and swirled lazily around the rim of the cup. The bloated body seemed to pulse as it bobbed, half submerged. He was certain that the movements of the parboiled spider were deliberate, that it was simply biding its time. Any minute now, the spider was going to crawl out of the cup and scuttle across the table on its remaining five legs and he would scream in terror like a little girl. He forced himself to look away from the spider that stretched languidly in its china Jacuzzi and picked up the cards. His hands felt like they were encased in oven mitts.

"Okay then, so I just shuffle the deck and then lay out three cards, right?" he said hoarsely, keeping his eyes on his hands. The stars and moons started their slow swirl on the backs of the cards again but that was better than watching the zombie spider come back to life. He squeezed his eyes to slits while he shuffled, wishing that Mabel would just go home so he could sit alone quietly and sort out what was going on in his crazed brain.

Mabel's gaze went back and forth between the cards in his hands and the spider's slow dance in her teacup. Phin could see every smear and speck of dust on her thick glasses, and it made the magnified eyes behind them seem cloudy and distorted. He carefully laid three cards side by side on the table.

"Right. Now you tell me what they say." Mabel waited eagerly as Phin stared at the three cards. One showed a knight brandishing a sword while riding a horse; the second had a woman prying open a lion's mouth; the third showed three women holding up goblets and dancing in a circle. The cards weren't saying anything that Phin could hear, though the colors in the images were growing brighter, and he could have sworn that a figure in one of the pictures was looking right at him. He wondered if he was hallucinating and glanced up at Mabel in case she was seeing the same thing as he was. Nope. She was staring at him expectantly with those humongous, magnified eyes.

Phin sighed, took a deep breath and dared to look at the cards again. The images had grown deeper and more three-dimensional, and as he squinted the horse began to move, its powerful legs pumping as it propelled itself and the knight right out of the card and into the next, startling the woman and the lion. The lion promptly bit the woman's hand off and the three women from the third card rushed in to fill their cups with her blood. The knight and horse were long gone by the time the lion had finished eating the hand, and the woman had fallen to the ground in a faint. The three other women huddled together in their own card, cradling their blood-filled cups and eyeing the lion warily.

Phin gaped at the scene through a haze of dust that the horse had left behind. He could hear the lion growling and smell the blood that glistened on the grass and glanced up just in time to see Mabel take a sip of her spider tea. He felt his gorge rise as he imagined the spider swimming into her mouth. He shut his eyes tightly for a moment and when he opened them the three cards had reverted back to their original images; no amputated hand, no blood, even the knight had returned. Phin's heart was pounding so hard and fast that his chest hurt.

"So are you going to tell me, or what?" Mabel said, finishing her tea and setting the cup back in its saucer. "Riva always said that your first impressions are usually the right ones. That the longer you stare at the cards, the more obscure the information gets."

Phin glanced at the cards, flinching when the knight's horse chuffed out a breath. "Well, um, I guess someone's going to come charging in and startle the woman holding the lion," he said thickly. "The lion will bite her but three women will save some part of her. Uh, so maybe that means that no matter how bad things get, she's always got friends that will come to her rescue."

Mabel beamed at him. "I knew you had the gift," she said, reaching out and squeezing his hands. "So the woman is me, right? And I suppose the three women might be Dee, Lydia and Tammy. Or maybe Fiona. Doesn't matter, I guess. No matter what happens, they'll always be there for me. I am getting older, you know, almost sixty-eight. It's nice to know I've got friends. Thank you so much, Phineas."

He kept his eyes on her face as she chattered, hoping that the cards would remain static if he ignored them. But no such luck; the knight had noticed Phin and had turned his horse to face him. The knight held his sword high and Phin saw the glint of a spurred boot heel. He snatched his hands away from Mabel's, grabbed the three cards and shoved them back into the deck before the horse could leap out at him. He quickly wrapped the cards in the piece of green velvet and pushed them towards Mabel.

"Ok, I'll put them away in a minute, but now I'd like you to read this," she said, handing him her teacup. It wavered and rippled as he reached for it, and he held it in both hands to make it stop moving.

Phin stared at the bloated remains of the spider in the bottom of the cup. One of the spider's remaining legs peeled away from its wet body and waved at him. A shiny black eye winked. Phin clamped his teeth together to keep from squealing. He felt like he'd fallen into Alice's rabbit hole and wondered if this was what an acid trip felt like.

SEVEN

"And then she handed me her cup with this cooked spider in it and asked me to read her fortune," Phin said, sitting on the only cat-hair-free spot in the room – a wobbly, straight-backed wooden chair. Dee laughed from the sofa where she was surrounded by three cats, all of which were vying for her attention. She petted and scratched each one in turn and Phin could almost feel their combined purrs from across the room rumbling through the bottom of his chair.

"Mabel has always put a lot of trust in tea readings and Tarot cards," Dee said. She pulled a plastic bottle out of her purse and shook it. It rattled and the cats set up an excited chorus, begging for the crunchy treats they knew were inside. "There was a time when she couldn't do anything without first calling Riva for a reading. She'd sit at home for days, afraid of doing the wrong thing, always needing to be told what to do next. It took Riva a long time to convince her to just live her life, that the cards could only give advice."

"But she was so serious about it and then when I made something up, she believed me."

"She just figures that if Riva left this all to you, then you must have the gift too." She pushed a greedy Castor aside so the other two cats could get to their share of the snacks. "You could probably tell Mabel anything and she'd be happy to fit it into whatever was going on at the time."

"Just like I said! I made it all up," Phin said miserably. He watched the cats lick their paws and swipe them over their ears and faces until their fur was sleek and shiny. They then tucked themselves contentedly against Dee, kneading their paws against her thighs.

"I looked at the pictures and described to Mabel what was going on in them. Nothing else." He suddenly felt queasy as he remembered the knight on his horse and the lion that had bitten off a woman's hand. Nothing else, indeed.

"Exactly! That's what the cards are all about, Phin. You look at the pictures and give your impression of what's going on."

"But I didn't get any kind of impression. They're just cards with pictures. I just described the images and Mabel lapped it up."

"You linked the three images together and applied it to her situation."

"She did that herself."

"So what?"

"You're not making any sense."

"She came to you with a concern. You told her fortune and she was satisfied. If her concern had been different, you would have told a different fortune."

"You can't be sure of that," Phin said, exasperated with her logic.

"Of course not, but then neither can you. Who says you don't have the ability to pick the very cards that apply to her needs? Maybe you could sense her fears about her forgetfulness and her future and were able to zone in on the right answers."

Phin glared at her for a moment, tempted to tell her about the little blue jar and its possible contents. If she'd known he'd been hallucinating the whole time Mabel had sat in his kitchen, she might not be so ready to label him psychic. He watched her roll one of the cats onto its back. She stroked its belly and then rubbed her cheek against the cat's silky head. Phin's eyes started to itch again and he had to look away.

Orion jumped off the sofa and sauntered over to the aquarium. He batted at something lying underneath the elevated glass tank, then picked it up and carried it over to where Phin was seated, dropping it at his feet. Phin recognized the small orange scrap: a dried goldfish tail, lightly mangled. He smiled wryly as Orion head-butted his leg and walked off, tail flicking in his wake. He supposed that was the cat's way of saying, "So long, and thanks for all the fish." Maybe cats had a sense of humor after all. He frowned, as he realized he was starting to think of the cats by their given names, instead of the generic "Stupid." He picked up the scrap of goldfish and dropped it into his empty cup. Dee laughed as he mimed pouring water into it.

"So how long did the fish last?" she asked between giggles.

"A couple of days at least, though I could have sworn I saw one limp across the tank just yesterday. None of the plants were damaged and there was no water on the floor. I'm still not sure how they managed that."

"Cats are pretty agile and they hate to get their paws wet."

"So, the cats teleported the fish out of the tank using their magic psychic powers. Must be something in the air in this house." Phin grinned at her fresh spurt of giggles, enjoying the way her face lit up. "Why did Riva bother to keep the aquarium if she couldn't put any fish in it?"

"When I asked her about it, she said she liked having water in the room, that the plants growing in it kept things lively. As if all these cats didn't do that on their own." She shook herself and pushed furry Castor off her lap. He curled up next to her with his identical orange brother Pollux and resumed cleaning his paws.

"Um, Mabel insisted on paying me," Phin said hesitantly. He'd been embarrassed when Mabel tried to shove twenty dollars into his hand. He thought he'd fended her off but found two tens hidden underneath the teapot when he cleared the table later.

"Well, of course. It adds value to the reading when it's paid for. It keeps balance in the universe." Phin's blank expression encouraged her to try again. "Look at it this way – if she's paid you for a reading, you're a professional. Therefore it's a valid reading. Whatever you tell her is true and will happen."

70

"But that makes no sense," Phin argued. "I told you I made it all up. There was no reading, just me making shit up so she'd stop bothering me." He glared at Dee's amused expression and crossed his arms. "It's like some bad joke."

"There's something you have to understand about Mabel and all the others who came to Riva for readings. These women are looking for a little affirmation in their lives." She held up a hand as Phin opened his mouth. "They usually forget all they've heard the minute they walk out the door. They might cling to a small scrap of information but most of the time they're satisfied that they've gotten their money's worth."

"But they're being swindled. Who needs cards and tea? I could just whip up a bunch of fortune cookies and hand them out at the door every time they show up."

"You're not taking into account the entertainment factor. This is a small town, with not much going on. They run out of things to do, things to talk about. They love all the spiritual gossip. None of their friends in Minnow Bay or Castle Creek has their own local fortune teller." She smiled as Phin winced at the term. "Well, you're more like the local hippy witch doctor," she said as she looked around at the changes in the living room.

So much of what had contributed to Riva's ambience had disappeared. The silk scarves, beaded curtains and glass angels, the crocheted doilies and scented candles were all gone. The small round tables that had held her glass menagerie were folded and stacked in one corner. There were colourful throws on the two sofas and Dee recognized the small television that Riva had kept in her bedroom. There were also two posters tacked on the wall that Phin must have found packed away in one of Riva's many closets. They were a manic swirl of psychedelic colors that were probably meant to be viewed under special lighting.

"Where did that come from?" she asked, pointing to a tiny bleached animal skull on a shelf. "I don't remember seeing it before."

"I think it's a fox, but pretty small so maybe just a pup. I found it under a stack of old lumber out back. Most of the skeleton was crushed by the wood, but the skull was intact so I cleaned off the dirt and brought it in." Phin leaned over and picked up the skull, placing it on Dee's palm before she could protest.

"I've always been fascinated by animal skulls," he continued. "I suppose most kids are at some point during their childhood. When I was eight, my father found a nest with three baby bird skeletons. They were perfectly preserved and he helped me set it up on a shelf in my room. The bones were much too fragile to handle and he bought me a magnifying glass so I could get a closer look without damaging them."

Dee couldn't help but marvel at how small the skull was, though its sharp teeth made her shiver and she handed it back promptly. She rubbed the palms of her hands against her jeans as if the skull had left a sticky residue on them.

"I've been thinking of using it on my next walking stick, maybe attaching it at the top or something," Phin said musingly, as he stroked the tiny snout before setting it back carefully in its place.

Dee stood up and went to the nearest bookshelf, pretending to read the titles. She felt jittery. Bones always did that to her. She'd had a recurring dream for years about a giant pile of bones that suddenly started to shake and move, separating itself into smaller piles that became arms, legs and ribcages. These slowly assembled themselves into human skeletons, over which flesh would glide, muscles and sinews seeming to grow out of the bones until they looked nearly alive. She always woke up before the skin finished coating the glistening flesh, so she never got to see the faces, never knew whom – or what – she was dreaming about. She shook herself to get rid of the creeping nerves in her limbs and took several books off the shelf.

"If you plan on staying awhile, you should read some of these books," she said, as she riffled their pages. "They'll help you understand what it is that Riva's clients are looking for in a reading." She looked back at him, relieved to see that he was no longer holding the skull.

"Here, have a look at this," she said, handing him one of the books she'd selected.

"Hey, this picture is the same as one of those cards Mabel brought out yesterday," he said uneasily, taking only a quick peek at the cover of *True Tarot*. He was afraid to look directly at the picture in case it moved. The strange effects of the suspicious tea that Mabel had brewed seemed to have worn off. Nothing was sparkling in the air and nothing inanimate had so much as twitched since he'd woken up this morning, but he wasn't taking any chances.

"That's the Fool, part of the Tarot. Each card has a meaning of its own but that can change depending on what other cards come up with it."

"It's just a guy taking a walk off a cliff and a dog biting his ass."

"But depending on what you had asked the cards, if he turned up he might have something relevant to say to you. There are lots of different decks designed by different people. Some of them claim certain meanings depending on what they painted into the pictures." She walked out of the room for a moment and came back carrying the same green velvet covered cards that Mabel had shown him.

Phin felt a prickle of unease as he watched her unwrap the bundle and lay the fabric on the table between them. He kept his gaze averted, feeling foolish for letting something as lame as a deck of cards unnerve him.

Dee gazed thoughtfully at the cards as she shuffled them several times, and then set them face down on the square of velvet. She turned over the top card. "All right, what do you see in this image?" she said to Phin, as she settled back onto the sofa's cushions.

He glanced at the figure in the card. It didn't move. So he took a longer look. "Ok, a man holding a ball."

"What do you think is happening?"

"I don't know; he's just holding it and looking at a star in the ball. Maybe it's a crystal ball. He's dressed a little funny."

"Good, that's a start. Does it say anything else to you?"

"Not really," he said. "Just a dark-haired man maybe holding a crystal ball of sorts with a glowing star in it."

"You see how it works now?"

"No," he said, exasperated.

"The more you looked at it, the more you saw. First it was just a ball, and then it became a crystal ball with a glowing star."

"But what does it mean?"

"I don't know. You're the one doing the reading, you tell me."

"All right, I will." Phin bent over the card, studying it. The star really seemed to glow, even pulsate a little. And had the man in the card just glanced at him? Even if he had, that was nothing compared to the aggressive antics of the knight on the horse, so Phin calmed down and took a deep breath. "Ok, a dark man will come into your life and give you a glowing star in a crystal."

"So now it's a dark man. See how you changed it when you really looked?" She leaned in closer. "There are so many ways to interpret the cards, there isn't only one right answer."

"Well, what do *you* see?"

"I see exactly what you see. At least this time, I do. The next time I see this card it may mean something else entirely."

"I know, I know – depending on who's there, and what they're asking, right?"

"Right! Now you're getting it. The last reading Riva did for me, she also said I'd meet a dark man. When I first saw you, I thought that's whom she'd meant. Now, I'm not so sure," she said quietly, picking up the card and studying it. "Maybe she meant someone else since you seem to think there's still a dark man in my future."

"I don't think anything. I'm just making it up, like with Mabel. And really, all I'm doing is describing what I see in a picture. A silly-looking one at that."

"But why would you say the same thing Riva said?"

"What if I'd said I saw a boy in a skirt and tights serving up a volleyball?"

"But you didn't. That's just it. You said the first thing that occurred to you, instinctively. Now, you shuffle and pick a card," she said, handing him the deck.

He shuffled as he'd seen her do and turned over a card.

"Ah, the Hermit," Dee said, nodding. "Look at him; he's carrying a walking stick, like you do. He's also holding a lantern and if you look closely there's a glowing star in *it* as well."

"So what's that mean?"

"Well, maybe there's a connection between the two cards, if only in the star. But I'd have to say the Hermit looks more like he's using it to light the way, as opposed to just looking at it, so my guess would be that whenever my dark man shows up, he'll give you a glowing star, or maybe try to take one from you."

"I don't have a glowing star, whatever that is."

"It could be anything. The star is most likely symbolic of something else."

"So, not only do I have to guess at what the cards mean, but whatever happens will only be symbolic of what I read in the first place. This makes less and less sense all the time."

"It's not an exact science, Phineas. Most of the time your clients will tell you what they need to hear. Your job is to just dress it up with magic and serve it to them. Trust me, they'll eat it up every time."

"Do you?"

"Well, I believe that there are many possible futures."

"That doesn't answer my question."

"It's the only answer I've got," she said, gathering up the cards and wrapping them in the velvet cloth once more. She glanced at Phin. He was watching her intently. There had been so little magic in her life lately. When Riva had told her there would be a dark man coming into her life, she hadn't dared to hope that things would change, that her life might come to mean more than just working at a run-down bakery and caring for her mentally ill mother.

"Look, as long as you're staying in Riva's house, the women in this town are going to keep coming to your door for advice. Riva made a decent living out of it, why shouldn't you?"

"So, if I decide to keep the house and live here, I have to fleece the locals," he said, shaking his head disgustedly.

"But they expect it, so it's not like you're taking their money and giving nothing back. Just have a look at some of these books I picked out. They'll be a good start."

"Um, Mabel said something about seeing me on the full moon. What do you think she meant?"

"Riva always held some sort of get-together on the full moon."

"Like what?"

"It varied, I'm sure you'll come up with something," she said, smiling at his anxious look. She got up to leave. "Don't worry, there's still a week until the moon is full. I'll help you if you want."

Yeah, I want, he thought, as he walked her to the door. He watched her as she walked down the path. She was wearing jeans today, a marked improvement on the baggy slacks she wore at the bakery. They showed a form that was more voluptuous than the one he'd imagined was hidden under the frumpy uniform. She turned once to wave to him before disappearing around the bend.

Phin closed the door and returned to the living room. He picked up the books she'd left for him to read. He still found it difficult to look directly at the cover of *True Tarot*. Neither the Fool nor his dog had so much as twitched, but Phin didn't trust what he might see if he looked too closely. He quickly flipped through *Worlds Within*, but it seemed like dry reading, scientific studies on paranormal abilities. He supposed that Dee was trying to show him that it wasn't all flaky, but he put it back on the shelf, along with *Could You Be Psychic?* and *Crystal Magic*, which promised to be a tad too fluffy for his taste.

He scanned the titles of the other books in the bookcase, his eye settling on *Modern Voodoo* and then flicking to the fox skull on his left. Didn't bones get used in voodoo fortune telling? It was a slim volume. He wiggled it out and took it back to the sofa, absently picking up the fox skull as he walked past it.

The room was darkening in the corners, the shadows slowly creeping and spreading inward. Phin reached up to light the lamp he'd set up behind the chair. He turned the book over in his hands, noting that it was yellowed around the edges, though its otherwise pristine condition told him that no one had likely ever read it. The book's spine crackled as he opened it, sounding like the snapping of many small bones.

EIGHT

Dee carried the tray into the sun porch. She set it on the table next to Lydia and adjusted the blanket covering her mother's lap. Lydia opened her eyes and smiled at Dee, reaching up to stroke her cheek.

"Hi sweetie, did you have a good day at work?"

"My day's not over yet, Mom," Dee said with a smile. "I've made lunch. Mabel should be here soon too. Do you want some tea?" She poured it without waiting for an answer. "I've been to Riva's house a couple of times since Phin arrived," she continued, "and he's made some changes to the place but it looks good. It's actually a lot less cluttered. He wants to make sure that anyone who was a friend of Riva's gets something of hers. So he's going to have some sort of yard sale, only he won't be taking any money, just giving her things away."

"That's sweet; he was always such a good boy," Lydia said, carefully picking up her teacup and taking a small sip. "Mother liked him and said he'd make a fine man one day."

"Mom, he stayed with Riva one summer to help out and you probably only saw him twice, if that. I doubt Gran even met him." Dee pushed her mother's plate closer so she could easily reach the egg sandwich and fruit salad. Lydia had eaten the same lunch for weeks; soon she would tire of egg sandwiches and Dee would have to tempt her with something else, otherwise Lydia would eat nothing but fruit salad.

Lydia nibbled on her sandwich and sighed deeply. "Oh, Dee, I'm so tired. Why am I so tired all the time?"

"I don't know, Mom, just eat your lunch and then you can have a nap." She stroked her mother's thin, graying hair and kissed her temple. They went through this same ritual day after day. Doctors had come and gone, each one quick to dismiss Lydia's depression as post-traumatic stress brought on by the disappearance of her mother twenty-five years ago. Dee had come to question their certainty when nothing had changed after a dozen years and Lydia continued to alternately stare at the wall for hours or cry plaintively for her mother. The doctors had prescribed a stay at a hospital, claiming that the change might snap her out of her fugue, and that she'd benefit from the therapeutic programs.

But Dee knew better. Her grandmother, Delia, had begun to behave strangely when she was barely sixty. She'd become forgetful and confused, blaming others for moving or hiding possessions that were usually in plain view. Sometimes she'd lapse into an almost catatonic depression for many days, coming out of it only to weep inconsolably for many more. Dee was afraid for her mother. She was afraid for herself as well. If your grandmother and mother both suffered from mental illness, what were the odds that you would make it through life sane and rational? Her doctor had assured her that there was no guarantee that she would follow in the footsteps of the other women in the family. He'd pointed out that Mabel was healthy, mentally. But Dee wasn't so sure.

Mabel might be sane but she saw things differently than others did. When the sun was shining and Mabel told you it would rain before nightfall because she'd seen George the grey squirrel jumping from tree to tree instead of racing along the power lines, then you could be sure it would rain. Mabel had always been a little different than the other adults during Dee's childhood.

When Dee was ten years old, Mabel had given her a set of baking pans for her birthday. Dee had thought it was a joke and had waited for her real present, but Mabel only told her to remember that she didn't like raisins in her muffins. The tins had sat unused for three years at the back of Dee's closet until the winter that her grandmother disappeared. Lydia had been hospitalized when the search for the three women had been called off after they'd been missing for nearly three weeks.

The snow that winter had been deep, and the temperature had dropped until the trees crackled and snapped from the bitter cold. School had been cancelled for several days until the roads could be cleared and Dee was stuck yet again with her aunt Mabel. They couldn't even get to the hospital to visit her mother. So, out of boredom, Dee dug out those baking pans and started poring through recipe books, looking for something she could bake for her mom's homecoming. She'd always enjoyed baking with her grandmother and thought she might miss her less if she learned to bake for herself.

Mabel found her hours later with several versions of the same cake, each one lighter and tastier than the last. Dee had made copious notes on the experiments and changes she'd made to the recipes, excited by the magic she'd wrought. Mabel had been unsurprised and merely reminded her to go easy on the raisins.

Dee topped up her mother's tea and urged her to eat more of her sandwich but Lydia shook her head and picked at her fruit salad. "So that boy is back, eh?" she mumbled around a grape. "Is he staying at Riva's again?" She glanced at Dee. "Or I suppose he could stay with us if you'd like. He could sleep in Mother's room until she gets back."

"Mom, Phin is a man now, not a boy anymore," Dee said sharply. "He inherited Riva's house so he already has a place to stay." She tucked the blanket snugly around her mother's legs again. "And besides, Grandma isn't coming back. It's been twenty-five years, remember?" She had confused Lydia by changing the routine. Mabel almost always made lunch for Lydia, but Dee had needed to escape work for a while after her encounter with the stranger who'd come through the bakery door that morning.

She had just finished loading the ovens with the day's bread when the bell over the door had tinkled. Her stomach had lurched at the sight of the dark man from the Tarot cards that both Riva and Phin had read for her. She hadn't clearly seen his face at first; limp black hair hung in front of his eyes and stuck to the sweat running down his temples. He'd been wearing far too much clothing for the hot weather. His long black coat dragged on the worn linoleum and hung open to show a black tee shirt and black jeans over dusty cowboy boots.

"Can I help you?" she'd said, watching him warily as he stood there, panting in the damp heat.

"Yeah, I'm looking for Riva. No one seems to be home at her place," he'd said with a smile. It was a poor effort, merely stretching his lips into a tight grimace. "Don't worry," he'd continued, waving a hand in front of his face as if he were shooing a fly, "I know she's dead so you won't be giving me any bad news." He'd smiled a little more widely, but the effect was just as grim, tightened lips disappearing into a thin line.

"Then I don't know why you'd be looking for a dead woman." Dee had felt sorry for him, standing there in the sweltering heat and had wondered if she should offer him a cool drink.

"Okay, I didn't start that right," he'd said, shuffling his feet and taking a deep breath. "Look. I know she's dead. We haven't heard from the lawyers yet. I'm here for my father. He was her cousin and that makes me her second cousin. Riva had something that belonged to my Dad. I need it back." He'd spat out each sentence as if it took tremendous effort to do so.

"Well, then you'll have to speak to Phineas Marshal. He's the new owner of Riva's house."

"What do you mean, new owner?" he'd demanded, his voice rising.

"I mean, Riva left the house to Phineas and he lives there now."

"Who the hell's Phineas? Why didn't she leave the house to her family?" he'd asked, raking his fingers through his hair. The act had exposed his face, showing clear pale skin. He appeared to be no more than thirty, with sharp cheekbones and a few wispy hairs on a pointed chin.

Then he'd looked directly at Dee with eyes of the deepest brown velvet she'd ever seen. "That house should have gone to my grandmother, Ella. How am I supposed to get my Dad's stuff back?"

"Um, well…" She'd swallowed hard, unable to tear her gaze away from those eyes. "I could introduce you to Phin, and well, you could just ask him for it, whatever it is, I guess."

"How can I be sure he'll give it back? I mean he *owns* the place now, right? He might think he owns everything in it too. There are probably lots of things in that house that should go to Ella so she can keep them in the family."

"I'm sure he'll want to give it all back. In fact, he's been getting rid of a lot of Riva's stuff recently, so it should be all right. What is it you're looking for?"

"It's a special crystal with magical properties, been in the family for generations."

"Why didn't your father come to get it himself?"

"Oh, he's been dead for three years but he talked about it all the time when I was a kid." He'd stared at Dee for a moment and then abruptly stuck out his hand. "I'm Eric Minkley, by the way. I'm staying at that place by the highway."

"I'm Dee, short for Delia." She'd blushed. She almost never used her grandmother's name, but this strange man had made her feel, well, strange. "Look, I'll give you Phin's phone number. Just describe to him what the crystal looks like. He's packed up most of that stuff, but I'm certain he'll be glad to dig it out and give it back to your family." Dee had handed him a scrap of paper and he'd taken it from her hand with a grateful, if tense, smile. He'd then walked out into the searing afternoon sunshine and hadn't looked back.

Dee watched her mother stare out the window at the birds in the yard. Lydia had dropped her sandwich, but her hand still hovered an inch below her chin, fingers curled as if she were still holding it. Riva had always been able to shake Lydia out of her fugues and now Dee missed her friend more than ever.

Dee would ask Mabel if she'd ever heard of Riva having a magical crystal that belonged to a relative. Riva had never really talked about her family at all. She'd once mentioned an aunt named Ella a long time ago but Dee didn't remember any details about her except that she lived in Vancouver.

Dee's cheeks flushed again at the thought of Eric's deep brown eyes. She felt as if they had looked deeply into her and taken hold of her breath. Riva had seen a Dark Man in her future, or maybe it had just been Darkness. Phin had told Dee that she'd soon be meeting a Dark Man.

Was Eric the man from the cards or was Phin still a possible candidate? Both Phin and Eric had dark hair. Eric dressed all in black, but Phin exuded an air of shadowy secrets.

Either one could be her Dark Man.

NINE

"Now hold hands with the person on either side of you, so we're in a closed circle. Everyone gaze at the candle in the centre of the table until you feel like your eyes want to close." Phin watched them stare at the flame until their eyelids drooped. Mabel was the last one with her eyes open. Before they closed she winked at him. He frowned at her serene smile. Did she wink because she had confidence in him, or did she know he was mostly making it up as he went along?

When they had arrived at the house in ones and twos an hour ago he'd had tea ready for them in the kitchen, following Dee's instructions. She'd said not to bother with food, that everyone would bring something. She had baked enough rolls, pastries and cookies to feed everyone and still keep Phin in leftovers for a week. Mabel had been in charge of chips but had not been told they were for dipping in the sauces that Tammy and Fritz would bring, so had bought flavoured chips and nachos. As Mabel daintily sampled a barbecue chip covered in guacamole, Josie had arrived bearing an enormous tray of carrot sticks, celery, and sliced peppers, which she set on the table where everyone had helped themselves, sampling the guacamole, salsa and hummus dips with something other than flavoured chips.

Phin had made the tea using loose leaves and a set of tiny cups that Riva had only brought out for special rituals. He'd stuffed himself on the fresh veggies and chips, claiming to be too full to try out the three pies sitting off to the side. Fiona had coloured the pie crusts with vegetable dyes, so that the blueberry pie had a pale blue crust, and the rhubarb was topped in bright pink. The third one looked like some little kid's mud pie, dirty brown and lumpy. It smelled like peanut butter – which he loved – but he wasn't brave enough to try it. Lydia had brought a huge bowl of yellow gelatin jammed full of flowers that she claimed were edible. There'd been no room left on the table so she'd put it into the fridge for later. Phin didn't think he could eat it; it looked more like a decorative centrepiece than like any food he'd ever seen.

They'd all stood around chatting amiably while they sipped the reddish tea, then spent a hilarious twenty minutes interpreting the various images and designs that the wet leaves had shaped at the bottom of their cups. According to Mabel, Phineas would be blessed with six more kittens by autumn, which elicited howls of glee from everyone but Phin. The house was filled with the warmth of their chatter and attentions, and though he was apprehensive about the ritual to come, he felt accepted and welcome.

He'd spent the previous week reading books from Riva's extensive library. *Séances through the Ages* and *The Path of Ritual* had helped him understand the importance of atmosphere and symbolic props and why people needed to believe he was in control of the elements and spirits. He'd found journal notes on past séances that Riva had held – mostly light, fluffy affairs where she conjured up ghosts of dead rock stars, actors and favourite saints. She had followed the same pattern each time, answering questions that people asked about those ghosts she had brought into their midst, and deflecting queries about close friends and family that had passed on.

Phin intended to change that aspect of the ritual by focusing on Riva. He would call her to come and tell them that she was in a better place, that she was in Heaven or wherever they expected she had landed. When they realized it was impossible and that he couldn't contact their dead psychic friend, they'd never ask him to tell their fortunes again. They might then leave him alone so he could work on the house without their constant interruptions. He was feeling worn out from the daily fear that someone would discover his shameful secret.

Dee had helped to set up the living room for the séance and had contacted all the people who would most likely want to attend. She had made him dig out all the candles he'd stuffed into boxes and left out on the porch. They'd placed them all over the room, along with several sticks of fragrant incense. The wooden table from under the window had switched places with the sofa. It had two leaves that flipped up to convert it from rectangle to circle. Dee had draped scarves over the lamps, as Riva had always done, but she'd used darker hues, lending the room a more shadowy, dusky feel.

She'd also helped Phin dress for the occasion. He'd balked at the closet full of caftans and shawls that Riva had dressed from, but Dee found him a simple dark blue velvet robe covered in black satin stars. Then she had trimmed the sides of his beard, leaving a long swatch on his chin, which she twisted into two thin braids. She'd even brought makeup and had lined his eyes in black kohl.

By the time Dee had left to pick up Lydia and Mabel, the sun was setting and the living room had begun to glow warmly with candlelight. Wisps of incense smoke trailed throughout the room, and cats wound their lithe bodies around the legs of the nine chairs Phin had set up around the table.

While he'd waited for the first of his guests to arrive, Phin had nervously moved several candles to better spots, and then put them back in their original places. He'd poured himself a large shot of rum and downed it in one gulp. He'd gone over his notes once more to be certain he wouldn't forget anything. Dee had warned him not to be too locked into a schedule, as the unexpected always seemed to happen during these séances. But Phin was determined to give them something completely different than what they were used to. He would *be* the unexpected.

As he'd paced around the room, trying to immerse himself in the ambience that he and Dee had created, he'd spotted the fox skull sitting on its shelf next to a low candle. The skull had taken on a ruddy cast in the glow of the tiny flame bobbing next to it. Phin had reached for it and cupped the tiny skull in his hand, studying its delicate lines. It had felt warm – warmer than it should have been in the cool room – but he told himself that it had been sitting next to a candle flame for an hour.

He'd then carried it over to the desk, and rummaged through several drawers until he found a thin length of leather. He'd wound it through and around the skull, then knotted the ends and slipped the loop over his head. The fox skull had settled on his chest – snout down – just a few inches below the stiffly braided beard. Phin had grinned fiercely at what he'd seen illuminated by twin candles fixed in sconces on either side of the mirror. The dark caverns of his eye sockets matched those of the fox's skull, to grisly effect. Riva's girls would not see the mystical fortune teller they expected, they would not get the same old familiar séance, instead, they would encounter the gruesome mask that the mirror now reflected.

Phin cleared his throat. "Everyone take a deep breath now, and then let it out in a hiss." Everyone at the table did as he said, and the room filled with a sibilance that sent the cats scurrying out of the room.

"Good. Is there anyone here who wants to talk to someone on the other side?"

There were several murmurs but then Dee spoke up, right on cue.

"We'd like to hear from our friend Riva, who was taken from us suddenly." She squeezed Phin's hand, her signal for him to follow the next part in their rehearsed sequence. He didn't respond and she glanced sideways at him. His eyes were closed, his brow furrowed. She squeezed again, harder, and gave his hand a little shake for good measure.

"Uh, Spirits of the Beyond, hear our plea," he said in a rush. Phin was getting confused. He and Dee had decided on a series of hand squeezes as their signal to each other. Unfortunately, Rebecca, who sat on his other side, was also trying to convey something to him and had been squeezing his left hand repeatedly. He was losing track of where he and Dee were in their hand-squeezing sequence.

Phin was finding it difficult not to be distracted by Rebecca, a younger version of Tammy, her mother. From the moment she was introduced to Phin, she had been vying for his undivided attention. She was visiting her parents for a few weeks to recover from her latest shattered romance. Rebecca was several years younger than he was and very pretty, with her mother's striking green eyes. Tammy had taken over the seating arrangements, contriving to seat her daughter next to Phin, though the name card had clearly shown that Mabel was to sit at his left.

"Um, we'd, um, like to speak to our departed sister, Riva," Phin continued. He tried to ignore the hand squeezes coming from both sides now, since both women had intensified their attempts to get his attention. He wished that Mabel had been on his left, as they'd decided, since she'd have at least been calming.

The room was very quiet, with only the sound of nine people breathing and the occasional sigh and fidget. According to Dee and Mabel, the night of the full moon was appropriate for conjuring and talking to ghosts, and was generally a time of high spiritual energy. He was taking their word for it, since it was all bunk. In his world, the full moon was only a backdrop for werewolves and other make-believe beasties.

Phin wondered what to do now. Dee had told him that the spirits would come and take care of whatever it was he asked of them. He didn't believe that any more than he believed that cards and tea leaves could predict the future but had been willing to suspend disbelief long enough to see what would happen. He remembered Dee telling him to be firm when talking to the spirits, as they would ignore him if he sounded uncertain or nervous. Maybe he'd better try again.

"We demand to speak to Riva. Need we ask again?" He felt a hard tug on his right hand and winced, wondering if Dee thought he'd overdone it.

"This boy has grown into an impatient man."

Phin's eyes snapped open. Mabel sat directly across from him. Her eyes were wide open but had rolled back and showed only the whites.

"We remember the boy. We thank the boy for his service."

Everyone was staring at Mabel now. Her voice wavered, and was higher pitched, that of an older and weaker woman. Fiona and

Tammy were trying to disentangle their fingers from hers but she gripped them tightly. Dee shook her head at them and they settled, keeping the circle closed, though they pulled their bodies as far from Mabel as they could while still holding hands.

"Um, who is speaking to us?" Phin ventured.

"Some of you may remember me as Cora, though much time has passed."

"Cora? Is my mother with you?" The first words that Lydia had spoken since she'd arrived at the house came out in a choked whisper.

Dee twitched and nearly let go of Phin's hand as she turned to her mother. "Mom, shhh! Only Phin can ask questions, otherwise the spirits will get angry and leave."

Lydia said nothing more but began to tremble as if a cold wind had suddenly whipped through the room. She huddled into her shawl and Dee and Josie scooted themselves as close to her as they could.

"Is the boy still here?"

"This is Phineas. There's no boy here." Phin began to sweat, wondering what was going on. What was Mabel up to? Did she know more than what she'd let on? She couldn't. Mabel couldn't have kept herself from blurting out the truth if she had known it. But there couldn't actually be spirits talking through people. That was just some kind of trick. Everyone knew that séances were faked.

"We were certain that, in time, the boy would forget. We regret his involvement. He must let it go."

Mabel's face betrayed nothing. Her expression was wooden. Only her lips moved and her eyes remained rolled up, the whites reflecting the tiny flame from the single candle on the table. Drops of sweat had begun to bead along her hairline and the muscles in her neck and arms where knotted with tension.

Phin was losing feeling in his fingers. Dee and Rebecca held his hands so tightly that his bones were grinding against each other, but he hardly noticed. His attention was focused on Mabel. Was someone really talking to him through her? That was impossible. Wasn't it?

"Um, thank you Spirits of the Beyond for your attentions. Is there any other message you have for us?" He was afraid to ask but Dee had said that was the formula to use. They always had something else to say but you had to coax it out of them.

"Yes, Riva warns that the crystal is dangerous and that Carl was never meant to have it."

Phin was about to ask who Carl was, when Mabel gasped and slumped forward, her forehead thumping loudly on the table. Tammy and Fiona reached for Mabel, sitting her upright and rubbing her hands and cheeks. Her glasses sat askew on her nose. She shook her head and looked at Phin, grinning widely.

"Wow, did you get all that?" Mabel said excitedly. "That was Cora! Ow, stop fussing, Tammy, I'm ok." She pushed Tammy's and Fiona's hands away and straightened her glasses.

"Mabel, do you think Mother was there too?" Lydia leaned forward anxiously and held her breath.

"I think so. I could sort of feel her and Fran off to the side."

Fritz pushed his chair back loudly and stood up. "Oh, come on now. You don't mean to tell me you think you channelled those three old women. You all need to let go of that, it's been nearly thirty years." He gestured to his wife and daughter to get up. Tammy and Rebecca glared at him and stayed put.

"Fritz, I told you that you wouldn't like a séance. You should have stayed home with Lola and the puppies."

"I thought it would be different without Riva and her crazy ideas, that a man would bring a bit of reason to this house and you'd stop relying on mystic tricks to run your life. And now it's just all continuing with this stupid voodoo shit." Tammy rolled her eyes at his pompous tone and returned her attention to Mabel. Fritz huffed into his mustache and stomped from the room, slamming the back door on his way out.

"Do you know what happened to them?" Lydia asked. Dee draped an arm over her mother's trembling shoulders, pulling her closer.

"Well, not really," Mabel answered slowly. "I mostly got that they were pretty much ok where they are."

"Do you think maybe they're alive?" Fiona blushed as all eyes swiveled towards her. "Oh, I know it's been a long time…" she faltered and smiled sheepishly.

"Honey, Fran was ninety-two when she disappeared. That would make her almost a hundred and twenty. Not impossible, but unlikely, since she was so sick with her arthritis back then." Mabel patted Fiona's hand and turned back to Phin. "What boy do you think Cora was talking about?"

"Probably Carl, whoever he is," Rebecca said, earning a grateful smile from Phin. She gazed at him adoringly and scooted her chair closer, ignoring Dee's glare.

"But she was speaking to Phin when she said something about a secret being held too long," Fiona said, "And that you'd done what they'd told you to do."

"Uhh, I'm not sure what she meant by that," Phin said, trying to avoid looking directly at any of the faces turned towards him.

Mabel shook her head. "You know the spirits are never specific. They often tell you things meant for other people. I'm sure that Cora was talking to Phin as if he were Carl, if that's who the message was for."

"But what do you think she meant by a secret?" Fiona said, insistently. "I mean, it sounded to me like it had something to do with us, otherwise, why would Cora bring it up at all?"

"Why don't we ask the cards?" Mabel said. She stood up and went to a side table where several packs of Tarot cards had been set out for the evening. She picked out her favourite deck and brought it back to the table, putting it in front of Phin.

He shuffled it a few times, but his hands shook so he handed the cards back. "You go ahead, Mabel. You seem to have the thread of the issue, you'll most likely get a better answer to your questions."

Phin sat back, glad that Dee was engrossed with Lydia. He hoped she hadn't noticed his distress at Cora's words. Did Cora mean that he should confess his secret? Tell them about his part in the disappearance of Cora, Delia, and Fran? He'd tried for so long to forget about his involvement. Over the years, every time it came to mind, he told himself that someone had shown up, just like they'd told him would happen, and that they'd had their ritual. Years later, when he'd finally learned to use one of the library computers, he'd searched news archives for stories about Cricket Lake. Every article he'd found that referenced the disappearance confirmed that the women were never seen again. There was no mention of any ritual.

Mabel cut the deck of cards into two piles.

"This one is for whatever secret Cora is talking about, and this one is for Carl," she said, then flipped over the top card from each pile.

Phin twitched as he was confronted again with the three dancing women holding their golden goblets. He wondered briefly if they were still filled with the blood from the woman who'd lost her hand to the lion. Were the cards confirming that Cora's secret was about the three women he'd once driven to a remote cabin in the woods on a stormy winter night?

Mabel jabbed the card with satisfaction. "Aha! There they are again. Or should I say: there you are again," she said, looking in turn at Dee, Tammy, and Fiona. "Phin read this card for me the other day. It's about my friends, and how they'll always be there for me."

"But this is supposed to be about the secret that Cora told us about. Not a confirmation of our friendship." Dee spoke without lifting her eyes from the other card. "It's more likely to have something to do with Cora, Fran, and Delia."

Mabel frowned and peered more closely at the card, her nose nearly touching it. "The one on the left does sort of look like Fran did when she was younger. But I've only ever seen a picture of her at that age, so I can't be sure. The one in red has her hand on

Fran's butt. Could that be it? That they were secret lesbians? Wow, that would explain a lot."

"Mabel! Get some sense, will you?" Fiona exclaimed. "I knew them all, and there was certainly nothing like that going on. Think, now. Three women disappear, never to be seen again. They could have planned it. Maybe that's the secret, that they were the ones with a secret, one which we'll never learn."

"But why did Cora say that Phin had held the secret for too long, then?" Rebecca hadn't let go of Phin's hand, though he'd tried to shake her off a couple of times.

"Um, I don't think she was necessarily talking to me, or about me," he said hopefully.

"That's right," said Dee. She finally looked up from Carl's card and frowned at Rebecca's and Phin's entwined hands. She could just see the fox skull out of the corner of her eye, swinging back and forth every time Phin moved his head. She wished he hadn't worn it. Bones brought a sinister element to their usually lighthearted get-togethers.

"It just looks like three women sharing a toast, big deal," Josie said glumly. She looked at her watch, wondering if her boys had tied up the babysitter yet. She didn't usually stay away for more than a couple of hours, just in case things got out of control at home.

"You have to look past the obvious," Mabel said to her. "Twitch your mind a little. Phin's got the hang of it. What do *you* think it means, Phineas?"

"Well, if it's about a secret, it looks like there are three people involved. But we sort of know that already. So maybe they're celebrating about having kept the secret for so long?" Phin hoped they'd buy that line of reasoning and drop it. He'd have to think about the whole divulging-of-the-secret thing. He couldn't just tell them he'd been the one to take their friends away and had never told anyone about it. Time had worn his screaming conscience down to a whisper but tonight the volume was rising again, as if twenty-five years had never happened and he had just today driven away from those three old ladies.

If the storm had prevented the others from meeting the women at the cabin – or worse, if he'd left them at the wrong cabin – they'd have likely died of the cold. Not the worse way to go if you're going to kill yourself.

Should he have refused to leave them there? Called the police? If the three women had gone out there to commit suicide, did that make Phin an accomplice of some sort? Could he be charged, kind of like leaving the scene of an accident? If he told the group now, they'd probably run him out of town. Just when he was starting to think it might be nice to stay.

"I'm sure we'll find out what this all means soon enough," he said, desperate to buy himself some time. "What about Carl's card?"

"Oh that one's easy," Dee said, picking it up to inspect it more closely. "This one came up the other day. It's about a dark man and a globe."

"Hold it," Mabel interjected, "That was a different reading. This is about Carl, whoever he is." She smiled smugly at Dee, who stuck out her tongue and smiled back.

"All right then, fine. Maybe Carl wants a globe. There was a young man at the bakery yesterday looking for something his father had loaned to Riva."

"A young man? You didn't say anything about a young man. How young?" Mabel leaned forward eagerly.

"Whoa, Mabel. He said he was looking for a crystal that Riva borrowed from his father a long time ago."

"Was he dark? I mean, could he be Carl?"

"He was dressed completely in black, but he introduced himself as Eric, so he couldn't be Carl."

"Maybe Carl sent him as a decoy, or a messenger." Josie stood up as everyone's attention focused on her. "Doesn't really matter unless we know what Cora meant by a crystal. Look, I should get going. The sitter usually calls at least twice when I'm away, and I haven't heard from her yet. I'm worried that the boys may have trussed her up and put her in the root cellar again."

"We could ask Eric," Dee said, as everyone else stood up and started folding chairs. "He might know this Carl."

"That would be just too much of a coincidence. Maybe we're reading too much into this." Fiona gathered the tarot cards together and set the deck with the others.

"I'm with Dee on this one," Mabel said. "This is like finding a fresh clue in a mystery."

"But how will you find him again?" Phin asked.

"If he was serious about finding his father's crystal he'll probably find you," Dee said. "I gave him your phone number."

TEN

Phin woke to the soothing rhythm of rain on the roof. The sun had barely come up, and the bedroom was patterned in shadowy shapes and dark corners. He stretched until his bones cracked, and then snuggled deeper into his blankets, lulled by the drumming patter. Rainfall had always been one of his favourite sounds.

One of his oldest memories was of sleeping in his grandmother's screened porch the summer he was five. It had rained all night, and every time he'd woken up the thrum of the raindrops on the tin roof had been like a lullaby that had sung him back to sleep. He'd wet himself in the night, and the next morning claimed that the rain had dripped onto his bed and soaked him. He hadn't noticed his grandmother's smile as she folded the dry blanket that had covered him.

It was too early to get up yet, so he bunched his blanket more tightly under his chin and rolled over into a wet spot. He drew back sharply and sat up. That's when he noticed that the sound of the rain hitting the roof was punctuated by several other dripping sounds. He reached over and turned on the bedside lamp, and heard the wet plop of a huge drop of water just as he saw it splash onto his blanket. The wet patch of fabric was darker than the rest of the blanket and had spread over nearly a quarter of the bed.

Phin threw back the covers, swung his feet over the side and stepped into another puddle. Before he had time to move his feet out of it, a drop struck him on the nose and trickled into his mouth. It tasted mouldy. He spluttered and stomped across the room to slam open the door. Castor and Pollux had been sleeping on the other side of the door, just as they had every night since he'd started closing it when he went to bed. They both hissed and ran, skirting yet another puddle that lay in the middle of the hallway.

Phin realized with dismay that he could now hear an entire percussive symphony of drips, splashes and trickles as the deluge outdoors seeped through the gaps in the roof and into his house. He stumbled towards the kitchen, cursing loudly as his feet encountered one cold pool of water after another. He ransacked the kitchen, pulling out every bowl, pot and bucket he could lay his hands on. He then worked his way out from the kitchen, setting out catch basins in the middle of each puddle. They began to fill quickly, and he hoped the storm wouldn't last long or he'd have to spend the day bailing the house.

He had to move an entire bookshelf to get at the river that was trickling down the wall in the living room. Fortunately, none of the books was wet, but the stack of metaphysical magazines on the floor next to the shelf was already soaked and starting to swell. He pulled a blanket off the sofa and shoved it against the bottom of the wet wall to catch as much of the running water as he could.

He hadn't yet put away the chairs and table from last night's séance. Water splashed up from where drops hit the table surface, sprinkling his forearms as he put three plastic cereal bowls down to catch the rain.

He stripped the bed, noting with relief that the water hadn't seeped too deeply into the mattress. He moved the bed away from the dripping water and set another pan out to catch it. That made it eighteen leaks, including the stream behind the bookshelf, and he wondered if it was worth climbing up into the cramped attic space to count how many places the roof was actually compromised.

He'd been warned about the roof by nearly everyone who came to the house. Aside from the recent windstorms, Mabel had told him there'd been a couple of minor earthquakes in the last year and that Riva's house had suffered the worst in the neighbourhood, with toppling bookcases and broken dishes. He'd noticed the cracks running through most of the ceilings in the house, and had planned to patch them. He'd added that chore to his growing list of everything that was wrong in his new home.

Riva had mentioned the earthquakes in passing in one of her journal entries, noting that the cats had all vacated the house several hours before each tremor and hadn't returned until after dark.

The cats were making themselves scarce now, he thought, as he turned on all the lamps in the living room to drive back the gloominess. Water dripping into bowls and pots drowned out the thunder of the rain outside. He drew back the curtains from the window above his carving corner. The sky was a deep leaden grey, with dense low clouds endlessly draining themselves of water. The constant downpour hammered the leaves in the trees, as if a strong wind buffeted them from above.

Phin picked up the walking stick he'd been working on all week. Tiny footprints marched in a crooked downward spiral around the bottom third of the staff. They were crisscrossed with an even smaller set. Phin had tried for wolf prints, but suspected that he'd achieved something more like a cat's. Several days ago, while preparing for the séance, he'd discovered a book on symbols and had been carefully carving various designs into the top part of the staff. He'd tried to incorporate images that not only were pleasing to look at, but that represented aspects relating to walking. The book claimed that certain symbols would bring protection and strength, and would keep the traveller from becoming lost. Phin had tried to puzzle out why a shape or an image could be responsible for keeping a person safe but eventually decided that it didn't matter. The walking stick was turning out to be the best he'd done. He'd blended the carved symbols with the natural whorls and grain of the wood, achieving a harmonious design that made him smile with satisfaction every time he picked it up. Except this time.

A pungent scent filled his nostrils, a scent that came from this corner. His carving corner smelled of cat pee. He walked through the living room to be certain of where it was coming from. The rest of the room smelled musty, as he would have expected from all the dampness, but only the corner with his wood and carving tools carried that distinctive ammonia smell. He fumed and muttered as he picked up each piece of wood and delicately sniffed it. It was only when he leaned over the box of curled shavings that the scent became the sharpest. He peered closely at the mass of wood parings, noting with disgust that they were darker in one corner of the box.

"She said the stupid cats peed outside," he grumbled as he carried the box out to the back porch to be dealt with later.

The huge pile of boxes and bags of Riva's possessions that had nearly filled the small porch had shrunk considerably. He'd invited all those who had attended the séance to help themselves to something of hers as a memento. He'd also managed to pawn off the more rickety pieces of furniture and dainty dishes that Riva had collected. Tiny tables with glass tops and spindly legs were useless to a man who was used to sturdy, functional furniture. He'd destroyed one such table simply by dropping a stack of books onto it one day. Its legs had buckled and collapsed into kindling.

Phin went into the kitchen to brew a pot of strong coffee. He didn't think he'd ever get used to people giving him money for making up fortunes for them, though it was hard to ignore the crinkled bills sticking out from under the edge of the toaster, especially with the house's lengthening repair bill.

He opened the fridge for some cream and was confronted with the usual assortment of containers and wrapped foods. A sheet of thin plastic film covered half a pie, and he grinned at the memory of its taste. Fiona's peanut butter pie. He'd politely declined, and joked about having it on toast until he'd finally had that first bite. It had melted in his mouth in a burst of creamy peanut butter, cheesecake-like wonder. Smells like breakfast to me, he thought, as he set it on the table and poured himself a cup of coffee. There was a stack of Riva's journals sitting on top of the fridge and he took them to the table to read while he devoured the pie. Luckily, the table was one of the few dry areas in the house, so he was able to comfortably eat his breakfast while he read.

He'd only briefly skimmed the few pages relating to a period in Riva's life when she'd begun to explore metaphysics and the possibility of "communing with departed spirits," as she'd put it. He wondered if her need to talk to the departed stemmed from her involvement with the three women who had disappeared. His skin goose-pimpled as he recalled last night's "visit" from Cora, and her warning about Carl. He swallowed his mouthful of pie with difficulty and drained his coffee in one gulp.

Were there really spirits out there, watching the living, just waiting for an opportunity to be heard? Phin hoped to speak to Mabel soon about her experience. Dee had mentioned that her family had a history of mental imbalances. Mabel had to be almost seventy. She might simply be succumbing to an inevitable mental decline, an age-related dementia, like her mother had, doomed to end her days imagining ghosts, phantasms and dead friends coming over for a visit and a chat. Or she could be as sane as he was, and really had become a spirit channel last night, a speaker for the dead.

Phin was 42 years old and had never encountered a ghost in his entire life. He'd never heard a voice from someone who wasn't there, had never had a dream that foretold a coming event. His life was based on reality, on what he could see and touch. His parents had never even taken him to church. They had instilled in him a need to question and refute any idea that had even the slightest suggestion of flakiness. As a young adult, out on his own, he'd delighted in being the skeptic, in poking holes in others' beliefs and theories. It hadn't gained him any popularity, but he felt safe knowing he'd never fall victim to someone else's superstitious nonsense.

It had been fun to play-act the voodoo priest last night, though from what he'd understood from all the reading he'd done on the subject, voodoo was an actual religion with millions of followers. It was nothing like what he'd seen in the movies, with zombies rising from graveyards and human sacrifices by mad cannibals. Sure, in real life voodoo practitioners sacrificed the odd rooster as an offering, but corn cakes or rum would do just as well for summoning a spirit. He hadn't planned for it to actually work, but without drums, dancing, or sacrifice last night, Mabel had fallen into a spiritual trance, just as was described in the books. Was she simply a good actor?

Phin squinted at Riva's tiny handwriting as he finished the last bite of pie. He was reading entries that dated from before she'd begun her career as a fortune teller, several years after he'd spent the summer here at her home. There was no mention of her plans with the three women that night, or of giving him her car. She'd likely thought it best not to put it in writing.

What if Cora, Fran and Delia had thought that there really was a solstice ritual happening at the cabin? What if Riva had involved him in a conspiracy to kill the three women by having him drive them to a secluded cabin to await their deaths in a December snowstorm? It was possible. If Riva had been held in such high regard by her clients they wouldn't have questioned her plans for an out-of-the-way ritual. But what would be her motive for murder? And what of the possibility that the three women had planned to disappear? They'd been old, probably dying of something incurable and had decided to end their lives.

He'd once thought that if he found out he had some incurable disease he'd find some way to kill himself before he suffered an agonizing, drawn-out death. He'd just end it, simply, like those ladies probably had done. If everyone thought that way, no one would ever suffer needlessly. Anyone who found out they were going to die would check out before the going got rough, instead of trying every desperate treatment or gimmick they could get their hands on.

But could he really do it? Would he have the courage to have someone drop him off in the middle of winter, with no way to get back to safety? He shuddered, and was about to close the journal when Carl jumped out of the page at him.

"Carl called last night. He was very angry that I'd been given the crystal instead of him. I told him that it was important that it be kept safe. He said it would be wasted on me; that it held powerful magic that would dwindle and fade if it wasn't used.

"The crystal is much too dangerous to give to Carl. He'd try to force the magic to his advantage, use it to tap into power he'd never be able to control. I hate having it in my house, it's creepy, but I promised Ella that I would guard it. I just hope that Carl doesn't try to take the crystal. I'm not sure if I can protect it from him if he tries, let alone defend us all from the nasty forces he'd unleash."

Phin closed the journal and set it on the stack. So Carl wanted a crystal that had been given to Riva for safekeeping. Was it the same crystal she had mentioned in a much later entry, penned only a few weeks before she died? She'd written that it held powerful magic, great divinatory powers, and that she was thinking of using it, as she felt that her "sight" was fading and needed a boost. Maybe she had used the crystal, whatever that meant, and it had killed her. But he had seen several crystals in the house. Could it be one of them? No, if it were that powerful and valuable, Riva wouldn't have left it out in the open. Phin shook his head and smiled ruefully. He couldn't believe he was actually entertaining the possibility that there was not only a magic crystal in the house, but that a ghost had told him not to give it to someone he'd never met. And who was Ella?

Dee had said that this Eric was looking for a crystal as well. Could Carl have sent him? Phin pressed his fingers to his temples, trying to puzzle it all out: Ella gives a crystal to Riva, which Carl feels should have been given to him; Cora – a dead woman channeled by a possibly demented Mabel – says not to give the crystal to Carl; some guy called Eric shows up looking for a crystal.

Phin got up to pour some more coffee, hoping that a fresh caffeine jolt would clear his head. It was still raining heavily outside. He reminded himself to empty the bowls and pots soon. The coffee was bitter, probably simmered too long. He winced as he drank it down quickly, and turned when he heard a soft meow. Orion sat in front of the stove, looking down at a perfect set of furry moth wings, nearly five inches across from tip to tip, chocolate brown, each with two white spots rimmed in black. They had been neatly severed from the moth's body, which was nowhere in sight. The cat patted the wings gently with his paw and looked up at Phin, who sighed and picked them up, holding them gingerly by their fuzzy edges. He wondered how the cat had found a moth in a rainstorm; neither the cat nor the moth wings were wet. If they hadn't felt so fresh, he would have thought that the cat had been saving them for a rainy day.

He thought of Mabel as he set the kettle on the stove, and how proud of him she'd be. He folded the moth wings into the bottom of a teacup, glumly staring at them as he waited for the water to boil. He glanced down at Orion as the cat brushed against his leg on his way out of the kitchen. He wondered if Riva had trained the cats to bring her their kills to use in divination, though he'd never heard of cats being trained that way before. So far they'd brought him an eviscerated crow, a broken-legged spider, and now a pair of severed moth wings.

As far as he knew, cats did whatever they wanted to do, whenever they wanted to do it. He'd heard that they could see more than humans could; that they could sense when an invisible entity was in their presence. But you'd have to believe in ghosts before you could believe that cats could see them.

He could ask Mabel about that when she showed up for her next reading. He shuddered at the memory of her first visit and hoped he could get her to just have her tea leaves read next time, skipping the creepy Tarot cards. He'd been steering a wide berth around the cabinet where they were kept, they made him uneasy. He was pretty sure the images wouldn't move if he looked at them now, but in the future he'd keep a close watch on Mabel and what she dropped into his teapot.

As he poured boiling water over the moth wings, he wondered if he should be worried about the violent nature of the cat's offerings. The wings shrivelled and melted together to form an ugly brown clump at the bottom of the cup. Dust and tiny hairs swirled in the muddy water and Phin watched the concoction darken until it resembled something scooped out of a puddle. He sniffed at the rising steam, trying to decide if it smelled more like mould from a wet basement or a very old pair of sweat-drenched running shoes. He took a tentative sip and grimaced at the rank taste, deciding that it tasted like a very old pair of sweat-drenched running shoes that had languished in a mouldy, wet basement for too long. He closed his eyes, pinched his nostrils closed, and drained the cup in one gulp.

After several moments, during which he had time to wonder whether moths were poisonous, he leaned over the sink and drank deeply from the cold-water faucet. He then took the teacup to the table and sat staring at its soggy contents. They had settled into three distinct masses, surrounded by several tiny bits in brownish clusters. He took a deep breath and tried to quiet his thoughts, as Dee had told him to do. One of the clumps looked a bit like a rat staring at one of the other clumps, which looked like a clothes hamper. Phin shuddered at the thought of finding a rat in his clothes hamper and then remembered he now lived with five cats.

So, no rats in the clothes hamper.

He blinked hard and looked again, this time seeing a large parcel wrapped in string. Was he going to receive a parcel? A gift? A delivery?

Dee had said that the bits you saw in the bottom of a teacup didn't always represent actual things, that sometimes they were meant to symbolize feelings or events. Phin closed his eyes and asked himself what he was feeling. He wasn't certain, so he opened them again. Maybe his uncertainty was the answer, he thought, as he frowned at the mush in his cup. He allowed his eyes to unfocus, and immediately felt a prickle of unease run down his back. He sat up straight and glanced out the window at the backyard, certain he'd heard something outside that had caused his nervous reaction. He avoided looking at the marijuana plants, crumpled at the feet of the thistles. In their weakened state they hadn't been able to withstand the rain and had been hammered into the mud.

Phin pushed back his chair in disgust. This was stupid. He'd drunk a cup of moth wing tea – risking poison – and then tried to divine his future from the dregs. Apparently, he was feeling uncertainty, and maybe a touch of danger. Or maybe he was about to receive a parcel, or he'd somehow find a rat that had run the cat-gauntlet and found its way into his clothes hamper.

As he carried his cup to the sink, he heard the front door open. He'd almost forgotten he was expecting Dee to come for lunch so they could hash out last night's séance together.

He quickly rinsed out the teacup, poking at the drain until all the mushy bits of moth wing had disappeared.

ELEVEN

Dee realized too late that she'd walked into Phin's living room without knocking. Riva's door had always been open to Dee. She'd been letting herself into this house for most of her life. She'd always loved the front entrance, with its tiny stained glass window and the recessed alcove in the hallway where Riva had always kept a bowl of mints. The bowl was empty now and the stained glass was smudged and dusty.

She knew that Phin spent a lot of time in the kitchen, but going through the back door would seem too abrupt, even though she knew that was the entry most other people used. She felt her face flush, and wanted to kick herself for acting without thinking, for carelessly intruding on his privacy, and for feeling self-conscious and flustered every time she came anywhere near Phineas Marshal. She'd left the bakery earlier than usual just so she could meet Phin for lunch, but had rushed home first so she could clean up and change into some casual clothes. She hoped that Brent could manage alone and wouldn't scare off too many customers.

She wished she could sneak out and try again, but the wind had helped her close the door a little more loudly than she'd intended. She took a deep breath. Phin had most likely heard her grand entrance, so she might as well keep going and hope he didn't mind. She left her umbrella by the door and took off her wet shoes.

The living room was dim, though it was just after noon, but she could see well enough to weave her way around the furniture. She also saw the water dripping and splashing into the half dozen or so pots and bowls throughout the room. Some of the leaks had snaked along the ceiling, changing direction as they encountered bumps or cracks and were now dripping on the carpet next to their half full pots. Dee adjusted their positions as she walked by, feeling the carpet squish under the socks she now wished she'd removed. This wasn't the first rainstorm that had soaked Riva's carpet.

The room still held some of the ambience from last night, with its dark fabrics draped over the lamps and half-burned candles covering every available surface. Castor and Pollux watched her from the dry safety of the sofa, yawning and stretching. She scratched their ears as she walked by and was rewarded with their deep, rumbling purrs.

"Hello," she called, as she went from the duskiness of the living room and hallway into the brightly lit kitchen. "Sorry I just barged in, I've really got to get me some manners and learn how to knock," she joked.

Phin turned from the sink where he'd just managed to rinse out the teacup before Dee could see what he'd brewed. He wasn't about to admit that he'd parboiled an insect.

"Hello back at you. It's all right to walk in when I'm expecting you," he said, smiling stiffly. "It's when I don't know you're coming that it could be a problem. You never know when I'm going to spend the day walking around in my underwear. You wouldn't want to see that." He refilled the kettle and put it on the stove to boil. He was beginning to like this new habit of making tea for anyone who came through the door, it gave him time to think of something to say.

Dee took off her coat and hung it on one of the hooks on the back of the kitchen door. She was wearing faded jeans and a pale green tee shirt that showed off her curves. Phin found himself staring, so he busied himself with cups and spoons until she was sitting at the table.

"So, what do you think of my new décor?" he asked with a grin. "I've always admired waterfalls, now I've got several."

"You know, the roof is probably leaking in only a couple of places, but it runs along the attic floor and spreads out all over the house. Riva had several large buckets somewhere around here. I'm surprised you haven't found them yet."

"I did. Last week I filled them with yard waste and left them at the curb. They were taken along with the trash."

"Too bad. Those bowls you left on the table in the living room are going to fill up fast."

"I'd forgotten about those. You're right, I should empty them out before I've got a mess on my hands." He chuckled at her raised eyebrow and crooked grin. "Okay, before I have a *bigger* mess," he said as he headed for the living room.

Dee poured herself some tea and took a careful sip, glancing at the journals on top of the fridge. Phin had probably been reading them. She was tempted to take a peek, but told herself that they were his property now. If he decided to throw Riva's journals away she'd ask for them, but until then it was hands off.

"Do you think that Mabel was really visited by the ghost of Cora last night?" Phin asked, as he came into the room carrying a pot that was brimming with water.

"You know what I believe."

"Actually, I don't. You've said you believe in the power of divination, using cards or wet tea leaves, but this whole ghost business…" He emptied the pot into the sink and set it on the counter before turning to Dee. Her brow was furrowed, and her bottom lip was caught between her teeth as she contemplated her answer.

"When my grandmother disappeared with her two closest friends, this whole town fell apart. Everyone felt the loss. Fran had been a third grade teacher here for forty years. She'd taught almost all of us our times tables at some point. Cora ran most of the committees we had in town and she had a huge family. We all called her Auntie Cora." Dee shifted in her seat and took a long sip of tea. "Mabel came to stay with us for a couple of weeks after they disappeared. She'd done that off and on since I was three, when my father ran off to the States.

"Mabel was like a second mother to me, but in a distant sort of way. She was always staring at nothing and wandering off in the middle of the night. She was prone to nightmares and terrors, and woke her neighbours so many times with her screaming that they were probably relieved when she came to stay with us for days or weeks at a time." Dee reached for her teacup. It was empty and Phin hurried to fill it again.

Phin was not comfortable with the subject of the missing women and some dim part of his mind kept expecting Dee to accuse him of leaving her grandmother to freeze to death out in the woods. But he was also curious enough about Dee that he was willing to take the risk.

"I think there was so much shock involved when her mother went missing that Mabel went numb for a while. So did Mom. It was like having two statues in the house. The whole town was grieving, but I swallowed all that and took care of my mother and my aunt. After all, they'd just lost their mother. At least I still had mine."

"Yeah, I understand how they must have felt. For weeks after my mother died I could barely move. Then, as if that wasn't bad enough, for months afterward I kept thinking I heard her calling me, or I'd see her walking down the street and make some poor stranger nervous by following her for several blocks."

"That's exactly it!" Dee said excitedly. "Mabel would claim that she'd seen Gran getting on a bus or in a taxi, or she'd hear her mother calling from behind the big peach tree out back, and go sit there for an hour. Eventually, she started seeing and hearing other people too. That's why some of her nightmares were so spooky to me and mom. Mabel would get out of bed, pack a bag, get dressed and run out the door. She'd wake up somewhere along the highway out of town in the middle of the night, half-dressed and usually in her bare feet. Those nights were scarier than the ones where she woke up screaming. She'd remember every detail of those dreams. That's why Riva claimed they were more likely prophesies than dreams. All that detail had to come from a vision of some sort.

"I was just a kid, and Mom was no help, so Riva stepped in. She had moved here about a year after Mabel did – they'd been friends in Vancouver. They decided that Mabel's problem was likely more psychic than psycho. That's about when they started playing with Tarot cards and tea leaf readings."

"So Riva didn't come by it naturally?"

"Who knows? She certainly took to it naturally enough once she started helping Mabel. Riva would go to some Gulf Island once in a while for metaphysical workshops, and she went on a couple of month-long retreats out in the woods somewhere with some psychic guru."

Phin's attention was piqued. "Could that be Carl?"

"I don't know. Maybe. She never talked about the guy much, so he could be Carl. She always came back from these retreats glowing, in more ways than one. Mabel teased that he was her lover, but Riva denied it. It bloomed into a huge fight and they didn't speak for days. Maybe there's something about it – or Carl – in one of her journals, but it hardly seems to matter now."

"I haven't seen his name mentioned yet," he said, feeling sick that he was lying to her yet again. "But she may have called him something else, like Petunia, or Forsythia."

"Actually, Dogbane would be a more accurate name for that guy. He and Riva eventually had some kind of falling out and she never took another metaphysical class. She became the local fortune teller and the tourists came to rely on her as much as the locals did."

"What about Mabel? Didn't Riva start all that because of her?"

"Mabel couldn't 'bring on the wiz at will,' as she liked to say. Predictions and prophecies came to her haphazardly and she claimed her thoughts just got too jumbled when she tried to read cards or tea leaves. That's why she needed Riva to help her focus and make sense of the images that came into her head."

"So Mabel is the true psychic, but Riva studied and made a career out of it."

"In a way, yes, and every time that Mabel made some sort of cryptic comment to someone, that someone usually took it to Riva for interpretation. They'll probably look to you now for that sort of thing."

"Unless we convince them that you're the most reliable interpreter of Mabel's pronouncements."

"Oh no you don't," Dee said, laughing. "You're the new fortune teller in this neck of the woods. I wouldn't dream of intruding. Besides, you'll need some sort of income if you're going to stay." She stopped laughing as Phin stood up abruptly.

"I'd better check the bowls again. They fill up pretty quickly." He grabbed the pot off the counter and ducked out of the room in a hurry.

Dee rubbed her eyes with the heels of her hands. Stupid. She'd gone too far and made him uncomfortable. Again. She'd asked Mabel on the way home from the séance last night if she could sense whether Phin was going to remain in Riva's house, or if he'd just fix it up to sell and leave, which was his original plan. Mabel had said that if Phin changed his mind he'd probably let them know. Then she'd kissed Dee on the cheek before heading towards the middle of town, to her apartment above the bakery.

The rain cascaded down the kitchen window, blurring her view of the back of the yard. Dee closed her eyes and listened to the pounding on the roof. She smiled at the various indoor plinks and splashes that accompanied the downpour. She hoped the rain wouldn't do too much damage. It really was a lovely little house. She'd spent so much time here that it felt like a second home to her. Maybe she'd offer to buy it from Phin if he decided not to stay. She had some money saved up. Once he'd finished fixing the place up, she'd talk to him before he put it up for sale.

Phin came back and silently poured more water into the sink. Dee's innocent comment had confused him, stirring up the torrent of conflicting emotions that he'd been feeling all week. He'd never settled down long enough in one place to become part of a community, yet here he was being offered one, all wrapped up in a neat package, complete with a job. It wasn't the sort of job he was used to, but so far it had been fun. And then there was Dee. She was warm, funny and seemed to genuinely like him. How bad could it be to at least consider staying?

He clamped down hard on that thought. It could get very bad if she found out the truth about what went on twenty-five years ago. And it would eventually come out if he stayed. It was enough that Riva had kept the truth from all her friends for so many years, but he'd already been here a couple of weeks and had neglected to mention that he knew where her grandmother had gone, even if he didn't know what had happened to her.

"How's your tea? Is it still hot enough?"

"Yes, it's fine." Dee fidgeted in her seat, unable to meet his eyes. "Is the ghost issue any clearer for you?"

"Not really, but I'm willing to play along for a while. I've got to pay for this roof somehow, don't I?" he joked. A silence stretched between them while they sipped their tea. Then a new leak erupted above the table and a large drop of water splashed into Phin's teacup. He groaned as he realized there were no more catch basins and the teacup would have to do.

"Oh God, you're going to have to repaint all the ceilings too, aren't you?" Dee exclaimed. "There are several gallons of white paint in the storage room at the bakery. Sam had been planning to renovate before he died, and now Brent couldn't be bothered. There should be enough to do this whole house, and Brent would be glad to get rid of it, if he even remembers it's there." Dee was babbling, hoping to fill the gulf of silence that separated them.

"That would be helpful, but let's wait until this storm stops before making plans." Phin felt pulled in two directions. He wished he could just give it up, sell the house right now, and leave this mess for someone else to clean up. It would be so easy to walk away, just like he'd done so many times before. Walk away, and never look back.

If only he weren't so desperate to feel like he was someplace where he belonged. If only Dee and her friends hadn't made him feel so welcome. If only she weren't so lovely.

"So let's continue about last night," Dee said, a little too loudly. "Let's get out the Tarot cards."

"Wait! I've got another idea," Phin said, jumping up and running out of the room again. He returned with a green drawstring pouch. He sat down, grinning at a bemused Dee while he picked apart the knotted cord. "I flipped through quite a few of Riva's books last week, trying to get a feel for what I should do at the séance. I was looking for something a little less traditional than cards, palms and tea, a little less girly maybe." He finally managed to untie the knot and loosen the drawstring. "She had these books: *History of Hoodoo and Voodoo*, *Spells and Amulet*, and *Bones of Fortune*."

He tipped the bag, and a handful of small bones rattled onto the table.

Dee squeaked and her chair's legs chattered on the floor as she pushed herself back. She squeezed her eyes shut for a moment and took a deep breath. Phin was grinning widely at the pile of bones, and was unaware of her discomfort. She willed her racing heart to slow, forcing herself to watch as he poked the bones with a finger, separating them into smaller piles. They're only bones, she told herself, and tiny ones at that. They weren't moving by themselves. They weren't at all like the bones in her nightmares. She knew they weren't going to suddenly assemble into skeletons and grow into people she might know. She kept her distance anyway.

"I went back to the woodpile where I'd found the fox skull, and salvaged what I could from the rest of his skeleton. A lot of the bones had been broken when the wood fell on him, but these were all ok." He scooped them up in one hand and shook them.

"Are you going to use them on one of your walking sticks?" Dee asked hopefully.

"No. I've found a much better use for them." He dropped the bones on the table with a flourish. They scattered widely, several of them sliding close to Dee. She flinched.

"These bones can tell me anything that tea leaves or Tarot cards can."

"But Riva's clients are used to those styles of divination," Dee protested. "They might not believe you can read bones the same way."

"What does it matter whether I'm reading clumps of wet tea leaves in a cup or piles of little bones on the table?" He picked up one of the tiny bones and examined it closely. "I'm just making it all up, remember? How about I test them and read your fortune?"

"No, you can't," she said, desperate that he not link her in any way to the bones. She thought quickly as he raised his eyebrows questioningly. "Remember, the person who's having her fortune read has to drink the tea first," Dee faltered, realizing that she'd said exactly the opposite of what she'd meant. She hardly had time to regret her words when Phin scooped up the bones again and poured them into a pile directly in front of her.

"Of course," he said, winking. "It adds to the drama if you toss your own fortune." He looked back and forth between her face and the pile of bones, urging her with his eyes to pick them up.

Dee felt trapped. She knew her reluctance to touch those bones stemmed from her nightmares, which fed her fear of bones and anything to do with them – including voodoo. Riva had once loaned Dee several books on voodoo, hoping they would ease her phobia and help with the nightmares. Dee had only made it through the first few pages of *Bones of Fortune* and had returned *History of Voodoo and Hoodoo* unopened. Nothing could convince her that bones wouldn't breed dark magic.

She looked at Phin's face. He'd cut off the braids from his chin, leaving jagged tufts of stiff hair, and he hadn't managed to wash off all the kohl she'd lined his eyes with. They'd left ashy smudges above his cheekbones. It might have looked ghoulish in the watery light that came through the window, except for the boyish grin that lit his face with excitement.

Dee told herself that she didn't have to touch the bones if she didn't want to. She would tell him it was silly and that everyone would be uncomfortable around such dark symbolism. She almost told him that using the bones might be bad luck. She even opened her mouth to say that the bones might bring on more curse than fortune. But Dee knew that those were her own fears so she said nothing. She had to encourage his new discovery, give him the confidence to fill Riva's place and become part of the community, maybe part of her life. What she wanted more than anything right now, a need more powerful than her fear of the bones, was for Phineas Marshal to stay in Riva's house.

So, before she could change her mind, she took a deep breath and picked up the bones with both hands. She cupped them for the barest trembling instant before dropping them back onto the table's surface. Her frantic psyche tried to convince her that a million ants were crawling under the skin of her palms and moving up into her arms. She willed herself not to run to the sink and wash her hands.

Phin leaned forward eagerly, his nose poised inches above the scattering of bones. "Hmm," he said, stroking his scruffy chin, "that's interesting."

"What?" she said, barely breathing through her clenched teeth.

"Shush, I'm just practicing my part in all this. People are going to expect a bit of drama, aren't they?" He frowned deeply and sniffed the bones, his nostrils flaring. He looked up sharply and widened his eyes. "I see a bakery. Your bakery," he whispered, and dropped his gaze back to the bones.

"I don't have a bakery. I mean, I suppose in a way I wish it were my bakery." She leaned towards him the tiniest bit, in spite of her nervousness. "What else do you see?"

"Not much else, except that you seem happy. That's about it." He picked up a bone and scratched at a black stain that could have been dirt, or maybe dried blood. "Maybe you'll buy the bakery from Brent someday."

"Not likely. Even if I had enough money for the outrageous price he'd want for it, I'm not sure it's salvageable." She watched as he picked up each bone and inspected it before putting it back into the bag. "Besides, you just made that up, didn't you?"

"Now look at who doesn't believe," Phin said. "It was like you said before: tell them what they want to hear. Isn't that a fortune you'd want to hear? And who knows…maybe it'll come true."

"What I can't believe is that you could get a positive reading from something so negative. I mean, I believe voodoo is evil magic so it shouldn't have anything good to say to me."

"Isn't it all about what you put into it? Reading bones is no different than any of the other divination systems out there." He grinned as he hefted the tiny sack of bones. "Look, as far as I can tell from what I've been reading, it's only evil when evil people use it. Just like all magic."

"I don't know. It still feels too dark to me. I'll stick to the cards or tea leaves."

"Cards, bones, tea leaves, whatever. They're just tools. I feel more comfortable using these bones. They're manlier."

TWELVE

Phineas shivered as a cold stream of water ran under his collar and down his back. The temperature had dropped several degrees in the last half hour, chilling his already wet skin. Heavy grey clouds had darkened the sky and sagged with the promise of more rain to come. He hoped that the bowls and pots he'd laid out at home hadn't all filled up and converted his new home into an indoor pool. If he was very lucky, he'd still have dry clothes to change into.

He carried two plastic five-gallon buckets in each hand, and had stopped twice on the way back from the bakery to empty rain water pooled in their bottoms. Dee had insisted he take them after he'd lugged a set of five antique nesting-tables to her house. She'd carried the box of glass animals, and they'd laughed as they'd run the last block when the box had started to disintegrate in the rain.

Dee had invited him to have dinner with her and Lydia but he'd declined, saying that he had to get back to bailing the house before it sank. So they'd dashed to the bakery for the buckets and a dozen fresh rolls double-wrapped in plastic, which Phin had tucked into the front of his shirt.

He ducked his head as he trotted down the side of the house, mindful of the grasping cedar, and cursing as the buckets lodged him between the house and the hedge in the narrow space. The back yard was a soup of mud and drowning plants. He nearly lost his footing in the slippery muck when the leaden sky lit up in a crackle of lightning. He fumbled for the doorknob and gratefully let himself into the kitchen.

Phin slapped the light switch, but the bare overhead bulb did little to brighten the dreary afternoon. He dropped the buckets with a clatter, and unbuttoned his shirt. It was drenched, but the plastic bags had kept the rolls dry. He kicked off his soggy running shoes and peeled off his socks, rolling them into a ball and squeezing them out into the sink.

There wasn't much water dripping in the kitchen; he scanned the ceiling, following one long wet line that ran towards the centre of the room. Several large drops glistened and hovered a moment before gravity interfered and splattered the stack of journals on the table. He scooped them up and poured off the worst of the water before swiping at the rest with his damp shirt. The journals were soaked, the paper already swelling and warping. He dumped them on a chair, and slammed a bucket onto the table.

He was certain he'd tossed the journals on top of the refrigerator before Dee had arrived. They hadn't been on the table when he'd thrown the bones for her reading. Had Dee taken a look at them before they'd left for town? Maybe he should have given them to her in the first place. After all, she'd been Riva's friend. What business did he have reading about the woman's thoughts and feelings? That was something for a close friend to deal with. On the other hand, Dee didn't need to accidentally discover that her best friend had sent her grandmother to an isolated cabin in the woods so she could freeze to death in a snow storm.

He'd been gone more than an hour, maybe Tammy had dropped by with more cat-loaf. He opened the fridge to see if anything new had been added, but it was still full of the offerings his new friends had brought to the séance last night.

"I must have left the damn journals on the table after all." His voice was small against the percussive rain beating the window so he snapped on the radio and turned it up loudly. The station was having a Led Zeppelin revival and Phin sang along lustily to "Stairway to Heaven" for probably the thousandth time in his life. He'd never tire of it, he was sure, and as the final cymbals clashed he kicked his running shoes into the corner in a thumping accompaniment.

He was rummaging through the fridge, looking for beer, when he remembered he should be putting those buckets in the attic under the main leaky areas. Beer would have to wait.

He headed for the hallway, where he stepped into a puddle of cold muddy water. Wincing, he lifted his foot and shook it, and saw a row of diminishing puddles leading to the living room.

Muddy puddles. Made by muddy shoes.

He wasn't imagining things after all. Someone *had* been in the house and had moved Riva's journals to the table. He froze as he realized the intruder might still be in the house, maybe hiding in the living room's shadows.

Two maple branches leaned against the wall near the back door. He'd yet to strip them of their bark but they were clean of smaller branches. Phin held one in front of him like a spear as he padded quietly down the hall. He flicked on lights as he went and leaped into the living room, swinging his weapon in a wide arc.

There was no one there. But someone definitely had been.

Riva's journal cabinet stood open, its contents dumped, and the pages ran black with the ink Riva had used to pen her thoughts. Phin stared, horrified at the smeared mess. Every journal was damp, the pages moist, the ink wet and spreading. They were ruined. He tried to gather them up and stack them, but the pages were soft and tore easily. His skin soaked up the black ink that lifted from the pages, leaving stains on his fingers.

Had Eric done this? Dee had said he might be in contact about a crystal. Phin's eyes darted to the pedestal where Riva's crystal ball had rested. Gone. Definitely Eric, but why tear up the place? How could he not realize that Phin would suspect him? Dee had said he seemed shy and reserved, though a little weird, but he couldn't be stupid enough to think he could get away with breaking into a house, destroying property and stealing, could he?

Riva hadn't mentioned Eric in the few journals Phin had taken the time to read. And now they were all gone. There wasn't a single journal left dry.

If Riva had written anything about young Phineas driving Delia, Fran and Cora to their deaths, that info was now gone, the ink dissipated to illegible smears. Those very words could have run from these pages onto his hands. He remembered having nightmares in which he'd somehow killed the women himself and couldn't wash their blood off his hands. He shuddered at the comparison. It would be days before the black ink would fade from his fingers.

But only he and Riva had known his secret, and now no one could ever read those damning words. He'd let the journals dry out, and then burn them in the barrel out back. The others might be upset to hear Riva's journals were gone, but Phin could almost hear Mabel telling him it was an omen, a sign for them to let Riva go. He rubbed his hands hard on his damp trousers – already splotched with ink – and glanced at the corner where he kept his tools.

He'd been so worried about Riva's journals that he'd forgotten about his collection of carving knives. He'd bought them over many years, each one carefully chosen, and each one a little more expensive than the last. They were his pride and joy, and his blood boiled at the possibility that Eric had taken them.

Two steps took him to the corner. The first thing he saw was the new walking staff. He was meant to notice it.

It leaned against the wall where it had for the last week, but was a far different staff than when he'd last looked at it. The leafy vines that he'd so painstakingly, so patiently carved into the dense wood had been gouged repeatedly, and the wood was pale and fresh where large divots had been crudely cut out. The top edge – which he'd tapered to fit into the base of the fox skull – had been sheared off, and several curls of wood still hung down from where a gouge had bitten deeply. The fox skull itself was nowhere in sight. The leather pouch that held his tools was wadded into a soggy ball, and knives, gouges and chisels littered the wet carpet around it. He gathered them up and set them back onto the table. His two best knives were missing.

Those knives would be almost impossible to replace out here in the boonies. Herman's Hardware carried only disposable utility knives with thin blades that snapped off if they bit too deeply into even the softest wood.

He slammed the mutilated stick against the wall, and felt a sharp sting on the back of his hand. Blood welled up from a shallow slash, and he looked down to see one of his knives stuck point-down in the carpet, still vibrating from the impact.

The other pierced a sheet of paper, high on the wall. There was an overturned kitchen chair that Eric had probably used to hang his message. Phin righted the chair, stepped onto it, and pulled out the knife, snatching the paper before it fluttered to the floor. It was half a page from one of Riva's journals, torn away before the water could dilute the ink and warp its message.

Phin set his knives on a dry corner of the table and brought the scrap closer to the nearest lamp.

"All that summer I plotted a young man's seduction. And these many years since, no one has guessed that I corrupted an innocent. I haven't slept well since. It was selfish and wrong to use Phineas, another mistake that has likely tainted his entire life."

Eric had lucked out and found the one passage that damned Phin. Now the little creep thought he'd found a secret involving Phin and Riva. Riva hadn't provided details but the entry was suspicious enough for Eric to use it as a threat. If Eric spread it around someone would figure it out. And even if no one guessed the ugly truth, Phin didn't think he could lie if Dee were to ask him outright what Riva had meant.

He crumpled the note and jammed it into his back pocket. His heart felt like a hollow pit. His inheritance had been a trap.

He sank down onto the sofa and a furry orange face popped out from underneath, next to his feet. The cat's ears flattened as it struggled to squeeze the rest of its plump body out from the tight space. It jumped up onto the cushion and pressed up against Phin's side. He slid sideways, but the cat followed until Phin was trapped between the cat and the sofa's arm. It meowed piteously and pushed its head against Phin's hand. Its littermate promptly appeared from around the corner and nimbly leapt up as well. They greeted each other with a head butt and then settled comfortably next to Phin. Their rumbling purrs and warm bodies were strangely comforting, and even though dampness from the sofa cushion was slowly seeping through the backside of his jeans, he stayed where he was.

He scratched a furry head and Castor's purring went up a notch. Phin smiled, realizing that he could tell them apart. They were exactly the same orange shade and pattern, but Castor's fur was a bit longer, and his eyes a shade darker than his brother Pollux's.

Phin had also not had any allergic reactions to the cats for days now. He'd gotten used to them in more ways than one, and found that he was becoming worried about what would happen to them when he sold the house and left town.

What kind of game had Riva been playing by leaving him this house and luring him back? Maybe she'd wanted him to tell her friends what had happened the last time he'd been here. Riva had lived among them with the secret for all those years, and had probably felt it would finally be safe to let them know once she was gone. She obviously didn't care about what happened to Phineas. It had been more important to give her friends some answers than to protect him.

THIRTEEN

Winter Solstice, twenty-five years ago
Chilliwack, British Columbia

Riva watched the boy clump down the steps of the Greyhound bus, ducking his head. He'd grown several inches in the few months since she'd last seen him. Phineas slung his backpack over his right shoulder as he clumsily wrapped a scarf around his neck. He grinned and waved when he spotted her and hurried over, his smile dimming as his eyes scanned the parking lot behind her.

"Where is she?"

"She?"

"Leyla. I...I mean the Buick," he stammered. "It's just, I mean, I sorta named her last summer, you know."

"Hmm, Leyla. I like it." She took his arm and steered him towards the parking lot. "Now, remember what I said on the phone. This has got to be our little secret. No one can know about this."

"But Mom already knows you're giving me the car. I had to tell her why I was coming out here again. And it's not like I'll be able to hide it."

"Yes, of course. I was talking about the other thing, the little job I need you to do for me."

"Oh yeah, no problem. You know me. I'm good at those little jobs." He grinned again, hitching his pack. "Sure is cold up here. It was raining when I left Vancouver. Mom tried to pitch a fit when she checked the weather forecast and found out there might be a snow storm coming. I told her I'd drive safe. She even gave me some cash for a cheap motel if I need it."

Riva led him to a rusty white hatchback and unlocked the passenger door. She watched him toss his pack in the back and clamber in. As she slowly walked to the other side of the car, she wondered if she hadn't made a big mistake promising her friends that Phineas would help. Would he balk at the "little job" she had for him?

She sighed as she got in and shut the door. The starter ground as she turned the key, turning over several times before the engine caught.

"Why are you driving this bucket of bolts?" Phin asked.

"This is Fran's car, I'm just borrowing it for the day. Leyla should be packed and ready to go by the time we get there."

"Packed?"

"I need you to drop off something before you take the car home. That's the job. It's a bit of a detour, but I think you should be able to get back to the main highway before dark. It'll take us less than an hour to get to Fran's house and then it's no more than two hours out of your way to drop them off."

"Them?"

"It's a bit complicated, and I have to remind you again that you can't tell anyone about this."

"This is starting to sound like a spy movie: Your mission, should you choose to accept it...you know, like James Bond."

"Mission Impossible, maybe?" Riva reached up and adjusted the rear-view mirror.

"So what's in the secret package?"

"It's not a package, it's a person. Three people, actually."

"Oh." He frowned at the road ahead for a moment. "You mean I'm just driving some people somewhere, like a chauffeur? What's so secret about that?"

"Phineas, no one can know where they went."

"Won't people wonder where they are?"

"Oh, they'll be back. No one can know for a while, that's all." She glanced sideways at his face, hating to lie to him, and quickly added, "They'll tell people when they're ready. You, on the other hand, have to promise never to tell anyone. Not where you've gone, not who was with you, nothing except that you came up here to pick up a car that I gave to you as a gift for all your hard work last summer."

"Seems like a big gift, just for giving someone a ride. Not that I'm complaining. I'm just not sure I get it."

"Today is the winter solstice. Do you know what that means?"

"Sure, it's the first day of winter. That's why Mom was freaking out about me driving back to Vancouver by myself. She's thinking I'll drive like an idiot in the snow and get creamed on the highway."

"Ok, think back to a certain ritual from last summer. Remember what happened that night?" He didn't answer, and Riva glanced at him. His cheeks had flushed scarlet and he was staring ahead to avoid her gaze.

"That's right. A ritual in the forest, a secret ritual." She waited but he still said nothing. "You kept that secret, didn't you?"

"Oh yeah," he finally muttered. He fidgeted in his seat, remembering the group of naked women he'd seen dancing in the woods.

"This is the same sort of thing, only you'll be leaving before anything weird happens." She tried not to smile at his obvious embarrassment, but knew he'd keep quiet. That was why it was important that he be the one to take Fran, Cora and Delia to the cabin, that no one in Cricket Lake guess that Riva was involved in the women's disappearance.

A shocking plan that involved a remote cabin that Fran had bought for cash many years ago from an old hunter who was now dead. There were no ownership papers involved and only Fran knew exactly where it was. It was a place where three women could kill themselves in privacy, far enough away that their families and friends couldn't stop them.

Riva blinked to clear the tears that blurred her vision, and slowed down to put some distance between her and the truck ahead. She and Phineas would be of no help to her friends if she lost control on the highway and got them killed.

"We're just a few minutes away from Fran's house. They'll be anxious to leave as soon as we get there, so there'll be no time for anything except maybe a bathroom break. I've packed a stack of sandwiches and a thermos of hot chocolate for you to take on the road, in case you get hungry."

"Are you kidding? I'm always hungry," he said, and laughed as his stomach growled in agreement.

Riva wished she didn't have to involve Phineas but he was the logical choice. The boy would take the Buick back to Vancouver. No one would look for it, since she'd supposedly sold it to a tourist from over the border a month ago. She also hoped that it would be some time before someone checked Fran's house and found this hatchback in her garage – the car that the three women had supposedly driven to a spa in Chilliwack.

Fran, Cora and Delia didn't want to be found, just left in peace. There would be questions, but their hope was that no one would miss them for a few days, and that by then it would be too late.

FOURTEEN

Dee stuck the "Back in 20 minutes" sign on the window and shut the door. No need to lock it. Nobody had been in the shop for at least an hour and there was really nothing to steal except a few muffins and this morning's bread. She pushed her damp hair off her forehead and pulled at the top of her blouse, flapping it to create a breeze. Didn't help much. The town's single coffee shop was just a block away and they made a passable iced tea. Time for a break.

You wouldn't know that there'd been a rain storm just yesterday. Everything looked bone dry, with not a puddle in sight. The sun glared off the storefront windows, and its searing brightness blinded Dee for a moment to the dinginess of peeling paint and crumbling sidewalks that had slowly eroded the town's quaint Main Street in the last dozen years or so.

There were a few people out on the street, ambling locals and early tourists passing through on their way to open their cottages for the summer. They brought most of their supplies with them, but often forgot the most basic of items. According to Annie – who worked at the small grocery store – most tourists bought at least one of what she termed the top three: insect spray, condoms or the fudge that her mother made every week.

Dee nodded to a woman who was supervising her profusely sweating husband as he rearranged the back of their van to accommodate a stack of garden pots and several bags of soil. They had come every summer for at least ten years and rented one of the tiny cottages that would likely be torn down if the town council sold the lakefront. The couple would probably find another cottage to rent in Castle Creek or Minnow Bay, two other local towns that competed with Cricket Lake for tourist dollars.

The brilliant sunlight and green leaves did nothing to cheer Dee's mood. Brent hadn't shown up for work again, the second time this week. If Mabel hadn't come by to help out for a few hours early this morning, Dee would have been hard pressed to deal with all the customers that had come into the shop, while also baking the bread, cookies and biscuits they'd come in to buy. She'd offered to pay Mabel, but her offer had been waved away.

"Nothing better to do," Mabel had said as she carefully set a pie into a box and taped it shut. "It's too hot to stay upstairs with that morning sun beating in, hotter than down here if you can believe it."

"You could always move. Mom and I have lots of room, and you know she'd love to have you around." Dee had been trying to convince Mabel to give up the small apartment above the bakery for years, with no luck.

"Not a chance. If you'd had a sister, you'd know what it's like to live with one. Lydia and I get along well, as long as it's from a safe distance. Besides, this is my home and I like it."

Standing on the sidewalk in front of the bakery, Dee could hear music drifting down from Mabel's open windows. It sounded like the opening theme song for one of the many soap operas she watched daily. Dee thought of going up to thank her again for her help in the shop this morning, but knew the heat would be unbearable in the tiny apartment. Though Mabel complained about the heat, she really didn't seem to mind it much, and spent hours in front of her television working on the many craft projects that paid her bills.

Mabel received a large box of craft supplies each month from one of several American companies: pre-cut wooden figurines with tiny jars of paint, bags of colourful beads and rolls of thin wire, or bolts of fabric with markings to show her where to cut. Each box had a sheet or two of instructions, and a cheque to pay for the last batch she'd put together. She slipped each instruction sheet into a plastic sleeve and stored it in a binder. Over the years, she'd filled four such binders, each project repeated several times as the same holidays came and went year after year.

Mabel made Halloween decorations in July, stitched and stuffed Easter bunnies in November, and assembled gaudy, beaded jewelry in between major holidays. Her tiny living room was crammed with boxes of supplies, and the walls were lined with shelves covered in finished projects: rows of bobble-headed dogs that had arrived without their fur, their pink plastic skins pitted to show where she should glue on the eyes; stacks of colourful quilt squares to piece together; strings of fake pearls with matching earrings; ranks of wooden soldiers, brightly painted and wearing glued-on caps.

Dee, whose birthday was in June, had received at least three furry red heart pillows over the years with the words "Happy Birthday" stitched on in silver thread where it normally would have read "Happy Valentine's Day."

The oval coffee table where Mabel worked was scarred and streaked with a chaotic rainbow of dried paints. Her ever-present glue gun dripped molten plastic onto the table – and the carpet – which hardened into clear scabs that couldn't be removed.

Dee decided against a visit. The pies would be ready in half an hour and she needed to get them out of the oven before the dinner rush when everyone would be in a hurry to get home to their families. She crossed the street and walked the short block to the coffee shop. The bell jangled over the door when she opened it. It was cooler in here than it was outdoors, but not by much, and the steam from the many pots of coffee made the air feel almost liquid, so thick Dee could taste coffee with each breath she took.

She stood in line behind a group of giggling teenage girls baring more skin than Dee had ever dared to at their age. They leaned far over the counter, showing off their high cleavage to Josie's oldest son, Matt. He blushed and made a nervous joke, sending the girls into a fresh fit of laughter. Dee couldn't remember when Matt had started working at the café. It wasn't that long ago that she'd babysat him while his parents went out on a much-needed date. He'd grown into a handsome young man with the beginnings of a patchy mustache streaking his upper lip.

The girls took an eternity placing their orders, changing their minds several times, and counting out handfuls of loose change to pay for their elaborate, expensive drinks. Dee felt fat and overdressed in their presence, envying their lean, tanned legs and glossy hair.

Café du Monde. Café of the World. What a joke, she thought. The cracked counter top hadn't been replaced when the old ice cream parlour was converted ten years ago, and splinters of wood caught at the fabric of her blouse when she leaned against it. The new owners had kept the original tables and chairs, and most of them tilted in one direction or another, creating an unpredictable wobble that wasn't helped by the wadded paper napkins that customers had shoved under the legs.

Faded posters had been glued to the plaster walls a long time ago, exotic scenes from far-away places that no one in town had ever visited. Many of them were torn where children had picked at their edges and pulled off strips. The pale, yellowing images were ignored now. No one even glanced at the majestic mountain peaks of Switzerland, the brilliant lights of Las Vegas, or the colourful market scene with baskets of exotic produce that no one had ever tasted in Cricket Lake.

In spite of the run-down atmosphere and the unstable seating, the coffee shop was packed. It was the only place in town where people could meet to socialize since the old Legion Hall had been torn down.

"Iced tea with lemon, please," she said to Matt. "How do you like your summer job? Seems kind of hectic."

"It beats taking care of my little brothers while Mom works." He smiled absently, already making eye contact with the man behind Dee while he gave her a handful of change. She dropped it into her purse and turned to weave her way to the door.

Her waxed paper takeout cup was soon sweating and slippery, and she lifted a corner of her blouse to wipe it dry, nearly dropping her drink when she spotted Eric watching her from the back of the room. His brown eyes regarded her with apprehension, as if he'd hoped she wouldn't notice he was there.

He wore the same long black coat as before and had a matching backpack on a chair next to him. Was he leaving town? Dee hesitated. She really had to get back to the bakery, but it wouldn't hurt to at least ask him if he knew someone named Carl.

As she took a step toward Eric, a burst of warmth exploded in her chest, spreading through her body and leaving her light-headed and leaden at the same time.

Her vision swam and she closed her eyes against stinging tears. The air was caustic and seared the back of her throat. What was happening? Dee felt like she was burning up, like she couldn't breathe. Her skin was drying up, the moisture evaporating, leaving it as scorched and arid as a desert.

"FIRE!"

Dee's eyes snapped open and she sucked in a lungful of the room's fresh coffee-flavoured air. Her eyes now felt clear and the burning sensation in her body had disappeared as if it had never happened. She glanced at Eric but he was staring over her shoulder and it took her a moment before she realized that people were screaming.

Eric sipped his latte as he watched Dee order her drink. Her skin was flushed and moist like the bread dough she made all day. The sun blazing through the shop's front window made a glowing halo of the cloud of flour motes that clung to her hair. They sifted down onto her clothes like dandruff when she moved. Good thing she wore a white uniform.

Eric held his mug in both hands, the hot ceramic helping him to stay focused. He'd missed last night's bus so hadn't slept a wink, expecting the cops at every moment. By dawn he'd been a wreck, though assumed that since he was still free Phineas probably hadn't guessed who his visitor had been yesterday.

He'd been packed and ready to check out of the Cot & Couch as soon as the front desk had opened. The bus back to Vancouver wasn't due until noon and he hoped he could stay awake until it arrived.

Eric had never had any intention of knocking on Riva's door and asking Phin for something that should never have left the family. He'd waited in the rain until Phin and Dee had left the house together. The door had been unlocked so he'd let himself in.

He'd searched Riva's living room from the bookcases to the sofas. But aside from a crystal ball – which was not what his father had described – and a few fancy rocks and fake gems, he'd seen nothing egg-sized and opaquely white that looked like it might grow brighter and emit sparks when you touched it. He'd taken them all anyway, in case his father's ranting obsession had caused him to change details over the years.

Riva's diaries had been drivel, except for one passage that had jumped off the page at him. It was like he'd been meant to find it, and he'd been elated to find such a shocking revelation about his cousin and her boy toy. Not so elated now. He wished he had thought to take the diary page with him, instead of going all melodramatic. He could have used the information to force Phin to give up the crystal but he'd left his only proof tacked to the wall as a cheesy threat and now had no leverage. And he still didn't know for certain that the crystal was actually in Riva's house.

Now he had to go home and question his grandmother all over again. Ella had always insisted that she didn't know what he was talking about when he asked about the crystal, but Eric knew she was lying. He'd overheard her and his father arguing about the crystal's power too many times over the years. She'd told his father more than once that the damn thing was dangerous and that he needed to forget about it.

Eric froze as Dee turned away from the counter with her drink. She wiped the condensation from her cup with a corner of her shirt, exposing a strip of pasty white skin. The fabric stuck to her damp belly when she let it drop. Eric grimaced in distaste but forced a smile when she glanced across the room and caught him watching her.

Dee's eyes locked onto his and he thought she was about to speak when her eyes closed abruptly and her shoulders slumped. Eric almost fell off his chair as the coffee shop erupted into a noisy symphony of shouting and footsteps. Everyone rushed to the window, where smoke was drifting over from a building across the street. Eric looked back at Dee in time to see her drop her cold drink on the floor and dash outside.

FIFTEEN

The oven ticked as it cooled, the half-baked pies sinking in their centres. Cherry juice oozed out of the slits that Dee had made in the crusts, congealing into a sticky red pool in the centre of each pie. The thermostat clicked, and the elements inside the cavernous oven warmed again. Before they could begin to glow red, the thermostat clicked once again and the ancient wiring shorted out and overloaded the circuits, shutting down the breaker and cutting all power to the ovens.

But not before a shower of sparks flared from the frayed wires attached to the side of the breaker box, and fell onto an open book of recipes. The paper quickly ignited, the flames hungrily devouring page after page of text written in Dee's large, loopy handwriting. Dozens of recipes, collected and transcribed over many years disappeared in an instant and crumbled to ash.

The fire grew, as if fed by the mere description of sustenance that the book contained, and the flames stretched upwards, licking at the layers of papers tacked onto a corkboard. Phone numbers, purchase receipts, utility bills and a calendar with photographs of wedding cakes fluttered as the flames caught their edges. They curled and blackened as they perished, falling away from their thumbtacks and floating on a current of smoke, still burning as they alighted onto paper sacks of flour, stacks of cardboard pie boxes, and the wooden shelves that lined the walls.

Grey smoke billowed, its edges tinged black as it rolled across the ceiling, spilling out through both doorways, escaping into the front of the shop and out the back into a staircase that lead to the upstairs apartment.

It filled the narrow space with choking, toxic fumes trailed by flickering tongues of flame that eagerly began to incinerate the old wooden stairs. The blaze roared unchecked and charred wood squealed and crackled as it blackened into coals. The sounds muffled the thumping that came from above, as Mabel pounded a fist on top of the television that had suddenly winked out in the middle of her favourite program.

SIXTEEN

The sun beat down on Phin's bare back, and his head was starting to throb from squinting in the bright light. He wished he'd remembered where he'd put his sunglasses. He'd found a pair of Riva's, but hadn't been able to bring himself to wear those plastic lavender frames. He wiped sweat from his brow with an already-soaked handkerchief, and stood up to stretch his back, grimacing as his spine cracked and popped in protest.

He'd been up since sunrise emptying water buckets and putting the house in order. He'd hauled out several bags of damaged books along with the ruined journals and dumped them in a corner of the yard to dry in the sun. He'd laid out the damp sofa cushions, blankets and towels next to the soggy mess, and hoped it wouldn't rain again anytime soon. Not that it was likely; there wasn't a single cloud to mar the perfect blue of the sky.

He'd then gone down into the basement to check for any other water damage, but none was apparent. He'd sighed in relief and was heading up the stairs when he spotted the several large packs of roofing shingles stacked in the far corner. Riva must have been planning on fixing the roof at some point. It had taken him most of an hour's heavy labour to lug them to the first floor and then up the ladder.

He'd been appalled at the state of the roof; no wonder the house leaked like a sieve. Nearly a quarter of the shingles were missing, loose, or broken, and he'd only had to prod most of them with the toe of his boot to loosen and send them skittering off the edge of the roof.

He squatted and pulled the lid off a little styrofoam cooler. One last cold beer in the box. Good thing he was nearly finished inspecting this mess.

Phin had spent several summers working for a contractor as a young man. He'd had no formal training, so was paid a pittance for carrying materials and cleaning up after the builders while they erected identical rows of houses in one growing suburb after another. As the work had progressed, they'd needed more and more workers to keep up with the demands of the endless families that were always waiting to move into the new houses. Phin was watchful and a quick learner, and after several seasons had become a valued assistant among the roofers, masons and carpenters. As long as he had the tools and materials, he could take on most building projects now.

Phin sat on the edge of the roof and dangled his legs over the side, sipping his beer. He looked past his boots at the wheelbarrow he'd placed below to catch the broken shingles he'd tossed over the edge. It had overflowed, and was hidden underneath all the broken pieces of shingling and the rotted wood that had had to be torn up. He'd have to find some way to haul all that garbage away, along with all the junk he'd carted out of the house and piled on the porch.

The lawn was a lush green from the two-day downpour. He smiled in smug satisfaction at the thought of the cats trying to find a spot of dirt to scratch among the nearly waist high weeds that now choked the garden patch. Some of those weeds were rustling and waving, as if from a breeze, though not a breath of wind was blowing in the baking heat. He wondered if there were still grass snakes in the area and whether the cats hunted them. He recalled catching and disposing of several that Riva had spotted in the basement that summer. She'd been terrified of their sleek, black-green bodies and had insisted that Phin check every window screen in the house for holes.

The weeds began to wave faster. There was a frenzied twitching, a moment of stillness, then a sinuous, black body wove out through the tall grasses. Phin recognized Orion, heading for the house with a limp, grey body hanging from his jaws.

Phin threw a piece of roofing shingle, hitting the ground in front of the cat. Orion stopped and looked up at him, eyes slitted and ears flattened. Blood dripped on his front paws.

"Oh no, you don't," Phin shouted. "You are *not* leaving that in my bed." He threw another fragment of roof, narrowly missing the cat, who dropped his bloody prize and disappeared back into the weeds.

Phin swigged the last mouthful of beer, and dropped the empty can into the cooler. What would happen to the cats when he sold the house? He couldn't force the new owners to take five cats as part of the deal, as had happened to him. He certainly couldn't take them with him. He hadn't made any definite plans yet. He hadn't thought about anything except finishing the house repairs so he could call a realtor and put it up for sale.

No, that wasn't true.

He'd thought plenty about Eric, and the secret they now shared. He'd never even met the guy, but he'd turned Phin's life upside down. Was Eric the dark man from both of Dee's Tarot card readings? Could a deck of cards have foretold that this would happen? Dee had looked at the image on the card that Phin had turned over a week ago – The Hermit – and had seen a dark man who would try to take a glowing star from him. Was that glowing star the crystal everyone was fussing about?

He stood up and shook his head to clear those thoughts. There was no way that a picture on a card could predict the future. He'd always made his own future. He'd expected trouble from the moment he had come to town, and trouble had finally caught up with him.

Eric was just a fluke coincidence in an already confusing situation. He'd broken into Phin's house, ruined half of Riva's library – not to mention every single journal she'd written – and destroyed Phin's latest, and best, walking stick. As far as Phin could tell, Eric had also stolen several items, including the fox skull and the crystal ball. The guy must be desperate for the damn crystal he thought Riva owed him.

Phin had also thought a lot about Dee, and how he hadn't felt so comfortable with a woman in a long time, maybe not ever. He'd allowed Dee to get under his skin, and that wasn't good. He'd had a part in her grandmother's death, had driven the old woman and her friends to a remote cabin and abandoned them. He might as well have killed and buried the three women himself. He'd agonized his whole life about that day, wishing he hadn't wanted that old Buick so badly, and wishing he had refused Riva's request. But there was no taking it back. If Dee knew, she'd be horrified. She'd hate him. There was no reason for him to stay. He'd been kidding himself that he could leave the past behind, but he'd never forget those three shadowy faces at the cabin window as he drove away.

And now Eric could spill the beans at any moment.

Phin gathered his tools and dropped them over the edge to the grass below. He took one last walk around the entire roof, testing for more soft spots or loose edges.

As he completed the circuit, he thought he saw smoke rising through the leafy canopy of the treetops. He moved to the front edge of the roof and saw a dirty gray plume curling up from the centre of town.

SEVENTEEN

Mabel smacked the top of the television with the flat of her hand. "Damn it," she muttered. "Not now, you piece of junk." Jason was just about to find out he was Thorne's long-lost son, and Brianna was going to tell Forrest that she'd never really loved him. Mabel hoped that Tammy was watching "Endless Sorrows," so she could fill her in later. Unless the power was out across town too.

It was silly really, how slowly her TV stories went. She'd guessed nearly a year ago that Brianna and Thorne were Jason's parents, and that Forrest was about as dense as a slab of marble not to notice that his eldest son looked nothing like him and more like his wife's former boss.

Might as well put away the paints and clean the brushes. Mabel snapped the tops onto the pots of red and green paint. She was picking up the jar of muddy water that her brushes had been soaking in when she caught a whiff of smoke.

"Oh blast! Dee's burned her pies." She hurried to the door, certain that Dee was stuck waiting on customers and that Brent still hadn't come in to work. She grabbed the doorknob, and let go of it instantly, hissing with pain. The doorknob was scorching hot! As she stared dumbly at the red welts forming on her fingertips, a thin wisp of smoke rose up from under the door. It twisted its way upward and was sucked in on Mabel's next breath. Its noxious taste burned the back of her throat, and she coughed sharply.

Fire!

More than just burned pies, she thought, as she heard the wail of the volunteer fire truck's siren approaching. Was Dee downstairs? Was she safe? Mabel coughed again, and backed from the door. She pulled an afghan off the sofa, and quickly wadded it against the open space under the door. It helped some, though the old door had never really fit properly, and grey smoke oozed into the room through the gaps between the warped door and its equally warped frame. No getting out that way.

Mabel crouched as low as her creaky knees would allow and waddled to the window. She peeked over the sill and saw the crowd gathered on the sidewalk, all staring at the building below her, heard them yelling too. The bakery really was on fire.

Her heart pounded painfully against her ribs as she craned her head to the left. She could barely see through the tears that streamed from her stinging eyes, but spotted the fire engine racing her way. Help was coming.

She pulled the top of her shirt over her nose, breathing shallowly through the thin cotton fabric. She dropped to her knees and swept everything off the coffee table into the cardboard box sitting next to it. Pots of paints, wooden cutouts, and stuffed animals waiting for their beady black eyes fell together in a jumble. She kept her head below the thickening pall of smoke as she dragged the box to the window.

A thin tongue of flame curved around the door and licked at the ceiling. Mabel felt a flutter of panic and sank a little closer to the floor where the air was clearer. She wheezed as she lifted the box to the window's wide sill and pushed it over the edge.

She heard Dee's voice, screaming her name. Thank you God, she thought, Dee's safe. The thought energized her, and she turned from the window for the other box, the one that had just arrived yesterday. It was unopened, and she didn't want to lose it. Bad enough she'd lose everything else, but there was a paycheque in that box.

She adjusted the tee shirt over her nose, and crawled back into the centre of the room. She blinked away hot tears, grimly reminding herself that the cards had said nothing about dying today.

EIGHTEEN

Dee pushed through the crowd gathered in front of the bakery. A siren shrieked in the distance, growing louder as it approached, but the fire truck was still several minutes away, it hadn't even crossed the bridge yet.

Dee stared in disbelief at the dirty smoke pouring over the bakery's window sills. "Where's Mabel? Has anyone seen Mabel?"

She lunged for the door to the bakery. No flames were visible yet but the door radiated almost as much heat as of one of her ovens, and its paint was beginning to blister. Her fingers barely brushed the red-hot handle before rough hands grabbed her from behind and spun her around.

"Are you crazy?" Matt shouted into Dee's face, gripping her upper arms tightly. "No one can go in there. It's too dangerous. Wait for the fire department, it's their job."

"But Mabel is upstairs. She won't be able to get out," she said, struggling to get free. She shouldn't have left the bakery while the ovens were on. She knew they were unreliable. The building was a tinderbox and the fire would eat it up.

She had to get Mabel out!

Matt stumbled as Dee managed to turn around in his grasp so he clasped her back tightly to his coffee-stained apron, pinning her arms.

"Damn it, Matt, let me go! Mabel's in there. We have to get her out."

"Not a chance. My mother would kill me if she knew I let you go into that fire." He panted as he struggled to drag her backwards, away from the smoke and flames.

Dee tried to squirm out of Matt's grip but her arms were tightly pinioned and she couldn't force her way free. "Let me go!" she screamed. "Everyone is just standing around. Someone has to get Mabel out." She was jostled and nearly fell as Matt shoved her against someone else. She recognized Eric's black coat and tried to shy away from his reflexive grasp.

"Hold her!" Matt shouted. "If you let her go, I'll hunt you down and rip off your face."

Dee twisted fiercely, but Eric held her snugly, and she could only watch as Matt ran off, away from the fire, abandoning Mabel.

The crowd surged away from the building, shouting in alarm, as something plummeted out of a second story window. A large cardboard box crashed to the sidewalk and burst open, spilling a jumble of stuffed animals and wooden cutouts. Streaks of green and red paint bled across the concrete as broken jars rolled across the ground. Everyone looked up as a small figure appeared at the window.

"Damn it," Mabel yelled hoarsely, "somebody get the next one." She tipped another box over the side. No one moved to catch it, and it landed on its corner, tearing open and adding its colourful cargo to the rest of the craft supplies that were strewn across the sidewalk.

Mabel coughed and leaned farther out the window, trying to avoid the hot wisps of smoke that rose around her.

"Mabel!" Dee screeched, trying to tear herself away from Eric. He squeezed her more tightly and pulled her farther away from the building. She tried to bite his arms, and kicked at his shins with her heels, but he was unmovable, stronger than she would have thought possible.

Eric was appalled to have to hold her so closely. She was so sweaty that she was slippery, and didn't seem to care that her blouse was pulling up and showing off her bare stomach. He had not doubt that Matt's threat was real and didn't dare let her go. He resolutely pulled her into the street.

Dee could hardly draw a breath. Eric held her so tightly that she couldn't suck in enough air to scream anymore. Over the approaching shriek of sirens and the growing roar of the fire she heard a metallic rattle, and Matt suddenly reappeared carrying a ladder that he'd taken from the hardware store across the street. He braced it against the building underneath Mabel's window and pulled off his apron, tossing it aside.

Matt hadn't abandoned her after all. He flashed a grin at Dee and pulled out a red and blue bandana from his back pocket. He covered his nose and mouth with it, and knotted the makeshift mask at the back of his head.

The sirens were louder – half a block away – but the fire truck had to negotiate its way past the knot of curious people who were watching a crazy man about to climb into a blazing building.

Dee could only stare mutely as Matt charged up the ladder into a thickening cloud of smoke.

NINETEEN

Phin nearly fell off the roof in his haste to get to the ground. He was certain it was the bakery that was on fire. The rat teeth gnawing his insides told him so.

Dee had complained that the bakery's ovens were well past their prime, but that the owner was unwilling to fix or replace them. Phin had asked her why she didn't just move to the city and get a job in a more modern bakery, she clearly had talent, and a passion for baking. She'd claimed that she couldn't leave Lydia alone, but he was certain she was just afraid to take a chance on a dream. She deserved better than to work for a contemptible man who had no interest in the business he'd inherited.

Phin kicked his bicycle in frustration when he discovered its tires flat once again, and set off at a run. The bakery wasn't far but the thought of Dee trapped in a burning building had him flying so that he arrived gasping for breath.

Even if he hadn't known the way there, he would have easily found it. A huge crowd had gathered in the street. They erupted into applause and cheers as he arrived, and he stopped abruptly, confused, until he realized they were all looking away from him. His chest heaved as he searched the crowd for Dee, shoving people aside and shouting her name. They grumbled but fell back at the sight of his red face and wild hair. He was streaming with perspiration and his eyes bulged as he desperately scanned every face, hoping to find her safe.

He heard her voice before he saw her. She was babbling and crying all at once, and he dove through the crowd towards her. She was struggling to free herself from the clutches of a man who was trying to pull her away from the burning building. Dee's hair had come out of the ponytail she customarily wore while working, and was pasted in stringy strands to her tear-stained face. Phin was transfixed, both terrified and fascinated by this fierce and wild woman.

"You bastard," she screeched, "let me go!"

"You heard the guy. He wasn't kidding and he's twice my size."

"You heard the *lady*," Phin planted himself in front of Dee. "Let her go." The man pulled back as Phin reached for him, revealing a tiny skull dangling from a leather thong around his neck. "Eric, you scumbag."

Eric's angry glare turned to fear when he saw that the man had recognized him by the fox pendant. He backed up, yanking Dee along.

"Dee, listen to me," he whispered harshly as he kept his eye on the wild man keeping pace with them. "You can't trust that guy. He should never have got that house. Riva only gave it to him because they were lovers when he was just a kid."

"Get him off me," Dee pleaded, still struggling to free herself. Phin grabbed Eric's forearms and jabbed his fingers in deeply. Eric bellowed in surprise and pain, loosening his grip. Dee burst out of his grasp, slapping at Phin's hands when he tried to catch her. She ran back to the ladder as Matt stepped to the ground, carrying Mabel easily, as if she weighed no more than a kitten. They were both gasping and coughing and several people from the crowd ran forward to help guide them all to safety.

The fire truck finally arrived and came to a stop in front of the bakery. The siren shut off abruptly in mid-wail, and in the sudden silence everyone heard the guttural cough and roar of the fire as it continued to consume the building.

The spectators scattered as several volunteer firefighters jumped out of the truck. Two of them unrolled thick hoses, which they hooked up to the large water tank on the back of the truck. Two others strapped on oxygen tanks, masks, and helmets before approaching the building to assess the danger. The fifth firefighter pushed back the crowd, shouting at them to move across the street. They obeyed reluctantly, drifting away to cluster in groups in front of the grocery and hardware stores.

Flames now shot out of the second storey apartment's window, where just minutes ago Mabel had tossed out her cardboard boxes.

The tiny shoe shop next to the bakery was also in danger, and the two owners had been running back and forth, carrying out boxes of shoes and dumping them in the back of a van, trying to save as much of their stock as possible. Smoke had started to drift into their shop, and they tried to run in one last time for another armload, but were stopped by the two masked firefighters who shook their heads and blocked the way.

Phineas gripped Eric's upper arm tightly and forced him to walk alongside him across the street and down the alley between the coffee shop and the hardware store. He shoved him against the wall.

"Hey, let go!" Eric tried to lunge sideways but Phin pushed him back and pinned a hand against his chest. His other hand reached for the skull that hung around the younger man's neck. It buzzed and tingled against Phin's fingers and he twitched as a wrenching jolt ran up his arm and neck, his hand closing convulsively around the fox skull. There was no pain, but a thick pressure settled behind his eyes and he saw Eric's features ripple as a misty, second likeness settled across his face, a pointed nose and reddish fur forming over his pallid skin. Dead black eyes yawned widely and invited Phin to have a look. Phin pulled the younger man closer until his eyes were inches from those deep wells.

"What the hell are you, crazy?" Eric said, flinching, and Phin glimpsed what the young man most feared – that he would become his father, a washed-out stage magician, reduced to plying his trade at kids' birthday parties, pulling rabbits out of hats and tissue-paper flowers from his sleeves.

Eric tensed and broke eye contact. Instantly, the pressure eased behind Phin's eyes, and the fox skull became just bone again. The fleeting sense of kinship was gone, leaving him both hoping and dreading that he would feel it again. He wondered then whether other animals' bones would imbue him with unique qualities and insights, and regretted having thrown out the dead crow Orion had put in his bed.

"You broke into my house, Eric, and you took something that was mine," Phin said quietly. "I want it back."

"You're crazy. I didn't go into your stupid house."

"You're lying, Eric. This fox skull is mine. I found it in *my* yard next to *my* house. I realize it matches your Goth-like outfit, but that doesn't give you the right to take it." Phin yanked the pendant over Eric's head and slipped it over his own. His chest filled with warmth when the skull bumped against it.

"That's bullshit, man," Eric sputtered. "Riva only left you that house because you were her little sex toy. Not everything in it is yours. I want my father's crystal back."

"Moron. What Riva wrote about had nothing to do with sex," Phin said. "And there is no crystal in my house except for a clear ball that used to sit on a stand that I might have parted with if you'd only asked nicely."

"Dee needed to know that you'd fucked your way into getting that house."

"Yeah, just the kind of long-range plan a seventeen-year-old boy is going to make. Seduce an older woman so she'll leave you her house when she dies. That's brilliant, Eric." Phin glanced up the alley but couldn't see anything past the backs of the spectators that lined the street. He wondered what Dee thought of Eric's story.

"Why else would Riva leave you her house? She and my father were cousins. Their mothers were sisters. That house should have gone to her Aunt Ella – my grandmother. My grandfather was a famous psychic and magician, and the crystal gave him power. Riva was never meant to have it, the crystal should have gone to my father. Now my father and Riva are both dead and that power is mine by birthright."

"You just don't get it, do you? You don't get power from an object; it's the other way around." Phin picked up the fox skull from where it lay against his chest and pointed the little snout at Eric. "Objects gain power from those who use them. It's like a residue left behind by our intentions, our dreams and our beliefs." Phin almost smiled as he realized he'd sounded like a line from one of Riva's flaky books. He dropped the skull, reached into the pouch hanging from his belt and pulled out one of his carving knives. The blade gleamed in the sunlight as he snatched a handful of Eric's hair and sliced it off near the scalp.

"Are you crazy?" Eric screeched, as he slapped a hand over the ragged patch above his ear. Sweat streamed down his face, and he blinked his eyes against the sting. "You could have cut me." He tried to grab the lock of greasy hair out of Phin's hand, but Phin pointed the tip of the knife at his face and Eric stepped back.

Phin held up the hank of black hair. "Now, you might think this is just plain old hair," he said, "but in the right hands, it could become a thing of power, just like that imaginary crystal you keep going on about." He wound the hair through the eyeholes in the fox skull, and it clung there, garish against the ivory of the bone. "I'd say that since this hair comes from you, it probably holds quite a lot of your energy, and since I'm keeping it now, wouldn't you say I now own at least some of your essence?"

"That's crazy," Eric snarled.

"So you keep saying, but *I'd* also say that you're at a disadvantage here. If you leave now, and never come back, I might just mail your hair back to you some day. Otherwise, I may be tempted to make it into some kind of voodoo fetish. You'd be surprised at the amount of control over someone that I can get with just a little piece of that person." He smiled wickedly at the uneasy look in Eric's eyes. "You thought you could come here and steal power from me. Way I see it, I'm holding all the cards now. You'd better leave, Eric, before I decide that I need another souvenir. Go home and talk to your grandmother. No one here cares about your family trinkets."

TWENTY

Phin splashed cold water on his face and ran his wet hands through his hair. He tilted his head and swallowed several mouthfuls before turning off the tap. His head was throbbing from too much time out on a hot roof in the sun, and also from too many beers. His panicked run to get to the fire had not helped either. His heart was still beating too quickly, keeping time with the headache.

Phin had never before threatened someone with a knife, or with anything else, for that matter. It had happened so quickly, and he couldn't remember deciding to do it before actually pulling the knife out of his pocket. He'd been thinking that Eric needed to be scared into leaving town, and suddenly he was slashing at the younger man's hair. He was ashamed of himself, but didn't think Eric would be bothering any of them again. The fox skull thrummed against his chest in a soothing pulse, almost as if it approved of what he'd done.

He opened the fridge and scanned its contents, each offering making him queasier than the last. He pulled out two slices of leftover pizza, chewing and swallowing quickly so that his taste buds did not have time to react to the congealed grease on the pepperoni. He went into the bathroom, limping on an ankle that had twisted during his wild run. He rummaged through the cabinet above the sink for the aspirin bottle, and swallowed four of the tablets dry along with his last bite of pizza.

Dee would hate him if she knew the real secret. She would wonder why he had kept it from her. He'd had plenty of opportunity to confess during the weeks since he'd arrived. Now Eric had ensured that no matter which version Dee ended up accepting, Phin would have to leave Cricket Lake.

He should just fill up his backpack and go now. There was no place for him here. To hell with the house. Dee and her friends could have it. They could empty it and sell it, or live in it. He didn't much care. They'd probably take better care of the cats too.

He'd need his carving tools, a couple of changes of clothes, pretty much what he'd arrived with. He could get work back in Vancouver, plenty of construction sites looking for help. That would do for a start. He could find another crappy furnished room to sleep in.

Phin had been living in one such room – at the bottom of a narrow, dirty alley – when the letter from Riva's lawyer had finally reached him. He'd had the letter for nearly two weeks before deciding to at least go and have a look at the house. He recalled delaying as long as possible; as bad as his situation had been, he'd had mixed feelings about going back to Cricket Lake.

Then, one morning before sun-up, he'd been lying awake listening to the swish of tires on damp pavement. His eyes were closed, and he could imagine the sound was a breeze rustling through the leaves of a tall tree. It was a game he'd played since he'd been a boy, transforming the reality of an unpleasant noise or smell into something more appealing, so that a car idling too long outside became a lawnmower cutting a lush lawn, its fuel fumes carrying a hint of freshly cut grass.

He'd been vainly trying to convince himself that the warbling pattern of a car alarm sounded just like birdsong, when a new sound intruded: voices outside his window. Again. He'd first heard these two voices a month before, and at about the same time of night. He'd shuddered in revulsion, remembering their whispered words, one threatening to cut the other's throat unless a certain service was provided. The second voice had pleaded for his life, and

148

Phin had been ready to call the police when he'd detected a note of eagerness in the plea.

"Blow me, or I'll slit your throat."

"No! I'll do it. Please don't kill me!"

"Why are you still talking?"

Zip.

The alley had been empty the next morning, the two perverse role-players having de-camped after their creepy sex games.

And here they'd come again. Phin had jammed the pillow over his head to drown out the moans and grunts. He'd been shocked the first time. The second time was just pathetic. That's when he'd decided to re-read over the letter from the lawyer. He'd thought nothing could be worse than having to listen to those two play out their twisted sexual game again.

Now he wasn't so sure.

Phin limped unsteadily through the living room and almost tripped over a cat lying in a patch of sun. Every available sunbeam was covered in feline. They purred and rolled, cleaning whiskers and paws.

"How the hell do you guys stand the heat with all that fur?" he growled at them, just as he noticed Orion lying under the aquarium.

It wasn't sunny under there.

He wasn't basking in the heat like the others.

Just lying there on his back.

Head tilted sideways and tongue lolling.

"Oh Christ," Phin said, stumbling to the other end of the room. He dropped to his knees next to the cat, and flinched as his tender ankle bent under his weight. "That mouse you caught got into some poison, didn't it?" he murmured. Orion's ears poked out from under the tank. The rest of his body was wedged underneath the bookcase that stood behind the aquarium's wrought iron stand.

Phin didn't think it very dignified to pull the cat out by his ears, so he flopped down on his stomach, and wriggled himself underneath the tank with the cat, who promptly woke up and slashed at Phin's face, snarling as he ran off.

"You're welcome," he muttered into the carpet. His cheek stung where Orion's claws had snagged him, and the pizza and beer were threatening to come back up. He turned over onto his back, too weary to crawl out and stand up right away.

Instead, he stared at the bottom of the aquarium, at the hundreds of tiny coloured rocks, and wondered why his entire life had gone so wrong. Everything he touched turned to dust; everything he did just got him into deeper trouble. All he wanted to do was have a normal life, in a place where he had friends, a job and a comfortable home. He'd thought he could find that here. His inheritance had begun to seem like a dream come true, a chance to settle down and stop wandering.

But now that dream was shattered. Maybe he'd been kidding himself all along. It was as if he were under one of those voodoo curses he'd read about where he was doomed to failure no matter how hard he tried. Was something like that possible? Could his involvement twenty-five years ago in a triple suicide have condemned him to a life of aimless wandering, just biding his time until death? Was he so responsible for those three lives?

A sudden flash of light made him squint. He stared at the bottom of the aquarium where he could just make out the edges of a piece of clear glass coming out of the sand as if someone were pushing it from the top. It flashed another searing bolt of light at him and he tried to close his eyes against it, breathless with the sudden thought that here might be the crystal that Eric had been so desperate to find. It settled on the bottom of the tank with a click, pulsing its white light rhythmically.

He began to panic as he found he couldn't shut his eyes against the powerful glow, and he remembered that Riva had been found dead on the floor near this very aquarium. She'd had a heart attack, and he felt his own heart racing with fear as he tried to bring up his hands to cover his face.

The light brightened even more, searing into his brain, expanding to fill the room with its white brilliance, blocking out everything from his sight. Then with one final flash, everything exploded, and there was only snow.

TWENTY-ONE

The cabin.

Thick snowflakes swirled and danced, cloaking the yard outside the cabin in a white shroud that obscured all landmarks. Cora, Fran and Delia pressed their faces to the window, their breath misting the glass and blurring the fading headlights of Riva's old Buick as it retreated in the gathering storm.

"Do you think he'll be back for us?" Delia asked in a quavering voice.

"He's not coming back, remember? We told him to leave us here." Cora took Delia's arm and gently steered her back into the room, closer to the fire. She settled her friend onto the bench and handed her a bottle of wine and a corkscrew. "That's why Fran bought Riva's car, so we could give it to him in payment. You know how young men are about fancy cars. In a little while he'll have completely forgotten about us."

"But Lydia will worry. You know how she gets." She closed her eyes a moment, and when she opened them she frowned up at

Cora. "I forgot again, didn't I? I'm feeling so stupid, stupid, stupid."
She jabbed the cork and angrily twisted until it pulled out with a
soft pop.

"You're not stupid," Fran said, as she lowered herself
gingerly onto the bench, hissing with pain. "You're an intelligent
woman who's made a difficult decision." Her gnarled hands
trembled as she tried to shake out a folded blanket. It wouldn't
open, and Cora took it from her.

"Don't worry, Delia. We've all talked about this for weeks
now. We've worked it out, it'll be all right." She shook out the
blanket and tucked it around Fran's frail legs, being careful not to
press on her swollen knees. Her head swam and she abruptly sat
down next to Fran.

"Are you all right, Cora?" Delia set aside the wine bottle and
looked around helplessly, clutching the corkscrew. "The boy should
be back soon, and then we'll go home."

Cora sighed, and smiled sadly at Delia, whose eyes had once
more clouded over with confusion. "Dear, the boy is not coming
back. We're staying here and having a picnic."

"It's too cold for a picnic. We should have brought hot
chocolate."

"Let's have a glass of wine. That will warm our insides for a
start." She heaved herself to her feet, pressing a hand to her
abdomen where the searing pain had bloomed once again. She
wouldn't be able to have much of the wine and hoped it would be
enough.

Fran reached up and gently touched Cora's back. "We're
doing the right thing, aren't we?"

"Yes, and none too soon," Cora said tightly. She took a
deep breath and smiled again at Delia, who was gazing into the fire,
having forgotten the bottle that sat next to her on the bench.

Cora took three paper cups from her bag and filled them
halfway with wine. Delia sniffed hers suspiciously then smiled
widely and drank it down in one long gulp. She held her cup out for
more.

"Wait until we've had a chance to toast this time," Cora
said, refilling Delia's cup.

Fran held her cup in one hand, while clutching the tiny crucifix around her neck with the other. Her eyes were closed and tears glistened at the corners. When she opened them, she saw that Cora was watching her anxiously.

"Don't worry, I've made my peace with this. There's nothing to fear. I know in my heart that God wouldn't want me to continue to suffer. I'm ninety-two years old, I've got to go sometime.

"I'm just grateful that I get to choose, instead of waiting in agony for who knows how much longer." She took a deep breath, and raised her cup of wine. "To us – three women who dared to live life joyfully, and choose to leave it peacefully."

Cora took a careful sip of her wine. "To our families – may they hold our memories dear."

"Families? Are the others coming out too?" Delia asked, frowning into her empty cup. "We should save some of this wine for Lydia and Mabel. None for little Dee though; she's much too young yet."

"No, Delia. Remember, it's just us three. Nobody else knows we're here."

"Sorry, I keep forgetting."

"That's okay, I'll just keep remembering for you. Would you like a sandwich?"

"Yes, do you have any egg salad?"

"They're all egg salad," Cora said, laughing. "You made them this afternoon." She unwrapped the sandwiches while Fran gingerly rummaged around in her tote bag.

"How many do you think we should take?" Fran held up an orange plastic bottle with a white label. "One usually gets me to sleep, though I wake up if the phone rings."

"I don't see a phone," Delia mumbled and bit deeply into her sandwich.

"There's no phone here, dear," Cora answered as she took the bottle from Fran's twisted fingers. She peered through the murky plastic. There were at least a dozen sleeping pills in the vial.

"I think three each should be enough. We just need to be deeply asleep so we won't feel the cold."

"I don't like pills."

"Delia, we've talked about this. Now think. Remember what your mother was like? You don't want to get like that, you told us so."

"She used to run out into the street without her clothes," Delia said, her sandwich forgotten. "My father would chase her and she'd scream that a man wanted to rape her. There was always one neighbour who would call the police, and they'd come and sometimes take both of them away. Mother would sometimes remember what she'd done and she'd be mortified and stay hidden in the house for days. They finally took her away when she tried to burn down our house. They put her into that horrible place."

"I remember her too, Delia. I won't let you get like her, I promise." Cora held out her hand to Delia. Three small white pills sat in her palm. Delia snatched them up and put them in her mouth, swallowing hard. Cora poured more wine and Delia gulped it down.

"Don't let me run naked outdoors. It must be at least thirty below out there. I'll freeze to death." She giggled and clapped a hand to her mouth. "Oh my god, I can't believe I said that." She stopped laughing suddenly and grabbed both her friends' hands. "You won't leave me, will you?"

"No dear. See? I'm taking them too," Fran said, and washed the pills down with the last of her wine. She whispered to Cora, who was massaging her abdomen. "You won't be able to keep them down, will you?"

"Not likely, but that's all right. I'll go to plan B." She grimaced and pretended to take the pills for Delia's benefit. In weeks past, whenever Delia had been lucid enough, she had made Cora promise endlessly that no matter what happened, she would help Delia follow through with their plan so she would never slide permanently into the same demented state that had left her mother raving madly for years.

Cora and Fran had reassured Delia repeatedly that they would all be together, and she would never go mad. They had been amazed that Delia had never let slip their secret plans. There was no way that Mabel and Lydia would have allowed them to take Delia out to the deep woods to kill herself.

The fire was low. It crackled and weakly spat a shower of sparks onto the stone hearth, where they hissed and glowed briefly before winking out.

Cora sat close to the fireplace, shivering as she stared into her lap at the syringe and tiny vial of morphine. A nurse at the hospice had slipped it into Cora's pocket weeks ago. Cora hoped it would knock her out quickly. The cold would take care of the rest.

She filled the syringe completely; it sucked up nearly the entire vial. She bared her thigh and quickly stabbed the large muscle. She pressed the plunger, and winced as the cold sting seeped into her tissues. When the syringe was empty, she tossed it into the dying fire, along with the nearly empty vial.

The cabin was getting colder by the second and the wind had picked up, howling through the cracks between the wooden planks and driving the snow into the room. It had begun to accumulate in tiny drifts in the corners, and wasn't melting.

Cora checked the others one last time. She shook them hard and pinched their frigid skin. She got no response from either woman. Their breathing was shallow and so infrequent that she could hardly tell if they still drew air. She pressed an ear to Delia's chest, and groped at her friend's throat, feeling for a pulse. It was there, though faint and very slow.

Cora pressed a cold kiss to Delia's forehead, then Fran's. She smiled at Fran's smooth, relaxed face, finally free of the agonizing pain that had crippled her for so many years. She glanced at the door, wondering if she should open it. A deep wave of lethargy decided for her. Besides, she'd promised Delia, who was afraid that wild animals would come and eat her. It had been dark for several hours, and the temperature had been dropping steadily. When the fire died completely, the freezing night would quickly claim the cabin.

Cora had barely enough energy to crawl under the blanket and wrap her arms around Delia. Her mind hardly registered that her friend was dead before dark oblivion claimed her too.

TWENTY-TWO

Phin knocked at Dee's door. He leaned heavily on the door frame, and shook his head to clear it of the wooziness he'd felt since waking up on the carpet in his living room. Except he couldn't have been asleep, since he came to with his eyes wide open, staring at a million tiny pebbles through the underside of the aquarium.

But he'd had that dream, so he must have been asleep, though his regular dreams tended to be a jumble of images and emotions, nothing like the clearly detailed vision he'd been shown. He'd been seventeen again, back at the cabin with the three old women. They couldn't see him, but he'd witnessed them drinking wine, taking sleeping pills, and preparing to freeze to death. He'd woken up with the bite of that cold December wind still on his skin.

Phin heard footsteps approaching on the other side of the door, and tried to smooth his hair with his sweaty palms. He wanted to turn around, go home for a shower, and maybe try to pull a comb through his snarled hair before showing his face to Dee. Too late, he thought, too late all around. He didn't know what he was going to say, only that he needed to see her one last time before leaving.

"I have something to tell you please don't shut the door," he said quickly through the tiny gap that showed one red-rimmed eye peering out at him. The eye disappeared and the door swung open. Phin stepped into the dim hallway and followed Dee's back to the living room. Her shoulders drooped and her feet scuffed along the bare wood floor. She was still wearing her baker's uniform, only it wasn't so white anymore – soot on her blouse, and grass stains on her knees. She smelled faintly of smoke, like he did. She passed the living room and kept going, towards the kitchen.

"Oh, hello Phineas," Mabel said, her voice rasping and weak. She sat on the sofa next to a crumpled and damp cardboard box, sorting through its contents while Lydia fussed over her, wiping at her face with a damp cloth. She pushed Lydia's hand away irritably. "Did you hear about the fire? I coulda been burned up. Josie's oldest boy carried me down a ladder. Quite a commotion." She pulled out a clump of necklaces, and began to untangle the beaded strands.

"Yeah, I got there late," he said. "I'm glad you're all right, Mabel, though I'm surprised you're not in a hospital."

"Are you kidding? You won't catch me anywhere near one of those places. Nothing but germ factories. Cesspools of disease. Yuck. A strong cup of tea will fix me up in no time." Mabel plucked the damp cloth from Lydia's hovering hand and handed her the ball of necklaces. Lydia sighed and bent to her task, loosening the knotted mass and laying the freed necklaces in a row on the table.

"I wonder if I shouldn't have had you make me up one of those voodoo protection thingies to hang over my door. Maybe it would have protected me from the fire."

"I don't think anything like that would have helped with those old ovens. I'm just happy that you're ok, Mabel." Phin accepted the large wad of damp fabric pieces that Mabel held out to him. She mimed taking one and smoothing it out on her knee, and Phin nodded. He copied her action, stretching out each square of fabric and stacking them as neatly as possible on the low table in front of him. The fabric was deeply wrinkled, and resisted flattening as he pressed down with his palms.

He looked around the room to avoid meeting her searching gaze. Above Mabel's head, a fading color photo in a wooden frame showed a woman hugging a young girl. The girl was smiling at the camera, and seemed to be looking right at Phin, but the older woman gazed at a point past his left shoulder. A shiver of recognition rippled up his back, and his teeth chattered as if the temperature had suddenly plunged in the warm room. The woman's vague, confused smile was unmistakably Delia's. Phin realized he was the only person left alive who knew where Delia was.

"Hey, speaking of tea," he said, tearing his gaze away from the photo, "one of the cats brought me a huge pair of moth wings the other day. I made tea with them, and read the, uh, dregs afterwards."

Mabel slapped his arm weakly and frowned. "What a waste. You don't make tea out of moth wings, fool. You could have poisoned yourself. What were you thinking?" She looked at him speculatively. "What did they tell you?"

"Aw, it was dumb. It looked like a rat in my clothes hamper, but then again it could have been a parcel wrapped in string." Phin swallowed hard, past the dryness in his throat, remembering the musty taste of the moth wing tea. He felt silly, talking about tea and sorting damaged crafts supplies. He wanted to go into the kitchen, where he could hear Dee bustling about, but at the same time also wanted to avoid the kitchen.

She knew something was up. Did Dee believe Eric's story? Phin didn't think he could keep the truth from her if she asked for it. If only Eric had kept his mouth shut.

Phin added the last square of fabric to the stack. He eyed the pile critically and gave it another squish. His tingling palm felt every wrinkle in the cloth, every thread in the weave. He could pick out the delicate perfume that Lydia wore over the pungent scent of scorched-everything. His senses felt curiously heightened but at least nothing was moving that wasn't supposed to.

If the crystal had been the source of Riva's so-called powers, he could understand why she'd want to maybe top-up once in a while. The initial experience wasn't one he'd want to repeat, but he was enjoying the buzz.

Dee came into the room carrying a tray with a teapot and four mismatched mugs. She poured and set three cups on the table, carrying the fourth to the chair farthest from where Phin was sitting. She turned her body towards her mother and aunt and wrapped both hands around her cup, as if they were cold, though a sheen of perspiration glistened on her flushed skin.

Lydia took a sip of her tea and sighed contentedly. "You should have given the moth wings to Dee," she said, her eyes on the web of knotted strands of beads spread across her lap. She picked at a tight knot, careful not to break the string.

"Come on Lydie, he didn't know any better," Mabel said. She turned back to Phin. "Are you expecting any packages? No way it could be a rat, not with all those cats around."

"Not really. No one knows I'm here, so who'd send me a package? And why should I have given the moth wings to Dee?" He glanced at her, hoping she would answer, but her lips were pressed tightly together and she kept her eyes on Mabel. Would she want to know the real story? Neither Eric's version nor the truth would paint him in a good light but Dee deserved to know where her beloved Gran had gone.

"Dee makes these little satin bags with a drawstring. You put the wings in one and carry it around for good luck. We all could use a bit of that around here right now." Mabel coughed deeply and pressed a hand to her chest. Lydia dropped the rest of necklaces to the floor and gently eased Mabel's head down until it rested against a cushion. She lifted her sister's feet up onto the sofa. Mabel protested but didn't resist as Lydia smoothed back her hair and laid the damp cloth on her forehead.

"Sometimes a package is just a symbol of something that's coming, like an announcement, or news that you're going to give or get." Phin turned to stare at Dee. She had set her teacup aside and was looking at her hands, twisting in her lap.

"Well, I guess I do have some kind of announcement to make," Phin said slowly. "It has to do with Riva back when I was seventeen." He moved over to squat in front of Dee. "Maybe we should talk about this alone. I heard what Eric told you, but I'd like to tell you about it myself."

"No. I don't keep secrets from Mabel and Mother. You'll tell all of us."

"It was unfair of Eric to say anything. He had no right."

"Don't talk to me about rights. She was old enough to be your mother." Dee's face was flushed with embarrassment, and she still couldn't bring herself to look at Phin.

"Riva's age had nothing to do with it. The others were much older. They were the ones we did it for. Well, actually Riva did it for the others. I did it for the car."

Dee's head jerked up. "What are you talking about? What car?"

"The one Riva gave me for driving the women out to the cabin."

"What cabin?"

Phin got to his feet, wincing at his stiff ankle, and pulled a wrinkled wad of paper from his back pocket. "This is from Riva's diary." He smoothed out the sheet and handed it to Dee. He hobbled over to sit on the stool that Lydia had vacated. "Here's the whole story, at least as well as I remember it. The winter after I'd spent the summer here, Riva called me and said I could have her car if I did one last job for her. I loved that damn car and had spent a lot of time polishing it for her over those two summer months.

"I was living with my mother. My father was long gone at that point, and Mom and I weren't really getting along. It was near Christmas break, so I got on a bus and came back here."

"Why didn't you tell anyone else you were coming?" Lydia bent over Mabel, fussing with a blanket. She covered Mabel's feet with it and Mabel promptly kicked it off again. She'd pulled the cloth off her forehead and had picked up the necklaces that Lydia had dropped on the floor, running them through her fingers as she listened.

"I didn't really know any of you that well, and besides, Riva told me to tell no one at all. She said it was a secret. I wasn't going to argue if she was giving me that car. So I came out, and there were these three old ladies." He glanced at Mabel and grinned apologetically. "Well, they seemed old to me at the time."

"Wait a minute," Dee said, shaking the paper at him. "This doesn't say anything about the winter or Riva's stupid car. She named you in this, Phineas. What happened that summer?"

"Nothing. She didn't ask me to drive them until the winter."

"Drive who?" Mabel was watching him intently, her eyes gleaming.

"This has nothing to do with driving, damn it!" Dee stood up and tossed the paper onto Phin's lap. "You and Riva were having an affair. She seduced you, or maybe it was the other way around. It's disgusting." She heaved in a breath and sat down abruptly, mortified at her outburst. Her heart was racing and she slumped in her seat.

"You're just jealous because you had a crush on him that summer," Mabel said.

"I am not, and I did not," Dee retorted, flustered.

"Or you're mad because he seduced Riva instead of you."

"Wait a minute," Lydia said. "Dee was only thirteen that summer, and much too young to be seduced."

"We're talking about Riva and Phineas," Dee said hotly, trying to deflect their attention.

"There was no seduction, except maybe by that shiny blue car," Phin said. He picked up the wrinkled paper by a corner and tilted his head to read the passage again. It *did* seem a little suspect if you looked at it with a dirty eye, though he wished Dee hadn't been so ready to accept Eric's interpretation.

"Eric broke into my place yesterday, probably looking for the crystal he asked you about."

"What do you mean he broke into your place?" Dee was becoming confused, not sure why Phin's story kept going off in different directions. "Why didn't you say something?"

"I knew he'd read Riva's journals and had found that passage. I thought that he'd guessed the truth. He got it all wrong." The women were all watching him, with varying expressions on their faces: Dee was still angry, and seemed determined to distrust anything he said; Mabel was smiling gleefully, as if anticipating a delightful surprise; only Lydia was neutral, her usual blank look masking any emotions that may have been hiding beneath the surface.

"Remember how you told me your grandmother and her two friends had disappeared that winter?" Dee nodded mutely and reached out to take her mother's hand. She clasped it tightly as Lydia leaned towards Phin.

"Well, um, I drove them to a cabin in the woods. Deep in the woods. During a snowstorm. Then I left. I left them there, with no way to get back." He pulled in a shuddering breath as Dee's eyes filled with tears and her face drained of colour.

"Riva made me promise never to tell anyone. I had no idea what was going on. I was just a dumb teenager who would have done almost anything for that car. My parents had split up and my life was turned around so many ways that I hardly knew what was right anymore. Riva called and I just came, without asking any questions.

"The old ladies, um, I mean, your grandmother and her friends told me there was going to be a ritual, and that others would be coming too. I didn't think to question them. Well, I tried, but they told me to mind my own business. I was just a kid, so I did what I was told."

Dee let go of Lydia's hand and stood up wearily. She scrubbed at her cheeks, smearing tears and soot, then simply left the room without looking at any of them. Phin numbly watched her go.

Lydia picked up the mess of beaded necklaces and resumed picking them apart, humming softly to herself.

"I tried really hard to just forget them, like Riva had told me to do. Whenever I worried about what might have happened to them, I told myself their friends had shown up and they'd had their solstice ritual and gone home." His eyes were locked on Mabel, the only person left who was still actively listening. He knew Dee had gone into the kitchen, and could probably hear every word, but he raised his voice just a bit so he could be certain she'd hear everything.

"When my mother got hit by a bus two weeks later I thought it was my punishment for what I'd done. I spent most of my life after that believing that I'd had a part in those three women's deaths, which of course I sort of did, didn't I? It was only later, years later, that I sort of realized that they had probably gone there to kill themselves."

"Mother was only in her sixties, about the age Mabel and I are right now," Lydia said softly, not pausing in her work as she spoke. "She was sick."

"She wasn't sick, Lydie, she was going crazy, like her mother had." Mabel sat up, and reached over to pat Phin's hand. "She had some kind of dementia. She was too young for it, but that doesn't matter. She forgot stuff all the time, left the house with the stove still on, sometimes looked at us as if we were strangers, and once walked all the way to the bank, made up like a two-bit..."

"Shush, Mabel," Lydia said without looking up.

Mabel reached into her box and pulled out a red satin heart-shaped pillow and pushed it under Phin's nose. "Here, sniff this. Does it smell smoky to you? I can't tell anymore, I'm too stinky myself."

"All of it smells smoky, Mabel. You might be able to wash some of the glass or plastic bits, but a lot of it got broken in the fall." He tossed the pillow back into the box and took both of Mabel's hands in his. "I'm so sorry," he said. "I didn't mean for any of this to happen."

"Dammit boy, it wasn't your fault." Mabel pulled one of her hands back and lightly slapped his arm. "Those old ovens were bound to fizzle one day. I'm just glad Dee wasn't in there when it happened."

"I'm not talking about the fire. I mean that winter. I ruined all your lives by helping those three ladies. One of them was your mother. You must all hate me now." He sat back and rubbed his hands roughly over his face.

"Don't be stupid, nobody hates you. If anyone's to blame it's Riva, for knowing all along and not telling. She saw how much we were all hurting and didn't say a damn word. She comforted us, helped us make dozens of phone calls, even took Dee for a month when Lydia had a breakdown over it. And not once did she even hint that she knew where they'd gone."

"I'm not sure Riva knew exactly where they went. I think they bought the cabin way ahead of time and didn't tell her where it was. They gave me directions as I drove. I was lucky to find my way back in the storm."

"That's right, there was a big snowstorm that night."

"The snow was so heavy I could hardly see where I was going. I kept getting lost. It took me almost three times as long to make the trip back as it did going out. They were probably dead before I made it anywhere near a phone. No one could have gone out to check on them until at least the next day."

Mabel scooped up the necklaces from the coffee table, and threw them into the box. "Mama had gone to stay with Cora while we painted the kitchen for Christmas. She was always so confused and we were worried she'd do something crazy, like paint all the appliances to match the walls while we were in another room. It was such a relief to be able to paint the place without Mama around that we didn't call her for days. They were going to some fancy spa they liked in Chilliwack. I can't imagine going to a resort to get your toenails painted but they did that sort of thing once in a while.

"They were due back on Christmas Eve but it was still storming so we didn't worry when they didn't show up. We just figured we'd celebrate with Mama on Boxing Day. She wouldn't notice the difference. When they were four days late we realized that no one had a phone number for the spa they'd supposedly gone to, and that's when we called the police."

Mabel closed the flaps on the box and pointed to the far corner. She'd packed away all the craft supplies, even the quilting squares that Phin had so carefully stacked. Phin picked up the box and set it where she indicated. The box was mushy from the fall and didn't sit flat.

"Mabel," he said, sitting next to her again, "why don't you go live in my house?" She shot him a look, her eyebrows furrowed together in suspicion.

"You really want an old lady living with you? I don't know that we'd be such good roommates. You've already got a houseful of cats. And I have a lot of junk, or at least I used to."

"No, I mean you alone. Well, the cats too, I guess. It's mostly their house anyway."

"Where're you going?"

"Come on, Mabel, you know I can't stay now. I took your mother and her friends to their deaths. The other two ladies were someone's mother or grandmother too. The whole town's gonna know soon enough."

"You're not going anywhere," Mabel said, grabbing his hand. "You're the best thing that's happened to this place in a long time. None of that was your fault, you were just a kid. Everyone should be happy that the mystery's solved. They weren't kidnapped and they didn't get lost. They chose to go away and die, that's all."

"That's all?! Are you kidding?"

"Phin, they were all sick. Mama was going nuts, just like her mother had. Cora had the stomach cancer, real bad. They didn't have those fancy treatments back then that they do now. She was dying, in a lot of pain and not looking forward to more of the same. As for old Frannie, well, she was just old. Her arthritis was so crippling she could hardly move most days. Cora'd go out to her place every morning she was able, just to help her get out of bed. I'm not surprised they made a death pact."

"Death pact?" Phin couldn't help but smile at the thought, though he realized that was exactly what they'd done. "Why didn't Riva drive them out herself? Why involve me?"

"I guess that way she could say she had no idea where they'd gone. No one suspected she had anything to do with it, and we didn't ask the right questions. She didn't ever have to lie about it. Kind of amazing that she was able to keep such a big secret, but she was used to it."

"So they told her what they wanted to do, and she found them a stupid kid to help them kill themselves," he said bitterly, reaching up to stroke the fox skull around his neck. His fingers touched the lock of hair entwined in it, and he pulled them back in revulsion. He glanced down at his chest and curled his lip in distaste at the sight of Eric's black hair sprouting from the skull's eye sockets. He slipped the leather cord over his head and wrapped it around the skull, trapping the hair in place, and then shoved it into his pocket.

Mabel watched with interest, one eyebrow raised questioningly. "That's a nice voodoo necklace you've got there, Phin."

"It's not a voodoo necklace," he said tightly, trying to ignore the tingling lump in his pocket.

He'd throw the lock of hair into the first garbage bin he came to. Or maybe not. If what he'd said to Eric was true, and it carried some of the younger man's power, why not keep it just in case? He remembered seeing something about a protection spell in *Modern Voodoo*.

Could hair taken from another person be used as protection against them? Maybe he could just bury it in the yard by the steps to prevent Eric from even approaching his house. He would have laughed at such a notion a month ago, but the last few hours had changed everything. Sudden visions of long-dead suicides could do that to a man.

Phin nearly jumped out of his skin at a tentative touch on his shoulder. He looked up at Dee, who caught his eye for the briefest moment before shifting her gaze to Mabel. Her look had held his for less time than could be measured, but he'd seen hurt and anger burning in her eyes, which he felt he deserved. He also thought he'd detected a trace of longing, and maybe gratitude. But he could have been wrong, and merely delusional.

"Take me to that cabin," Dee said quietly. "Mabel, please stay here with Mom. You two don't need to deal with any of this."

"But I want to come too," Mabel protested. "Lydie can take care of herself, she's no baby."

"She's very upset, and I don't want her left alone. We'll take the delivery truck. Brett won't even notice it's gone."

Phin realized the truck comment had been directed at him, even though Dee was careful to look only at Mabel.

"You're not leaving me behind, Dee," Lydia said.

"Mom, you're in no condition to go out."

Lydia huffed out a soft, dry laugh. "Come on, dear, we're all a little shell-shocked, and I doubt any of us is fit to drive, but I think I can decide for myself if I'm to go out or not."

"Good God, Lydia, that's the longest sentence I've heard out of you in months." Mabel jumped up and hugged her sister.

"Are you sure you want to do this? It could be a false alarm but I sure would like to know what happened to Mama, once and for all."

"Yes, Mabel, I'm sure," Lydia said, and then turned to her daughter. "Dee, we have a chance to finally know the truth. I'm not going to pass that up. I'll get the spare set of keys. Phineas can drive."

"Can't this wait until tomorrow? None of us has eaten and it's already afternoon." Dee realized she was now stalling. Was she trying to spare Lydia's and Mabel's feelings by leaving them behind? It surely wasn't because she wanted to be alone with Phineas, was it? She felt foolish for believing Eric's ridiculous story about an illicit affair between a teenage boy and a middle-aged woman, but she wasn't sure if she liked the truth any better.

Her mother and aunt stood on either side of Phin. It was almost impossible to look at them while ignoring him, though he was a full head taller than either of the two women and she could slide her gaze across his chest as she looked from one to the other. "You know, we have no idea what we'll find at that cabin. It could come as quite a shock."

"Dee, you were the one who suggested this trip," Mabel said. "We're all grownups here. We know exactly what we'll find there – a tomb. Unless someone else has come across them in the last twenty-odd years we'll likely find a pile of bones waiting for a proper burial.

"How about we have a quick wash-up while Lydia makes some sandwiches for the road? Maybe egg salad, they were Mama's favourite."

TWENTY-THREE

The truck jolted in every direction on the narrow, rutted road. Not much wider than the truck itself, the road sported a tall swath of stiff brown grass down its middle, which bowed as they rolled over it and whispered along the underside of the truck before springing up again behind them.

Low-hanging branches slithered and slapped against the windshield, impeding their view. A heavier branch made them all flinch and laugh nervously when it thumped hollowly on the roof.

Phin's hands were clenched tightly on the steering wheel. He was hunched over, and he peered intently through the window with a furrowed brow. His neck and shoulders ached from having held that posture for the last hour as he wove through the forest on little-used paths, backtracking repeatedly when he came to dead ends.

Nothing looked familiar. He'd only been through these woods once, in winter, and in fading light. Everything had been covered in a thin sifting of snow. Now he was surrounded by screens of green leaves and tree trunks layered in green moss and creeping ivy. Same scenery, different colour.

He might as well have been driving through any of the dozens of forests he'd ever hiked through. To Phin, one hiking trail bordered by trees and dense brush was the same as any other.

Mabel sat next to Phin, chattering excitedly and recalling forgotten memories of her mother and the two women who had disappeared with her that winter. She barked out directions to Phin.

"Take that one, on the left, right after that big birch tree."

"Mabel, I can't tell a birch from an oak," Phin growled through clenched teeth.

"It's right there, just follow the tire tracks."

"Are you kidding? There are no tracks, at least none that I can see. You're just leading us around in circles. This is hopeless. We'll never find it."

"I saw something through the trees, on the left. Just back up a little, you'll see."

The truck bumped and lurched through the ruts as he reversed, and branches drummed a tattoo against the sides and top. Phin looked where Mabel pointed but saw only more trees, more bushes, and no road. He stopped the truck and turned off the ignition.

"There's nothing there, Mabel. We're lost." Phin opened the door and stumbled out, groaning as he stood and stretched his back. The others piled out, Lydia and Dee coming to huddle close to Phin, while Mabel pushed aside branches and peered into the dim undergrowth.

"Mabel, there could be dangerous animals in there," Dee called fretfully, clutching Lydia's arm.

"I'm sure I saw something in there. And this really was a road some time ago. Look, it's just grown over. No one's been here in a long time." She pushed through the foliage and disappeared.

"Mabel, please come out of there. Phin, do something."

Phin sighed and followed Mabel into the brush. As the dense branches closed in behind him, he saw that Mabel had been right. There was a path of sorts though a thick layer of leaf mulch had hidden its edges. Grass and brush had crept in on either side of it, shrinking the path until it was barely noticeable. Branches and leaves crowded together, and the path was scarcely discernible beneath their tangle.

The air was close and moist, and the little sunlight that forced its way through the dense canopy created a random strobe effect that barely lit the way. Phin doggedly followed Mabel as she forged her way along the path. Brambles clawed at his skin, and his pant cuffs became studded with burrs. There was nothing here. It was just another false lead. They were never going to find the cabin. It could have burned to the ground years ago, and been obliterated by over twenty years of rampant forest growth.

Phin opened his mouth to call Mabel back when they stumbled out into a clearing. It was brighter here than in the brush, and he squinted as his eyes adjusted.

Thick moss grew all over the roof, spilling over the edge and clinging to the log walls. The windows were intact, but the panes were so filthy they were nearly opaque. The cabin looked on the verge of disappearing into the bush. Another twenty-five years and it would become just another green mound in the forest, eventually crumbling and settling into a dense hump.

A hatchet head lay on a wide, worn tree stump in the middle of the clearing. Its handle was nowhere in sight, and might have rotted long ago. Phin's hands twitched against his sides, as if they recalled wielding that very hatchet.

Mabel had crept nearer the cabin. She stopped next to the stump and gestured for Phin to follow. Her face was white but held a look of wonder and expectation.

"We should get Dee and Lydia," he whispered, then shook his head at the notion that he should keep his voice down. He could hear birds singing, small animals rustling in the undergrowth, and bees buzzing lazily among the spring flowers. The everyday cacophony of a forest clamoured all around them. There was no need to be quiet.

"You go get them. I'm not leaving until I see inside the cabin."

"We're not even certain that this is the right one."

"I saw the look on your face. This is the right one. You've been here before. Go get them. I'll wait right here."

She sat on the stump, next to the axe head. She scraped at its rusted surface with a fingernail, and then picked it up and

170

weighed it in both hands before dropping it to the ground. She smiled at Phin in encouragement and pointed back the way they had come.

Phin stepped between the trees, then glanced back at Mabel. She had fixed her attention on the cabin, staring with her lips formed into a half smile. She looked so small and vulnerable, a tiny old woman sitting on a chopping block, her white hair glinting in the sunlight. Phin wanted to run over and pick her up, carry her back to the car. They could drive back to town, forget all about this morbid joyride.

He was afraid to take his eyes off her, afraid that if he left her there she would be gone when he came back. Disappeared along with the other old women he'd brought to this cabin.

A faint shout came from the direction of the truck. Dee's voice was shrill, and carried a note of fear. They must be close to panicking, he thought, as he reluctantly tore his gaze from Mabel. He kept his head down so he wouldn't veer off the path as he went, heedless of the grasping branches that tried to hold him back.

TWENTY-FOUR

Mabel stood facing the cabin door, her hand hovering in front of the knob. Her heart fluttered in her chest, too quickly, seeming to squeeze the air from her lungs. She forced herself to calm her breathing. It wouldn't do to drop dead of a heart attack. That would just be too many bodies for Dee and Lydia to deal with at once. That is, assuming there were bodies in the cabin.

She took another deep breath to steel her nerves and gripped the doorknob. It was as rusted as the hatchet head in the yard, and its rough, pitted surface felt like sandpaper against her palm. She stood on her toes, craning her neck to see through the grimy panes of glass set in the door, but they might as well have been made of wood, for all the view they allowed.

"Mama, you'd better be in there," she whispered, and then turned the doorknob. Or at least tried to. Her hand turned alone with a rasp, and she hissed in pain as the gritty knob bit into her palm. The whole mechanism had rusted into one solid piece of metal.

"Serves me right, not waiting for them," she muttered, glancing back guiltily at the opening in the dense forest where she heard the others making their way through the brush and branches. She blew on her scraped palm to ease the sting and inspected it for damage. No blood, just flecks of rust and reddened skin. Good thing, since her other hand was still blistered from the fire. She turned to face her sister, her niece and Phineas.

Phineas. He'd changed a lot in twenty-five years, but then so had they all. It must have been hell for the boy to live with such guilt. He claimed to have more or less drifted around all these years, aimless and restless. No wonder.

And why did he come back? He must have been terrified to return here, where he might have to confront the ghosts of the three women he thought he'd helped to kill. Maybe that's what Riva had hoped would happen, that Phin would come back and solve the mystery for everyone.

"Hey, you were supposed to wait for us," Phin called as he stepped out of the forest into the tiny clearing.

"Don't worry, I couldn't get in, it's rusted shut. You'll have to kick the door down."

"Wait," Dee said, panting to catch her breath, "How do we know this is the right cabin? We can't just break into someone's camp."

"Oh, it's the right one, all right," Mabel said, glancing at Phin.

They watched him walk up to the door of the cabin. He tried to turn the knob, and then rattled the door to test its strength. The cabin trembled, and clumps of loose moss fell off the roof, but the door held shut.

Phin stepped back two paces, lifted one booted foot, and kicked the door just beneath the knob. The rotted wood frame splintered, freeing the jammed mechanism, and the door swung open with a tortured screech of hinges, banging against the inside wall. He held up his hand as it swung back to keep it from closing.

"Mabel, wait," Dee called, as Mabel pushed past Phin and stepped into the cabin. She backed out immediately with a squeal and bumped into him.

"Ugh, what a stink," she said, pinching her nose shut. "And there's a human skull on the floor. This is the place, all right."

Dee kept her eyes on Phin's back. He hadn't moved. He was so still that she wondered if he was even breathing. She tried to picture him at seventeen, as the polite young man she'd met that summer. She imagined his excitement when Riva offered him the car of his dreams in exchange for giving three old women a ride to this cabin. He would have trusted Riva and the women and not asked questions, just done what he was asked to do. Any misgivings he might have had would have been pushed aside when his mother was killed two weeks later.

"Phin?" At his nod, she started forward. If he had the strength to face this, she could at least summon up enough courage to follow him inside. If this was the place where Gran had died, they could finally put her to rest.

"No! Let's just leave. I don't like this," Lydia moaned, clutching at Dee. She tried to pull her daughter back towards the path, but Dee stood her ground, easing Lydia's fingers open.

"Mom, we came all the way out here to see. You can stay here if you want to, but I'm going in. I need to know, and I think you do too." She gently curled her arm around her mother's shoulders and steered her towards the cabin. "Phin, why don't you and Mabel go on in and open some windows. It looks pretty dim in there."

"Smells pretty bad too," Mabel said. "Probably some animal that crawled down the chimney and died."

"Um, Mabel," Phin whispered, "There are three dead people in there. Could explain the smell, right?"

"Maybe not, after so many years. There wouldn't be much of anything left rotting. Bugs and varmints would have taken care of all that. Come on, quit stalling. We don't go in now, Lydia's going to bail on us. I think it's important for all of us to see what's inside, don't you?"

"Yeah, I guess."

"Come on, boy, this is your chance to prove to yourself that it wasn't your fault. Then you can let it go and get on with your life."

Mabel gave him a little push and he stumbled into the room. She stayed close to his side, peering into the gloomy interior. She could just make out a crude fireplace and two wooden benches. A lump of wool blankets lay on a raised platform across the room from a filthy window that barely added to the light spilling into the open doorway.

Phin already felt trapped in the tiny room, the close heat of the place jangling his nerves. He was terrified of what they'd find under that pile of blankets. There was a smell of rotting flesh, but not as bad as he'd expected. Probably just a mouse or a squirrel, like Mabel said. He took another tentative step into the room. Mabel gave him a poke in the ribs and pointed to the window. He stepped up to it, grateful to have something to focus his attention on. Better the window than the lumpy blankets or the skull lying on the floor.

The window latch was jammed, as rusted as the door handle had been. He picked up a length of firewood lying under the bench and jabbed it through the glass pane. It tinkled as it broke, scattering shards of glass inside the cabin and outside on the mossy ground. Dee and Lydia rushed in at the sound of breaking glass, and then froze at the sight of the skull.

"Dee, is that what I think it is?" Lydia asked, backing out of the cabin.

"Mom, you have to be strong. We're going to do this. We've waited a long time to find out what happened to Gran. It's just bones, she's long gone." Dee laced her fingers through Lydia's and pulled her close.

"How do you know it's her?"

"Well, I'm not sure. Phin?" Dee's voice was shrill and she took a steadying breath.

Phin raised one shoulder and dropped it. It looked like Fran, Cora and Delia had had to huddle together to keep warm, but had probably frozen to death anyway after he'd left them. He could hardly breathe. His worst nightmare had come to life. Bad enough he'd come back to this town, but now he'd brought these women to witness his secret crime. A part of him wanted to bolt, another part was horrified that he'd even consider abandoning these three other women to the woods. But, under the fear and the horror ran a thread of relief that it was finally over.

"Lydia, Dee, come over here and look at this," Mabel's excited voice called from the far end of the tiny room. She held up a dust-coated, faded plastic tote bag. It had once been bright blue with yellow sunflowers. "This was Mother's bag. She bought it when we all went to Vancouver that time, remember?"

Lydia slowly walked towards Mabel, her eyes glued to the bag her sister held up for inspection. She snatched it from Mabel and looked inside. A cracked lipstick tube rested among mouse droppings and disintegrating tissues. Lydia reached inside, but shuddered as her hand touched the silky strands of a web and startled a fat spider. She upended the bag and shook it. The lipstick tube fell out, along with a pencil stub and tattered notebook, whose brittle pages crackled as they hit the floor, shedding their yellow, ragged edges. The spider scuttled away, running for the nearest corner.

"That's her notebook. She wrote down all the things she was afraid of forgetting."

"Don't touch that," Dee said. "All that mouse poop carries germs and diseases. We should have brought rubber gloves or something."

"But she might have left us a message in it."

"We've got some plastic bags in the car. We'll get them later and bring the thing home if you really want to read it," Mabel said as she nudged the blankets with a trembling finger. A tiny mouse ran out and headed straight for the open doorway. The three women screeched, and then laughed nervously.

Phin flinched at the sudden noise, and desperately wished that he could follow the mouse.

"Okay, girls," Mabel said, "I'm going to pull off the blanket."

"No, don't. I don't think I can stand any more." Lydia leaned against Dee. "Let's just take the notebook and go. I'm sure it'll tell us everything we need to know."

"It's probably just full of her endless lists: where she's put stuff; people's names; appointments. I don't think it's going to tell us about what happened here." Mabel turned back to the blankets. They were mouldy and rotten patches had fallen away, showing glimpses of colourful – though filthy – synthetic clothing. She reached out and gingerly took hold of a corner and pulled. It slid away, exposing a jumble of bones that shifted and clacked as they resettled. Most had been picked clean by insects and small animals, but scraps of sinew still clung to a few of the larger joints and kept parts of the skeletons intact. There were also many smaller bones scattered around them, and a few more further away, as if some animal had dragged them there. Phin glanced at the floor, backing quickly from the tiny bone that lay in front of his right boot.

Lydia moaned and her legs buckled. Dee struggled to keep her upright, and Phin rushed forward and caught her before she could fall to the floor.

"I'm all right. Which one is Mother?" Lydia asked in a whisper.

Dee tried to look away, tried to call Mabel back, tried to turn and lead Lydia out the door, but couldn't do any of those things. She could only stare at the grotesque pile of bones. When they failed to join together into a full skeleton and start growing sinew and flesh, she closed her eyes and pressed a hand to her chest, willing her heart to slow down.

"Do you want to go outside?" Dee asked hopefully.

"No. I think I want to see." Lydia pulled away from Phin, but didn't let go of his supporting arm.

"Hey look at all this," Mabel said, holding an old syringe she'd picked up off the floor.

"Mabel, put that down!" Dee cried in alarm. "You could stab yourself."

"Don't worry, sweet Dee, I'm being careful. And there's a little vial too; the kind that Fran used to have around the house for when her pain got real bad. Probably morphine. I know Cora used it too." She set the syringe on a hearth stone, along with the tiny vial, and picked up another bottle that had rolled in a corner. She tried to read the faded prescription label. "I think these were Fran's sleeping pills." She put it beside the other two items, and looked around the room. "There's a broken wine bottle under the cot. Wow, they really planned this, didn't they?"

Mabel straightened up and picked at the blanket, exposing a once-clear plastic container with a faded red lid. It had been gnawed at the edges but seemed intact. The plastic was milky with age, but clearly showed what it contained. A folded sheet of paper.

Mabel fought with the lid of the container, but couldn't open it. The heat of twenty-five summers had partially melted the plastic. She handed it to Phin, who managed to break off one of the corners and pry it open. He pulled out the paper between a finger and thumb, and passed the folded sheet back to Mabel.

Phin couldn't take his eyes off the syringe and the two small bottles. Morphine, sleeping pills, and wine. Just like he'd seen in his vision.

"Listen to this," Mabel whispered excitedly. "It's a letter from all three of them.

"*I, Cora Harper, being of sound mind, do declare my intention to leave this world. By this I mean to kill myself by drug overdose and the cold of a winter's night. I have been ill too long, have no hope of cure, and do not wish to face a long, drawn-out and painful death.*

"*I, Fran Belmont, have also decided to leave this life. I am old and tired and in constant pain. I leave no family behind, except friends whom I have come to think of as sisters. I leave my car to Riva and this cabin to Delia's daughters. The deed resides in city hall. Do with it what you will, my loves. I purchased it for this very purpose, and I'm sorry for what you may find here, but I had no other recourse. Everything else I owned, I have given to charity.*

"*Delia Berkeley, who is not currently of sound mind, has also chosen this path. She has repeatedly stated her wish to us that she wants to die before her mind leaves her completely, as her mother's did. In her lucid moments, we planned this together. None of us has been coerced. We just want to leave in peace.*

"*Riva Glen was our ally only in that she procured for us a vehicle and driver. She had no idea where we were going. The young man who drove us here is also innocent. He believes there will be others joining us soon.*

"*We are alone in this, and have not meant to cause others grief. Your love for us would have kept us alive long past the point where we could have enjoyed such devotion. Get on with your lives, and know that we are at peace.*'

"And they all signed it. That's definitely Mother's signature."

Lydia's hand trembled as she reached for the yellowed sheet of paper. Mabel gave it to her, and watched silently as her sister re-read and then folded it. She tucked it into a pocket and turned to Dee, who pulled her mother into her arms. Mabel stumbled to the pair and wrapped her arms around them.

Phin could not bear to watch the three women loudly weeping as they held each other. He bent and picked at several tiny bones that were stuck between the floor boards. He held them in his hand, and wondered if they had come from just one of the skeletons or if he was holding bones from all three of them.

They weren't much bigger than the bones that belonged to the fox, but somehow they were much more substantial, and he wondered how it would feel to throw these bones for divination. The thought made him shudder with revulsion, but he folded his fingers around them anyway and walked to the window, feeling their shapes pressing into his palm.

His thoughts whirled confusedly as he stared out at the bright day. It would seem he hadn't really abandoned three women to their deaths. They'd chosen to come here, planned it from the start, and no one else was to blame for their disappearances. In the vision that the crystal had shown him, he'd seen the three women just after he'd left them to drive away in the snowstorm. They'd seemed calm, serene and content to be left there alone.

"Phin, honey, do you think we could bury Mother and Fran and Cora out here?" Mabel asked, sniffing loudly and wiping her nose on the tail of her blouse. "We need a shovel, or something. And we can, right? I mean this is our place now."

"I'm not sure it's legal to bury someone outside a cemetery," Dee said uncertainly. "Besides, don't we have to contact the police first?"

"Let's bury them. We don't have to tell anyone anything. No one needs to know we've found them. We know, and that's enough."

They all turned to Lydia in surprise. Her voice was strong and steady. She looked at the three in turn, holding their gaze until they nodded.

"Good. We've agonized enough because of all this. Now we know what happened. They didn't suffer. They did what most people wouldn't have the guts to do – end their own misery. They didn't want to become burdens to us, even though we would have been glad to take care of them."

"Dear God, Lydia," Mabel exclaimed, "you just keep surprising me, what's got into you?"

"I guess I've spent too long locked up in myself. You almost died in that fire today, Dee lost her job, and now the mystery surrounding Mama's death is solved. If that's not enough to shake up a person, I don't know what can."

"Um, I can probably use that axe head," Phin said as he headed for the door. "I'll start breaking up the dirt if you want to show me where. The slate on that hearth is loose; the pieces will make good enough scoopers." He shoved his hand into his pocket and dropped the tiny finger bones, flinching at the clicking sounds they made as they settled against the fox skull. He pulled his hand out quickly when his fingers brushed the greasy hank of hair he'd taken from Eric. He briefly thought of burying the hair along with the three skeletons, but then decided it wouldn't be very nice of him to lay that kind of nasty energy to rest with Cora, Fran and Delia.

"Should we just wrap them in the blankets?" Dee asked. She eyed the jumbled skeletons warily, and wondered which one was her Gran.

"I guess so," Mabel said. "They've been lying in them all this time, they won't mind." She picked up the skull from the floor. She stroked its smooth contours, and peered into its eye sockets.

"Sweet dreams, Mama."

Dee tried to superimpose her grandmother's face onto the skull that Mabel held, and fainted when Mabel planted a kiss on the smooth, bony forehead.

****

"Don't you think three dozen cookies are enough for the four of you?" Delia asked as she pulled the last pan out of the oven. "And you've got that apple pie and a quart of ice cream. None of you will have any room for supper."

180

"We're not planning on eating supper, Gran," Dee said, giggling. She kissed her grandmother's soft cheek. "I'm going to be a teenager before any of my friends. That's cause for a celebration." She pulled a cookbook off the shelf. They had tried out nearly every recipe in it and Dee remembered the taste of each one she saw in its glossy pages.

"You and your girlfriends will be up half the night giggling about boys, or whatever it is you go on about all the time. You'll likely sleep through morning and wake up starved for some real food after all that sugar."

Dee smiled sweetly at her grandmother. "Would you make waffles for us when we wake up?"

"That's not what I had in mind, and you know it." Delia tried to sound stern, but failed. She never could say no to her granddaughter. She was delighted that Dee had asked if she could hold her slumber party here, rather than at her own house. "Good thing we bought that bottle of syrup this morning."

"But we didn't buy it, Gran," Dee said warily, slowly turning the cookbook's thick pages. "You said you preferred the other brand and would wait until they got it in." Her Gran got so confused sometimes, and it was hard not to correct her when she got things mixed up.

"No, I'm certain it's right in here." Delia opened the cupboard over the sink, rummaging around among the boxes of cereal and cans of soup. "Hmm, maybe I put it in the pantry," she said quietly to herself. She went out into the back hall towards the tiny room where she kept most of the extra dry goods.

Dee closed the cookbook and sighed. She pushed her hair off her face, realizing too late that her hands were smeared with cookie dough and flour. She shrugged and touched the cookies on the cooling rack. They were cool enough, so she layered them into a round tin and set the tin aside for later.

She hoped her Gran wasn't going to have one of her bad days. It would be embarrassing if she came out of her bedroom and tried to hang out with her and her friends. Gran sometimes forgot she was old.

Dee would have preferred to have her party at home, but her Mom and Aunt Mabel had set up the giant quilting frame in the living room and Dee's room was just too small for four girls. She'd overheard her mother and aunt discussing – while they sewed the layers of the quilt together with tiny stitches – that it might be time for their mother to move in with Lydia and Dee. As if the house weren't crowded enough already. She'd probably have to share her room with Gran. That would be the end of any sort of privacy.

Dee didn't quite get what was wrong with Gran. Her mother had explained that it sometimes happened that older folks got confused easily, and forgot how to do things that they used to do all the time. But Dee's friends didn't have grandmothers that sometimes looked at them as if they were strangers, or had had their drivers' licenses taken away for parking at a red light and walking away from the car.

She heard the television come on in the living room, and a game show blared into the room. She wandered towards the sound and found her Gran sitting on the sofa, knitting furiously. The blue scarf was several feet long and had so many dropped stitches that it was beginning to unravel in the middle, but her grandmother hardly noticed as she continued to ply her needles.

"Did you find the syrup?" Dee asked hopefully.

"Syrup? I bought a fresh bottle just this morning, dear. Check in the cupboard above the sink."

TWENTY-FIVE

"Shouldn't we say something?" Lydia asked quietly, squeezing Mabel's hand.

"Aw, Lydie, you know Mama hated all that funeral eulogizing crap. She would have wanted it simple and to the point."

"Funerals are for the people the dead have left behind. It's about a sense of closure." Lydia pulled Mabel close, and they huddled with Dee at the head of the mound of dirt that had already started to dry and crumble in the late afternoon sunshine.

"I keep thinking we should have counted those bones; you know, make sure we got them all."

"Stop it, Mabel," Dee said with a shiver. "We picked up every bone in that cabin. Phin even followed you twice around the outside, just in case. Besides, we can't even agree on how many are supposed to be there." She looked away from them, staring into the trees. "What if we'd found that some were missing? I'd have nightmares about a raccoon carrying Gran's fingers up that chimney to fill its cubs' bellies."

Lydia stared at Dee in horror for a moment, and then slapped a hand to her mouth, stifling a giggle. "Oh dear," she mumbled between her fingers. "Those cubs would be geriatric by now, wouldn't they? We'd never find them, I mean, how long do they live?"

Dee watched her mother laugh helplessly, and realized that she was right, twenty-five years was a long time. They were lucky they'd finally found Gran and her friends. It was a shame they'd had to wait until Riva died and Phin came back to show them the way. She looked down again at the pile of dirt at their feet.

It was pathetically small for a triple grave. The three sets of bones had made a disturbingly compact package when wrapped tightly in the blanket.

They'd decided against digging too deeply, since there was almost no danger of a hungry animal excavating bones that smelled mostly of dust and mildew. So Delia, Cora, and Fran were laid to rest with about three feet of soil on top of them. It had taken nearly an hour to dig the hole, using the axe head and pieces of slate from the fireplace. The soil was dense, and packed tightly with grass and flower roots that yielded only grudgingly to their chopping and scraping.

Dee had watched her mother closely throughout the entire ordeal, staying near her side and in constant physical contact. She wasn't certain which of them most needed the reassurance, but Lydia had been grateful for her daughter's attention, leaning into the hand that stroked her hair or squeezed her shoulder.

Mabel had kept up a constant chatter while she paced out the area for the grave and helped Phin to wrap the bones in their woollen shroud. Her white hair was plastered to her forehead in muddy strings, and she smeared more dirt as she pushed it off her face.

"I'm sure Mama knows how we feel. I'm guessing that wherever she is now, her mind's as sharp as when we were little and you'd try to distract her while I snuck into her bedroom to look for Christmas presents. Remember?"

"Yes," Lydia said, laughing softly. "She was on to us every time, and would always have some irresistible reason to take me into her room. I'd be in a panic trying to warn you without letting on that that's what I was doing."

"You always were a bad actress, Lydie. How could she not know? Your voice would get louder and more panicky as you got closer to the bedroom."

"I know, and I could never help staring at the exact spot where I knew you'd be hiding. I gave you up every time. She was such a good sport, pretending to be so surprised when she found you there."

"Do you think Gran will be all right here?" Dee asked, leaning her head on Lydia's shoulder. "I mean, shouldn't we tell someone we've found them?" She jumped at the sound of the cabin door banging shut and looked up to see Phin standing a few feet away from them, hunched and miserable, tightly gripping the plastic tote bag.

"I put everything in the bag: the bottles, the lipstick and notebook, even the syringe," he said, coming slowly toward them. He could still feel the six tiny bones in his pocket. He could have sworn they were moving around on their own and tamped down his frantic imagination. "If you called the police, they'd want to investigate, wouldn't they?" he continued quietly, glancing at the path that led to the road. He had a momentary urge to flee, to drop the tote bag and run back to the car. His shoulders slumped as soon as he had the thought, knowing that he'd never leave Dee, Mabel and Lydia in the woods. Never again would he leave anyone in the woods alone.

"No. We're not telling anyone about this. There's no one else that would be affected. Fran had no family, and Mama's entire family is right here. Cora's people are all far away from here. There's no reason to drag them into this. Nothing they could do anyway." Mabel eased her hand out of Lydia's and stepped up to Phin, squinting up into his face. "How many times am I gonna have to tell you that you did nothing wrong? You were a dumb kid, doing what you were told. You didn't force them to make this decision; you couldn't have stopped them. Even if you had told someone when you got back to town, it would have been too late to save them. Besides, not one of them was enjoying life any more. If anything, you were the only person who could give them what they wanted – dignity and control over their lives." Mabel's eyes filled when his chin trembled and a tear ran down his face, tracing a runnel through the soot and dirt on his left cheek. She wrapped her arms around his waist, squeezing him tightly as he wept into her hair.

"You're right, Mabel, we don't need to tell anyone about this place," Dee said. "It's ours and we can keep it our secret." She picked several wildflowers and laid them on the tiny grave. "Bye Gran. I understand what you had to do, and I'm sorry I was so mad when you went away."

"I guess we can open that box now," Lydia said as she plucked petals from a daisy and let them float down onto the dirt mound.

"What box?" Mabel said, letting go of Phin, who sniffled loudly and tried unsuccessfully to find a clean spot on his tee shirt to wipe his eyes.

"Mother gave me a key to a safety deposit box a few years before she disappeared."

"You never told me about that. What's in it?"

"I have no idea. She told me not to open it until she was long gone. I figured it was her will and stuff."

"Well she's been long gone, all right. Why didn't you say something?"

"I guess I always expected her to come back. Most times I forgot I even had it." She twined the daisy's stem around her fingers, and bent to pick another.

"Wouldn't you need to prove she's dead?" Phin pulled his tee shirt over his head, and used the inside to wipe his face. He grimaced at the grime that came off his skin. "A will isn't worth anything until someone officially dies, right?"

"I think you can have someone declared dead after they've been missing for several years," Dee said slowly, watching her mother shred another daisy over the grave.

"Let's just wait and see. We've had a long enough day." Mabel looked at them and grinned. They all had dirt caked under their nails and smeared all over their clothing. They were sweaty and three of them stank of smoke from the fire. "My home burned down, Dee has no job to go back to, and we've solved a twenty-five-year-old mystery. All in one day. I'm exhausted, filthy and starving."

"Mabel's right," Dee said. "Let's go. We'll eat the egg sandwiches that Mom made while we're driving home."

"It'll be like a wake," Mabel said, clapping her hands in delight. She grabbed Phin's hand and dragged him towards the path. "Come on boy, that includes you. We're going to have a picnic." She grinned up at him and winked. "You know, it's mighty peaceful here. Maybe in a few years I'll get you to drive me out to this cabin on some cold winter day."

"Not funny, Mabel," he grumbled.

As they ducked underneath branches to get back onto the path, Phin glanced back at the little clearing. The grave wasn't visible from where he stood. Just a tiny moss-covered cabin that no one had come across in a quarter-century.

He put his hand in his pocket and lightly brushed the tiny bones that lay there. They tickled his fingertips as if they conducted a mild electrical current, and he shivered and pulled his hand out quickly. It was too late to put the bones back with the others, though he didn't think he could give them up now anyway. He could feel a bond with these bones, a bond that connected him with the three women he'd just buried, kind of like the strange link he now had with the fox bones.

The fox's skull had allowed him to see Eric more clearly, and to understand the man's motives. Phin wasn't certain how that had worked, only that it had, in some creepy kind of way. He wondered if he'd ever use these bones – human bones, he reminded himself – and in what way they'd be useful, if at all. Maybe he'd only been drawn to them because of his connection to the women who had died in this place, though he could never tell Dee that he'd kept what were possibly her grandmother's bones.

He'd spent twenty-five years trying to forget that he'd abandoned three old ladies in the deep woods, but Phin knew that if he closed his eyes right now, he would still see their faces pressed against the cabin's window, their shadowy hands waving as he drove away in the snow.

PART TWO

Three months later

TWENTY-SIX

Late Summer, Vancouver, British Columbia.

Eric's hand hovered above the knob of Ella's front door, and he tried to force a more pleasant expression onto his face as the evening gloom gathered in the shadowed corners of the porch.

He hoped that she hadn't cooked fish and cabbage for dinner again. The house always stank of it for hours afterwards, but at least it covered up the smell of her talcum powder and all those flowers she kept in vases in every room.

Eric rested his forehead against the door. The paint was cracked and peeling but felt cool against his face. The sun had set an hour ago, but the still air was stifling and his tee shirt clung to his sticky skin.

"I fucking hate August," he muttered. He took off his coat, rolling it into a bundle that he planned to drop inside the entrance. Ella hated that coat and said it made him look like a thug. Eric was certain that it also made her just a little afraid of him and he needed for her to be calmer than she'd been on his last visit just a few days ago.

She still had no idea he'd read the letter that Mabel had sent to her about Riva dying suddenly last spring. Eric also hadn't told her that he'd visited Riva's house in Cricket Lake. He'd meant to casually mention it to catch Ella off guard and shake her up a little, maybe shock her into telling him more about the crystal than the same old story she'd been feeding him all his life.

But he hadn't needed to bring that up at all.

He'd sat in Ella's too-hot living room sipping weak tea and asked if there was a chance that any of his father's or grandfather's things might still be up in the attic. She had looked up at the ceiling with a worried frown, and there had been real fear in her eyes when she'd seen that he'd noticed. She'd become flustered and confused, glancing up at the ceiling repeatedly as she tried to deflect his questions. By the time Eric had left, she'd changed her story several times, stating that the crystal had been given to a stranger, that Riva had taken it after all, that she'd thrown it out with the trash.

Eric didn't know what to believe any more, but he was tired of her lies and was determined to ferret out the truth once and for all. Either there was a magical crystal that would give him power and fame, or his father had been a raving lunatic and the stupid thing didn't exist.

He was more certain than ever that Ella was hiding something, and that the answer would be found in her attic.

TWENTY-SEVEN

Ella woke up with a gasp and pressed trembling fingers to her forehead. The room was dark and her head was pounding. She struggled to remember what she'd been doing before she fell asleep, but it was like running away from monsters in a dream, the harder she tried, the more her thoughts became mired in sludge.

A streetlight cast an eerie glow throughout the room, and she massaged her temples as her eyes adjusted to the dimness and shadows. She was in her living room and had fallen asleep in her favourite chair. She never fell asleep in her chair. Ella was a creature of habit and would no sooner have slept in that chair than she would have worn her slippers to the mall.

She glanced upwards. The usual muted thumps and creaks from her unseen tenant in the attic sounded different tonight. The stranger who'd taken up illegal residence in the attic was as routine-driven as the benefactress she'd never met. Ella had noticed that she snuck in at almost exactly the same time every night, crept along the same path, and settled in the same corner of the attic until sunrise.

A crash overhead startled Ella and she lunged to her feet. She grabbed the edge of the coffee table, spilling her nearly empty cup of tea. She closed her eyes and swayed a moment as waves of dizziness washed over her in time with her thumping headache.

"I must have caught that summer flu," she muttered weakly, opening her eyes and blinking hard to focus on the cup that rolled back and forth on the table. Pale red tea dripped onto the carpet, but a few drops were left in the cup, along with some white grit that had no business being there. She rubbed a finger into the sediment and brought it to the tip of her tongue, crinkling her nose at the familiar bitter taste of her prescription sleeping pills.

"The little bastard drugged me." She breathed deeply, focusing on her anger at her grandson as her memory came flooding back. She straightened up slowly, tipped her head up and squinted at the ceiling as if she could see into the attic, where she could now hear the sound of something heavy being dragged across the splintered boards. Panic caused her heart to thud painfully against her ribs and she took several more deep breaths to calm herself.

When she could trust her shaky legs to hold her up, she let go of the table and patted the pockets of her dress. The key was gone, Eric had taken it and gone up into the attic. She shouldn't have trusted his sudden new interest in her welfare. She'd always been suspicious of his motives, but it was so nice for a change to have a grandson who would make his grandmother a cup of tea on a summer evening.

Ella was tired of this business with the crystal. She wished she'd never heard of the stupid magic rock in the first place. Her son had been obsessed with it, thinking it would impart some sort of powers to him, and make him something more than the insipid man that he truly was. Carl had tried to follow in his father's footsteps, but had not had Nico's stage presence or charisma. He'd wanted the same fame that his father had garnered as a psychic and illusionist, but had not had the talent to impress even a small child.

The Great Nico had been a popular man who had spent most of his adult life entertaining audiences with his feats of magic and sleight of hand. Ella had been happy to stay in the background, to be the wife who cleaned his costumes and props between shows and created hand-lettered posters to be displayed in the lobby of the theatre downtown.

Ella had adored her husband, even when he began to change after one of his many trips abroad to search for yet more ways to astound his fans. Ella had always thought of those trips as pilgrimages. Nico would research the great magicians of the past and visit their homelands to look for what he called icons – the stage props and magical gadgets that had been used by the men he'd admired.

She had happily tolerated this hobby. Even when Nico had filled their attic and spare room with stacks of dusty books crammed with handwritten incantations and symbols, broken boxes with trick lids or hidden compartments, and trunks of moth-eaten black capes and top hats, she had encouraged his need to seek out past links to his passionate devotion to magic. Treasured finds – such as a broken handcuff once belonging to Harry Houdini – had been displayed in a glass case in their living room, a revered prize to touch when he needed to commune with an inspiring hero.

But a smooth ovoid crystal he'd found on his very last trip had made Ella uneasy from the moment he'd brought it into the house. He had warned her not to touch it – not that anyone could have forced her to – and had kept it locked away in his study. He had taken the crystal out occasionally, sitting alone in the dark with it cupped in his hands, staring into its glowing depths, and Ella had begun to fear those days because of the nightmares he had afterwards. What had been even scarier was that he welcomed those nightmares, claiming he was being shown visions that increased his psychic powers.

Ella had been stunned as his newfound psychic sense increased, and she could hardly open her mouth without him spouting the very words she'd been about to utter. She worried about the darkening of his usual joyful outlook and his fixation with the crystal. Ella had begged him to return it to its previous owner, but Nico had said the man told him that the sale was final.

When she'd found him lying dead on the floor one morning, she'd known that the crystal laying a few feet away from him had been responsible. She'd thrown it into the scummy pond at the very back of her yard, but had fished it out a few days later, afraid that it would attract some unsuspecting stranger.

She'd wondered then why she had never been drawn to its power the way that Nico had, but had eventually decided that women were less susceptible to its lure, which was why she had sent it away with her niece Riva years ago.

Lovely Riva. Ella bit back a sob and clutched the front of her dress as her heart sped up again. Had Riva succumbed to the crystal's nastiness after being exposed to it over so many years?

Now that Riva was dead, Eric was the only family that Ella had left. Not much consolation for an old lady. She should have been more careful with that letter Mabel sent her, but it had never occurred to her that her grandson would snoop through her mail.

Ella's head still felt foggy, and her legs shaky, but she knew she had to get Eric out of the attic. He might not find the crystal he so desperately wanted, but it would be disastrous for him to discover her real secret.

She edged past the table to the living room door, holding onto the wall for support. She gritted her teeth as she fought the waves of exhaustion that threatened to overcome her and wondered how many pills Eric had crushed into her tea. Her legs felt as stiff as tree stumps, and she had to think about each step and force her feet to keep moving, otherwise she might just slide down the wall and go right back to sleep.

The hallway wavered in and out of focus, and the tiny tables that lined the walls appeared to move like so many mobile obstacles determined to trip her up. She flicked a switch, flooding the hall with light, and she winced at this new assault on her throbbing head and tender eyes.

"Come on, old girl," she murmured to herself. "You can do this. It's only ten feet or so to the back room, maybe fifteen mini shuffle steps." Her vision was irritatingly cloudy as she made her halting way down the hall. She could hear Eric up there, stomping from one end of the attic to the other, pushing over boxes, and slamming down trunk lids. She twitched at each slam and stomp, and prayed he wouldn't notice the almost invisible seam of the door to the crawlspace beside the chimney, where she was certain the young woman had taken refuge. It was the only place to hide in the one-room attic.

Ella reached the end of the hall safely, exhausted and more than a little woozy. Her legs shook and her breath was ragged. She knew she should sit down and rest, but was afraid she'd pass out. She wondered how the sleeping pills were interacting with her heart medication. Her pharmacist had cautioned her against taking the two at the same time and she'd swallowed her heart pill just minutes before Eric had let himself into the house.

The door to Nico's old office was ajar, and she could see the inverted vee of the step ladder taking up half of the floor space. She pushed her way into the room and let go of the door, shuffling towards the ladder, praying she wouldn't trip on the way.

She clutched at it in desperate relief, and sat on the bottom rung to catch her breath. She could hear Eric cursing loudly as he banged around, thinking she was sound asleep.

Ella strained to hear any other sounds from above, specifically toward the north end of the attic and the tiny crawlspace. Unless Eric knew where to look, he'd never see it, never discover its occupant.

Ella had only glimpsed her tenant once, in a burst of lightning during a heavy thunderstorm two weeks ago. She'd been fretting at the window, wondering if her flower beds would survive the pelting rain, when a brief flash illuminated the drenched form of a young woman clambering up to the roof of her back porch. She didn't think the woman had noticed that she'd been spotted and Ella had heard her clamber through the north attic window.

She had picked up the phone to call the police, but when she had heard no more sounds from above, decided to let the young woman keep her refuge for the night. She had lain awake until dawn, watching the ceiling, and had wondered if that was the first time the woman had slept in her attic.

Ella wasn't afraid that the stranger would come down into her house, since there was a heavy padlock on her side of the attic door, a padlock she'd installed many years ago to keep her nosy son and grandson from ransacking her belongings. She briefly wondered if the woman had robbed her, realized she didn't care. She'd never again need those old clothes or Nico's collection of obscure magical gadgets.

Weeks went by and she got used to the soft, creaking sounds coming from above every night. She had come to feel comforted by this unseen presence in her house, even though they had never met face to face.

Ella heaved herself to her feet once again and peered up into the dark rectangle in the ceiling. She had not been in the attic for at least a dozen years, had not had the strength to drag the ladder into the house, let alone set it up and push up the heavy trapdoor while perched atop its highest step.

Nine steps to the top. Her arthritic knuckles protested as she gripped the sides of the ladder and started to climb. The rungs were narrow and didn't give much purchase to her slippered feet. Barely halfway up her creaking knees began to tremble, and a terrible vertigo threatened to topple her sideways. She froze, unable to continue climbing or to back down. Too many fears crowded in on her at once and her heart raced like a runaway train.

She was terrified of falling off this ladder.

She was afraid of her grandson.

Ella pressed her forehead to a cool rung and tried to breathe deeply, but it felt as if a band had been wrapped tightly around her chest, squeezing out more air than she could draw in. The smart thing would be to carefully retrace her steps down the ladder, go back to her chair and just hope that Eric didn't find the concealed woman. Maybe she wasn't even there. Maybe she'd seen that Ella had company and had decided to stay away tonight.

The tinkle of glass.

Lots of glass. Her head whipped up at the sound of what could only be the old chandelier toppling off the cabinet where it had lived since she'd had the horrid thing replaced with the simple light fixture that still served her today.

That cabinet leaned against the front of the chimney, far too close to the hidden crawlspace. Eric was a cruel man. Ella shuddered to think of what he would do to the young woman if he found her. She had to get him out of the attic.

"Eric, you come on down from there," she called, hating the weak shrillness of her voice. She clamped her teeth together and forced herself to move up another step.

"Ella? What are you doing? I thought you were asleep."

She heard the clomping of those ridiculous cowboy boots come toward her. She couldn't remember when he'd started wearing all black, but it had happened at about the same time that he'd taken to calling her Ella.

"You drugged me, stole my keys, and now you're breaking my things. Come out of there right now!" Her heart pounded against her ribs and dark spots were crowding in front of her eyes, but she bit down hard on her bottom lip, tasting blood, and heaved herself up another rung.

"What are you talking about? You asked me to get one of your pills because you felt poorly," he said, his mocking voice almost on top of her. "Besides, I'm your grandson. One day all this will belong to me anyway, so why don't you tell me where you hid the crystal."

"I told you, I sent it away with Riva years ago, when you were a little boy." Eric's face glared at her out of the hole in the ceiling. His face dripped with perspiration, and his lank hair stuck to his neck. It was very warm atop the ladder. It had to be baking hot in the attic.

"That's a lie. I went to that stupid hick town where she lived. Some idiot hippy is living in her house. He doesn't know anything about it." He glanced over his shoulder. "It's got to be here somewhere."

"I swear to you that I got rid of the evil thing," she croaked. "I couldn't keep it around here. It was too dangerous." She reached up for another rung but missed when the ladder juddered. An icy pick of fear lanced through her body as she saw the black boot swing back to kick the ladder again. It connected a second time and shook her other hand free. She tipped backwards, her feet slipped off the rungs, and then she was weightless.

All of her fears left her in a rush and she only had time to wonder whether Riva had ever hated her for sending her away.

TWENTY-EIGHT

"Dee, come and look at this," Mabel called across the room. Her voice barely carried above the whine of the power saw and thump of hammers beating nails into drywall. Six men worked at various tasks throughout the new building, dividing the shell of the ground floor into two large rooms.

Mabel turned back to the sign she was painting, tilting her head as she eyed it critically. *Voodoo Café*. "Can't tell if it's straight," she muttered, and leaned in for a closer look at her handiwork.

"Mabel, you're dripping paint all over the floor." Dee stepped over a toolbox as she crossed the bare floor. She felt self-conscious as she walked, avoiding eye contact with any of the men who smiled at her as she passed.

"It's just plywood. They'll be covering it up with tiles tomorrow anyway. What's a little paint?" Mabel smiled up at her niece. "So, what do you think? Is the colour right? Should I add little skeletons in the corners?"

"Don't you dare!" Dee exclaimed. "The name's bad enough as it is."

"Well, I like it. Besides, we all agreed to it."

"I didn't have much choice. I still think *Delia's Tea Room* would be nicer."

"But not as interesting."

The din of construction stopped abruptly and the two women realized they had been shouting to hear each other over the noise. Six men trooped outside with their lunch boxes and sat on the bare patio, leaning against the building to eat their sandwiches in boisterous companionship.

"They sure are cute, aren't they?" Mabel said, winking at Dee.

"Stop it. They work for us, so don't harass them." She blushed as Mabel smirked and turned back to her task. "And don't get any ideas about matchmaking either."

Dee slowly turned in a circle, taking in the large space that was the main room of the new café and bakery. She was still rather stunned that her dream was finally a reality, and that they had managed not only to demolish the burnt-out remains of the old bakery, but to erect a whole new building, all in barely three months. It hadn't come cheap, but thanks to what they had found in Delia's safety deposit box, they'd been able to hire a contractor who took care of purchasing all the permits and materials they'd needed, as well as bringing in an army of workers to make it all happen.

She still couldn't believe that Lydia had managed to keep the deposit box a secret for twenty-five years, though she understood Lydia's need to pretend that her mother might come back. To open that box would have meant that she'd given up hope of ever seeing her again. So she'd kept the key in a safe place and forgotten about it. She had dug it out when they got back from the burial at the cabin and presented it to Dee.

They'd all gone to Vancouver the following day, found a lawyer, and signed all the necessary paperwork to transfer the rights of the contents of the safety deposit box to Lydia and Mabel, the beneficiaries of Delia's estate.

The box had held a treasure. A thick pile of Canada Savings Bonds, yellowing at their edges. Alone, they had bought the piece of land the burned-out bakery had sat upon. Brent had been glad to be rid of it, and let it go for the cost of several years back taxes.

There had also been a fully paid-up insurance policy, and several stacks of wrinkled tens and twenties. There'd been more than enough to pay for all the materials and equipment they'd needed to realize Dee's dream, and Cricket Lake's town council had approved all their building plans.

It had been Mabel's idea to include Phin in their partnership. Lydia had agreed wholeheartedly, as had Dee, until the time came to name their new venture. Dee had wanted to name it after her Gran and call it *Delia's Tea Room*. Mabel wanted *Cricket Café*, in honor of their local lake, and Phin favoured *Voodoo Café*. Lydia claimed to have no imagination for that sort of thing. She was happy to stay in the background, ordering baking supplies and keeping the books in order. She even refused to help choose among one of the three names.

So they drew straws.

They flipped coins and tossed bones.

They consulted the Tarot, and drank endless cups of tea so they could read the leaves. And to Dee's dismay, every method pointed to Phin's choice. She argued that it would attract negative energies, that it would scare away customers, and that it was simply in bad taste.

Mabel was happy either way, and had easily discarded her cricket motif, seeing many more decorating possibilities with Phin's voodoo theme.

"Do you think we'll be ready on time for the festival?"

"I don't see why not," Mabel said, as she carefully outlined the letters on her sign in black. "Those guys are happy to work overtime for the extra pay. If they manage to finish the walls this afternoon like they said, and get the floor tiles down tomorrow, there's no reason we can't open by Friday."

"But what about the business license? We can't sell so much as a cookie until that stupid piece of paper gets here, and our grand opening is on Saturday. That's only three days."

"Who needs to sell anything? We'll have a party, with free tea and cookies. Make a big cake, a couple of jugs of lemonade. We can set up a table and have Tarot or palm readings." Mabel pointed her brush at Dee. "I know it doesn't coincide with the full moon but maybe Phin could hold some sort of ritual for the grand opening. I'll go over and ask him later."

"I wouldn't count on that, Mabel. Phineas wasn't thrilled to hear that he was expected to host a séance every full moon. He's been a good sport about it so far but I doubt he'll agree to an extra one."

"Are you kidding? They've all been great, especially that first time; it was the best séance we'd ever had. Riva never managed to contact Cora, Fran and Mama, but Phin got it right away."

"I don't think Riva wanted to contact them. Remember, she was an accomplice in their disappearance."

"Aw, Dee, she was no more responsible for that than Phineas was. Those old gals would have found a way, with or without Riva's help." She put down her paint brush and hugged her niece. "You have to forgive her and let it go. We can't change the way life happens, we can only find ways to live with the results and make the best of things."

"I suppose you're right," Dee said, pulling back and smiling fondly at her aunt. "I'm going to check on the ovens. Even though they're brand-spanking new, I'm still a bit paranoid about leaving them unsupervised for too long."

"Yeah, don't you go burning down my new apartment," Mabel said with a grin. "I haven't even moved in yet."

"I wish you wouldn't live up there, Mabel. You know it makes me nervous to know you'll be above the ovens again."

"Don't worry about me, Chickadee, I can't wait to go home. I miss my view. Besides, I've got that fancy fire escape off the little balcony out back."

Dee left Mabel to her sign painting and went back to check on the bread. She'd made far too many loaves, since she wouldn't be able to sell them, but she'd thought it wasteful to turn on the bread oven without making enough dough for a full batch. She'd leave them out during the festival as samples, or donate them to the church group for making sandwiches.

She sighed with pleasure as she walked into the spacious kitchen. She'd insisted it be completed before the front of the shop, and had ordered the appliances delivered two weeks before the display cases so she could start working as soon as possible. The three ovens had been installed on the north wall, and the two refrigerators – which gleamed in matching burnished steel – faced them from across the room. Two long counters ran along the other walls, with a table running parallel to them through the length of the kitchen. There were racks of shelves above the counters, already half filled with baking supplies and stacks of shiny new pans of every size and shape.

The kitchen should have been sweltering, but it was almost cool in the room, even with the biggest oven running at full capacity. Since they'd started from scratch, Dee had insisted on having an industrial air conditioning and heating system installed throughout the building. No more stifling days in July where the glazing would ooze off the donuts, or freezing winter mornings trying to get bread dough warm enough to rise.

Dee opened one of her many new cookbooks and flipped through the stiff pages. They were crisp and spotless, and she smiled wistfully as she thought of all her old recipe books with their stained and crinkled pages. She missed them mostly for all the notes she'd made in the margins where she'd substituted ingredients or doubled and tripled recipes for the bakery. She smoothed her hand across a glossy photo of oatmeal raisin cookies, knowing that soon it would get splashed and then wrinkly, or become sticky from the occasional glop of jelly that fell on the pages.

She nearly dropped the book when the oven timer rang shrilly in the quiet room. She pulled on a pair of oven mitts, which like everything else in her new kitchen felt stiff and awkward. The oven door opened smoothly, without the familiar squeal of old hinges.

The bread was perfect, each loaf browned evenly, no matter where it sat in the spacious oven. Dee hummed happily as she slid each one out of its pan and set it on a gleaming rack to cool.

Two dozen loaves of perfect bread filled the air with their fragrant aroma. The old oven had not made such a consistent batch in many years and Dee sighed with satisfaction. She would test the other two ovens by making a variety of cookies for the festival. They'd keep well in the refrigerators until Friday.

She reached for the stack of new mixing bowls. Her fingers had barely connected with them when she was startled by a shout from Mabel. The bowls tipped off the shelf, bounced on the counter and hit the floor with a deafening clash of stainless steel.

Dee rushed out of the kitchen, her heart in her throat, sniffing the air for a whiff of smoke. The front room was empty and she could see through the large plate glass window onto the patio where Mabel stood with the six workmen. They were watching something to their left and they all turned to follow the sheriff's car with their eyes as it raced by with its lights flashing.

TWENTY-NINE

The darkness was absolute. The sliding panel had been well-made. Not even a sliver of light penetrated into the tiny space where she hid. It was also too quiet. Nothing since the old lady's thin scream and heavy thud followed by the rattle of boots running down the ladder.

Penny Rodgers cowered in the dark, straining to hear through the floor of her hideaway. No sounds had come from downstairs for a long time, and she wondered if Eric had even called an ambulance for the woman he'd called Ella.

The air was getting stale in the crawlspace where she'd jammed herself when she heard someone opening the trap door into the attic. It was horribly hot too. Sweat poured off her face, and her tee shirt clung to her clammy skin. She couldn't see the walls around her, but knew precisely how small the space really was. If she lay on her back, her head and feet would almost touch the walls. Good thing she was only five foot four or she'd have had to curl up in a fetal position just to fit.

Penny wished she'd taken the time to peek through one of the downstairs windows as she sometimes did before coming in. If she had known that the woman's grandson was visiting again, she would have waited until he'd left before climbing up to the attic for the night. But by the time she'd realized he was in the house, she was already up here, too late to risk climbing back out.

If the old woman had suspected that she had a tenant in her attic she'd never let on. She might have been deaf, but Penny didn't think so since she'd heard her talking to people on the phone. So she must have known and didn't care. Either way, Penny had eventually relaxed and decided that the woman didn't mind if she slept in her attic.

She shifted her hips carefully, trying to find a more comfortable position without making noise. The floorboards were old and many of them creaked when she walked on them. When she'd heard someone rattling the lock on the other side of the trapdoor she'd thrown her books and food onto her blanket, bundled it all together, and skittered across the floor to the tiny space where she now hid. She'd slid the panel shut as quietly as she could, but Eric had made so much noise coming in that he wouldn't have heard her anyway.

Penny waved the hem of her drenched shirt to create some sort of breeze. She had to get out of the attic but was terrified Eric would hear her leave. She didn't think he'd closed the trapdoor and was afraid of falling through it in the dark. She patted the floor around her for the flashlight and gripped it tightly. Did she dare turn it on? She'd never hesitated to use it before, but what if Eric suspected she was here and had snuck back up the ladder? The panel that hid her might not be as light-tight as she assumed.

What was she going to do if Ella was dead? She couldn't live here any longer, that was for sure. It had taken her weeks to find this place. She'd followed at least a dozen elderly women home to see where they lived, hoping to find a suitable place before her funds ran out and she had to give up her cheap room. She'd been desperate, afraid she'd end up on the streets again, sleeping in homeless shelters with the winos, junkies and bugs.

Her stupid little part-time job pouring coffee wasn't going to net her enough money to get her own apartment, but with a resumé with no address – and no real skills – no one was ever going to give her a decent job.

She flinched at the wail of an approaching siren. Eric had finally called an ambulance. Doors slammed, and she heard several muffled voices right below her feet. Penny pressed her ear to the floor, straining to hear: heavy thuds, squeaky wheels, the rattle and clank of an aluminum ladder being folded and leaned against the wall.

She held her breath, and heard Eric tell someone that he'd just arrived to visit his grandmother and had found her on the floor. He claimed that he'd told her many times to wait for him if she wanted something out of the attic, but she was stubborn and very independent. Penny bit her lip. Part of her wanted to run down there and tell on Eric, but who'd believe a stranger that had been hiding in an old woman's attic? She'd probably just get herself arrested.

That thought was enough to chill the sweat on her skin and set her teeth chattering in fear. She had to get out of the attic and away from this house before someone caught her.

There wasn't much to pack since she hadn't taken much when she'd left her aunt's house nearly six months ago. She filled her backpack by feel, stuffing in whatever came to hand, hoping it would all fit. She rolled up the blanket and tied it to the pack, then ran her hand over the floor for any stray bits. Her fingers brushed a bag of potato chips, knocking it over, and she instinctively grabbed it, crunching the chips left inside, a sound she was sure could be heard all over the house. Her heart slammed against her ribs and the blood rushed to her head.

When she was able to think she pressed her ear to the floor again, but the voices had moved toward the front of the house. They were leaving. This might be her only chance to escape without notice. She slowly slid back the panel, wincing at every squeak and scrape. Her sweat-slicked hands slid along the wood, leaving splinters in her palms.

Light seeped into the crawlspace. The trapdoor was still open, revealing a rectangle of light that illuminated nearly the entire room.

She paused to listen again. She could hear voices in the distance, not through the hole in the floor but from the window at the front of the house. She turned to that window to face a darkening sky reflecting the ambulance's pulsing red light. They'd gone outside. Ella was probably lying on a gurney, covered in a white sheet, being shoved into the back of an ambulance.

Penny crawled out into the open space of the attic. She felt exposed in the light, certain she was being watched from below. She stood and carefully skirted the hole in the floor, peeking down to make sure no one was there. The ladder was out of sight, but there was a large pool of blood on the floor that she wished she hadn't seen.

She hoisted her pack onto her shoulders, hoping she'd managed to find everything in the dark. The sooner she was away, the safer she'd feel. She edged toward the window, eyeing the broken glass and toppled boxes from Eric's rampage. It was not easy to avoid the detritus, but she didn't think anyone could hear her from outside the house.

The window that looked over the backyard was still open the usual half-inch she always left it. Penny slid her fingers into the gap and lifted, praying the squeal from the old window couldn't be heard from the other side of the house. She peeked out to make sure the coast was clear. Red and blue lights flashed from the street. The police were here along with the ambulance, all the more reason not to be seen.

Penny stepped out onto the porch roof. The window jammed when she tried to close it and she cursed in frustration. No time to fuss with it. She crab-walked to the edge of the roof and peered along the side of the house toward the street. Lights still flashed but no vehicles were in sight.

There was no one in the narrow, grassy alley between Ella's house and the brick building next to it. Penny climbed down to the porch railing with practiced ease, holding onto the drain spout for balance. She dropped to the ground and the weight of the full pack – and breathless fear – caused her to land harder than she expected. She pressed against the side of the house, rubbing a tender ankle while she decided on her next move. She could sneak through the backyard while everyone's attention was focused on the action out front.

That would be the smart thing to do.

Just leave. Forget all about Ella, the woman she'd only glimpsed through windows, fantasizing that it was *her* grandmother in there. It had been enough to know that she wasn't alone in the house, that the woman downstairs probably knew about Penny and didn't mind having her there. Not like Aunt Margaret, who'd thrown Penny out the moment she'd found out that after two years of university there wasn't anything left in the trust fund Penny's grandparents had left.

Ella had been a stranger but had seemed more like family to Penny than her own blood. No, she couldn't leave without at least knowing whether Ella was alive or dead.

Unruly bushes bordered the old lady's property. Penny shrugged the cumbersome pack off her shoulders and ducked underneath the lowest branches, hoping the leaves were dense enough to conceal her while she spied on the front yard.

Two paramedics were sliding a gurney into the back of an ambulance. No one seemed to be in any rush. Did that mean that Ella was dead?

Eric stood nearby with his arms crossed tightly over his chest and his hands shoved into his armpits. He shook his head at the police officer who was asking questions and writing in a notebook, and periodically glanced at the upper level of the house.

Penny crept closer, trying to hear what the policeman was saying. A twig snapped under her knee and she froze. No one turned toward her, but she could have sworn that Eric's eyes swiveled her way for a moment. Probably her imagination, but it was too dangerous to stick around. If they found her spying on them from under a bush they might assume that Ella had heard something in her attic and had climbed up the ladder to investigate.

Penny shuffled backwards, scraping her knees and forearms along the way, until her foot nudged her pack. She awkwardly slipped her arms through the straps, hissing as they rubbed against her abraded skin. She glanced up at the window one last time as she tip-toed through the backyard, silently saying goodbye to the home she'd only known for a month. She'd stayed here too long anyway. She could sleep at a shelter for a couple of nights until payday and then maybe splurge on a room at the YWCA again while she figured out where to go next. And maybe when Aunt Margaret read the letter...

The letter!

She ducked behind a tool shed and threw off her pack, pawing through its contents and tossing them aside in a frantic search for the letter she'd spent nearly a week composing. She'd torn up the version where she'd apologized for calling Aunt Margaret a bitch for making her leave – no point in reminding her of that – and also the one where she accused Margaret of spending the trust fund Penny's grandparents had left for her education. Instead, she'd chosen to write about how Margaret was the only family she had left in the world, and how she'd come to realize they needed to be there for each other.

It wasn't in the backpack. It wasn't in any of her pockets. The letter was probably still in the cigar box along with her passport, the money she'd been saving up, and the only existing picture of her mother. Her hands remembered picking up her clothes, books and food – everything that had been on the floor of the crawlspace. But she was certain the box was still on the narrow shelf that jutted out from the back wall. She had to get it back. Aside from the passport, that letter not only admitted Penny had been living in a stranger's attic for the past several weeks, but had Margaret's address written on the envelope. She had to sneak back into the attic.

She was jamming her stuff roughly back into her bag, biting her lip to keep from screaming in frustration and fear, when she heard the ambulance and police car drive away.

Too late. Eric was sure to go back into the attic to find whatever it was he'd been looking for earlier. He'd notice not only the open window, but the open crawlspace, which he'd most likely search as well. He'd probably give her passport to the police, along with the letter, which would lead them to Margaret – who'd have nothing at all nice to say.

THIRTY

Phineas swiped a hand across the misted greenhouse pane and peered through the wet glass, watching for Mabel. She was several days late for what she liked to call her mid-moon reading, but she'd had that awful summer cold and had been lying low. She'd called half an hour ago and said she was on her way, and Phin wanted to have the flower baskets ready for them to take to the café after they'd finished with whatever reading Mabel saw fit to test him with. She'd insisted he practice several types, to see which worked best for him. As far as he was concerned, reading tea leaves was for little old ladies, and Tarot cards still made him nervous. Mabel said she didn't get the whole throwing bones thing, but Phin still felt it was his most comfortable way of telling fortunes. If you had to read fortunes at all, why not pick one that suited you?

He plucked another slug off the edge of a basket and placed it in the bucket with its mates. He hated to kill them but saw no other way to keep them from ravaging his garden, inside or outside the greenhouse. He wondered how anything survived in the greenhouse at all. The thermometer showed thirty degrees Celsius and was still climbing. The plants didn't seem to mind the heat, though the most delicate would wilt until evening when the sun was low and the air had cooled.

With all the work that needed to be done at the new café, he'd hardly had time to spend in the garden. The tomato and squash plants lined up against the house had overgrown their pots, and some had fallen over. If he'd liked tomatoes and squash even a little, he might have remembered to water and fertilize them regularly. As it was, they only got wet when it rained, or when Mabel or Dee visited and took pity on them and, as a result, the vegetables were puny and inedible.

Phin wished he'd moved the sunflowers outside before they'd gotten so tall. He hadn't realized they'd grow so much in only a couple of months, but they were like hormonal teenagers on a growth spurt; sometimes he could almost imagine they were stretching while he watched. He'd staked them and he'd tied them to nails that stuck out of the greenhouse's frame, and now the bright yellow blooms were as big as dinner plates and were mashed up against the glass ceiling. If he untied them, they'd probably fall over from their own weight and snap their stems. He was awed by their size, and planned to harvest their seeds so he could plant them all around the house the following spring.

At least there'd be more room in the greenhouse when he took the four flower baskets to the café. He picked up two of the baskets by their wire hangers and backed out the door. The air was noticeably cooler outside the greenhouse, though it was still a hot summer morning. He was dripping with sweat and his hair was glued uncomfortably to his neck in itchy clumps. Hercules came running across the yard and rubbed against his shins as he walked to the porch.

"Hey big guy," he muttered to the grey cat. "Careful there, you're going to knock me over." He tried to summon a frown, or a growl. He even thought of aiming a kick in the cat's direction, but told himself that he'd probably drop one of the flower baskets. Truth was he was starting to enjoy the attention the cats gave him. Okay, that thought brought the frown. He did not enjoy cats, though if he had to like even one, Hercules would be it. He was huge, scruffy and solid grey. He greeted Phin whenever he saw him, and then went on his way. He didn't fawn for attention like the twin orange fluff-balls who never ventured outdoors. Hercules also never brought him the sacrificial bloody offerings that were Orion's trademark. Peg wasn't so bad for a cat, though he suspected he might only feel sorry for her because of her missing leg.

There were plenty of large sturdy hooks around the edges of the porch roof, though the wood was rotten and barely held them in place. Phin yanked hard on each of them, pulling out every third one or so in a small explosion of rust and bits of wood. Several remained, enough to hold the baskets until he and Mabel were ready to take them downtown.

He gingerly hung the two baskets he'd brought out of the greenhouse, then turned and headed back for the other two. When he'd hung all four he stood back to survey the effect. Two of the baskets overflowed with red geraniums, and the other two with yellow marigolds. They made a startling, colourful contrast against the drab faded blue of the little house.

"Wow, that thumb of yours has gotten really green," Mabel piped up from behind him. He hadn't heard her coming down the path along the side of the house. She gazed appreciatively at the blooms from behind her thick lenses. "I thought you were going to grow some of those Supertunias. Didn't you buy seeds for them?"

"I couldn't get them to flower. I think the strain's been tweaked too many ways and it's made them weak. The buds got too big for the stems, which broke before they bloomed. So I went for the old standbys."

Mabel wore a voluminous white blouse with no sleeves, baggy hiking shorts and thick walking shoes. She was all bony knees and elbows, and if she hadn't been wrinkly and white-haired, Phin would have thought she was a little girl dressed up in her mother's clothes. He snorted a laugh at that thought, which earned him a grin from Mabel.

"Glad to see you're in a good mood, Phineas," she said, as she walked past him and stomped up the porch steps. "I'm almonst a week overdue for my reading. Hope it's not too late, though it's kinda hot for tea, don't you think?" She veered to the left, where a furry bundle was curled up on a cushion. She stroked the cat's head, and was rewarded with a rumbling purr.

"Do any of the other cats have fleas?" she asked Phin. "Peg seems to have a lot of bites around her ears."

"Fleas? That probably explains the welts on my ankles." Phin scratched an ankle with the toe of his sneaker. "I'm even more allergic to fleas than I am to cats."

"They've never had fleas before," Mabel said, eyeing Phin suspiciously. "Haven't you been dusting them?"

212

"Dusting? What are you talking about?"

"Riva had a tin of crushed herbs and spices she made up every spring. She dusted the cats every couple of weeks from spring until fall, and they never got fleas. Your house must be overrun by now if you haven't been keeping it up."

"How could I have known? It's not like the house came with an instruction manual. Can't we just shave them all and vacuum the house or something?"

"Not unless you want to be slashed to death by Hercules. He'd never allow that sort of indignity. No, you'll just have to start dusting them and hope for the best. They always smell like cinnamon for a few days after a treatment. I'll ask Tammy if she has the recipe and we'll make up a batch next time I come over."

Phin grimaced. He'd have to keep a close eye on Mabel and her cat dust. He didn't want to chance another of her mysterious concoctions. Who knew what five hallucinating cats might get up to?

"Come on, old Peg," Mabel murmured to the cat. "Let's go inside. I know where he stashes the catnip." The cat jumped off the chair, landing awkwardly on her single front leg, stretched languidly and, after a vigorous scratch, hobbled after Mabel into the dim, cool kitchen.

"How about we do one reading your way and one my way," she said to Phin over one shoulder. "Then compare the two readings to get an idea of whether one is more accurate than the other."

"How could we tell? It's a prediction, so we won't know which one is right until one of them comes true." He fished through a drawer full of receipts, broken tools, dried-out pens and mysterious utensils until he found the lumpy drawstring bag that held his collection of small bones. It was heavier now that he'd added the finger bones he'd taken from the skeletons at the cabin with the tiny fox bones. He hoped Mabel wouldn't notice the difference between the two types of bones. He'd hate to have to admit he'd been telling her fortune with pieces of her mother.

"We're just faking it, according to you, so let's wing it and see," she said with a wink as she brought out the Tarot cards with a flourish.

"Aw, Mabel, couldn't I just read some tealeaves?" Phin still cringed at the thought of touching those cards. None of the characters in the scenes had moved since that awful day Mabel had made tea using Riva's collection of questionable herbs, but they'd left a bad taste in his mouth – in more ways than one. Since then, he'd found most of the images on the cards to have a sinister aspect, even those which depicted happy scenes.

"We did that the last time, and the time before that," she said, as she unfolded the velvet cloth that covered the cards. "I miss these cards. Riva read them for me all the time. I'm used to the way they tell me my life story."

"Fine. I'll shake the bones, and you shuffle the cards."

"My reading, so I should do both."

Phin was reluctant to let Mabel touch the handful of bones. He watched her small hands manage the oversized cards by leaning them on her stomach as she shuffled. She divided the deck into two piles, and turned over the top card on each one.

"Ok, that's the Page of Swords. I haven't seen him for a long time," she said musingly, bringing the card closer until it nearly touched her nose. "He usually means some young person will come around and try to hurt someone close to me."

"What do you mean, usually? I thought the cards answered whatever question you had at the time. It can't have a specific meaning."

"Who told you that?"

"Dee, or maybe you. I don't remember."

"Phineas, there are dozens – maybe hundreds – of books on interpreting the Tarot. You could spend a lifetime studying and learning the meanings of the symbols in the cards."

"So anyone could just read a book and learn the meaning of the symbols? Why didn't anyone tell me that before?"

"It's all in the interpretation. I have a question, I pick a card while I think of my question, and then you interpret what comes up."

"But I'm just telling you what I see in the pictures, like Dee told me to do."

"All right then, what do you see?"

"A young guy holding a sword."

"Does he seem friendly?"

"Not really, he's holding it up like he's about to swing it at someone. I suppose it could mean someone wants to hurt you, since you're the one who pulled the card."

"Spooky, eh?" Mabel grinned at Phin, and patted his hand. "You don't really have to believe in it. As long as you go through the motions and read the fortune for me, my faith in you, along with the magic, will make it work."

Phin watched her as she picked up the card from the top of the other pile and examined it closely. He marveled at the way someone's life could revolve around interpretations of pictures on cards pulled randomly out of a deck. But Mabel came around twice a month – between the new and full moons – demanding he tell her what he saw in the cards, except when he could convince her to use tea leaves or bones. She always went away satisfied with what he'd told her, trusting that he'd accurately foretold what the next few weeks would bring her.

He realized she was frowning at the card she held, and he reached over and plucked it out of her hand before he'd had time to think.

"I don't like that one," Mabel said with a shiver. "The Moon always bothers me. It's never good news." She stood and went to the stove for the kettle.

"Hold on. Give me a chance to look at it before you tell me what it's supposed to mean." Phin stared at the image of two dogs on a riverbank, howling at the moon. A lobster was crawling out of the water toward them. He agreed with Mabel – kinda creepy. "Well," he started tentatively, "this seems a bit sneaky, like something – or someone – isn't quite as it looks."

Mabel had her back turned as she filled the kettle with water. He could see goosebumps raised on the backs of her arms, though it wasn't exactly cold in the room. She set the kettle on the stove to boil. She heaved a big sigh as she came back to the table, as if the simple, familiar act had helped calm her.

"I'm wondering what this could relate to. I mean, everything in my life is pretty good right now. Sure, the bakery burned down, along with everything I owned, but then we found Mama and buried her, and now I'm about to get a new home. My whole family is all right too, and my friends are healthy. The only thing I can think of is what happened at the lake with those boys."

"What are you talking about? What boys?"

"Didn't you see the Sheriff's car yesterday? He would have raced right past here. Josie's two youngest boys. They got poisoned or something, and he – the Sheriff, that is – took them to the hospital in Hope. They've roped off the beach and someone said the boys told them there's a bunch of dead fish all along the south edge of the water." She paused for breath, and went to the cupboard for the teapot and some cups.

"I thought it was too hot for tea."

"This is more for comfort. I'll use tea bags, you don't have to read them."

"So, why do you think this card symbolizes what happened at the lake? And is someone testing the water, or whatever it is they do? Are the boys okay?"

"We haven't heard from Josie yet about the boys," she said glumly.

Phin pushed the cards to one side and draped them with the green velvet so he wouldn't see them in his peripheral vision.

The kettle whistled and Mabel poured boiling water into the teapot. It sat on the table between them, and Phin could feel the heat radiating off the little pot. He shook the bag of bones and poured them into his hand, listening to the satisfying clicks they made as they tumbled together.

"All right Mabel, you wanted to compare cards and bones. So far, you've got a bad person coming around to hurt one of your friends, and some vague sneakiness, maybe about the same person." He held out the handful of bones, though he didn't want to.

"Are those clean?" she asked, leaning forward and sniffing daintily.

"Yeah, I boiled them well, so no fleshy fox bits and no blood. Just shake them and drop them on the table." He put the bones into her cupped hands, and held his breath as she rattled them and poured them from one hand into the other.

"You know, not many people are going to feel comfortable holding these bones," she said after a moment. "Couldn't you just have them blow on the bones while you hold them in your hand? Like the way you do to put luck into dice before throwing them?" She made a little pile out of the bones and pushed them across the table towards Phin.

He gathered them into one hand, and squeezed them gently in his fist, breathing deeply. The fox bones vibrated in a sharper, almost jazzier way than the finger bones did, and even if they hadn't been shaped differently he could still have blindly picked out one

216

kind from the other. They blended well together, combining their energies into a warm, almost sensual hum.

"Do you think it would work? You're the one who told me the person having their fortune read had to touch the cards, or drink the tea."

"Who knows? Give it a try. As long as you intend to read my fortune, I don't see why the bones wouldn't get it right." She sat expectantly, and stared at his cupped hand.

"What do you want to know?"

"I didn't really ask a question for the cards, so we'll do it the same way and see what they have to say."

Phin closed his eyes and thought about what the bones would want to tell Mabel. He tamped down the habitual voice that told him to just throw them in the garbage and get a real job. This reading was for Mabel, and she believed, therefore he had to trust that she would get what she expected. Hadn't he had that proven again and again in the past few months? He realized that his resistance to this magical stuff was wearing down, and he wondered just what that crystal had done to him.

Mabel leaned across the table and blew on his closed fist. "Well? Are you getting anything? I hope it's something good."

Phin opened his eyes as he felt her breath on his hand. He'd had a sudden feeling of peace, a sense that all would end well, though he couldn't have told her exactly what that meant. "The cards told you mostly about what was wrong in your life. I didn't hear anything about how it would work out, or that there was anything you could do to fix it." He spread the bones on the table and touched them one at a time with a fingertip, enjoying the buzz that each one gave, almost like a purr from one of the cats. "The bones show that last part. You can't really *do* anything, but I get the feeling that it'll all have a happy ending, that someone will find a solution."

"See, I knew you could do it," Mabel exclaimed, and heaved a sigh of relief. She reached out to prod one of the bones, but Phin scooped them all up and poured them back into their sack. He pulled the strings to close it and crammed the pouch into the front pocket of his shirt.

The bones thrummed against his chest and he flinched, not from their buzz but because Mabel was staring at the bulge in his pocket with a puzzled frown. Could she tell that there were more than just fox bones in the pouch? She'd held them in her hand only briefly, but Mabel had surprised him too many times with her keen insights and ability to see things that no one else could. Phin knew then there was no way he'd ever let anyone touch them again.

"I need a new name," he blurted. He'd meant to distract Mabel, but realized that it was true. If he could attach a special name to his fortune teller role, it might help him to shift more easily into character when someone wanted a reading. If he had to do something so outrageous, why shouldn't he have a whole new name to go along with it?

"Funny you should bring that up," Mabel said with a grin. "I meant to tell you about the research I did on the Internet the other day." She chuckled at Phin's look of surprise. "Didn't think an old gal like me could manage that, did you? Fritz sat me in front of his computer and started me off. He might be a grouch but he's always willing to help when it comes to that computer stuff." She pulled a much-folded sheet of paper from the back pocket of her shorts and smoothed it out on the table.

"I typed in your name and you wouldn't believe how many interesting references came up."

"Uh, Mabel, I'm looking for something other than my real name, remember?"

"Did you know that in Hebrew your name means oracle?" She nodded at his skeptical look. "Yep. Not only that, but in that story 'Jason and the Argonauts,' Poseidon had a son named Phineas who had the gift of prophecy. Mind you, Zeus was so pissed that Phineas was telling people all about the gods' secret plans that he blinded him as a punishment." She beamed at him. "Amazing, huh? You've actually found a calling that matches your name."

"Oh come on!" Phin sat back in his chair and crossed his arms. "That's just coincidence. You could take any name and find a connection to whatever you wanted."

"No way. I checked all my friends' names and not one of them had anything to do with prophecy, not even Riva's."

"My father used to tease me that Mom had chosen my name from some counter-culture comic from the sixties," Phin muttered, reluctantly leaning forward to peer at the paper.

"See, that's another famous Phineas," Mabel said triumphantly. "Phineas Freak was one of the 'Fabulous Furry Freak Brothers'". She ran her finger down the list on her page. "There's

218

also Phineas Trout, who was a news reporter in *Willy Wonka*, and Phineas T. Bluster from the 'Howdy Doody Show,' though he was named after P.T. Barnum, the guy who ran the circus."

"Yeah, he's the one who said that there's a sucker born every minute," Phin reached over and took the paper from Mabel. He frowned down at the list of names, bemused at how many she'd found: an oracle and a prophet; a puppet and a comic book character; a fictional reporter and a circus shyster. He sighed and slid the paper back across the table.

"You've got a strong name with mystical connections. It's no wonder you're so good at reading fortunes." She reached over and patted his hand. "It's best to keep your own name, dear. Say, maybe one day you could channel one of your namesakes at a séance. It would be pretty entertaining, though you'd have to do it yourself since I probably couldn't do a man's voice."

"Why don't we just keep doing it the way we have so far, and see how things go," Phin said wearily, and rubbed his eyes with the heels of his hands.

"I've got a bunch of ideas planned for our grand opening on Saturday," Mabel said while she poured them each a steaming cup of tea.

"Don't go too crazy. I'm not so sure we'll get that many people out and Dee doesn't think the café will be ready on time."

"We still have two days. The workers will have finished painting and putting in the floors by tomorrow. We might not have much to display or be allowed to sell yet, but I'll be there early in the morning to help Dee clean up whatever the workers have left behind. Then I'll decorate while she bakes some last-minute goodies." Mabel clapped her hands delightedly. "We're going to have so much fun. You're going to be a big hit at the ritual, so get lots of sleep tomorrow night." She grabbed his hand and squeezed it affectionately.

"What are you talking about?" He eyed her warily. "What ritual?"

"The one we're having after it gets dark on Saturday night," she answered with a smile. "It was your idea to name it Voodoo Café. Did you think our grand opening was only going to be about free cookies and tea?"

THIRTY-ONE

Eric snapped another photo with his cell phone. The flash was blinding in the small space and briefly illuminated the open cigar box on the narrow shelf. A stack of empty fast-food containers sat in a corner next to a ball of rolled up tee shirts. It was a pathetic collection. Cast-offs left by some stranger who'd been holed-up in his grandmother's attic. A woman, according to the passport. How long had she been here? Who was she? Ella must have known that someone was hiding up here. It explained her panic about him being in the attic.

Eric picked up the cigar box again and backed out of the crawlspace. He'd put it back where he'd found it just long enough to take the photos, proof that someone else had been in the house in case he needed to show the police. He cast another glance around the attic, climbed down the ladder and turned off the light. He'd give it another quick once-over in the morning before leaving.

He'd been so certain he'd find the crystal when he heard that Riva had died, but had now searched both Ella's and Riva's houses and had found nothing, no crystal and no information about whether one even existed. Maybe his father had been wrong after all. He'd certainly sounded crazy when he'd ranted on about the powerful magic that should have been his inheritance. Carl had accepted his mother's claim that she'd thrown out or sold all of Nico's stage props after he'd died. Carl had never had the nerve to accuse Ella of lying.

But Eric had no such qualms. He'd been willing to do almost anything to get the truth from her. And now Ella was dead, though that was her own fault. She should never have climbed that ladder.

All he'd found in the attic was junk: rotting cardboard boxes and trunks full of mouldy clothes, crappy souvenirs and the props that Ella had once insisted she'd thrown away. Eric barely remembered his grandfather's face, but he'd never forgotten his fascination with The Great Nico's collapsible top hat and black satin cape, his vanishing bird cage, levitating balls, multiplying flower bouquets, and all the fancy boxes and bags with their secret compartments. They all seemed cheap now, any aura of magic they'd once held rubbed off by years of dust and mould, and his jaded eye saw nothing but faded worn-out garbage.

Shortly after the ambulance and police had left, he'd gone into the attic again to erase any evidence that he'd been up there earlier. The room had looked like a tornado had hit it. He had ransacked every box, trunk and armoire in his determination to find either the crystal or any papers his grandfather had left behind. Ella would not have made such a mess, would not have torn open everything.

Eric had decided to leave the busted chandelier where it had landed. Ella could have accidentally knocked it off the top of the rickety armoire when she'd opened the ill-fitting door. Easy to assume that she'd been upset and rushing down the ladder to get a broom to sweep up the shattered glass.

It was while he was dumping an armload of old clothing back into a trunk that Eric had noticed the gap in the wall next to the chimney. The sliding panel was cleverly made and concealed the space behind it when closed.

He'd nearly whooped with joy when he saw the cigar box sitting alone on a rough wooden shelf. He'd hoped it held secret papers left behind by his grandfather. But instead he'd found proof that someone had been living in the attic.

Someone who'd probably heard him arguing with Ella, and who had made a getaway when he'd been downstairs dealing with the police and paramedics. Left in a pretty big hurry too, judging by the open window and stuff left behind. Good for him, since he now had something for when the police came back with more questions.

Detective Feister. That prick had been way too nosy, asking why Ella would have been climbing up a ladder to the attic so late at night instead of waiting for her dutiful grandson to go up there for her, and how such a frail old lady could have dragged the ladder into the house in the first place.

Eric sat on Ella's worn sofa and sorted through the cigar box again. A passport, a photo of a woman holding a little girl, a letter dated two days ago, and two hundred dollars in crumpled twenties. He stuffed the bills into his pocket and turned over the photo.

"Jenny & Penny" was scrawled on the back in smudged ink. The woman looked weird, like one of the slow kids that used to go to his school, all dreamy-eyed and slack-mouthed. The kid looked all right, more normal. He set the photo aside and unfolded the letter. It was addressed to "Aunt Margaret," and signed "Your loving niece, Penny." It told of a great job in a café, and of the beautiful room she was renting from a sweet old woman across town. It described Ella's house, but a lot of the details were wrong and obviously made up. This Penny was pretending to be living with his grandmother as a boarder, when in fact she'd been squatting illegally in her attic. The name in the passport was Penelope Rodgers, and she was twenty-one. She sort of looked like the woman in the photo; except, again, normal. So Penny's mother was a retard. Wow. No wonder she was messed up and living in some stranger's attic.

He thought about calling the police and handing over the letter and passport, but didn't want them to know that he'd gone into the attic so soon after Ella had died. He wasn't worried about the footprints that he'd tracked through the thin layer of dust on the floor. He'd already told the police that he'd been up there many times in the past to fetch things for his grandmother, which would also explain his fingerprints all over her stuff. It was that other set of footprints they'd be more interested in investigating, the smaller ones that belonged to Penelope Rodgers.

His heart nearly stopped when he heard a soft thump overhead. Could she have come back for her papers? She must be desperate. His lips turned up in a feral grin as he tucked the letter and photo into the passport and slid them into his back pocket.

Penny had hidden her backpack behind the shed in Ella's yard. She'd been waiting in the dark forever, it seemed, and the last light had been turned off in the house half an hour ago, after the ambulance had left.

She peered up at the open attic window – her window. This would be the last time she climbed onto the roof of the back porch, the last time she'd see the familiar boxes and old furniture that cluttered the dusty room. She'd actually miss sitting in the tiny crawlspace, reading by candlelight until her eyes were tired and she couldn't stay awake any longer. She'd never dared light it in the main room with its uncovered windows. Penny had felt secure in Ella's attic, protected from the horrors of sleeping in parks, or even worse, in shop doorways. She'd felt safe from the prying fingers of the men – and sometimes women – who had shared space with her at the various shelters she'd had to stay in after Margaret threw her out. There'd always been someone either trying to crawl into her blanket with her or trying to take her stuff.

She had to get her cigar box back. It held all the money she had, and her passport. So stupid! Until a few weeks ago she would never have taken it out of her backpack. She'd carried everything she owned with her wherever she went. But she'd felt comfortable in Ella's attic, too comfortable it seemed. She'd started leaving her stuff there when she was at work, and had always assumed it would be there when she got back at night.

All right, make this fast, in and out, and then get the hell away. Penny climbed onto the worn wooden railing one last time, braced herself against the side of the house and scrambled up onto the porch roof. She crouched next to the window and listened to the night sounds. Nothing except the familiar creaks and groans of the house, and wind soughing through the trees.

She ducked through the window into the room and stood up. It wasn't completely dark; a faint grey square showed her that the trap door in the floor was still open. Eric must have a light on downstairs that she couldn't see from the back yard. It lit the room enough to see that he'd cleaned up most of the mess he'd made earlier.

Penny kept her back to the wall and inched past the faintly glowing hole in the floor as quietly as she could. She held her hand over her flashlight as she clicked it on, to minimize the beam she aimed into the crawlspace. The shelf was bare. No cigar box. She started to tremble and screamed when the attic room behind her flooded with light.

"You must be Penelope," Eric said as he climbed into the room. "I should have known you'd come back."

"That isn't my name," she choked out, blinking in the sudden glare.

"Fine then, Penny, whatever."

She pressed her back against the wall. He stood between her and the window. "I just want my stuff and then I'll go."

"Oh, you mean the box with your passport and that cute photo of you and the retard."

Penny's heart slammed against her ribcage. She'd never shown that photo to anyone. "She was not a retard," she said weakly.

"What are you doing in my grandmother's attic? You know squatting is against the law. I should call the cops."

"No, please don't. Look, I just want my stuff back. You don't need it. I promise I'll leave and never come back."

"I don't know about that. Some vagrant has been living in my grandmother's attic, and now my poor sweet granny is dead. How do I know you didn't kill her?"

"What are you talking about? I heard you…" Penny clamped her lips shut.

"You heard what?"

Penny took a deep breath. "I didn't hear anything," she muttered.

"What I want to know is this – how badly do you want that cigar box?"

"What do you mean? It's not like you can use any of it. You can keep the money. I just want my passport back."

"Let's go downstairs and talk about Jenny, and your Aunt Margaret, and Ella."

Penny stared at the window, her only way out. Even if she could get past Eric, would she be safe? Not likely, since Eric had her only real piece of identification and all her money. He only had to give her passport to the police and they'd be out looking for her in an instant. And what about the letter she'd been writing to Margaret? She'd already addressed the envelope. She squirmed, knowing that was the greater danger. Margaret had no love for Penny and would relish the task of helping the police to track her down.

Running away wouldn't work. She had no money in her pockets – it was all in the box. The photo of her and Jenny was the only one left in existence and the thought of losing it left her throat dry. She didn't think she could leave it behind. When Jenny had died, Margaret had torn up every picture of her sister that she had found in the house. Penny had been only ten years old but had managed, in her grief, to hide this one photo.

Eric gestured impatiently. Penny felt tears sting her eyes as she sat at the edge of the hole in the floor and reached for the ladder. She'd only gone down two steps when she saw Eric's big boot coming toward her. She braced herself, certain he was about to kick the ladder and send her to the same death he'd dealt to Ella, but he simply stepped onto the top rung and followed her down.

THIRTY-TWO

Dee stood on the patio outside the new building. A waist-high wrought-iron railing surrounded the newly laid flagstones which would hold the four tables and eight chairs that were due to arrive on Monday. She eyed the sign one of the workers had put up before leaving yesterday afternoon.

Mabel had managed to make each letter of "Voodoo Café" look like an assemblage of bones. As much as she admired her aunt's talent with a brush, Dee felt a little uneasy with the results.

She could see Mabel through the window, sweeping the gleaming white tiles that covered the floor. There were several stacks of folding tables and chairs that they'd rented for the weekend leaning against the far wall, next to the little alcove that Mabel had insisted they would need for private readings. The alcove was just big enough for a tiny table and two chairs. Mabel planned to hang a curtain in an exotic animal print to hide it. Dee just hoped it wouldn't be too gaudy. Between Phin's dark brooding theme, and Mabel's penchant for bright colors, Dee didn't hold out much hope for her own understated preferences.

Mabel noticed her and waved. Dee sighed and pushed open the door, which swung smoothly on its new hinges. She tried to find the happy, optimistic feeling she'd had for the past weeks as they'd built the café and realized her dreams, but her heart was heavy and her throat squeezed around each breath a little too tightly. She should have been elated that she'd soon be able to take care of herself, her mother, and her aunt while spending her days at the best job in the world.

"Why are you wearing a kerchief?" Dee asked, trying to inject a cheerful note into her question. "You just got your hair done this morning."

"Aw, it's so humid today my hairdo was starting to frizz, so I thought I'd wrap it up to try and keep it under control and now all my new curls are flat." She pouted comically but Dee only stared at her with a stony expression.

"Why so glum, chum?" Mabel set aside the broom and offered her niece a hug. "And where's Lydie? I was only gone ten minutes and the place was empty when I got back. I bought more paper towelling and garbage bags, but they didn't have any more of those little wipe-things I like. I've swept the floor twice, but it's going to need mopping, what with all this plaster dust." She stopped for a breath and looked up at Dee, frowning with concern. "You don't look so hot. What's happened?"

"Oh, Mabel, it was terrible," she began, and burst into tears. She turned her back to the window, suddenly feeling exposed to the street outside. She put her hands up to her face and wailed like she hadn't since she was a child.

Mabel hustled her across the room, and led her through to the kitchen. She pushed her into a chair and handed her a crumpled tissue from her pocket. She ran the water in the sink until it was icy cold, and filled a tall glass while Dee sniffled behind her. "If you hated the sign that much, you should've said so," she joked, as she handed her the glass of water. "I suppose I could tone it down a little, but I wanted to have something to really wow the tourists."

"It's not the sign." Dee took a long drink of water and wiped her eyes again. "I had to take Mom home. She was going on about the grave again. You know how she keeps wanting to go back and plant some flowers?"

"Nothing wrong with that, Dee," Mabel said gently. "She's finally got a place to focus her grief. It's better than when she was zoning out for weeks, living inside her head. Remember that?"

"This was different," Dee insisted. "Tammy came in and Mom asked her to help her plan a wake. Tammy had no idea what she was talking about, and I kept trying to pass it off as a joke. Mom got mad and slapped me. Said I was being disrespectful of the dead."

"Oh crap."

"You said it. Tammy got uncomfortable and left, and then Mom really lost it. She demanded we drive out there so she could be sure the grave was still intact. She wanted to give them a proper burial. I said we already had. She said we'd just dumped them into an embarrassing mass grave." Dee began to cry again, and Mabel handed her another wrinkled tissue.

"I thought we'd explained that all to her when she got upset last week."

"She said we were ungrateful, and had taken the money for the bakery when we could have used it to build a monument or a tomb or something."

"But we can't let anyone know that we found them, or that we buried them out in the woods. Can you imagine the fuss? The investigation? The police would want to know how they got up there, and how we found them after all these years."

"Mabel, I know all that. We talked about it, but Mom either doesn't remember or changed her mind."

"Lydia isn't thinking straight. She knew as well as the rest of us how it would affect Phineas, and agreed that we'd rather have him here with us, and not have to explain his part in all this to the police. Seems more like she's got it all mixed up in her head, and she can't see past just wanting to honour Mama's death. She can only focus on the grave. It's her only connection to the past and what happened."

"But she can't go blurting it out to everyone. We'll get into trouble if people start asking questions. Do you really think Tammy is going to ignore Mom babbling about burying old skeletons?"

"I know Tammy likes her gossip, but she knows Lydie is a little nuts and isn't going to believe much of what she says. Especially if she's ranting about finding her mother's decomposed body in an abandoned cabin deep in the woods."

"Sounds a little crazy when you put it like that," Dee said with a wry smile. She looked around her new, shiny kitchen. "Mabel, do you think we did the right thing here? Maybe Mom was right about the money. I mean, we kind of went a bit crazy ourselves, building this place."

"Are you kidding me? This is the best thing that ever happened to this town. They're finally going to renovate that old coffee shop down the block and restore it back into the old-fashioned ice cream parlour it used to be. I've heard they're going to frame some old black-and-white photos of the original shop from the fifties." She waved her hands in excitement. "And the shoe shop next door had to throw away all their stock. It was all water damaged and the whole place smelled smoky. Their insurance covered everything, but the owners couldn't be bothered to start all over again, so gave it to their two sons, who are going to open a game store. That makes three new places to attract more tourists."

"I don't know about that, Mabel. After Josie's boys got hurt, I heard a rumour that the town council is thinking of not selling the lake property after all."

"We don't know for sure that anything is wrong with the lake – the boys were ok."

"Someone said there were some dead fish on the beach. Sounds pretty toxic to me."

"Might all be for the better if they don't sell it. I didn't like that they wanted to sell the whole lakefront, and take away our right to swim and fish."

"So we hope the lake is okay and the land gets sold. That way we get lots of tourist dollars and the town survives, but we lose access to our own lake. Or, we hope the lake is polluted, and all the tourists go vacation in another town. That way we get our lake back, but it's of no use to us." Dee shook her head bleakly. "Either way we lose."

"Not according to Phineas," Mabel said, smiling widely. "I finally had my reading with him yesterday. We did a kind of test between the Tarot cards and those little bones of his. The cards had nothing but bad news, and said that someone sneaky was going to try and hurt someone close to me. But the bones said that it would turn out all right, that all I had to do was wait for a happy ending."

"What kind of a test is that?" Dee took Mabel's hands in hers. "I'm not sure we should trust those bones. I think they encourage bad energies, maybe even evil ones."

"Would something evil have told me that everything would turn out all right?"

"Maybe you just heard what you wanted to hear."

"Now you're sounding like Phineas. We've spent a lot of time trying to convince him that there are mysterious magical forces out there that are willing to help us guide our lives, if we can only trust them. Just because certain divination methods have a bad rep doesn't mean they're not valid if we use them for good."

"It still seems evil to me and makes me more nervous than you can imagine. I hope you and Phin are careful."

"Don't worry, Chickadee." Mabel grinned at her niece. "I say evil-shmevil."

THIRTY-THREE

Penny squinted up at the clear blue sky. Not a cloud in sight. She had drunk the last of her water on the bus, and was roasting in the baking heat that rose from the asphalt.

Eric had walked her to the station as soon as it was light. The bus wasn't scheduled to leave until three o'clock so she'd managed to snooze on a bench for a while after Eric had left. The smug bastard had known she wouldn't bolt. Every instinct had screamed at her to run but she was so tired, and he'd kept talking about the photo and the letter until she'd become convinced that she had no choice.

She'd dozed on the bus too, and her head had snapped up when the driver had called out "Minnow Bay". Penny had stumbled down the steps in a daze and the bus was gone by the time she realized she had the wrong town. She didn't have money for another bus – which wouldn't come until tomorrow morning anyway – so she'd backtracked for nearly an hour before she saw the sign: *Cricket Lake 5km*.

The whole place was likely a broken down hick town, no better than the worst neighbourhoods in Vancouver, where every other corner boasted its very own wino. There'd be no television –

let alone cable – and if she wanted cream in her coffee she'd have to go out back and milk the family cow. Everybody was probably related in eight different ways and she'd be the most normal person they'd met in years, which would make her stand out as a weirdo.

At least she didn't look too citified, with her scruffy jeans and worn-out sandals. Her tee shirt was new-ish; she'd found it in one of Ella's trunks a week ago when the night got cold and she needed something warm to wear. She'd piled on several layers of shirts that night, trying not to sneeze from the dust and musty smell of the enormous fur she'd wrapped over the layers. She'd been careful to put everything back where she'd found it, so no one would suspect that someone had been snooping through the attic.

She'd kept the tee shirt, figuring Ella wouldn't miss one shirt among so many clothes. It was pale blue, with several rows of strange symbols printed on the front that she knew were runes, thanks to the pamphlet that had dropped out when she'd unfolded the shirt. The pamphlet had been badly translated from who-knew-what original language. It claimed that anyone could tell the future from the runes on the shirt, though it was unclear to Penny as to how you went about doing it. The booklet was somewhere at the bottom of her pack, jammed in with everything she owned – minus what Eric had taken, of course.

She was starving. She hoped she wouldn't arrive too late to buy a meal. She tried not to think about the stupid quest Eric had set her on, and she cringed every time she tried to come up with a way to ask the stranger named Phineas to give her a magic crystal. She'd told Eric no way, but he'd said he was certain he could have her charged with murdering his grandmother unless she cooperated and helped him out. He was right, in a sense. If she hadn't been hiding in the attic when he was snooping around, Ella wouldn't have climbed up the ladder to protect her and "fallen". If she could get Eric's property back, she'd get hers back in return. Not exactly a fair trade, but she didn't seem to have a choice.

If only she hadn't carelessly left that box in the crawl space. If only Eric hadn't found it before she managed to get it back. She wished she'd had the nerve to force him to give it back, but one thing she'd learned from her short time living on the streets – if you started a fight with someone bigger than you were, you generally lost, big time. Eric had to outweigh her by at least fifty pounds, and she had no fighting skills.

How had her life gotten so fucked up? She was homeless at twenty-one, with a part-time minimum wage job that she'd probably lost by now since she hadn't shown up for her shift this morning. And now she had to go and find some stupid so-called magical rock just so she could get her stupid passport back. Eric wouldn't even tell her what he wanted the crystal for – not that she cared. Who even believed in magic these days anyway?

All he'd given her was a map showing where he wanted her to go, a return bus ticket and just enough money for a couple of meals and a night at some place called the Couch & Cot. She could probably take off, head for Alberta and hide, but she'd seen enough cop shows to understand how easy it was to track people these days. No, she had to finish this lame task, get her stuff back, and find some way to start her life over again.

"How the hell am I going to figure this out?" she whimpered. She'd never felt so alone in her life. She had no friends, and no family that wanted her. Even the road she walked on was deserted. She hadn't seen a car for miles. Trees lined the edge of the pavement, one side rising in a steep hill.

She guessed that she had walked most of the five kilometres since the road sign, and that she should be seeing the bed and breakfast that was across from the bus stop she should have waited for.

As she came around a bend she saw a mini waterfall coursing down into the ditch at the side of the highway. Penny shrugged out of her pack and hopped over the ditch, leaning her head directly under the water. She shivered, surprised at how cold it was. She didn't dare drink any of it, but let it splash over her sunburned skin.

Her tee shirt was soon soaked, the runic symbols on the front darker and more pronounced. And were they getting warmer? Penny looked down at her chest, noting that five of the runes were brightening, glowing like embers in the gloomy light. She touched one with a finger and felt a jolt of heat blaze onto her chest where the wet shirt touched her skin. It spread in a burst, sending warm tendrils through her abdomen and into her groin. She gasped out loud at the pleasurable feeling and reflexively clapped a hand to her chest, causing the other four runes to also touch her skin. The resulting blast of heat flashed through her entire body, pulsating in her abdomen and dropping her to her knees as an intense orgasm rocked through her.

She hadn't had sex for more than a year – hadn't really had much sex at all – and certainly had never experienced a climax that would feel good enough to make her fall down. She gasped and giggled, trying to catch her breath. She realized the pamphlet that had come with the tee shirt might have been obscure, but accurate.

"The pleasure of water will answer the wish you pose." She couldn't remember posing a wish – unless you counted whining – but the water certainly had given her pleasure. She looked down at the front of the shirt, and took note of the five runes that had faded and now blended with the others. She'd definitely have to reread that pamphlet, she thought, as she rose on shaky legs and continued on towards Cricket Lake.

THIRTY-FOUR

Phin realized he'd been staring at the aquarium for so long that his coffee had grown cold. He tore his gaze away and set his mug on the coffee table before dropping onto the sofa. He glared at the shelf of books that sat at eye level, reading each title aloud in an effort to distract himself from the compelling pull coming from the crystal that lay submerged in the aquarium across the room. He felt the pull deep in his chest, a twisting lurch that tried to force him back to his feet.

He barely remembered coming into the room. In fact, he'd been avoiding the living room for the past week, but the crystal seemed to call to him more desperately each day. He wondered if Riva had felt drawn to the damned thing in the same way he was. If she had, he could understand how she'd been finally lured to it that last time. He could also understand why her heart had failed her, since his was beating at such a frantic pace that he feared it would burst right through his chest.

He nearly screeched when something cold and wet slid across the back of his hand. It was only a cat nose, and he would have shoved it away, but Pollux wasn't taking no for an answer and forced his head under Phin's hand in a pushy demand for attention. Phin petted the long, silky fur and waited for his racing heart to calm. If he hadn't been so determined to dislike the cats, he would have dragged Pollux onto his lap and gripped him close for comfort.

"I don't get it, cat," he muttered. Pollux purred more loudly and stretched out against Phin's leg. "It's almost like a drug, one hit and you're addicted." He glanced towards the aquarium and then squeezed his eyes shut, certain that he'd seen a pale green glow pulsating from the water. "Ok, maybe two hits."

He wished he hadn't lain under the tank that second time, testing the first experience. He'd been sure that the vision caused by the crystal had been a fluke, a flashback from the mysterious tea Mabel had brewed the previous week. He'd waited until after midnight so there would be no chance of someone coming to the door and finding him lying on the floor on his back, communing with a fish tank.

Later that night, while he was retching over the toilet in an effort to purge himself of the revolting images he'd been shown, he reminded himself that Riva had been found dead, and that he'd be stupid to try it again. He'd stayed awake all night, shaking and moaning, unable to rid his mind of the vision of the three skeletons crawling out of the earth. They'd looked much as they probably had the spring after he'd abandoned them, when their bodies would have begun to decompose and melt along with the snow as it thawed. They'd been whispering his name, calling to him and rubbing at their rotted breasts in a parody of provocation that had shocked him out of his trance and sent him scrambling away from the crystal's brilliant glare.

He'd sworn then to never again look at the crystal and to find some way to rid himself of the aquarium. But two days had passed and he'd been drawn to it over and over, wondering where it had come from.

It wasn't until he'd pulled out his little bag of bones and poured them into his palm that he'd realized there was another effect the crystal had left behind. He only had to think of a question while he held the bones, and the answer popped into his head. They got very warm and he could have sworn that they softened and tried to melt into his hand as he thought of something to ask them. He'd tested the theory over and over, skeptical as usual, but it appeared something had been left behind by the crystal, just like the first time he'd encountered it. So far, it had helped him resolve a twenty-five-year-old mystery, and now seemed to have sharpened his sixth sense, giving him a stronger ability to divine the future.

Had Riva used it to strengthen her abilities? She'd mentioned in her journals that her powers had been weakening and that she feared she'd have to use the crystal again. How many times had she subjected herself to its nastiness just so she could gain a bit of power?

The crystal's siren call reminded him of the several times he'd quit smoking cigarettes, and how desperate the urge had been to abandon his resolve and run to the nearest store to buy a pack of smokes. He had given in to his cravings for cigarettes many times and had hated himself for being a weakling. Years after he'd finally kicked the habit, he'd still sometimes wake up reaching for his cigarettes and feel a pang of loss when he realized he didn't smoke anymore.

There was no doubt in Phin's mind that the crystal was dangerous, even though it had given him what some might consider a gift. Some gifts came with too high a price, he thought, as he forced himself to look again at the aquarium. He slitted his eyes and considered the other aspects of the tank, noticing the water level was very low and that the plants were barely surviving in the few inches of brackish water.

He was certain that he'd topped up the tank recently, but there was a full bucket of water on the floor next to it. He remembered filling the bucket yesterday, but couldn't recall why he'd left it just sitting there. He stared at it for a moment, feeling a sense of déjà vu, certain that he'd stared at this same bucket of water before. Hadn't he meant to fill the aquarium with that bucket just this morning, when he'd noticed it sitting there?

Phin lurched to his feet and stumbled across the room, aiming for the bucket. The glow coming from the scummy water intensified, its green hue brightening to a blinding white in the seconds it took for Phin to reach the bucket. He stopped, stunned by the glare and momentarily confused by the searing attack on his senses. The light softened, and he smiled at just how lovely and shiny the crystal was as it peeked out from among the coloured pebbles.

If the tank had been big enough to hold him he would have crawled in at that moment, but then Pollux butted his shin, annoyed that his attention had been diverted, and the spell was broken. Phin gasped and snatched up the bucket of water, sloshing it all over the cat and his own feet. His hands trembled badly as he poured the water into the tank, trying not to disturb the pebbles that covered the crystal.

As the water level rose, his anxiety slowly dissipated, and by the time he'd emptied the bucket he was able to drop it to the carpet and stumble away from the aquarium. He pulled up his tee shirt to mop away the tears and sweat, and noticed the cat desperately trying to lick itself dry over in the far corner.

"I'd bring you a towel," he rasped in a voice not quite his own, "but you'd probably claw me to death at this point." He shuffled to the washroom on trembling legs, intent on an icy shower. He glanced over his shoulder apprehensively, but felt only a muffled longing at the sight of the still-rippling water. Nothing in his life had prepared him for this, but if all it took to prevent the crystal from attacking him was a few extra inches of water, he would be forever diligent in keeping that aquarium filled to the brim.

THIRTY-FIVE

Penny turned the pages of the flimsy booklet as she walked toward the centre of town, trying to make sense of not only the individual descriptions of the crudely drawn runes, but of how they were supposed to fit together into an answer. So far the badly translated pamphlet had given her: "friends in making," "to trusting good," "many to holding closely," "having for courage" and "wanting gone." There was no company name or address at the back of the pamphlet, and no website or email to contact if she were so inclined.

She growled in frustration and jammed the booklet into the back pocket of her jeans. She'd be only too happy to dismiss the whole thing as a party trick, except for the part where five glowing runes on a wet tee shirt had caused her to have an orgasm. There was probably some sort of chemical in the dyes they'd used on the shirt that reacted with water.

The tee shirt was still damp when she'd arrived at the Couch & Cot late yesterday afternoon. They'd had a nearly full house but, true to their name, there had been one last cot for her to rent for the night. She'd had to share a room with a flatulent old woman who giggled every time she farted, but at least she'd managed to get a shower, a meal and a dry bed to sleep in. She'd draped the tee shirt over the back of a chair to dry overnight, and now it lay rolled up at the bottom of her pack.

Penny hadn't spent much time at the inn this morning, staying only long enough to share breakfast with the owners, her elderly roommate and a family with three rowdy children. The family had come to Cricket Lake hoping to rent a cottage by the water, but had arrived to find the lake roped off. There'd been some sort of toxic spill and no one was allowed near it. They would stay for the day, since there was a festival happening, but would leave early enough to find accommodations at another lake. Penny declined the man's offer of a ride into town, making her escape while he and his wife rounded up their over-excited children.

Penny wondered just how many of these little towns existed in the province. She'd always thought there wasn't much civilization off the main highways and that most of the areas outside the cities were crawling with moose and bears. There had been several maps tacked to the walls of the common room, and her eyes had widened in surprise when she finally found Cricket Lake sited within the bottom part of British Columbia. It had taken her more than six hours to get here from Vancouver, if you counted the walk from Minnow Bay. As she ran her finger along the map, she calculated that you could travel for a couple of days before reaching the top of the province.

When she'd asked for directions, she'd been told to simply walk up the road, and that she should slow down when she reached the grocery store or she'd miss the town altogether.

They weren't kidding, Penny thought. The grocery store was halfway down the two blocks that made up downtown Cricket Lake, and she paused to examine the fruit stand that had been set up outside the store. There was a basket of shiny red apples, just the one kind. At the fruit market next to the coffee shop where she worked, Penny could have selected from at least eight types of apples from around the globe. The most exotic fruit she could see here were bananas.

The sidewalks were cracked and the street pavement was buckled, though that wasn't much different from the city, where street crews worked year-long in a continuous attempt to keep the roads smooth and pothole-free. There weren't many cars on the street, driving or parked, and most people just walked from store to store. It was like some sort of movie set built for a small town in the seventies. Colourful plastic pennants hung limply from utility poles and car antennas, and giant cardboard crickets leaned up against buildings that sported posters in their windows offering discounts during the festival.

She moved to the side to avoid stepping on a penny, curling her lip in distaste as she passed it. She routinely threw them away herself, leaving them for others to pick up, though she never could understand how anyone could think of them as good luck. They only reminded her of the incessant taunts she'd suffered as a child. "Hey Penny, gotta penny?" She'd had so many of them thrown at her that she'd grown to hate their coppery stink.

Two teenagers on roller skates sped up to her, waving wildly as they approached. Penny tensed and gripped her pack more tightly. She'd encountered too many teens on the streets in Vancouver who were high on whatever drug was making the rounds. They invariably hit on her for money, aggressive and in her face, and she'd more than once given in rather than risk a beating.

"Hi, I'm Annie," the first one said, as she skidded to a stop in front of Penny. "This is Matt. We work at that crappy coffee shop you just passed. We've got some specials today and hope you'll come on by and see us." She thrust a coupon at Penny, who grabbed it out of reflex. They beamed at her expectantly and she realized they were waiting for an answer.

"Um, I'm Penny. I got into town last night. Just sort of passing through, I guess."

"That's great. Enjoy Cricket Fever!" Annie chirped with the enthusiasm of a cheerleader, and Penny wondered if the girl was like this all the time. They obviously weren't going to try and grab her stuff, at least not in a public place – though that hadn't stopped a lot of the kids she'd run into in the past few months – and she dared to relax enough to smile back at Annie and Matt. Their own smiles went up a few more notches and they waved and rolled off to accost another unsuspecting tourist.

She couldn't imagine Eric wandering around this town. He'd look completely out of place in his black clothing and creepy attitude, she thought, but that was probably why he'd sent her instead of coming here himself. She blended in a little better. She couldn't put her finger on just what made these people look so different from those in the city, apart from their outdated clothing and hairstyles. Maybe it was the way they smiled at everyone, confident in their safety, certain that no one was out to grab their purse or pick their pocket.

Penny spotted a wooden bench on a grassy area between the grocery store and an old-fashioned bank. The bench was shaded by a huge tree and she sat down, grateful for the shade, watching people going in and out of the building across the street. The sign proclaimed it the Voodoo Café and Penny held her breath a moment as she remembered what Eric had said about the man she was supposed to find. He hadn't been able to give her many clues, except she was looking for some kind of freaky hippy guy who thought he was a voodoo witch doctor. Eric hadn't mentioned this place but it looked like an obvious place to start.

She pushed off the bench and crossed the street. As she reached the café, she saw another sign in the window announcing their grand opening. The door opened and a woman with fluffy red hair bustled out, followed by four yapping little mutts. They lunged at Penny, and she kicked out a foot reflexively, causing one of them to yelp in fright, though she hadn't connected with the little rat-dog. The woman yanked back on the leashes and glared at Penny as though she'd started the ruckus.

Penny quickly slipped through the door before it closed and found herself immersed in the most wonderful smell in the world. She caught a whiff of paint, but it couldn't compete with the scent of freshly baked bread and the several platters of cookies and pastries that sat on trestle tables lined up along the back wall of the big room. There were also several urns that probably held coffee and tea, and a huge glass pitcher of lemonade that was covered with beads of condensation.

Penny's stomach growled loudly. She'd only picked at her breakfast. She picked up a paper plate from a stack and looked over the cookies, wondering how many she could afford. Her hand hovered over the peanut butter and chocolate chip, but passed them up for oatmeal raisin. They were still warm, so she took three. Then someone tapped her on the shoulder and she spun around, dropping the plate and cookies on the floor.

"Sorry, kiddo. Didn't mean to scare you." The old woman blinked at her through immense, thick glasses. She wore some sort of long yellow scarf that was wrapped around her head like a turban. It was coming loose, and her springy white hair was poking out in several places. She noticed Penny staring at her head and tucked one of the stray strands back in.

"Um, I'll pay for the cookies," Penny stammered. "I'm really sorry. I guess I'm a little jumpy." She scooped the plate and broken cookie bits off the floor and dumped them into a garbage bin.

"Don't worry about it. There's nothing to pay for today. My name's Mabel and I'm one of the owners here." She thrust out her hand and grinned widely.

"I'm Penny." She shook Mabel's hand and returned her smile. "So what's with the fake turban?"

"It's a gimmick to impress the tourists. Makes me fit more into the theme of the place, like a fortune teller." Mabel took Penny by the sleeve and led her back to the table. She took a clean plate, piled it high with cookies and handed it to Penny.

"There's no charge for stuff right now, at least until our business license shows up, so help yourself." She leaned close to whisper hoarsely. "Dee – that's one of the other owners – is determined to show off all her best baking today. That way everyone who has a taste will be bound to come back when we're a real business. She even made a couple of peanut butter pies, so save some room for that.

"That table over there has a pan of bacon and egg lasagna. You have to try it, it's my specialty. We won't be selling it as a regular bakery item, but this is a special occasion so I went all out. I was going to make my sister's famous flower jello too, but Tammy said she got sick after the last one and I'm not allowed to make it 'til I make absolutely sure all the flowers in it are edible."

"Thanks, Mabel. These are delicious," Penny mumbled around a mouthful of cookie.

The bell over the door tinkled and the family from the Cot & Couch burst into the room. The three kids made a beeline for the cookies, and Penny skittered sideways to avoid being bowled over.

"I'll be right back, kiddo," Mabel said, patting her arm. She marched over to where the children were grabbing handfuls of cookies and cramming them into their mouths before their parents could stop them. They froze at the sight of the tiny woman decked out in bright yellow, but relaxed when she gave them each a plate so they could carry their cookies.

Penny wandered toward the other table, intrigued by the thought of bacon and egg lasagna. It sounded like all her favourite foods rolled into one pan. She helped herself to a huge serving. It was the most delicious lasagna she had ever tasted and she wolfed it down while she spied on the old woman in yellow. Mabel must have been nearly seventy, but she darted around the room like a woman half her age, greeting people as they came in the door and making sure everyone sampled the cookies and other warm treats.

The building that housed Voodoo Café seemed brand new, with its scent of fresh paint and the obvious lack of counters and shelving. It felt more like a community hall than a place of business and Penny felt strangely at ease even though she was among strangers. It reminded her of when she was living on the streets and regularly attended free dinners at the local church hall. There'd been no pressure to socialize, since the main goal was to feed the homeless people who came in half starved. Sure, there'd been the inevitable sermon from the young, earnest pastor, but she'd learned to follow the lead of the other diners, smiling attentively while they ate and then drifting out the door before anyone spoke to them directly.

Everyone here was treated as if they belonged and she could hardly tell the tourists from the locals. She wondered if anyone here would know how she could find Phineas Marshal, but how did you ask someone to direct you to the local witch doctor? She could tell them she was on a quest to find a magical crystal, or a secret mission that was a matter of life and death, but they'd probably think she was crazy and run her out of town.

It sounded like a bad role-playing game, and she would have laughed and caught the next bus home if it weren't for the nasty weasel that had her passport and the only existing picture of her mother.

Penny was stuffed after several cookies and two helpings of bacon and egg lasagna. She needed something to wash down all that food, and made her way to the table that held several stainless steel urns.

Only one held coffee. The other three were filled with tea: orange pekoe, mint, and Earl Grey. She'd always preferred tea to coffee and poured herself a cup of the Earl Grey.

"You know, I could make a pot of the real stuff," Mabel said as she hurried over before Penny had the chance to take a sip. "I've got some fresh leaves, and I'm dying to use my new teapot." She pried the paper cup out of Penny's fingers and dragged her to an alcove that held a tiny table and two chairs. She pushed her into one of the chairs.

"Wait here, I'll be right back."

"Don't worry about me, Mabel. I'm sure you have lots of other people to take care of." She watched the little woman scurry off and disappear into another room, only to emerge minutes later with a tray holding a teapot and two cups.

"I have to get off my feet for a few minutes," Mabel said with a sigh as she set the tray on the table. "Good thing Dee anticipated that I'd want a pot made up. I'm going to read your fortune. I need the practice, and besides, I've got a feeling about you, kiddo." She peered at Penny intently, and grabbed her hand. "Maybe I should look at your palm first, though Phineas is the one who's been practicing."

Penny stiffened at the mention of Phineas. Could it be this easy? She'd been in the café for half an hour and someone had already mentioned the name of the guy she was supposed to find. She held her breath as Mabel brought her nose within a millimetre of her palm, frowning and muttering to herself.

"Yep, I knew it," Mabel said triumphantly, cupping Penny's hand in both of hers. "You're someone special."

"Oh, come on, Mabel," Penny said weakly, "I'll bet you say that to everyone."

"Well, I've only just started to read palms. We should really wait for the tea to be ready. I'm hell on wheels when it comes to tea leaves. You should stick around, or at least come back later on. We're having a ritual tonight. If we're lucky we can talk Phineas into holding another séance." She grinned at Penny and then whipped her head around as the door chimes rang again. "Aha! Speak of the devil."

"Is that him?" Penny whispered, staring at the man who had walked in the door. He was of average height, with a long salt and pepper ponytail. He was dressed like anyone else, in jeans and tee shirt, and carried a frayed backpack, much like Penny's own. His eyes shifted across the room, taking in the people crowding at the tables and stuffing themselves. He nodded at Mabel, who was trying to wave him over, and headed briskly through the door that led to the kitchen.

Penny wasn't sure what witch doctors were supposed to look like, but this guy had dark circles under his eyes and a tightness around his mouth that she'd seen countless times among the homeless. He was either a kindred spirit or someone she should steer clear of.

THIRTY-SIX

Phineas backed away from the doorway that led to the main room of the café. Mabel and Dee had led him to believe that only a few people would show up for the Grand Opening Ritual – as they'd dubbed it – but the bell over the door had rung at least three times since he'd stopped counting heads when he'd reached twenty-two.

He paced the length of the kitchen again, rehearsing the measly four lines he'd managed to write about putting the ghost of the old bakery to rest and inviting in a new spirit of welcoming goodness. The whole ritual idea was meant to be light and fluffy and he'd been pretty pleased with himself when he'd come up with his script. Now he wasn't so sure, but he didn't have time to make up anything else.

It would have worked with the usual group of locals who'd come to the three séances he'd been forced to preside over so far. The regulars were easy to please, happy to sit and hold hands while Phineas and Mabel conjured spirits by candlelight. Riva had set a pattern for the monthly séances years ago, an easy rhythm that Phin had reluctantly continued. After the three group sessions – and countless private readings – he'd started to think he just might get used to his new role as local diviner. He had to make some kind of living, didn't he? He was just the supply meeting the demand.

He'd been nervous about taking the whole embarrassing schtick outside the safe confines of his living room, but Mabel's enthusiasm had propelled the idea into the main event of the weekend. He'd pleaded with her to no avail. She'd said he had to branch out, and that Voodoo Café was going to be about more than good bread and a wide selection of teas.

He went into the bathroom off the kitchen and stared at himself in the mirror over the sink. He looked the same as he always did before a séance, with the black eyeliner drawn on thickly and his hair loose and draping over his shoulders. He was wearing his usual black velvet vest over a floor-length blue robe but he felt faintly ridiculous, especially tonight, with more than a couple dozen extra bodies watching the performance. Probably tourists who would go home with the amusing story of the long-haired idiot who made a fool of himself by spouting mumbo-jumbo and behaving like an untalented extra in a bad B movie.

"The natives are getting restless."

Phin squeaked in surprise and turned to find Mabel peering up at him. She'd re-wrapped her turban and applied the most lurid red lipstick he'd ever seen. She'd also put on a set of false eyelashes that were magnified by her thick lenses into mega-caterpillars. Phin felt the corners of his mouth twitch, and when she slowly blinked, he couldn't help himself and burst out laughing. Her eyebrows shot up and the caterpillars became furry arches, reminding him of Orion's reaction to the neighbour's dog wandering into his yard last week – instant Halloween cat.

"Quit snickering and get out there already," she scolded. "This is no time to be primping in front of the mirror. You look fine, though I wish you hadn't shaved the beard. I liked all the beads and stuff you put in it."

"Too itchy," he managed between giggles. "What's with the caterp…I mean eyelashes?"

"What? You think you're the only one who gets to be exotic?" She deepened her voice and affected a bad Slavic accent. "I am Sintalla, nomadic gypsy traveling from far away to tell your fortune. Give your hand, and I will see your whole life in the palm."

Dee popped her head around the door, looking flushed and breathless.

"Are you two ready?" she whispered. "I hope you've got something special planned; these people are expecting a show."

"What do you mean a show?" Phin said, his gaze anxiously flicking between the two women. Dee was dressed more conservatively, in a new baker's white uniform, though Phin noticed that its more modern cut was very flattering to her curves. "I thought it was just some kind of inauguration. I say a few words, and give a quick voodoo blessing – if there is such a thing."

"Come on. It'll be fun." Mabel grabbed his sleeve and tugged him forward. She winked at him, but those outrageous lashes just weren't as funny as they'd been a moment ago. "Follow my lead. We can make it up as we go along and no one will know the difference."

"They'll think we're loonies and never come back."

"Are you kidding? They've been munching happily on Dee's goodies all day. Even if we fail miserably they'll all come back for the food, so we have nothing to lose."

Phin stumbled into the room and froze, staring at the mob that had gone silent at his entrance. Mabel nodded to Tammy, who struck a match and lit several white candles and then turned out the lights. There was a murmur of anticipation as people settled themselves into the chairs set in a circle around the room. There weren't enough for everyone, so several had to content themselves with sitting on the floor or leaning against the wall.

Mabel strode to the centre of the circle and turned to look at everyone. She nodded meaningfully to Phin, who had no idea what she wanted until she pointed to the floor by her feet.

"Welcome to Voodoo Café," she began, as Phin shuffled into place next to her. "Today we've given you a taste of what will be offered from our kitchen. You've all met Dee, our illustrious baker." She waved a hand towards Dee and everyone cheered and clapped.

Dee blushed, but couldn't contain a shy smile at the appreciative response to her hard labours. She'd been up since dawn and was exhausted, but glowed with excitement at the realization of her dream.

Mabel clapped the loudest, bursting with pride at her niece's accomplishment, and had to clear her throat and sniffle before she could continue. "Dee first learned to bake when she was thirteen and has been dazzling us with goodies ever since. You won't find a finer pie, bread, pastry or cookie in this province, and I've only set that limit for her because I've personally never been beyond its borders."

Everyone laughed and clapped again, and Phin relaxed a smidgen, amazed at Mabel's ability to engage a crowd. They hung on her every word, though it might have been the ridiculous getup that kept their eyes riveted to her. No one paid him much attention, but he was wearing dark clothing in a dark room, and hadn't so much as twitched a muscle since he'd been standing there.

"But Voodoo Café is not just a bakery," Mabel continued. "As the Café part of the name implies, we're also going to offer a wide variety of tea and coffee to help wash down all those delectable treats." She paused to smile at Tammy, who brought one of the tall candles and placed it on the floor in front of Mabel and then went to sit in the circle next to her daughter, Rebecca.

"Now, some of you are probably wondering – what's with the Voodoo in our Café? Well, Cricket Lake has a number of talented people who can divine the future, tell your fortune and forecast events. We believe that there are forces all around us that can be tapped into to help us live our lives more fully. They're always there, but not many people can feel, see, or hear them well enough to know what they want to say to us." She glared at a pair of teens who were lounging against the wall and snickering.

"Some of us use tea leaves, interpreting the patterns they've made at the bottom of the tea cup. Others read the messages in Tarot cards." She turned to Phin and placed her palm on his chest. "This is Phineas Marshal, our local witch doctor." She smiled encouragingly when he grimaced at the term. "He reads the bones of small animals, divining their message according to how they fall. It's a similar method to the tea leaves, in that he studies the patterns that tell a story."

Phin winced inwardly at her description, and at the sudden sharp tingle from the bones in his pocket. Were they reacting to her words, or to his reaction? Only he knew that Mabel was wrong in that the bones in his pocket hadn't all come from a small animal, but from a human as well. Quite likely three humans.

He still felt jittery from his encounter with the crystal this morning, and wished he didn't have to appear at the café today. He felt exposed and uncomfortable with so many people watching.

"To commemorate the opening of this newest addition to our fine town, Phineas will now bless the café, ensuring many years of service to our community and its guests." Mabel faced the candle, and poked and tugged at Phin until he stood on the other side, facing her. There was a ripple of chuckles around the circle as she grabbed Phin's hands and lifted them so that his palms faced her. She then raised her hands until her palms were nearly touching his, and took a deep breath before nodding once.

Phin took that as his cue and tried not to panic. This was just a show, he reminded himself. If he could fake it for a few friends he could improvise for a larger group. He closed his eyes and steadied his breathing, concentrating on the reassuring thrum in his pocket.

"We call upon the spirits of sweetness, the ghosts of goodness, and the ancestors of awesome taste to come and join us in sanctifying this place of feasting. Many have come here today to partake in the delectable offerings and to warm their hearts with fine company. We have given to them freely, as a sacrifice in your honour and as a gift of welcome within these walls. We seek your presence, your blessing and your inspiration."

Phin paused and opened his eyes. He'd heard a subtle shift in Mabel's breathing, and instinctively reached out and grasped her hands in his. Her eyes were open too, but showed only whites, and she grimaced and squeezed Phin's hands as if she were in pain. She opened and closed her mouth several times, but made no sounds. She pursed her lips, frowning, and tried again.

"Are you the one living in Riva's house now?"

"Is this Cora?" Phin asked. He glanced at Dee, who shook her head, though he'd already known the answer would be no. This voice was thin and wheezy, and tinged with an edge of anxiety that hadn't been there when he'd encountered Cora at their first séance. Besides, Cora would remember him.

"No, this is Ella. Answer the question."

"Yeah, I'm Phineas, and I live in Riva's house. Did you know her?"

"No time for chit chat. Pay attention." Mabel was trembling, and she'd broken out in a cold sweat. *"Whatever happens, don't give that bauble to my grandson. I'm counting on you. The young woman will help."*

Mabel's legs gave out and she sagged sideways. Phin stepped around the candle and grabbed her before she fell. Her face was streaming with perspiration and her false lashes were coming unglued and drooping. She blinked several times and shook her head until they let go and fluttered to the ground.

"Mabel, are you ok?" Phin steered her toward the edge of the circle of chairs. Several people abandoned their spot, and Mabel dropped gratefully into the nearest chair.

"Wow," she said, grinning at him. "That was Ella! Did you hear her? I think she knew you."

"I don't know anybody named Ella." Someone thrust a glass of water at him. He grabbed it and passed it on to Mabel, who drank thirstily. Dee sat on the chair next to Mabel and put a protective arm around her shoulders, shielding her from the press of people who were peppering her with questions.

"Did you really channel a spirit?"

"Does it hurt?"

"That was pure bullshit! Do you really expect us to believe this woman talks to ghosts? She's a fraud. Get your stuff, we're leaving."

"Can you contact my sister Barbara? She died last year."

"Is it like a voice in your head?"

"Can you teach me to do it too?"

Mabel basked in the attention while Phin vacillated between wanting to stay near Mabel and wanting to run from the crowd. He was stunned. If he hadn't seen her do this once before, he'd have thought she was putting on a performance. But he knew in his gut that Ella was real. She had spoken directly to Phin. Twice now, a dead woman had told him not to give something away. There was no doubt in his mind that she'd been speaking of the crystal, and

Eric. But her grandson? That would mean that Ella was Eric's grandmother. So how did she know about Cricket Lake? Maybe she was somewhere with Cora. He shivered and wished he had never come to this place.

The bell over the door jangled as a few people left, having had enough of the strange ceremony. Tammy turned on the lights and blew out the candles.

Mabel jumped to her feet, slapping at Dee's hands as she tried to push her back into the chair. "Tammy," she called, "make sure everyone fills out a ballot for the draw for the free reading before they leave." She beamed in satisfaction at the faces around her, some staring in awe, others smirking but clearly enjoying themselves. Everyone was having a good time and most had headed back to the tables where there were still plenty of sweet treats and drinks to be had.

All except one lone figure that leaned against the far wall next to the alcove, staring intently at the little knot of people in the centre of the room.

THIRTY-SEVEN

Penny shivered in the cool dawn air. She'd hardly slept a wink, curled up all night in the bushes behind Phin's house. She couldn't afford another night at the inn so she'd followed him home. Her clothes were moist with dew and she had at least a dozen bites from insects she couldn't identify.

She hadn't had the nerve to talk to Phin after the show, not with so many people around. He'd also been a little too creepy in his witch doctor getup, though she could have sworn that he'd been terrified at the beginning. Was he faking it? If so, he'd have had to know something about Eric and Ella to pull off that scene with Mabel. If not, Ella's ghost had told Phin to hold onto the crystal.

Penny pulled the crumpled piece of paper out of her pocket and read it again – *Good for one private psychic reading of your choice, by Mabel or Phineas*. She couldn't believe her luck when Mabel had read out her name during the free draw. The older woman had winked at her and for a moment Penny had wondered if she'd fixed the draw. It didn't mention a time or a place, so she'd decided to march right up to his door as soon as it was light and cash in her ticket.

Her stomach growled loudly and she dug through her backpack for the goodies she'd taken from the café. There had been so much food on the tables that it had been easy to wrap some up and ferret it away for later. But she'd used her pack for a pillow; the two buns were squashed almost flat, and the cookies had crumbled and were barely contained in the napkin she'd wrapped them with. No matter. She was starving, and they tasted just as good crumbled as they had when they were whole.

Penny twitched and dropped the rest of the cookie bits when she heard a door slam. She crouched and scooted forward to peek through the bushes. Someone had come out of the house onto the back porch. So much for sneaking out of the bushes and knocking on the door.

She recognized Phin from last night, though he was dressed normally, in cut-off jeans and a faded psychedelic tee shirt. He still had black makeup smeared around his eyes, and his hair looked like he'd been the one sleeping in the bushes. He carried a mug in one hand and in the other held a mouse with its tail pinched between his thumb and finger. He chased a huge black cat down the steps and flung the mouse after it.

"Keep your kills outdoors," he shouted after the cat. "I don't need presents, and I don't like to wake up next to dead bodies."

The cat sniffed the mouse, batted it once, then walked back to the porch, butting his head against Phin's leg as he passed. Phin stood a moment, frowning at the stiff mouse, then shook his head and followed the cat up the steps. They disappeared into the house together and the door slammed shut.

Penny breathed a sigh of relief, though she was more nervous than ever now that the moment had come. There was no putting it off. He was awake, and it was time to pay him a visit. She groaned at the stupidity of it all. She'd been sent by one weirdo to fetch a magic crystal from another weirdo and now Ella's ghost – real or fake – was mixed up in the mess.

She stood up and pulled her winning ticket out of her pocket again. At least she had an excuse to knock on his door. She slung her pack over one shoulder and carefully picked her way out of the bushes, wincing at every scrape. She passed by a greenhouse that held a jungle and skirted around several plants in too-small pots that looked about to fall over. The guy must like gardening.

Penny paused at the bottom of the steps, trying to convince herself this was a bad idea and that she should just run like hell. But she couldn't go back without Eric's crystal. He'd turn her in to the police. She could try to tell them that she'd heard Ella accuse Eric of spiking her tea, but there was no way they'd believe her.

She had no choice. She had to at least try the direct route, so she took a deep breath, climbed the steps, and lightly rapped on the door. It took all her self-control not to bolt when the knob turned and the door opened, revealing Phin's scowling face.

"You better not be selling something this early in the morning," he growled, eyeing her suspiciously.

"N-no," she said, and thrust the ticket at him. "I won the draw last night. Well, one of them, anyway. Um, I get a free psychic reading, right?" She clutched the strap of her pack tightly and shoved her other hand in her pocket to keep from biting her nails in panic.

"It's Sunday morning, and not even seven-thirty. Couldn't you have at least waited until this afternoon?" Phin grudgingly stood back and let her in.

"I'm hoping to catch an early bus back to Vancouver," she mumbled as she slipped past him and stood, shuffling her feet, in his kitchen. "I'm sorry. I don't really get all this stuff, but I think it's cool and just want to try it this once, so I guess I'm lucky I won the draw, right?" She clamped down on her tongue when she realized she was babbling, and quickly sat in the chair that Phin was pointing at. She tried not to squirm as he watched her with a puzzled look.

"Do you like tea?" he asked abruptly, "or do you prefer the cards?"

"Um, tea's good," she said, wondering if he meant those Tarot cards Mabel had mentioned. She'd have liked to see them, but really wanted a cup of tea after her dry breakfast. She watched him fill a kettle and set it on the stove to boil. While the water heated, he took a blue teapot from a cupboard and half-filled it with hot water from the tap. He swirled it and poured it out, and then set it on the table.

Penny tried not to smile at his fussy preparations. He reminded her of an old lady, carefully measuring loose tea out of a jar and dumping it in the warmed pot. When the kettle whistled he filled the pot and brought two cups to the table before finally sitting across from her.

"Give it a couple of minutes to steep," he said. "Do you have a question you want to ask?"

"Question?" she squeaked. "What do you mean?"

"You tell me," he said, testily. "You're the one who's all fired up to get her fortune read so early on a Sunday morning. What do you want to know?"

"Oh, I don't have anything specific to ask," she mumbled. "I just thought you'd tell me about my future, or something."

"Fine." He poured them each a cup and thumped the pot down.

Penny reached for hers, to give her hands something to do, but stopped when he shook his head.

"You have to let the leaves settle or you'll end up swallowing them all and I'll have nothing to read. Besides, it's too damn hot to drink right away." He stretched and yawned. "So where do you live in Vancouver?"

"Oh, just around," she said, alarmed at his question.

"Around where? Which part of the city?"

"Um, sort of in the east end, I guess." She hoped he wouldn't need specifics. She didn't want to admit she was basically homeless, carrying around her entire life in a backpack. "Why do you want to know where I live?"

"Just making conversation," he said, rolling his eyes. "It helps to know a bit about you before we start."

"But I thought you'd get all that from the reading."

"It's not like that. I don't suddenly know everything about you, just what you need to know at this time." He leaned over and peered into her cup. "Your tea's as ready as it's going to get. Sip it and think about what it is you want to know."

Penny picked up the dainty china cup and sipped the pale reddish tea. It was still almost too hot to drink, but was delicious and soothed her parched throat. She forced herself not to gulp it down, but drank it in small sips until it was empty. She tried to think about why she was here, something specific that she could tell him, but was bewildered by everything that had happened in the past few days. Her mind was a jumble of images: the cozy attic that had been her home for several weeks; peeking through the window of Ella's house and watching her as she knit; Eric's angry face as he threatened to give her up to the police; Mabel speaking with Ella's voice last night. Another image came as she stared at the clumped tea leaves at the bottom of her cup – five glowing runes on a soaked tee shirt. She felt her face heat up at the memory, the blush increasing when she noticed Phin watching her with interest.

She pushed her cup across the table and leaned back in her chair, crossing her arms tightly across her chest. "So what does it say?"

Phin looked at her a moment longer, trying to remember her name. He was sure that Mabel had introduced her at some point yesterday, but he'd hardly paid attention. He picked up her teacup and glanced into its depths, seeing a tiny speck of leaf surrounded by several larger clumps. "Depends on what you're asking," he said again. "You're either surrounded by friends who'll protect you, or enemies who are threatening you." He saw her eyes widen in alarm, and then her face crumpled and she burst into tears.

"Well, um," he stammered, and jumped up to fetch a box of tissues from the top of the fridge. He slid it across the table and plopped back into his chair. "I could be wrong, of course. It's not an exact science, is it?"

Penny snatched a handful of tissues and covered her face. All the fear and uncertainty that had been choking her came pouring out and she wailed and sobbed until she could hardly breathe. She was embarrassed to be crying in this stranger's house. She kept her head lowered and peeked at Phin through a blur of tears. He watched her with a neutral expression.

Finally, she sniffled and blew her nose loudly. "It's both, I think," she said quietly.

"Both what?"

"The two things you said, about friends and enemies, though I don't really have friends. The runes said I would, but right now all I have is enemies. Well, only one, really, but he's going to turn me in to the police, so you could count them as enemies too."

"Are you in trouble with the police?"

"Not yet," Penny said. She was so tired and so afraid. Would Phin turn out to be a friend or an enemy? Only one way to find out, she thought, and took a deep breath.

"There's this piece of shit who killed his grandmother in Vancouver a few days ago. That's Ella, the one that Mabel was talking about last night. Or maybe Ella was the one doing the talking, I can't tell anymore. So now he's threatening to pin it on me, unless I bring him something from here." Phin was watching her with a confused expression, and she realized she probably didn't make much sense. She was going to have to tell him everything. There was just no other way to bring up the crystal and ask for it than to spill it all.

"Who the hell *is* Ella anyway?" Phin asked. "What was she talking about?"

"I think she was trying to stop me," she said. "It's stupid and complicated. This guy wants me to get something from you. He said you stole it from him, or maybe his cousin did and then gave it to you, I'm not sure anymore. He wants it badly enough that he killed his grandmother because she wouldn't tell him where it was." She stopped and took a breath, uneasy at the dark expression that had settled on Phin's face.

"So," he said, sighing. "This is about that damn crystal, isn't it? The piece of shit you're referring to wouldn't happen to be called Eric, would he?"

"Yeah," Penny said in surprise. She had twisted her handful of tissues into a shredded mess. She wadded them and put them on the table, eyeing the teapot longingly. Phin took the hint and reached for the pot.

"So let me get this straight," Phin started, as he poured them each another cup of tea. "Eric killed his grandmother because she wouldn't help him get the crystal." He winced when she nodded. He'd told Eric to ask his grandmother about the crystal. He felt a pang of guilt at the thought of having been complicit in the killing of another old lady but grimly tamped it down. Phin wasn't sure if he could cope with another dead granny on his conscience.

"How do you fit in? Did you see him kill her? And how's he going to manage to pin it on you?"

Penny watched Phin over the brim of her cup as she sipped. He looked very angry, and she wondered if she'd gone about this the wrong way. What if he called the police? And even if by some miracle he gave her the crystal, could she trust Eric to give her back her belongings? What if this was just the beginning and Eric decided he had another stupid quest to send her on before he set her free? Either way, she had nothing to lose by telling Phin the truth.

"Okay, here's how it happened," she began, reaching for more tissues to keep her hands from trembling. "My aunt kicked me out last spring when my trust fund ran out and I couldn't afford to continue school. I lived on the streets for a while and then found this nice dry attic in some little old lady's house. Ella's. I stayed there, not giving her any trouble, and then her grandson started coming around more often than usual. They'd argue downstairs, and sometimes he'd come and rattle the lock on the attic door. Then a couple of days ago I heard the lock open and hid in the space next to the chimney so no one would see me. I knew it probably wasn't Ella, since she was really old and had never come up there before."

Phin held up a finger. "Could you hear what they were arguing about?"

"Not really, until later, when he was up in the attic with me. She started yelling up the ladder at him and he got really nasty. She accused him of drugging her, and he said he'd own all her stuff someday so she might as well tell him where the crystal was. There was another name too, Rita or something like that, and he mentioned you. At least I think it was you." She smiled shyly, remembering Eric's mention of a hick town with an idiot hippy. Phin didn't strike her as an idiot, though he made a credible hippy.

"Where is Eric now?" Phin asked quietly.

"Probably still at his grandmother's house."

"So, you were in her attic and heard them arguing. How did he kill her?"

"He'd drugged her, but I think she was trying to climb up the ladder to stop him from finding me, and then she fell."

"Doesn't mean he killed her. She was woozy from the pills and fell off the ladder."

"But that's not how it happened," Penny said anxiously. "I heard him kick the ladder before she fell."

"Did you see him do it?"

"No!" She jumped to her feet and grabbed her pack. "You don't have to believe me, but it's the truth. I have to go." She turned to the door to find it blocked by two fat orange cats. She blinked, sure she was seeing double, but they both sat placidly, watching her with their matching green eyes.

"Don't mind them. They're just hoping you'll feed them." Phin spoke quietly from his chair. "Their names are Castor and Pollux. I used to call them both Stupid, but it's hard enough telling them apart without having the same name.

"Why don't you sit down and finish your story. I'll feed the cats and get us both something to eat afterwards. If you're hungry, that is."

Phin got up and went to the fridge, moving slowly so as not to spook the young woman. He wanted to hear the rest of what she had to say, but was seething with rage at the continuing bullshit that was Eric's interference in his life. He pulled out a pan of catloaf – as he'd come to name the unappetizing concoction that Tammy continued to deliver – and carved off a chunk. He dumped it onto the turkey platter that served as the cats' food tray and cut it into smaller pieces. By the time he was finished, all five cats were milling around his ankles, meowing piteously. He set the platter on the floor and sat back in his chair. He tried to suppress a grin as he watched the young woman staring open-mouthed at the sea of furry bodies surrounding the platter.

"So Eric and Ella were arguing, she tried to climb a ladder up to the attic, fell off, and died. You were next to the chimney, and he found you?" Phin watched her, amused, as she slowly turned back to him with a look of wonder on her face.

"You have five cats."

"Yeah, doesn't everybody?"

"Sorry, I mean, you just don't seem like a cat person."

"They came with the house, kind of like the furniture."

"Eric said you were living in Rita's house. Are you renting it from her?"

"Her name was Riva, and she's dead. She left me this house. I moved in last May, and Eric showed up a week later."

"But she's like, his cousin or something. Are you related?"

"That's another long story. Let's get back to yours, okay? How did he manage to get you involved in this?"

"When he went downstairs and the ambulance came and took Ella away, I snuck out but forgot something." She indicated her backpack with a wave. "That's pretty much all I own and I thought I'd grabbed everything, but there was one stupid little box that I kept paper and stuff in. He found it, and when I went back for it later, he was waiting for me. End of story."

"What's in the box that you had to have so badly?"

"My passport, a letter with my aunt's address, and the only existing picture of my Mom."

"Ouch," Phin said with feeling. "I can see why you'd go back. Let me guess – now he's holding your papers hostage and is blackmailing you."

"Yeah, he even took pictures of my stuff in Ella's attic and said he'd give it all to the police unless I came out here to fetch a stupid magic crystal."

She shuddered, suddenly cold. She'd told Phin everything and he hadn't picked up the phone to call the cops yet. She turned back to watch the cats, unnerved by his pensive gaze. They'd polished off every scrap of meat from the platter and were busy licking their paws and wiping their whiskers clean.

"Did you have some of that lasagna from the café yesterday?" Phin's muffled voice came from the fridge, where he'd gone to rummage around again.

"You mean the one with bacon and eggs in it?" Penny's mouth watered at the thought and she smiled hopefully.

"I'll heat some up, and then we'll see if we can't come up with a plan."

"You're not going to give him the crystal, are you?"

"No, it's too dangerous. Besides, Ella told me not to. You heard her."

"Do you *really* believe that was Ella talking?"

"It's not the first time I've heard someone speak through Mabel, and the last time it happened another woman told me not to give the crystal away. That makes twice that a ghost has told me to keep it from Eric. I can't ignore that."

"You people are all weird."

"Well, it seems to me that we both have a problem with Eric, so you'd better include yourself in our group. I thought I'd got rid of him a few months ago, but it looks like he's not about to give up without a fight."

The microwave dinged and he brought a fragrant plate of lasagna to the table. He popped another in to heat up and found some forks and napkins.

"You know, I'm sure that we were introduced at some point yesterday, but I forgot your name."

"Penny Rodgers," she said as she dug into her lasagna.

"Well, Penny, we're going to need some serious help with this," he said, sitting across from her with his own plate. "When we're done here, we're calling Mabel."

THIRTY-EIGHT

"But it's not safe. Your apartment isn't even finished yet."
Dee fluttered around Mabel, who was dragging a huge suitcase
towards the front door.

"It's finished enough for me," Mabel retorted, wheezing as
she lugged the heavy case. "I've got a bed, a couch and a TV up
there already, and Tammy said she'd send Fritz over with their old
dinette set tonight." She pushed the suitcase against the wall and
turned to her niece. "The three of us have been driving each other
crazy since I've been here. It confuses Lydie. Seeing me here every
day reminds her of Mama. That's probably why she's obsessed with
the grave and keeps asking to go and visit."

"She'll get used to it. She'll forget eventually, like she forgets
everything else." Dee's chin trembled and she clutched at Mabel's
sleeve. "Can't you stay for a few more weeks? At least until things
settle down at the café. I don't want to leave Mom alone while I
work. Who knows what she'll get up to?"

Mabel hugged her. "You're just afraid she'll end up like her
mother, but they're very different people. Mama was very outgoing,
which was why she ended up wandering all over town, sometimes
not very well dressed, if you know what I mean." She winked at

Dee, who grimaced at the memory of chasing down the road after her naked grandmother. "Lydie hardly moves off her chair, and just stares out into space for hours at a time. Her whole life is happening in her head, and she'll only go out if we make her do it. She's not going to run around naked in the streets.

"You'll see. Everything will go back to the way it was before the fire happened. I'll be upstairs while you work, and we'll take turns coming over here to make sure she eats. Both Tammy and Josie have offered to check in on her once in a while too." She stood on tiptoe and kissed Dee on the cheek. "Chickadee, I need for things to get back to normal. Besides, I've got a triple shipment of craft supplies arriving any minute, and you don't want that spread out all over your house."

Dee smiled at the thought of three times the amount of mess that Mabel was able to generate with *one* craft box. She agreed that they were too crowded in the small house, but she'd gotten used to the air of optimistic hilarity that Mabel carried with her everywhere she went. If she hadn't been here when Lydia had gone back into her fugue state, Dee would probably have joined her in her endless demented daydreaming.

"Will you at least come back for dinner tonight?"

"Aw, you know once I get over there I'll be so busy settling in that I won't want to leave." Mabel tilted her head in thought for a moment. She understood Dee's distress about Lydia, but she'd long ago accepted that her family was always going to produce a certain amount of craziness in its women. She thanked the stars that it seemed to have skipped Dee, but the signs had shown up in Lydia a long time ago.

It wouldn't be long before Lydia needed full-time care, but Dee would never recognize that if Mabel continued to live here and help out full-time. Mabel swallowed the lump that threatened to close her throat. She had to leave in order to let things fall apart, so Dee could let go of Lydia and maybe learn to live her own life.

"I have an idea," she said. "Why don't we put that big pot roast in the oven right now with some carrots and onions? We can make a huge batch of potato salad, maybe some biscuits and gravy, and have a big lunch instead. Then I can take some of the leftovers with me, since there's nothing in the new fridge for breakfast."

"That sounds great," Dee said with a sigh of relief.

"I love you Dee. You know that, right?" Mabel took Dee's hand and steered her toward the kitchen.

"I love you Mabel. You know that, right?" They laughed at the soothing ritual, words they'd repeated a hundred times.

At the kitchen door, they stood together and watched Lydia as she gazed out the window, her cup of tea forgotten and grown cold. Her hands lay limply in her lap, and she smiled wistfully at the chattering starlings that filled the trees in the yard. It was a sight Dee had gotten used to, her mother silent and still, only vaguely engaged with her surroundings. She didn't acknowledge their presence as they chatted quietly while they prepared the roast and vegetables for lunch. They worked around her as if she were part of the furniture, confident that they weren't disturbing her vacant meditation.

Lydia didn't react when a loud knock came at the front door, but Dee and Mabel both let out startled squawks at the sudden intrusion.

"That better not be that family of Bible thumpers coming around," Mabel grumbled as she headed for the front hall. "I almost had to throw them out of the café last night. They were sure we were having some sort of satanic ritual."

The morning sun streamed through the screen door window, backlighting the two figures that stood waiting on the steps outside. Mabel frowned and prepared to send the holy rollers packing. There was no need for people like that to be bothering folks on a quiet morning. She had never been one for church – none of her family ever had – and she wasn't about to let some moralizing, self-righteous do-gooder ruin a perfectly good day.

"You've got nothing to say that I want to hear," she said, as she swung open the door and nearly swept Phin off the step. "Oh, sorry, Phineas," she continued, and grabbed his arm to steady him as he leaned backward over the flowerbed.

"I'm not selling anything," he said, laughing as he regained his balance. He waved at his companion. "I think you met Penny yesterday, right?"

"Hi kiddo! Nice to see you again." Mabel had liked the young woman from the moment they'd met. It didn't hurt that they were nearly the same height, and saw eye to eye. She noticed now that those pretty hazel eyes were red-rimmed and swollen, and frowned at Phineas. "What did you do to her?"

"Whoa," he said, putting both palms up to fend her off. He turned to Penny. "Tell her you're okay, before she decks me."

"Well no, I'm not really okay," Penny said, her lower lip trembling. "But it's not his fault," she hurried to add, as Mabel leaned toward Phin.

"Can we come in?" he asked. At Mabel's nod, they stepped in and followed her pointing finger into the living room, while she went to the kitchen to make a pot of tea, her first order of business in any crisis.

Phin dropped onto the sofa, and Penny sat on the edge of a chair across the room from him with her pack on her lap. She wrapped her arms tightly around it and stared at the floor, blinking hard to stop the tears.

She wondered if she'd done the right thing by telling Phin about Eric's plan, or whether she'd just ruined her chances of getting her stuff away from the slimy creep. What if Phin and Mabel decided she wasn't worth helping and sent her back empty-handed? She could see Eric's face in her mind, smirking as he gave her up to the police, the vagrant he'd found in his dead grandmother's attic.

Penny snuck a peek at Phin. He had leaned his head back and closed his eyes. Despite his gruff manner, she'd felt comfortable enough to open up and tell him everything. Her Uncle John had been the same way, not as gruff but someone who really listened.

Mabel came back with a tray holding a teapot and several cups. She set it on the low table and sat next to Phin. Another woman hovered in the doorway. Penny didn't remember her name, and wondered if she was Mabel's daughter.

"All right," Mabel started. "Let's have some tea, and then you can tell us what's up, all right?" She poured them each a cup and handed the first one to Penny. "Who wants to start?" She looked at Penny, who held her cup with trembling hands and pretended to sip the scalding brew. So she turned to Phin, who rolled his eyes and put his cup back on the table.

"Remember Eric?"

"He was that nice young man holding Dee back from the fire, right?" Mabel glanced at Penny, who had nearly dropped her tea and was staring at her with wide eyes. She looked terrified and ready to leap off her chair.

"Yeah, that's the one," Phin said through clenched teeth. "Your nice young man killed his grandmother on Wednesday, and is trying to pin the deed on our new friend here." He nodded towards Penny and gave her an encouraging smile. When she just stared at him mutely, he continued. "He's got something that belongs to her, and is planning on using it as proof that she was the murderer."

"What if she is?" Dee piped up from the doorway.

"I didn't k-kill anyone," Penny blurted, jumping to her feet. She turned and faced Dee. "He drugged her, and when she climbed the ladder he kicked it and she couldn't hold on because she was dopey. I heard her scream and fall, and then the ambulance came and took her away."

"I believe you," Phin said quietly. "Sit down. It's all right." He raised an eyebrow at Mabel, who took her cue. She led Penny back to her chair and pressed the tea cup back into her hands.

"When Eric showed up here a few months ago, he was looking for a supposedly magical crystal that had belonged to Riva. He thought it should have been given to him." Phin looked at Dee while he spoke. She stood with her lips pressed tightly together and her arms crossed. "He trashed my house the same day as the fire. He dumped all of Riva's journals on the floor trying to find information on that stupid crystal. He thought he'd found an old secret that he could use to force me to give it to him."

"But he didn't get what he came for, so I thought he just went home."

"He was tearing apart Ella's attic looking for a crystal. I heard her tell him that she'd sent it away so he wouldn't ever get it." They all turned to Penny at her quiet words. "I thought she'd said it was Rita, but I guess I heard wrong."

"Wait a minute," Mabel said. "Isn't Ella the woman who came through at the ritual last night?" At Penny's nod she continued. "And she said not to give some bauble to her grandson. It that what this is about?"

"I guess so. If that was really her. Did you contact her ghost, or something?"

"I didn't contact anyone. Sometimes during our séances a spirit will want to give us a message. They seem to like me as a mouthpiece." Mabel paused a moment, staring at Penny. "You must be the young woman she said would help. Funny how all this stuff turns out, eh?" She smiled and poured fresh tea for everyone.

"That still doesn't tell us how you know he killed her. Where were you that you could hear all that?" Dee smiled to soften her words, but her eyes demanded an answer.

"I was hiding in the attic," Penny said. She'd stopped shaking and her tears had dried up. She looked from Mabel to Phin. Both were smiling with encouragement. Maybe the runes had been right, and she'd found allies after all.

She faced Dee and cleared her throat. "I've got nowhere to go. No home. No family except my Aunt Margaret who hated me so much she kicked me out. So I followed some old lady home one day and moved into her attic. I never met her, never went into the rest of her house, just snuck in and out for almost a month. It was really quiet there until two weeks ago, when her grandson started showing up once in a while. I could hear them arguing down there every time he came to visit. Then last Wednesday he drugged her so he could steal her key to the attic and snoop around. I hid from him, and that's how I heard everything."

"But how did he know you were there?" Dee persisted.

"I was in such a rush to get out of there when he finally left the attic that I forgot some of my stuff. I should have been more careful. I was so stupid. I remembered to grab my blanket, but not a box with a letter and my passport." She answered Dee's sympathetic smile with a wry grin of her own. "He caught me when I went back for them. He gave me enough money for the bus and a night at that inn at the edge of town. I was supposed to call him yesterday to tell him what bus I'd be coming back on, but I didn't have the crystal yet. I don't know why he thought I could get it when he couldn't."

"I'd say he was desperate." Mabel was fascinated, but one detail nagged at her. "If you only had enough money for the bus and one night at the inn, where did you sleep last night?"

Penny blushed and ran a hand through her tangled hair. "I slept in the bushes at the back of Phin's yard." At his raised eyebrow she added, "I know, it's creepy, but I'm not a stalker. If you think Eric's desperate, think about how I felt, having to follow you home so I could talk to you this morning. The cops are going to be asking questions. I need to get my passport back before he decides to give it to them to save himself."

"So he's been expecting your call," Mabel said. "I wonder what he's thinking about, now that you're overdue."

"Probably already gave my stuff to the cops," Penny answered glumly.

"I doubt it," Phin said. "It's too soon. He *really* wants that crystal. He's going to give you enough time to get it to him. He won't risk losing it by getting you arrested before you can hand it over."

Mabel slapped her hands on her knees and stood up. "I'd say we have a bit of time before the fat hits the fire. Dee and I were putting together a big lunch when you arrived and the roast will take another hour or so." She turned to Penny. "Why don't you come into the kitchen with us? I'll introduce you to my sister Lydia, and you can help me peel some potatoes."

"What can I do to help?" Phin asked.

"You could be a dear and take my stuff to my new place. Might as well take Penny's bag there too." She held up her palm to stop Penny's protest. "You're staying with me while we sort this all out." She grinned at her as they trooped into the kitchen. "Good thing my new couch is a pull-out."

THIRTY-NINE

The morning fog had mostly dissipated, with only a few wispy tendrils snaking along the still water. Tammy hurried the dogs along the beach. She didn't want to get caught on the wrong side of the cordoned-off area.

Josie's boys had returned from the hospital yesterday afternoon, still nauseated and weak, but their doctor had pronounced them free of anything dangerous. They'd clearly ingested something toxic but it was nothing their own bodies couldn't handle at this point.

Tammy wasn't worried that the dogs would get sick from the water. They all hated to get wet and would never venture into the lake. She'd once tried to teach them to fetch and had thrown their favourite toys far out into the water, but the dogs had stubbornly stayed on the shore, whining at the floating toys, until Tammy had to wade out and fetch them herself.

She ducked underneath the flimsy barrier and unfastened the leashes from each of the four dogs' collars. "Go on babies," she urged them with a laugh. "Do your thing, but make it snappy, we want to be out of here before anyone sees us."

The dogs ran off in a frenzy of barks and yips, excited at being back in their favourite place. They had been cooped up for days in Tammy's yard, fenced in because she had no time to walk them with everything that had to be done for the festival. They'd been restless all night and had woken her earlier than usual, so she'd decided to sneak a walk around the lake as soon as it was light.

She shivered, but not from the cool morning air. The beach was deserted and a bit spooky this early in the day. She gazed out over the water, where the sunrise was reflected in a wash of pastel blues and pinks. It *looked* normal enough. She prayed the tests would confirm that.

Tammy could barely hear the dogs' barking, and whistled for them. "Come on, you beasts," she muttered affectionately. "Pee and get back here." She quickened her pace when she realized they weren't coming back, and the tenor of their barks was getting more excited and high pitched.

"Uh-oh, sounds like you found yourselves another squirrel." She hoped that wasn't the case, since the last one that Prince and Lola had cornered and caught had been ripped apart. She'd had to clean blood out of both dogs' coats. Fritz had been furious that she'd allowed them off the leash, and she picked up the pace, hoping she wouldn't have to sneak them into the bath before he woke up.

She picked her way through a snarl of reeds and brush that the local residents had been fighting with for years. Too boggy to get to in the spring and too large to burn when it was dry for fear it would set fire to the local homes. So they attacked it with pruning shears and machetes as soon as the ground was dry enough to walk on, but it was an endless, summer-long task that everyone dreaded. It was the only part of the shoreline no one would miss.

She wondered what would happen if the lake was really toxic. Josie's boys might be all right now, but something in the water had made them sick enough to be hospitalized.

Tammy could see the dogs ahead, on the other side of a particularly large, prickly bush. They sounded almost hysterical with excitement and she could see them rolling around and chasing each other. She'd carefully parted the branches and was about to step through when the smell hit her.

Rotting fish.

"Oh no, babies, not that," she wailed as she stumbled out in time to see Lola leap onto a pile of dead fish. The dog rolled over and wriggled ecstatically among the sludgy remains. Prince was running around, barking encouragement at the two puppies, Shandy and Misha, who were sniffing uncertainly at each others' reeking fur.

"Get out of there!" Tammy shrieked, wrinkling her nose in disgust at the abominable stink. The dogs were covered in slimy, decomposing fish, their long coats matted with gore and sand. They barked excitedly at Tammy, proud of what they'd found, and ran to her. Too late, she realized that her new jumpsuit was doomed, as the dogs jumped on her and rubbed the rotten slime against her legs. The powerful stench overwhelmed her senses and she promptly threw up all over Prince, who yipped and leapt aside. The others crowded around him to sniff this new scent that had been added to the mix.

Tammy fell to her knees and burst into tears, retching between sobs. Fritz would have a fit. He was already angry at the extra vet bills that Lola's pregnancy had incurred. This would be all the proof he'd need that she wasn't responsible enough to raise poopoms, and she'd never be allowed to breed Prince and Lola again.

There was no way she could bring the dogs indoors to bathe them. The smell of rotten fish would permeate the house for weeks. I'll have to hose them down in the back yard, she thought in despair. They'll howl and yip in terror, and the whole neighbourhood will think I'm slaughtering my poor babies. And by the time the stink is out of their fur, Shandy and Misha will be too old to sell.

She felt a slimy nudge at her side and cringed away from the cold, sticky nose that sought her hand. Lola whined, aware of Tammy's distress. The dog backed away and barked once, wagging her tail in a wiggle that never failed to entice her mistress into playing with her. Tammy smiled wanly at her once-lovely dog and raised her hand to wipe away tears, stopping just in time to avoid smearing her cheeks with reeking fish guts.

She pushed herself to her feet, nose wrinkling in distaste at the state of her new outfit. It would have to be thrown out, along with the dogs' leashes and collars, another expense Fritz would hold against her.

Lola barked and ran ahead of her in renewed excitement as she approached the pile of fish and called the other dogs back. They had mashed the edges of the decomposing pile into sludge, and Tammy's feet slid in it repeatedly as she grabbed at dogs that had completely lost all sense of obedience and ran around her in circles, delighted that their mistress had decided to join them in this new game. She shrieked and threatened them, and would have kicked a few rumps if she hadn't been afraid of slipping and falling into the squishy, stinking mess.

She finally managed to round up all four dogs and clip them to their leashes. They sat at her feet, panting contentedly and trying to lick the gore off their coats, while Tammy stared sadly at the pile of rotting fish that steamed in the rising heat, catching her breath and trying to ignore the bile rising in her throat again.

The lake was in worse condition than they thought if the fish were dying in such huge numbers. It had been stocked with small-mouth bass to make it more appealing to those tourists who might like to spend the summer with a line dangling in the water.

Tammy wondered if she should mention the dead fish to someone when she got back to town, but decided it would be wise to avoid drawing attention to her stinky adventure. Her lip curled in distaste at the chore that awaited her, and she was about to turn and head home when she noticed that one of the fish had no head or tail. She inched forward for a closer look. Most of the decomposing fish carcasses had been gutted and she recognized at least two kinds of fish not normally found in Cricket Lake.

Her suspicions were aroused. She searched the immediate area and found two white plastic grocery bags shoved underneath a dense bush. One was filled with styrofoam trays and crumpled plastic wrap bearing labels from the grocery store's meat department. The other held two large blue bottles. Someone had dumped fabric softener in the lake and left this reeking pile of fish to rot in the sun, in a clumsy attempt to scare anyone who might want to buy the lakefront property.

It was a plan worthy of adolescents.

"Josie's boys."

FORTY

"So what's wrong with Dee's mother?" Penny braced one end of the metal shelving while Mabel hooked her end inside the display case. She then moved to Penny's end, and together they shoved it into the proper notch, levelling the shelf.

"She's got that Alzheimer's disease, the one where they lose their memories," Mabel answered. "She's my sister, you know."

"Dee?"

"Lydia. That makes Dee my niece." She measured the distance between the shelf and the bottom of the case. "Do you think there's enough room for another shelf in here?"

"Depends on what you're going to put on them, I guess. Cakes are taller than pies. Bread can be tall too, if it's puffy."

"The bread is going on those racks against the back wall. We have two display cases, why not put two shelves in one and only one in the other?"

"Not that anything will be sitting in there for very long," Penny said, as she patted her full belly. She'd been helping in the bakery since just after dawn, when she and Mabel had heard Dee downstairs starting the ovens for the day. She'd learned how to knead bread dough, covering herself and everything around her with flour. Dee had been patient with her but distant, all business while Mabel joked and teased, making rude shapes out of the dough to make Penny laugh. They'd become fast friends overnight, having stayed up far too late organizing the new apartment. Mabel had claimed that it was good luck to have a guest on her first night in her new home.

"I thought only really old people got Alzheimer's," Penny said, stacking the cardboard wrapping from the shelves out of the way.

"Not really. Lydie's a few years younger than me, almost sixty-two, but she's been like this off and on for almost twenty years. This is the worst she's been for a while, and it scares Dee."

"Aren't you scared to get it too?"

"Naw, we would have seen signs of it in me by now. I'm a little forgetful sometimes, but nothing like Lydie. Dee won't get it either – she's different than Lydie was at her age – but she's still afraid she'll go crazy too."

"Lydia didn't look crazy, at least not while we were all eating together. She even talked to me, though she called me Rebecca a couple of times."

"Rebecca is Tammy's daughter. She lives in Mission but was about the same age you are now when she left here. That confuses Lydia." Mabel eyed the two display cases critically. "I wonder if we should wait for Dee. This is her place after all, and here we are deciding where everything goes."

"We could just set it up and get rid of all the packaging. That way she won't have to worry about all the mess and we can always change the shelves if she wants it differently. It'll be a surprise."

"I like the way you think, kiddo," Mabel said, and hugged her briefly. "It'll look just the way she had it in the sketch she made after the fire. Get that string, and we'll bundle it up." She pulled up the edge of her shirt and wiped her forehead. "It's going to be hot again today. I'm glad Dee had them put in that fancy air conditioning. Cost her a bundle, but it's worth it. It's already baking hot out there." She giggled and clapped her hands. "Get it? Baking hot out there and we're the ones in the bakery." She hooted with glee at her corny joke while they flattened and tied the cardboard.

Penny lugged the bundle through the kitchen and out the back door. Mabel was right about the hot day, she thought, as a wave of moist heat engulfed her. She dumped the paper bundle in the bin and hurried back into the cooler building. On her way through the kitchen, she found two glasses and filled them with cold water from the tap. She drank one down and refilled it before carrying them out to the front. She paused at the doorway, watching Mabel struggle to put in a shelf by herself. The woman was shorter than Penny's five-foot-four, and triple her age, but somehow seemed stronger and more alive than she did. She had an enthusiasm that Penny couldn't resist, and she wished that she'd had someone like Mabel in her life while she was growing up.

"Here, drink this and then I'll help you put that last one in," she said, thrusting out the glass of cold water. Mabel drank deeply, and then moved out to the middle of the room to examine their handiwork.

"I think the best thing about these counters is how shiny and smooth the glass fronts are. The old display cases were all scuffed and scratched. There was even a crack in one of them, but that old skinflint Brent wouldn't replace them."

"Dee didn't own the other bakery?"

"Oh no, she'd just worked there since she was a teen. This place is all hers. Well, ours, I guess. Dee will do all the baking, I'm in charge of running the café part of it, and Lydie will take care of the accounting and ordering." She frowned and ran her fingers through her wiry hair. "Well, maybe Lydie won't be doing much bookkeeping; lately she can hardly keep track of which day it is."

"I'm pretty good with numbers," Penny said shyly, "I mean, I never got past high school, but I always got good marks in math. I'm the one who balances the cash at the end of the day at the coffee shop where I work – where I used to work." She glanced at Mabel. "I guess I'm kind of between jobs now."

"I'm sure your family misses you at home. Once Phineas helps you end this whole crystal affair you'll be heading back, won't you?" Penny's expression turned sour. "Or maybe not?"

"There's nothing for me to go back to," Penny said bitterly. Her eyes misted and she rubbed them in frustration, determined not to cry again. "My Aunt Margaret and I haven't gotten along for years. She blamed me for Uncle John leaving after my Mom got killed, and then when my trust fund ran out last year she dumped my stuff out on the lawn and told me to take a hike."

"You were just a kid when your mom died?"

"I was ten. Mom got killed by a bunch of boys in Stanley Park. They must have driven her there, because she could never have gone that far by herself." She turned to the display cases and rubbed the already sparkling glass vigorously with a cloth.

"Did the boys get caught?"

"Yeah, but they were all teens and only one of them was charged with her murder. He'd be out of jail by now. It was all over the news – how she got into the car willingly and none of them could be charged with rape."

"Why would she get into a car with a bunch of boys? Doesn't seem like a sensible thing for a woman to do."

"I guess I didn't mention that she was special." Penny never spoke of her mother. Calling herself an orphan was usually enough to stop anyone's questions, but she felt like she could tell this odd little woman anything.

"Okaaay, sorry if I'm being dense, but I'm not following you," Mabel said carefully.

"They like to call it mentally challenged now, but when I was little everyone called my mom a mental defective, or retarded." The tears started to fall, great drops splashing onto the pristine glass faster than she could wipe them away. "You think Dee is worried about losing her mind? When I was a kid, the teachers at school thought I was a genius just because I wasn't like my mother. They'd point me out to everyone and marvel at how normal I was. Every day I woke up wondering if I had become a retard overnight. No one thought to explain to me that my mother had been born that way and that it wasn't some contagious disease.

"My mom never had a clue about how she'd gotten pregnant, so she couldn't even tell Aunt Margaret who my father was. She was like this big kid with a new doll when I was a baby. She followed me to school every day and waited on the playground until I came out at recess. The teachers had to explain to her every single day that it wasn't time for me to go home yet. She'd pout and demand I play on the teeter totter. We looked ridiculous because she outweighed me by at least a hundred pounds and couldn't figure out why we couldn't make the teeter totter work. I'd just sit up there with my feet swinging, embarrassed as hell because all the kids were laughing at us.

"After recess she'd make a fuss again because she'd already forgotten I had to go back inside, and then she'd be out there playing until lunch time and it would start all over again. The classroom windows all looked out onto the playground and everyone could see her out there, sitting in the sand box.

"So no, I don't have anyone waiting for me. I don't have a home, and if I don't bring some stupid magic crystal to Eric he's going to tell the cops I killed his grandmother." She sniffed loudly and sagged against the display case.

"So you're a vagrant who's being framed for murder."

"And my auntie has disowned me."

"And you don't know who your father is."

"Well," Penny said, averting her eyes and blushing, "you know how I said Uncle John left after Mom died? He took her death really hard, and wanted to go out to the jail and pound on those guys. I was only ten, but I heard all the screaming fights he and Margaret had about it, and he told her everything.

"See, Margaret had married him when she was only seventeen to get away from her retarded sister, but then their parents died in a car crash six months after the wedding, and she was forced to take in her sister – my mom – who was only thirteen. They'd left everything to my mom, since they figured that Margaret had a husband to take care of her, and that their retarded daughter would always need care.

"Mom was confused and wanted to go home, and would wander and get lost for days at a time. The police would bring her back dirty and half-starved, and not able to tell anyone where she'd been. When she got pregnant a year later, Margaret wanted to send her away but would have lost Mom's trust fund. Uncle John had control of it as long as Mom lived with him and Margaret."

"And when Jenny died, Margaret found out that John was your father," Mabel said quietly. "I can't decide if that's tragic or hilarious."

Penny stared at Mabel, open-mouthed with surprise. But Mabel wasn't laughing, so Penny continued. Now that she'd started, she felt compelled to finish the story.

"After Uncle John left, Margaret went to a lawyer, thinking that she should inherit her sister's trust fund, but found out that John had taken Mom and me there shortly after I was born and changed the papers to make me her beneficiary.

"Margaret had never worked and John was gone, so she was stuck with me. The fund would support us both until I turned 21. That was last fall. There was less than a thousand bucks left in it when I got to it."

"So she kicked you out, you had nowhere to go, and you ended up in Ella's attic," Mabel finished for her. She took Penny's hand, pulled her towards the tiny alcove, and gently pushed her into a chair. She was outraged at Margaret for neglecting her, at John for abandoning her, at Eric for threatening her. But anger never changed anything.

"Let me see your hand," she said gently. Penny slid a limp hand across the table and Mabel turned it over, exposing the palm. She ran a finger along the bold lines that stretched across Penny's young skin. She didn't know much yet about reading palms, but could at least recognize the signs of a long and healthy life. "I should make a pot of tea," she muttered. "Easier for me to see what's coming for you in the bottom of a tea cup."

"What do you know about runes?" Penny leaned forward suddenly, staring intently at Mabel.

"It's some kind of Viking alphabet, I think."

"Don't some people use them to tell fortunes? Like, instead of cards, or tea, or palms. Runes can tell you stuff just like all the others, right?"

281

"Probably, but I don't know anything about it," Mabel answered, curious about the change in Penny's bright gaze. "Maybe Phineas knows. We can ask him when he gets here. He's coming later to build some shelves along that wall over there."

"No! Don't ask Phin! I mean, forget it." She sat back, flustered and blushing.

"It's all right, kiddo. He's actually quite nice; that getup he had on that night is just a costume he wears when we have séances and stuff."

Penny wasn't about to tell some old guy she barely knew that she had a magic tee shirt that gave you a hard core orgasm while it told your fortune.

No way.

FORTY-ONE

Phineas cursed and nearly steered his bicycle into the ditch. The fat raccoon he'd swerved to avoid just waddled a little faster and disappeared into the thick brush that lined both sides of the road.

The six-foot staff Phin had been balancing across the top of the handlebars spun sideways and whacked him hard on the left shoulder before clattering to the pavement. He braked hard and stopped before his front tire could roll over the staff, though he did manage to mash one of the crow feathers he'd tied just underneath the grip. Some of the smaller shells and bones broke off and rolled away into the gravel. He swore again. He'd just finished the walking stick this morning and had hoped to get it to the café in one piece.

He was wearing a backpack full to bursting, the saddle bags on either side of the back wheel were crammed with his tools, and the basket in front was piled high with the books Mabel had asked to borrow. He slid the kickstand down with the toe of his sneaker and braced himself while the ungainly baggage settled and the bike steadied.

He swung his leg over the seat and picked up the staff. It was scuffed and scraped along one edge from the asphalt, but the carvings were intact. A bit of sanding and a vigorous buffing would restore its smooth lustre. He bent to pick up the tiny bones and shells that had fallen off and inspected their surfaces. They'd separated cleanly from the glue, which remained attached to the wood, pitted with the shapes of the various items that it had held. He pulled at one of the tiny bones still attached and it came off easily.

"The damn glue's too brittle," he muttered. He picked at it with a fingernail. He'd have to try another type of glue, something more flexible, maybe a rubber compound.

But the café was closer at the moment than home was and Mabel was waiting for the books from Riva's library. He'd also promised to start the wooden shelves she'd asked him to build along the wall on either side of her little alcove. She wanted to display homemade craft items for customers to buy, and had encouraged him to include some of his carvings. She'd have to wait now for one of his walking sticks, but he'd brought a dozen wooden whistles and twice that number of the animals he liked to carve. The smaller items were easy and quick to make, and would satisfy Mabel who wanted to showcase local artists at the café. They'd start with his carvings and her seasonal crafts, and then invite other craftspeople as they found them.

He straddled the bike again, and drew back the kickstand. Maybe he could weld some rings to the side of the bike to hold his walking sticks. He'd already made several modifications and repairs to the bicycle, the least of which were the two new tires and inner tubes that he'd bought from Herman's Hardware. The heavy leather saddle bags he'd found in Riva's basement were old and tattered, but easily accommodated all his favourite tools, as long as he distributed their weight evenly. They'd been designed for a motorcycle, and the wide strap between them had been too long for the bicycle's narrow frame, but a short plank of wood installed behind the seat had solved that problem, separating the bags and lifting them off the ground and away from the back wheel.

Phin pushed off and the bicycle wobbled a moment before gaining momentum and balance. He had sketched a few designs for a trailer for the bike, but was having trouble figuring out how to hitch it to the back. There was no library in town, probably the only thing he missed about Vancouver. Dee's home computer was years out of date and barely ran the simplest programs, let alone a decent internet search, and he didn't relish the thought of approaching Fritz. He could always ride his bike into Chilliwack for a library visit. He could also look into setting up a computer at home.

Home. He couldn't remember when he'd started to think of Riva's house as his home. Maybe when he'd decided there was plenty of time to fix the roof before winter, or when he'd become concerned when he hadn't seen Hercules for two days last month. The big cat had finally come limping into the yard with a torn ear and infected eye. Mabel and Dee had come at Phin's panicked call and had fussed over the big tom, though Mabel had chastised Hercules for challenging whichever wild animal had mauled him this time.

He slowed as he approached the bakery, awed by the sense of *belonging* he felt within this tiny community. He'd lived near downtown Vancouver for most of his adult life, surrounded by thousands of people every day, but he'd made more friends living in Cricket Lake for a few months than he'd made in his entire life in the city. Nearly everyone he saw on the street was someone he knew.

But then there was Eric. Just when Phin had thought he'd heard the last of him, along comes Penny Rodgers, dragging the spectre of that idiot into his life again. Phin wondered what Eric actually knew about the crystal, and whether he'd ever stop trying to get his hands on it. The guy was trouble, especially if he was capable of killing his own grandmother and pinning the blame on an innocent girl.

Penny had been nearly hysterical when she'd realized that Phin would never give Eric the crystal, but once she understood that he, Mabel, and Dee were on her side she'd cried so hard she could hardly breathe. She'd calmed by the time the Sunday roast was ready, and ate enormous helpings of everything on offer, along with several cups of strong tea.

They'd discussed the issue at length, convincing her that Eric would come to them when he got tired of waiting for her to call. After they'd had lunch, he'd walked Mabel and Penny to the new apartment above the bakery. He'd left them there, confident that Mabel was the one person who could help settle the distressed young woman.

Phin rolled up to the bike rack he'd set up at the side of the café. He nestled a tire into one of six slots, and secured the bicycle with a shiny new combination lock. Mabel had assured him this was a small town and that his bike would be safe without a lock, but he was a city boy and wasn't comfortable leaving his stuff just lying around for anyone to take.

He unfastened the saddle bags and set them on the sidewalk, and was sizing up the stack of books when he heard the bell tinkle over the door of the café, accompanied by a chorus of yapping dogs.

He peeked around the corner and spotted Tammy storming out of the café with her four dogs tangling their leashes in their haste to keep ahead of Mabel's broom. Their fur looked damp, and Phin caught a whiff of lavender perfume that couldn't quite hide a strong underlying scent of rotten fish. They all bared their teeth when they noticed him, and the male lunged to the end of his leash. The yappy little rat-dogs had never liked him, and the feeling was mutual. He poked at them with the damaged staff, earning him a scowl from Tammy.

"Down, Prince," she snapped, trying to yank him back while the other three imitated their pack leader and rushed towards Phin, trying to bite his ankles.

"You know better than to bring those dogs into the bakery," Mabel shouted. "We could lose our license before they even give it to us. And what the hell is that smell?"

"That's what I was trying to tell you." Tammy pulled on the leashes, trying to rein in the dogs. They were in a frenzy, having been subjected to a dreaded hose bath and now an angry Mabel. Prince continued to bark and snap at Phin, and the puppies howled with fright and tried to reach their mother, who was hopelessly tangled on Tammy's other side.

"It's those kids' fault. They poured crap into the lake, and dumped a bunch of market fish on the sand."

"What are you talking about? What kids?"

Tammy gave up. They were attracting a crowd, which was freaking out the dogs even more. "Look, there's nothing wrong with the lake," she called over her shoulder as she dragged the dogs away.

"Whew, did you catch that stink?" Phin had retreated to the other side of the bicycle rack to protect his ankles.

"She won't get that out of their fur for at least a couple of weeks," Mabel said with a grin.

"What was she going on about?"

"Not quite sure, but she was kinda pissed and wasn't making much sense. She came barging into the bakery with the dogs, yelling about kids and fish. Then I got the broom and, well, you know the rest."

"She said there was nothing wrong with the lake," Phin said, nodding gratefully to Penny, who had come outside and was filling her arms and Mabel's with books from the bicycle's basket. He followed the women into the café and dropped the saddlebags to the floor. He shrugged off the backpack and handed it to Mabel.

"Is that what I think it is?" She opened it and lined up a parade of animals on the counter. She and Penny laughed with delight at the cross-eyed lion and a grinning trio of monkeys. The dolphin kept rolling onto its side, until Phin dug down to the bottom of the pack and came up with the tiny stand he'd carved for it.

"Wow," Penny said, "You're really good at carving stuff."

"Yep," Mabel agreed, "We're gonna sell a ton of these animals. The whistles are good too. Did you bring one of the walking sticks?"

"It had an accident on the way here. I'll fix it and bring it back later. Is Dee in the kitchen?"

"She went home to look in on Lydia, but she'll be back soon."

"These display cases look good," he said, running his hand over the smooth glass, then headed through the kitchen to check on the supply of lumber he'd stacked out back. He wanted to at least get the shelves cut and sanded before the end of the day. He could hear the women giggling over each new animal they pulled out of the backpack, and was glad to hear Penny laugh; her gaunt look reminded him they still had to deal with the problem of Eric and the crystal.

He idly wondered where he'd put the greasy hank of hair he'd taken from Eric, and how many ways he could use it to scare off the little weasel for good.

FORTY-TWO

Eric stared out the bus window at the passing greenery. His eyelids drooped with fatigue. He'd hardly slept since sending Penny to the boonies on Friday. She should have been back the next day, but hadn't shown up or called all weekend. Eric had been up since dawn, ready to head to Cricket Lake on the first bus.

But the police had other ideas, and Detective Feister had shown up minutes before he'd made it out the door. He'd had a few more questions, wanted Eric to help him understand why an old woman would decide to climb a ladder to her attic after taking an excessive dose of sleeping pills.

Eric had suggested that she may have heard noise in the attic and gone up to investigate, but Detective Feister had rejected the possibility of an intruder.

"No woman really ever goes into the dark room where the monster's waiting. That only happens in the worst horror movies." It was more likely that someone had lured her, or forced her in some way, to climb that ladder. He told Eric he'd be in touch.

Eric's left foot twitched, and he pressed it hard against the floor of the bus. It felt different than his right foot now, as if it were still vibrating with the impact from kicking the ladder. He'd checked the ladder and the boot itself for any sign that they had ever connected but had seen nothing, no leather bits or black dye on the ladder and no scuff marks on his boot. He'd almost thrown the boots away just in case they might be considered a murder weapon, but decided he was just being paranoid.

Eric checked his cell phone again, willing it to ring, hoping to find Penny on the other end but worried that Detective Feister might call with more questions.

"Nosy bastard," he muttered, and shifted uncomfortably in the small space.

"Excuse me?" The man seated next to him shot him a look of surprise. "Are you talking to me?"

"No." He'd steadfastly ignored his seatmate's many attempts at conversation on the trip from Vancouver to Chilliwack, but now the guy was gawking at him with a stupid smile.

"I'm talking about the cops," Eric finally said, and turned to stare out the window again, hoping that would be the end of it.

"I'm Bobby Fraser."

"Eric Minkley." Eric pretended not to see the hand that Bobby had extended.

"I'm a journalist," Bobby said, pulling his hand back. "Well, at least I'm hoping to become a journalist. You see, I was editor of my high school yearbook and now of my community college newsletter, so I've had some experience in reporting the news." He pulled out his wallet and produced a business card with a flourish. When Eric didn't take it, Bobby merely nodded and put it back.

"My creative writing teacher suggested I find some real stories to write about, not just stuff happening within my school, so I talked to my dad who has this friend that told him about some place up north where weird things have been happening." He paused for breath and pulled out a much-creased map, flapping it in Eric's direction.

The guy was starting to get on his nerves, and Eric was about to tell Bobby Fraser to shut it, when his eye was drawn to a spot on the map, circled in blue marker.

Cricket Lake. Eric took a deep breath and forced a smile. "What sort of weird things?"

"Well, the first thing we know about happened in the mid-eighties, when three old ladies disappeared from Cricket Lake in the middle of winter. Then six years later, a bear strolled into town and mauled two kids – not badly, you understand, but they had to shoot the bear, and the animal rights people caused a fuss, as you can imagine. Then about ten years after that, a plane went down on the outskirts of town – again in winter – and no one ever saw the two people that were on it again." He took out a grimy bandana and wiped his forehead. "And now we hear some kids were poisoned a couple of days ago while they were swimming." Bobby folded the map carefully along the creases and put it away.

"Now, no one else bothered to put those individual events together, but I look for patterns, and I'm thinking that four major catastrophes in one small place bears looking into."

Bobby had Eric's complete attention. An environmental disaster in Cricket Lake could explain Penny's silence if the local hicks were busy moaning about their lake. She might not have had the chance yet to sweet-talk Phin into giving her the crystal. Eric would have to be careful in his approach. He gave his companion an appraising look. Bobby Fraser might provide the perfect cover.

"I've been to Cricket Lake." he said, "I could show you around, introduce you to a few people."

"That would be cool," Bobby gushed. He glanced at his watch. "We're only about twenty minutes away from the bus station in Chilliwack. I wonder if there'll be time to get some lunch before our connection to Cricket Lake."

FORTY-THREE

"Okay, kiddo, bombs away!" Mabel squeezed her eyes shut and spread her arms wide. She braced her feet and grinned in anticipation.

Penny shook her head at this strange little woman and smiled in spite of the embarrassed blush that crept across her cheeks. She regretted having told Mabel about the runes and especially about the tee shirt and its interesting side effect. She'd only wanted to know if runes were as reliable as tea leaves and Tarot cards when it came to predictions. But Mabel was relentless. She wasn't familiar with runes, and had asked so many questions that Penny had finally blurted out the entire story.

Luckily, she'd mostly finished her story by the time Phin had shown up, and Mabel had become distracted with the bag of tiny wooden animals. They'd then helped him stain the shelves he'd cut and sanded. She was enjoying immersing herself in the many tasks these people had to do to get their shop ready. It kept her mind off the real reason she had come to Cricket Lake.

Mabel opened one eye. "Well?"

"Okay, okay. I'm just nervous, is all." She held up the plastic plant spritzer and aimed it at Mabel's chest. She'd been dismayed when they'd arrived in the apartment and Mabel had unbuttoned her blouse and yanked off her brassiere, chattering excitedly about trying out the wet-runes-tee shirt, as she'd taken to calling it. She'd debated the water options out loud while Penny averted her eyes and hurriedly dug through her pack for the shirt. By the time she'd found it, Mabel had decided that wearing the tee shirt in the shower would be overkill. She'd also figured that a bucket of water would be too messy, and had opted for a plant spritzer.

Penny took a deep breath and sprayed the front of the tee shirt. It quickly became sodden and plastered against Mabel's skin, clearly outlining her saggy breasts. Penny tried to look away from the sight of those wrinkly nipples tightening and poking at the thin fabric, but six of the runes had begun to glow and she couldn't help but stare.

"Wow," Mabel whispered. "That water was cold for maybe half a second, then it got warm, really nice. Kinda tickles." She opened her eyes and gave Penny a wink. Her pupils were dilated and her cheeks were flushed. She looked down at the shirt, with its six glowing symbols. "Would you look at that? Check the book! Quick now, what does it say?"

Penny put the spritzer on the table and picked up the booklet. She looked back and forth between the tee shirt and the booklet several times, carefully comparing the images so she had the right ones. "Um, it says something about a problem with several solutions," she muttered, frowning at the book. "No, wait. I think it's the other way around. More like several problems with one solution. That makes more sense if you look at the order of the runes." She turned to Mabel, who was smiling wistfully, her gaze unfocused.

"Did you hear me?" she said more loudly, snapping her fingers in front of Mabel's eyes.

"Yeah, kiddo, I heard you," she said with a sigh. "I was just remembering something from long ago." She shook her head and sat on the sofa. "That wasn't much of an orgasm. I expected a lot more oomph, if you know what I mean."

"Well, it pretty much knocked *me* off my feet," Penny said shyly. "Not something I've had much experience with, you know, but I'm sure it was a lot more intense than what you got."

"I wouldn't worry about that. You youngsters have a lot more fire in you than us older gals when it comes to that sort of thing, so I'm not surprised. But it's been a while, and I'm a bit out of practice."

"Are you divorced? You didn't say if you had any kids."

"Nope, never been married, never wanted to. Lydia was, but her husband up and left when Dee was only three. I had a good job with the government in Vancouver, but Lydia had always been kind of fragile, and she really lost it when Craig left. Our mother was no help, so that's when I came back to Cricket Lake. Riva was really pissed, though she still called herself Rita back in the seventies."

"But Riva is Eric's cousin, or something. You were friends with her?"

"Friends? Hell, she was my girlfriend back then."

"Girlfriend?" Penny squeaked. "You're a lesbian?"

Mabel barked a laugh at Penny's shocked expression. "Don't worry, it's not contagious." She refilled their glasses from the pitcher of iced tea she'd made earlier. "What gets me in this whole weird, mixed up story, is what you said about Ella sending Riva away with the crystal."

"That's what I heard her say to Eric when he was in the attic. Ella didn't want Eric's father to get it, so she told Riva to take it far away so he'd never find it."

"I always thought Riva had followed me out here. She'd showed up a year or so after I came out. She was so mad when I left Vancouver I figured she'd never speak to me again. And then one day she knocked on Lydie's door, looking for me. I mean, we were best friends until she died, but we couldn't be together the way we'd been when we lived in a big city. It just didn't happen. No one would have understood. So we adapted, and our relationship changed." She smiled, as if at a fond memory. "Oh, I'm sure some people suspected, but it was long over and nothing ever happened between us again.

"I wonder why she never told me about Ella and that crystal, though she was good at keeping secrets. I keep thinking it's because she hid the thing and forgot all about it, but from what Phineas tells me there's no forgetting that thing in the house. I haven't known him very long, but he's changed since he arrived last spring. He has a darkness that wasn't there at first, but now that I'm thinking about it, I seem to remember a change in Riva too. Not all at once, but she'd never been one for all the divination stuff and then, in just a couple of years, she became the local gypsy fortune teller. I was so busy by then with my crazy mother it was a while before I noticed the change."

"Maybe the crystal is evil, or something."

"I've never believed that a thing can be evil."

"But something can be used for good magic or bad magic, right?"

"We're the ones who put the good or the evil into something, and things can absorb the energy of the people that own them so it could have been filled with bad juju."

"What about Riva?"

"I think she was using it somehow to help her see more deeply into the Tarot cards. Using the crystal's magic eventually killed her, or at least she wasn't strong enough to handle its power anymore and had a heart attack the last time she messed around with it. That's the theory, anyway."

"So if we find a way to erase its evil nature then Eric won't want it?" Penny asked hopefully.

"I wish it were that easy kiddo, but I don't have a clue." They sat in companionable silence, sipping their iced tea. The sun was setting, bathing the room in red and orange light. It wasn't as hot as the old apartment had been since Dee had insisted on having the central air conditioning extended to the upper floor, but Mabel missed every little detail of her old home, including the stifling heat in August.

"So," Penny began slowly, "the runes said there's one solution for several problems." She counted them on her fingers one at a time. "Problem number one: Eric is a bad man and we absolutely can't give him the crystal. Two: if I don't give it to him, he's going to tell the cops I killed Ella. Three: the crystal may eventually hurt Phin, the way it did Riva." She sighed and dropped her hands into her lap. "How can one thing fix all of those problems?"

"Don't forget about our toxic lake," Mabel said with a grin.

"That's a lot of problems to fix," Penny grumbled. "I don't know why you think that's so funny."

"Our fourth problem is giving me an idea. Something Tammy said today is the clue to our solution."

"That's the woman with the smelly dogs, right?"

"Yeah," Mabel said, and then jumped up and headed for the door. "We need to talk to Phineas."

"Uh, Mabel," Penny called sharply. "Maybe you should change first. I doubt Phin will want to see you in a wet tee shirt."

FORTY-FOUR

Eric tried to roll over onto his side, but the hammock swung alarmingly and nearly dumped him onto the porch. He froze and clutched the knotted edges of the stupid thing until it stopped swaying. The night was cool, and he pulled the blanket to his chin carefully, trying not to agitate the hammock again. He wished he'd spoken quickly enough when the owner of the inn had offered him the choice between the hammock and the sagging sofa but Bobby had beaten him to it, claiming a fear of heights. The slob was just as loud asleep as he was awake, snoring up a storm at the other end of the porch.

He and Bobby had had to wait two hours for the next bus to Cricket Lake. He'd dozed on a bench in the station and had nearly fallen off when his phone finally rang. It was a lawyer calling about the details of his grandmother's will. Eric had known she had a life insurance policy. He'd need that money, since he had no intention of returning to his crappy job at the video store once he had his hands on the crystal. It would probably take him a while to figure out how to use it, and he planned to take all the time he needed while he worked out how to tap its power.

The lawyer announced he had just left Ella's house, having followed directives Ella had given him several years ago. He had gone through the entire property, checking various items off a list that she had made of her more valuable possessions, and had also taken away the contents of the hidden safe in her bedroom. Eric was flabbergasted to hear about a hidden safe, and couldn't believe the gall of his grandmother at having kept such a secret from him. His mind had worked furiously as the man spoke, trying to remember if he'd left any incriminating evidence in the house. Luckily, he'd taken Penny's papers with him, stashing them in the inside pocket of his overcoat in case he needed to remind her of his hold over her.

The lawyer had instructed Eric to return any keys to the house that he may have, and that if he had not returned them by Thursday morning, all the locks would be changed, again on Ella's instruction. Eric had nearly choked, and it had taken all his self-control not to shout at the man that it was his grandmother's house and he had every right to come and go as he pleased. The man had then informed Eric that the house would be kept closed and in trust until the will was read, and that he'd be informed when all the heirs named therein had been contacted and a date set for said reading. The line had gone dead before Eric could ask the lawyer which damned heirs he was talking about.

They'd finally arrived at the Couch & Cot as the sun was setting and Bobby had suggested they share a room to save money. Eric had been too exhausted to argue. But the inn had been full and the owners had brought blankets and pillows out to the porch, apologizing for the inconvenience. Eric had asked them if there was a young woman staying in one of their rooms. They remembered Penny and told him she'd checked out Saturday morning.

Eric was too angry to sleep but too tired to think clearly, hatching one ridiculous plan after another, all doomed to failure. A mosquito buzzed around his ear and he swatted at it, setting the hammock rocking again. He scowled and tried to keep still. He debated sleeping on the porch floorboards, but with his luck he'd be bitten by a poisonous spider or a snake.

Where was Penny Rodgers? Had she bailed on him and run off, giving up on her identity papers? Eric didn't think she was ballsy enough to choose that course, but there was another possibility that gave him a sudden chill – what if she'd managed to get the crystal and had decided to keep its power for herself?

FORTY-FIVE

The moon was barely past full, casting a glow that lit up the night and gave a pearly sheen to the surrounding leaves and flowers. Penny kept a tight grip on the back of Mabel's shirt as they crept along the path to the beach. She wasn't convinced the night was any safer in the woods than it was in the middle of a big city. At least in Vancouver she could call the police if she was in trouble. What did you do out in the bush when a wild animal came at you? She'd heard that bears run pretty fast, and couldn't believe the old saying that, "they're usually more scared of us than we are of them."

Phineas followed behind Penny, pushing a wheelbarrow determinedly over roots and rocks and cursing under his breath. The barrow held a five-gallon bucket full of water which sloshed and spilled at every bump, sometimes splashing Penny's back and making her even jumpier.

Mabel's crazy plan was to throw the crystal out into the lake. She claimed that it was the only way to keep it from Eric, and that getting rid of it would probably save Phineas from a fate similar to Riva's.

She'd explained it all to Penny as they had walked the couple of blocks to Phin's house after dark. Penny had protested, saying that it was fine for everyone else, but how was throwing away the crystal going to help her? Mabel had grabbed her hand to hurry her along and said not to worry, that everything would work out. Before Mabel had knocked on Phin's door, she'd cupped her palms on either side of Penny's face and said, "Gotta hit him hard and quick, kiddo. Don't give him time to think of reasons not to do this." Then she'd given her a quick peck on the nose and run up the steps.

Phin hadn't been surprised to see them so late, since he'd become used to unannounced visits at all hours. He'd offered to make tea, but Mabel had been all business, outlining her plan and giving him no opportunity to speak until she was finished. He'd been shocked at her proposal and Penny couldn't tell if he looked more dismayed or hopeful at the prospect of ridding himself of the crystal. He'd wanted to wait until daylight to give him time to think about it, but Mabel was relentless.

"The signs point to this being the best solution to all of our problems," she'd explained. "You can't keep it here any longer. That young man, Eric, is determined to get it. He's already shown how desperate he is. He broke into your house, killed his own granny, and now he's blackmailing this sweet kid. You have to get rid of it."

Phin had led them into the living room and pointed to the aquarium. He turned out the light so they could see the sickly glow that came from the bottom of the tank and described what happened when the water level dropped.

"Water seems to mute its effects," he'd said. "The more water, the better. As long as I keep that tank topped up, you'd hardly know the crystal is there. But as soon as the level starts to drop, all you want to do is get as close to it as you can, to bask in that glow, and when when it's got you hooked it insinuates itself into your mind and shows you things you'd rather not know. You think it's helping you by giving you all these brilliant insights, but while it's doing its party trick it sucks out a piece of you that you don't ever get back."

Penny felt her skin crawling, and had edged away from the aquarium, but Mabel had been ecstatic, nodding her head and grinning while he spoke.

"I knew it," she'd retorted. "Everything happens for a reason. Tammy claims there's nothing wrong with the lake, but it'll take a while for people to believe that. We'll have a ritual where we use the crystal to magically cure the lake."

"No!" Phin had been emphatic. "We can't expose anyone to it. It's too dangerous and you never know who's going to be vulnerable to its call." Phin had then pointed out a glitch in their plan. How would they get the crystal from the aquarium to the lake without falling under its spell? Mabel had searched the kitchen and found a soup pot with an extra-long handle. She'd handed it to Penny, having decided that the young woman was less likely to be affected by the crystal's siren call. She'd then directed Phin to fetch a five gallon bucket, which they placed into the wheelbarrow and filled with water from the hose.

They'd wheeled the barrow to the sidewalk, then sent Penny inside to scoop out the crystal and bring it to the bucket. Mabel had stood sentinel at the front door, insisting that Penny call out everything she was doing so they'd know she was all right.

Penny had felt foolish calling out her position every half second. She'd never been one to talk out loud to herself, and that's exactly what it had felt like she was doing. It had seemed like a crazy plan, until she'd dipped the pot into the aquarium and scraped it along the bottom, looking for what Phin had described as an egg-sized piece of murky-looking glass. She'd found it right away, and could have sworn that it had jumped into the pot of its own accord, nestling into the bottom among the handful of colourful pebbles she scooped up with it.

She'd rushed through the house, sloshing water all over her feet, feeling increasingly lightheaded as she went, unable to call out to Mabel because she was holding her breath. She'd almost missed the bucket in her haste to rid herself of the thing, and the three of them watched crystal sink beneath the water, filling the bucket with its sickly glow. Penny had then turned and run a few steps before falling to her knees and throwing up in a flowerbed. Mabel had patted her shoulder until she'd stopped heaving and crying. Then she'd gotten stoically to her feet when Phin insisted they needed to go if they expected him to be able to resist it for much longer.

Mabel stopped abruptly on the trail and Penny nearly ran into her back. She peeked over the older woman's shoulder and saw moonlight reflecting off mirror smooth water.

"Okay, we're here," Mabel whispered. "I don't think anyone's on the beach, but I can't see past the dock. It sure looks creepy out here in the dark, doesn't it?"

Penny was still a little dizzy and she felt an uncomfortable pressure at the base of her spine. It was a dull throb that she feared was the crystal trying to tug her closer. She could only imagine how Phin might be feeling. He'd been connected to it in the same way for much longer. She hardly dared to look back at him, but forced herself to turn around.

Phin had stopped and let go of the wheelbarrow's handles. He was standing over the bucket, staring down into the water, and the glow from the crystal showed a face gaunt with tension and fear. But Penny also detected a sort of sick longing, and she realized Phin had raised his hand and was about to plunge it into the bucket.

"No!" she shouted, and ran back to grab his wrist. He tried to wrench free, but Penny held on with a frantic strength she didn't know she had. Phin stopped struggling and staggered back just as Mabel darted in to help.

"I'm all right," he said hoarsely.

"Come on then, let's get this over with." Mabel and Penny stayed next to Phin as he lifted the handles of the wheelbarrow and trundled it the rest of the way to the beach. They left the wheelbarrow on the dirt path, and Phin had to pick up the bucket and lug it through the sand to the water's edge.

"Wait a minute," Penny said slowly. "We can't just pour this out into the lake. The crystal will be too close to the shore. Some little kid might find it. We need to throw it far out into the middle." She looked at Phin, who was sitting on the sand with his head bowed. "How are we going to throw it if we can't touch it without getting zapped or something?"

Phin clutched the fox skull that lay against his skin under his shirt. Its familiar ticklish buzz had slowly amplified into a sickening pulse in the last hour. At first he thought it was simply reacting to his fear and revulsion at having to move the crystal, but as he sat on the sand he became aware of Eric Minkley's presence. The slimy bastard had once worn this skull, and it had absorbed enough of his essence to recognize when he was near.

"How about we make a sling and whip it out there?" Mabel sat on the sand next to Phin and untied one of her running shoes. She then removed her knee high nylon stocking and held it out to Penny, who eyed it dubiously. "Just put the thing into the sock, swing it around a couple of times, and whammo! It'll fly like stink."

"That's still too close," Phin said. "Besides, the first fisherman who casts too deeply might snag the stocking and haul it back out of the water. We can't take that chance."

They sat morosely on the sand, staring out at the moonlit lake, pointedly ignoring the bucket of glowing water that sat to one side.

"Too bad we couldn't just drop it somehow way out in the middle of the lake," Penny said glumly. "Maybe one of us could swim out and just drag it behind in the sock?"

"Wait a minute," Mabel said, and jumped to her feet. "Of course we can drop it in the middle. There are half a dozen rowboats tied to the wharf and I know of at least two people who wouldn't mind if I borrowed theirs for an urgent mission."

Phin jogged to the wharf, easily finding the *Blow Me Down* tied to a corner piling. He jumped in, swaying until it stopped rocking, and cast off. He'd never rowed a boat and felt like a fool as it spun and wove drunkenly, banging into the dock more than once and threatening to tip and dunk him into the lake. Finally, he managed to gain control of the oars and set the boat on the right course, following the shoreline until he reached Mabel and Penny.

He clambered out and held the boat steady in the thigh-high water while the two women struggled to carry the bucket between them. The three of them managed to manhandle it into the boat, though they spilled enough water to make Phin and Penny exchange a sick, knowing look. Penny scooped handfuls of lake water into the bucket while Phin rowed them out toward the middle of the lake.

"Do you think anyone can see us out here?" Penny whispered anxiously.

"Are you kidding?" Mabel stopped rowing to look back at her. "The way the moon's lighting up everything tonight, there's no way anyone could miss seeing the three of us."

"Mabel, it's nearly two in the morning. No one is sneaking around the lake at this hour."

"Except us, you mean," Penny said, and spat out a nervous giggle.

"Yeah, no one out here but us boat thieves," Mabel snickered, causing Penny to laugh again. Phin glared at them a moment before his mouth quirked and he slapped a hand to his mouth to contain his own hysteria. That was enough to set the women off again, and then they were all laughing helplessly at their ridiculous situation. Phin picked up the oars again and they gradually fell silent as they neared the middle of Cricket Lake.

The moon's reflection cast a striking contrast against the inky black water that undulated hypnotically in the little boat's wake. They sat quietly for a few moments once they'd reached the middle of the lake.

"All right," Mabel started, "this thing killed my best friend, and it's hurting you too, Phineas, I can see it in your face. It's bad and it's gotta go." She turned to Penny. "Kiddo, I know you think you need it to save yourself, but you've got us now. We won't let anyone hurt you."

"But if Eric doesn't get the crystal, he's going to tell the police I killed his grandmother," Penny whispered, glancing at the bucket sitting in the bottom of the boat. "The last thing I want to do is give it to him, but I can't see how dumping it in the water is a solution to my problem." She clutched at Mabel's hand and squeezed her eyes shut.

"My gut and my heart both tell me this is the right thing to do." She pulled the girl close and hugged her. "We have to do this and trust that it will all work out. Are you ready?"

"How deep is the water?" Penny asked as she peered over the side. She had to squeeze her eyes shut as vertigo threatened to overwhelm her. Her heart raced and she wished she were anywhere else than in this stupid little boat, in this stupid town.

"Well, the kids sometimes dare each other to swim all the way to the bottom," Mabel said, "but they always have to come up for air long before they get there. It's got to be at least 350 feet, so I'd say it's deep enough for our purpose."

"How do we tip this overboard without dunking ourselves in the process?" Phin snugged the bucket against the side of the boat, preparing to hoist it over the edge. He turned when he heard Penny whimper and nearly went over the side when Penny suddenly pushed past him and plunged her hand into the bucket of water. She pulled out the crystal.

Penny stared open-mouthed at the glow that pulsed out from her hand, holding her breath as the brightness increased until she had to squint her eyes nearly shut against the glare. She heard a familiar laugh and gasped as she recognized her mother's slurred voice coming from the centre of the brilliant light.

"My Penny, Jenny's Penny. Come on, let's play." A ghostly image of her Mom floated out of the glare, the same puffy face, close-set eyes, and sweet smile Penny remembered loving and hating with equal intensity.

Then she felt a sharp pain and the light dimmed and drowned as the crystal hit the surface of the water and quickly sank from sight. She realized that Mabel had slapped it out of her hand, and angrily pulled her arm back to hit the old woman, but stopped when she saw the tears running down Mabel's cheeks.

"You heard her too," she whispered. "You heard my Mom, didn't you?"

"Yeah, kiddo. No idea how that worked, but I heard her. Saw her face too."

Phin's hands were shaky, and he didn't trust himself to talk, so he clumsily rowed back to the wharf, while Penny cried in Mabel's arms.

She'd quieted by the time they reached the dock and Phin held the boat steady while the women climbed out and tied it to its post. He emptied the bucket and set it by his feet. They stood on the dock for a long moment, staring out at the spot where they'd last seen the crystal. No one felt even the slightest tug from it, and Penny crossed her arms glumly as she turned away.

"Eric is going to be so pissed at me."

FORTY-SIX

Penny cradled her cup of tea with both hands, and tried to pay attention to what Dee was saying, but all she had been able to think about for the past several hours was her mother's voice, calling her out to play. She hadn't slept since they'd dropped the crystal into the middle of Cricket Lake, and she was ready to ingest all the caffeine and sugar it would take to keep her awake until Phin showed up at the café and explained to her how that could have happened.

When her mother had died eleven years ago, her Aunt Margaret had thrown out anything that would remind them of the woman Penny now believed the only person who had ever cared about her. Margaret had sneered at her sorrow over her mother's death, claiming that retards couldn't really love people. They were like animals, and only got used to having you around.

But in that brief moment last night, when she'd held the crystal in her hand and heard her mother calling to her, she'd also felt a swell of emotion riding on the tide of that voice.

Her mother had loved her, unconditionally, exclusively and deeply. Penny finally understood that simple fact and that knowledge had changed everything. It didn't matter that her mother hadn't known how to spell her own name, or how to make the correct change for the bus.

That simple, trusting woman had been capable of the most attentive adoration, and most of the time Penny had felt nothing but acute embarrassment at her Mom's devoted love for the child she couldn't remember conceiving or birthing.

"Earth to Penny," Mabel called as she came into the room. Her hair was dishevelled, bristly white tufts springing in every direction. Dusky skin surrounded her puffy eyes, and she smothered a yawn.

"Honestly, Mabel, I don't know what the three of you were thinking," Dee said. Snooping around the lake in the middle of the night is just plain dangerous."

"We had a plan, which we carried out perfectly, without a hitch."

"You could have broken a leg," Dee went on as if Mabel hadn't spoken. "And rowing out to the middle of the lake! Anything could have happened. You could have drowned. I'm surprised you're not all sick with the same thing that Josie's boys got."

"Josie's boys are all right," Mabel said, yawning widely enough to make her eyes water. She rubbed them with the heels of her hands, knocking her glasses into her lap. "There's nothing wrong with that water, Dee. From what I gathered when Tammy came barging in here yesterday with those dogs – and we're going to have to talk to her about a no-dogs-in-the-café rule – those boys set it up to look like there was something wrong with the water when there really wasn't."

"And why would they do that?" Dee flung her hands wide in frustration.

"Because they're little boys who are about to lose a part of their home turf, that's why."

"They'd have to know that we'd all find out."

"I imagine they thought they had the perfect idea to scare away anyone who might want to take away their beach. If the lake was toxic and the fish were dying, who would want to buy it? A brilliant plan, if you're ten."

"I give up," Dee said, turning away to wrap two lemon cakes. The freezer was getting full but, with the new ovens, she couldn't help baking all her favourites. She sliced a third cake for the display case near the window. A sign announced that they would open for business soon but to come in for a tour and a free sample.

It was still early on what promised to be another scorcher. She hoped her business license would arrive in today's mail but until it was legal for her to sell her baked goods, she was happy to continue handing out a few freebies.

Dee wondered if her frustration with Mabel was partly due to her feelings toward Penny. The young woman had only been in Cricket Lake a few days and already Mabel seemed to have accepted her as part of the family. Mabel said she preferred to live alone, yet she showed no sign of moving Penny along.

"I think we did the right thing," Mabel said. "You were the one who was concerned about the change in Phineas. You worried that the crystal was corrupting him. Well, we got rid of it. There's no way anyone could get it from the bottom of the lake. It's nearly 400 feet deep."

"Closer to 500, from what I've heard," Dee mumbled.

"See? So Phineas is rid of it, that young man won't get it, and our lake is fixed and free of pollution."

"Mabel," Dee chided, "you said there was nothing wrong with the lake."

"Yeah, but no one else knows that yet. As far as they're all concerned, maybe we fixed it when we had a midnight ritual and threw an enchanted crystal into the lake or something like that…oh who knows, I'm sure I can come up with some appropriate nonsense if anyone asks."

"Maybe you can say you had another vision," Penny piped up.

"Ella returned to tell me that she'd foretold the problem with the lake," Mabel shot back, getting to her feet.

310

"She told you we needed to sacrifice a powerful magical artifact."

"She gave me an incantation to recite."

"And now Cricket Lake is saved," Penny said, pumping her fists in the air and bouncing across the room in a little victory dance. Mabel joined her and the two of them giggled as they danced around Dee.

"You two have had too little sleep and too much caffeine," she said, laughing at their antics in spite of herself. "Phineas said he'd be here early to finish the shelves, but he probably hasn't had any more sleep than you have. I doubt we'll get much work done in here today."

Penny stopped and bent over, hands on knees, breathing heavily.

"I'm a little dizzy," she said.

"You're just giddy from not enough sleep," Mabel said.

"A cold shower would probably help wake me up. I said I'd help Phin varnish those shelves." She straightened and looked at Mabel, who was staring at her with a smile spreading slowly on her face.

"I have an even better idea," Mabel said, heading for the door.

"Where are you going?" Dee asked.

"For a swim."

"Where? In the lake? You'll never catch *me* in that water," Penny said, frowning.

"Mabel! Don't you dare." Dee followed Mabel out the door. She turned back to Penny, unsure about leaving the young woman alone in her shop, but Mabel was already halfway down the block, walking at a brisk pace. "I'm going after Mabel. You wait here for Phineas, and bring him to the lake. Maybe he can talk some sense into her." She hurried away, shouting over her shoulder, "Lock the door when you leave and put up the closed sign."

Penny watched Dee chase after Mabel, then closed and locked the door. Anyone who wants free bread can come back later, she thought. She was worried about Mabel. The lake water had been freezing last night. She didn't think it would be any warmer today, and wondered if old people could have heart attacks when they jumped into really cold water.

She soon saw Phin's bicycle turn onto Main Street and rushed out to meet him. He was looking over his shoulder as he rode and nearly ran into her. She followed his gaze and saw the figure dressed in black striding along the sidewalk less than a block away.

Penny clutched Phin's arm tightly enough to cause him to wince in pain, and as Eric approached them she inched back until she stood behind Phin. "Mabel's gone to jump in the lake and Dee's freaking out," she hissed in his ear. "We have to stop her before she has a heart attack or something."

Phin cocked an eyebrow in confusion, looked back at Eric, who had slowed and was now arguing with his companion, and then nodded at Penny. He swung his leg over the seat, leaned the bike against a tree and set off at a run. Relieved to be turning her back on Eric, Penny followed Phin to the lake.

FORTY-SEVEN

Mabel pulled her shirt over her head as she hurried across the sand. She panted from the run, and wanted nothing more than to sit down and rest, but was determined to follow through with her plan before Dee found some way to stop her. If they were going to claim that the lake was now free from toxic pollution, she had to show her confidence by going for this swim.

"I swear, Mabel," Dee said, panic rising in her voice, "if you go near that water I'll tackle you and hold you down until Phineas gets here."

"Don't try to stop me." Mabel paused to kick off her canvas shoes and peel off her socks. She could hear a babble of voices coming along the path.

"What if Tammy was wrong, and there really is something toxic in the water? Have you even thought of that possibility?"

Mabel faced her niece, and was startled to see real fear in Dee's stricken expression. She faltered for a moment. Of course she'd thought of that possibility, but had discarded it. She had to believe that even if Tammy was wrong, the problem had been fixed by the positive intent that she, Phineas, and Penny had willed onto that crystal.

"If there was something wrong with the lake, we've fixed it and I aim to prove it, but my guess is there never was anything harmful in that water. Those boys tried to make it look that way, but Tammy said she saw salmon and cod in that pile of fish. Aside from the fact that there's no salmon or cod swimming in our lake, I can't think of any toxin that would fillet them before throwing them onto the shore."

"I don't care about that," Dee said. She took a calming breath. "This is about you throwing yourself into that water, toxic or not. You haven't been in that lake for years. You said you were getting too old to brave the cold water. Why can't you let someone else test your theory?"

"In case I'm wrong," she said with a wink, and before Dee could stop her, she rushed into the water, waded out and dove in. She came up spluttering and shivering. "Holy crow, that's cold!"

Dee clutched Mabel's tee shirt to her chest and debated going out there and dragging her back to shore. She was afraid that Mabel was beginning to lose control, and Dee couldn't bear the thought of watching her slowly deteriorate the same way her mother had. So much had changed since Riva died, and she wished everything could go back to the way it was. She'd even give up her beautiful new bakery if she could turn back time, though that would mean that Phin would never have come back, and she couldn't ignore the fact that he partly filled the space that had been left empty when her best friend died.

She still missed Riva desperately, and wondered if Phin was right, that the crystal had been responsible for her death. It that were true, then it was better off at the bottom of the lake.

Dee was relieved to see Mabel was finally wading back toward dry land. The ground dropped so steeply that the water was over most people's heads a mere twenty feet from shore. Mabel had worn her glasses into the water, and Dee could see her squinting to see through the now-distorted lenses. She looked so tiny, forging through the waist-deep water, and Dee felt a pang of love and gratitude for this woman who'd been such a constant figure in her life.

"Mabel," she called, "come on out of there before you catch your death of cold."

"Jump in, the water's fine," Mabel hollered back, but she was looking past Dee and waving her arms.

Dee turned to see who she was talking to and squeaked in surprise when Phin raced past her to the water. He ran in, wearing his shoes, bellowing a Tarzan call which was abruptly cut off when he leaped and belly-flopped right in front of Mabel. He thrashed in the frigid water, stunned silent by the cold. Mabel hooted with glee, and splashed him until they were both laughing hysterically.

Penny had been right behind Phin, but stopped at the water's edge, nervous again with this huge expanse of water. She backed up and crowded nervously close to Dee.

"Are they crazy? That water is freezing," she whispered.

"Yes they are," Dee answered. "The lake rarely reaches any more than ten degrees Celsius." She moved away from Penny, who was standing a little too close for comfort, but the young woman followed her every step. There was a rustling in the thick bushes that lined the narrow path leading to where they were standing, and Penny flinched as a male voice drifted towards them.

"Keep going. I saw them take this path."

Penny inched even closer to Dee, angling around to her other side, as if to get as far away from that voice as possible. Her face had blanched beneath her tan, and a haunted look came into her eyes. Dee glanced from Penny to the lake, where Mabel and Phin were coming ashore, and then to the path, where Eric suddenly appeared. He was accompanied by a shorter, heavy-set young man who was sweating profusely and trying to keep up with him.

Eric rushed up to where Penny cowered behind Dee. "All right, where is it?" he snarled and grabbed her wrist.

"Let me go," she said, her voice breathless with fear and anger. She jerked her hand away and backed several steps.

"Hey Eric, take it easy."

"Mind your own business, Bobby," he spat, "this is between me and the little bitch. She has something of mine and I want it now." He lunged for Penny again, but instead found himself face to face with a dripping, snarling apparition.

"I thought I told you never to come back here, Eric." Phin spoke quietly, but his words held a menace that chilled the air and commanded attention.

"And I told you that I wanted that crystal," Eric shouted into Phin's face. He held his ground but squirmed under Phin's fierce gaze, and when he dropped his eyes he saw the fox skull outlined beneath the wet fabric of his shirt. Eric took a step back, reminded of the last time he'd encountered Phin.

"Who might you be, young man?"

"Bobby Fraser, ma'am, at your service." Bobby turned to Mabel and stuck out a hand to shake, but jerked it back when he realized the old woman was standing there in her brassiere. "Uh, I-I'm a reporter from Vancouver. I came out h-here to cover the toxic lake st-story." He kept turning in place to avoid looking at the woman's chest, but she followed his every move.

"Well, Bobby Fraser, you're going to make me dizzy with all this spinning around. Stand still for a second so we can talk."

"Mabel," Dee said, thrusting her tee shirt under her nose. "Put this on, you're embarrassing him." Dee frowned at Penny, who hadn't left her side, and they stood uncertainly between the two pairs. She was afraid Phin and Eric might come to blows, and thought Mabel would probably be able to defuse their anger, but she was also concerned about this new stranger. Who was he and why had Eric brought him here?

"Why were you in the water? I thought it was dangerous, like, contaminated or something." Now that Mabel was dressed, Bobby had recovered.

"We fixed it," Mabel smiled triumphantly and threw her arm out to indicate the lake.

"But I heard it was full of toxic chemicals and that two kids had been poisoned."

"Do I look like I've been poisoned?"

"Well, no. You seem all right. How do you feel?"

"I feel great. Nothing like a brisk dip to wake you up." She winked at Bobby.

"How did you fix it? What did you do?"

"We had a magical ritual and called upon great powers to restore the healthy balance of our lake."

"Right," Bobby said, rolling his eyes. This whole story was turning out to be a wild goose chase, and these people were crazy. He clicked his pen and pretended to write a few words on his notepad.

"No, really," Penny interjected, "We went onto the lake last night and dropped a magic crystal into the deepest part of the lake and voilà – cured, fixed, whatever you want to call it."

"What?" Eric rushed to Penny and grabbed her by the upper arms. He shook her so hard her head snapped back and forth. "What did you do with my crystal?" He stopped shaking her when he felt fingers digging into the back of his neck. He let her go and twisted away from that pinching grip, facing Phin, who moved to stand between Eric and Penny.

"You heard her," he said with a tight smile that didn't reach his eyes. "The crystal is gone. We pitched it into 400 feet of water."

"But you had no right!" Eric screeched, his voice cracking on the last word. "It was my father's. It was supposed to be mine." He tried to push past Phin to get to Penny. "You bitch! I told you what would happen if you didn't bring it to me. The cops are going to get everything now. You'll go to jail for murder."

"I didn't do anything wrong," Penny retorted. "You're the one who killed Ella when you bashed her head open on the floor."

"Whoa, he killed someone?" Bobby flipped to a clean page in his book. "A toxic lake and a murder, you people sure have a lot going on up here."

Dee sighed. "The lake was never toxic. Some kids tried to make it look that way so the town council wouldn't sell this." She indicated the large expanse of water with a sweep of her arm. "And no one up here's been murdered. They're talking about something that happened in Vancouver."

"You mean the lake story really is a hoax?" Bobby's expression darkened. "You people are just pulling a publicity stunt so you can keep your lake from getting sold?"

"Not us," Mabel piped up. "There's a couple of things going on here and you're getting them all mixed up." She took a breath. "Yes, two young boys thought they could stop the sale so they pretended to poison the lake."

"Wait a minute," Eric interrupted. "If the lake isn't really poisoned, why did you throw my crystal into it?"

"Two kids got hurt. Doesn't matter that they did it to themselves," Mabel snapped. Eric sneered and opened his mouth to retort, but she held up a hand to stop him. "Water samples were taken and they'll show that everything is okay, so the sale will go ahead. Throwing the crystal into the lake was just symbolic. Outsiders won't care about our ritual, but the townspeople will see that we cared enough about the lake to sacrifice one of Phin's most powerful magical tools."

"But it was mine," Eric snarled. He couldn't believe that they'd thrown away what he'd been trying to get back for so long. He looked out onto the lake. The water's surface was like a mirror, reflecting the blue sky and puffs of white clouds that glided overhead. He balled his fists and took a step toward the water. He could see Phin's fierce grin out of the corner of his eye, and nearly screamed with frustration at this new violation. He hated water and had never learned to swim. He turned back to Penny and was gratified to see her cringe away.

"Fine," he said, pointing to the middle of the lake. "Go back out there, Penny, and get my crystal."

"Not a chance," Mabel said, stepping in front of Penny. "That water's damn deep and that stone is probably under a few inches of sand by now. No way anyone's ever going to find it again."

"Well, she's going to try. I sent her here on a mission, and as far as I can see she hasn't finished it yet."

"Don't be foolish, young man. She doesn't have to do anything you say."

"This says different." He pulled a packet of papers from an inside pocket and smiled smugly at the shock that registered on Penny's face.

Dee stepped forward, and before she could lose her nerve, snatched the papers out of his hand and thrust them at Penny. Penny promptly dropped them down her shirt and crossed her arms tightly over the packet.

"Hey," Eric roared, "that's evidence!" He lunged for Penny, but found his way blocked by Dee and Mabel.

Phin stepped between the two women and wrapped his arms around their shoulders, pulling them close. Mabel snaked her arm around his waist.

"Actually," Penny said from her safe position behind her three friends, "Evidence is the fingerprints you probably left on Ella's pill bottle. You stole these papers from me."

"I've got pictures of your stupid papers. I'll give them to the cops."

"Big deal," Dee said. "You fabricated a story to try and fool the police into looking away from you. You can't prove she was there. In fact, I can probably fabricate a better story, and prove she's been working for me for several weeks now."

Eric turned to Bobby, who was writing in his notebook at a furious pace. "You're getting all this, right? They're gonna try to forge some kind of papers to make people think she's been here all along."

"Buddy, you are so screwed," Bobby said as he paused and shook out his writing hand to ease a cramp. "You killed your grandmother. Do you think the cops will care where this woman was living at the time? This whole community will back her up, and if your fingerprints show up like she says, you're the only one they're going to be looking for." He stepped away from Eric and stood with the others. "Those pictures you took only prove their story that you stole her papers and then tried to frame her."

Phin waved a sodden hank of hair under Eric's nose. "Remember this?" It was wrapped with red yarn and sported several damp feathers which stuck to his hand. He'd prepared it when he realized Eric might return and was gratified to see the blood drain from the young man's face.

"You can't hurt me with that," Eric said in a weak voice as he backed away from Phin.

"Of course I can. There's nothing more powerful than a voodoo fetish made from someone's hair. We've had this conversation, remember? Why, with this I can probably cause all kinds of mischief for you."

Eric looked at them all in turn. His so-called new buddy had turned out to be a traitor, Dee had shown more backbone than he'd given her credit for, and Mabel now stood with her arms around Penny. He locked his gaze onto Phin.

"You bastard," he snarled. "If it wasn't for you none of this would have happened. Riva was my father's cousin. She should have left everything to me. I'm the only family she had left, and now you've destroyed the only thing I've ever cared about."

"You just don't get it, do you?" Phin shook his head and glanced at the lock of sodden hair in his hand, curling his lip in disgust. He tossed it at Eric's feet and wiped his hand on his shirt. The younger man snatched up his hair and stuffed it in a pocket before Phin could change his mind.

"The crystal is gone. Get over it. You've caused enough people trouble for nothing. Take your greasy hair and beat it."

"You're the one who's caused trouble," Eric said bitterly. "You've taken away my future, my destiny. You had no right to take my family heirloom."

"Well, that's not exactly true," Mabel said, stepping up to stand next to Phin. She cleared her throat. "Forty-odd years ago, my friend Riva got pregnant. She gave up the baby to her best friend from high school – who was newly married – and stayed out of their lives as best she could. When their marriage was breaking up the friend asked her to watch her boy – the boy that Riva had birthed – while they sorted themselves out." Mabel looked up at Phin. His face was tight with apprehension, and she took his hand and squeezed it. "So when you called Phin a bastard, you were more right than you know, since Riva never told anyone who'd fathered her baby, not even me."

320

"You're lying." Eric said it flatly, but he was staring at Phin, who suddenly looked a lot more familiar. The silvery hair highlighted a dark mop similar to his own, and the feral grin he'd glimpsed earlier was a copy of the one in the photo of his grandfather that hung in Ella's house.

"You mean that Phin is…" Dee faltered.

"Riva's son," Mabel finished for her. "It was supposed to be the secret I took to my grave. She made me swear in blood and everything. But I'm sick of this foolishness. There've been too many secrets, and this one is too big for me to keep carrying all by myself." She turned back to Eric. "Riva left her house and all her worldly belongings to her only son, Phineas. You haven't got a leg to stand on so you might as well go home."

"Oh my god," Dee moaned.

Mabel frowned at Eric. "You're a very strange young man. You helped save one old lady from a fire, and then kicked another old lady off a ladder and killed her. Gonna take me a while to puzzle that one out, that's for sure." She shook her head sadly and took Penny's hand, pulling her away from the water's edge. Phin and Dee numbly followed and they all made their silent way to the path leading back to town.

Bobby was left alone on the beach with Eric, though he might as well have been invisible. Eric stared out over the lake. His eyes were empty, his face devoid of expression. Bobby started to speak but thought better of it. He turned and followed the tracks the others had left in the sand.

FORTY-EIGHT

A moist breeze wafted through the open windows, mingling with the heady aroma of freshly baked bread, of sweet rolls and spiced tea. At the back of the room, a more exotic scent clung to the brocade drapes concealing an alcove. The richly patterned fabric had absorbed the fragrant smoke from countless cones of incense burned in the tiny space since the café had officially opened mere weeks ago.

The drapes parted and Mabel bustled out of the alcove, blinking rapidly in the brighter light, and trailing a fragrant plume of gray smoke. Her bristly white hair had escaped the beaded red scarf she'd wrapped around her head. She carried a tray with a ceramic teapot and two delicate cups to the long counter where Penny was putting a carved wooden whistle into a paper bag for a customer. The woman handed the bag to her son, who pulled the whistle out of the bag again and rubbed a thumb against the burnished wood.

"Sonny, don't even think about blowing that thing in here," Mabel said, narrowing her eyes at the boy. "Phineas used voodoo magic when he made that whistle. You never know what kind of trouble it's going to call. I'd rather we didn't find out in here."

The boy's mother glanced at Mabel, decided that the little old lady wasn't kidding, and quickly dragged her son out the door.

"Mabel, you shouldn't scare away the customers like that," Penny said, trying to smother a laugh.

"Can't help it. Those things make a godawful screech when youngsters start spitting into them. You'd think that Phineas would have learned to make a sweet-sounding whistle by now."

"I think he's feeling a little rushed. They sell as fast as he can make them. He hasn't had time to refine the design."

Mabel turned and smiled at the two young women who had followed her out of the alcove. They smiled back shyly and one of them slid a twenty-dollar bill across the counter.

"Thanks, young lady. I hope you got what you came for."

"It was fun. Did you really mean it when you said he might ask me to go out with him?"

"Well, remember what I said about what we saw in the tea leaves."

"I saw his profile." The young woman blushed and giggled behind her hand.

"Right, and I saw a cactus plant, and your friend here saw some kind of animal."

"It was a gorilla, or maybe a dog," her friend said helpfully.

"Perception has a lot to do with it," Mabel said, tucking the bill into a pocket. "We attract whatever we put a lot of energy into. This was your fortune, so if you saw his face, that's where your thoughts are going to go most often, and that's what's most likely to draw his attention."

"Are they really all so gullible?" Penny asked as she watched them leave, giggling and whispering on their way out the door.

"They got what they came for, didn't they?"

"But what if it doesn't come true? If he doesn't call her, she'll think you're a fraud."

"I didn't tell her anything. She saw what she wanted to. If she's convinced he likes her, she'll do all the work and make sure he notices her. A self-fulfilling prophecy." She grinned at Penny, her eyes crinkling with mischief.

Dee came out of the back room, carrying an enormous tray of puffed pastries, so fresh the icing still glistened. Mabel deftly plucked one off the tray as she passed by and bit deeply into the warm sweetness.

"Oh," she mumbled as she chewed, "this is marvellous, Dee. I love almonds."

Dee wiped the back of her hand across her damp forehead, smearing icing into her hair. "I'm thinking of doing something with all those blackberries we picked last week. They're taking up a lot of space in the freezer. Purple muffins might be fun." She smiled as Mabel's eyes lit up, her mouth too full to comment. "I'm glad Phin decided to let the back of his yard go wild. I know he hates how messy the blackberry brambles look, but I think he was convinced once he saw how many wild animals rely on it for cover and food."

She leaned against the counter and watched several customers admiring the displays. A young man sporting a pointed goatee picked up a walking stick and peered closely at the small bones and feathers dangling several inches from the top. The wood was stained a rich brown and densely carved with twisting vines and leaves. The raised designs had been buffed and burnished until they were as smooth as satin. The man flicked the small bones with a finger, and they clicked drily against each other

Mabel had found the walking stick tucked away in a corner of Phin's living room, along with two others he'd finished. Each was uniquely carved, one bearing complex magical symbols that he'd found in one of Riva's books, another covered in astrological signs and constellations, and the third boasting vines and leaves. Bones and feathers graced the top of two of the staves, dangling from several lengths of leather lacing, and Phin had glued pebbles to the last one, creating a textured grip.

Mabel had examined each one closely while Phin stood by, explaining that they might be too unconventional to appeal to anyone. He was just trying some new techniques, testing out different types of wood, seeing what went well together. She'd

324

ignored his protests and had bullied him into bringing them into the shop. "People might not put much value on a simple wooden walking stick, but they'll pay lots for a piece of hippy voodoo art." She had put outrageously high price tags on them, and two had sold almost immediately. She'd smiled smugly at Phin's astonished look when she gave him the money.

"Do you think it'll sell this time?" Penny asked, as she set a steaming pot of tea on a tray.

"Doesn't matter," Mabel answered, licking icing from her fingers. "It fits in with the décor."

"What décor?" Dee asked. "There hasn't been any time to decorate. We barely get the doors open each day before the place fills up."

"Aw, honey, it's all about ambience. Who needs fancy decorations when we've got the best baked goods in town and our own fortune-telling den?"

"Well, I was hoping for another coat of paint or at least a nice beaded curtain across the doorway into the kitchen."

"Maybe Phin can make you one out of some strung-together bones," Penny exclaimed. "There's ambience for you."

"Ugh. I don't get his fascination for that stuff. It's just too creepy for me."

"The customers seem to like it," Mabel said, pointing to the young man who had nudged his girlfriend's arm with the staff to get her attention. The girl frowned, and her lip curled in distaste at the sight of the swirling feathers and clacking bones. His smile faltered and he put the walking stick back into its niche, meekly following her to a shelf of colourful plaques. He cast wistful glances back at the staff as he dutifully held out his hands, which his girlfriend filled with tiny wooden animals.

"See what I mean?" Mabel adjusted her kerchief and stepped out from behind the counter. "I wonder if they've seen my cross-stitched Tarot tea cozies yet. I'll bet they'd like The Lovers, or maybe I'll show them the one with The Devil on one side and The Fool on the other."

Dee arranged several cookies on a plate and set it on Penny's tray next to the teapot. "The couple at table four asked for the tea of the day. I wonder if we should come up with a dozen or so that we can offer on a rotating basis."

"Cool. Maybe we could do the same with cookies." Penny couldn't get enough of Dee's cookies, and was the first to volunteer her services as taste tester for any experimental recipes.

Dee watched Penny as she wove her way through the crowd and out the door to the patio. She was getting used to having the young woman around and had come to rely on her skills and hard work. Penny waited on all the tables as well as handling sales of crafts and baked goods, leaving Dee free to bake, and Mabel to play hostess and tell fortunes.

Dee picked up a newspaper clipping from the desk behind the counter. Bobby Fraser had mailed it to her from Vancouver. She was careful not to smudge any icing onto the paper since she planned to have it framed and hang it on the wall for everyone to read.

"Shambhala may lie in the Gobi Desert, but Voodoo Café is the glittering oasis of Cricket Lake." Bobby had avoided any mention of Eric and his grandmother, magical crystals, or the problems with the lake, but had instead focused on Voodoo Café and the other businesses in Cricket Lake. He'd written about the quirky accommodations at the Cot & Couch, the local eccentrics and their monthly séances.

The café had quickly become the town's focal point, where everyone gathered to meet friends or catch up on the latest news. There was no lack of customers clamouring for tea and scones, Mabel's homey arts and crafts, or a peek into the murky future.

Dee could see Phineas carving on the patio and averted her gaze so he wouldn't think she was watching him. She'd been mostly avoiding him since she'd heard the news he was Riva's son. How could Riva and Mabel have kept such a secret all those years? And how could Riva have sent her own son to drive her friends to their suicide out in the forest? She and Riva had been so close. She felt hurt and betrayed that Riva had not trusted her. She shook her head, determined to push those thoughts aside. It was nearly time to head home to start dinner for Lydia. Mabel and Penny would see to closing up shop at six.

She carefully laid the newspaper article back on the desk, sighing with satisfaction. She could scarcely believe her dream had come true in such a grand style. Six months ago she'd been baking in a broken-down fire trap that had nearly killed her beloved aunt. She grinned as she watched Mabel steer her customers toward the counter, carrying several items they'd decided to purchase.

"I'm certain the walking stick will still be there tomorrow," Mabel said to the young man as she took his money. "You can come back and pick it up before your bus leaves."

"Oh, there won't be room in our luggage," his girlfriend said before he had the chance to open his mouth. His shoulders slumped and he took the paper bag she thrust into his hands.

"Leave us your name and email address," Mabel called as they went out the door, "and we'll let you know when we're ready with our mail order business."

"What mail order business?" Dee asked.

"I just thought of it now," Mabel answered with a grin. "Just imagine the customers we could reach. In the meantime, you should head home before Lydie gets it into her mind to call the cops and report us missing."

"Who's waiting for lemon cookies and ginger spice tea?" Penny called as she stepped out the door. The patio was crowded with chattering people enjoying tea and pastries. The round tables were covered with bright tye-dyed cloths, and the chairs were a shiny black. Mabel had painted long white bones on the chairs' arms and backs, making everyone look as if they were sitting in the lap of a skeleton. Dee had protested Mabel's idea, but not a single customer failed to admire her handiwork and remark on how much fun it made their visit.

A middle-aged woman waggled her fingers in Penny's direction before bringing her digital camera back up to her eye. She snapped several photos of her husband posing in the skeleton chair with his eyes closed and hands crossed over his chest. Penny dutifully smiled at their compliments on the entertaining décor, and told them – when asked how much they cost – that the chairs were not for sale. It was the third time in as many days someone had wanted to buy the skeleton chairs. She'd have to remember to mention it to Mabel. Maybe she could make up a few more to sell.

Phin sat at the far end of the patio, surrounded by a growing mound of fragrant wood shavings. Peg was at his feet, batting with her single front paw at the curls of wood as they fluttered to the ground. She had moved into the café on the day it opened, plying the customers for head scritches and limping upstairs each night to Mabel's apartment above the bakery. Mabel grumbled about the cat hair on her bedspread and threatened to have her shaved, but sent Penny to look for Peg if she didn't come up by dark.

"I'm brewing a fresh pot of Earl Grey, do you want a cup?" Penny took his mug without waiting for an answer, ignoring the mess and refraining from asking what he was going to carve on this new walking stick. She had learned that he preferred to be left alone to brood about his designs, and would scowl and stomp away to work elsewhere if anyone made the smallest suggestion. "When do you think we can go to Ella's house? Though I guess it's kinda your house now."

"The lawyer says I can pick up the keys next week once I've signed all their papers. We can have a look at the house after that and figure out what I'm going to do with it."

"They won't know, right? That I was living in the attic?" Penny asked anxiously. "I mean, I'm sure Eric told the cops, the lawyers and anyone else who would listen."

"Naw, they have his fingerprints from her pill bottle and tea cup, and he keeps changing his story. They're not looking for anyone else."

"Don't you find it creepy? Like, there I was in this old lady's attic, and then her grandson not only kills her but then sends me off to find you, who supposedly has this magic crystal that the grandmother sent away with some woman who turns out to be your long-lost mother. And then she left you her house, and now I'll be going back to it?"

"Ella left the house to Riva and had no idea I existed."

"You can't be sure of that. Mabel knew Riva had had a baby, so maybe Ella did too. It's all kinda twisted up, eh?"

"Well, don't worry about it. We'll figure it out," he said, and bent back to his work. He examined the wood closely, following the line of a cut with his thumb and nodding with satisfaction. The wood was good and dry, but not so dry as to crack along any of the deep cuts he was about to start.

Phin wasn't looking forward to returning to Vancouver to claim Ella's house. He was grateful Penny was going with him. She wanted to search the house from top to bottom, and was confident they would find information on the mysterious crystal, or even other treasures Ella had kept hidden from her son and grandson. Penny had blushed furiously when Mabel mentioned keeping an eye out for more souvenir tee shirts, but neither woman had seen fit to explain the cryptic remark to Phineas.

From Penny's description, it sounded like the house was old but in reasonable condition. Phin had no idea what to expect from such a sale and he felt like a fraud taking something from a woman he'd never met. The feeling was familiar, since he'd just barely finished going through another woman's stuff.

He wished he knew the circumstances that had led Riva to give him up to the parents who had raised him. And why had they never told him he was adopted? When he thought about it, it explained a lot about the distant relationship he'd had with his father.

Phin sheared off another curl of wood and dangled it for Peg, who ignored it and clumsily hopped up onto his lap. He put down his knife and stroked her warm fur, trying for a scowl but not quite managing it. Darn cats kept giving him reasons to like them. In fact, he'd been awakened this morning by a deep rumbling against his body. Castor and Pollux had curled up on either side of him on top of the blanket, effectively pinning him to the bed. He'd reached out to pet Castor's silky head and the cat had licked his hand. He'd been so surprised by the display of affection that he'd twitched, scattering the cats instantly.

He'd realized then that he'd had more affection shown to him – by cats and new friends – in the past few months than in his entire adult life. It was something he thought he could get used to. He glanced through the big window into the café where Dee, Mabel and Penny were busy chatting with customers. He marvelled at how these three women had saved him from his guilt over what had happened to three *other* women.

Mabel with her quirky sense of humour was always able to chivvy him out of his dark moods and remind him life was all about having fun. He felt fiercely protective of the older woman and hoped she'd been joking when she'd asked him to be ready to drive her out to the cabin one snowy night in her future.

He was glad Penny had decided to stay in Cricket Lake. He felt less awkward and singled out with her around as the newest resident in the small town. She had hardly stopped smiling since they had left Eric on the beach and didn't let a day go by without telling Phin he had saved her life. Phin wasn't so sure about that. It seemed more to him like it was the other way around. If she hadn't arrived when she had, there was no telling how deeply he might have fallen under the crystal's spell.

But it was Dee who filled his thoughts and distracted him from his work. She ran from him in his dreams and he could never catch up. He wished he could believe that she really meant it when she assured him she didn't blame him. But the distant look in her eye made him afraid that she'd never forget he'd been the one to take her grandmother away from her. Mabel had told him Dee was likely still in shock at the news he was Riva's son, and to give her some time to adjust.

Dee wasn't the only one who still felt unsettled about Mabel's startling announcement. Phin hardly knew how to deal with the idea that his own mother had been the cause of so much havoc in his life. Riva had given him up as a baby, sent him on a deadly errand when he was hardly old enough to know right from wrong, and then called him back to this place to face his demons and resolve a mystery that had plagued this town for more than two decades.

The café's door opened and Penny smiled at him as she approached with a full tray. Phin accepted the mug she handed to him and blew on the steaming tea to cool it.

It had been nearly two weeks since they'd dropped the crystal into the middle of the lake. He hadn't felt its pull since then, though he'd had at least one terrifying nightmare where it had floated to the surface of the lake and sent intense beams of searing light all the way to his house. He'd woken up standing in the living room with panic blossoming, staring at an empty spot on the carpet in front of the bookshelf. He hadn't calmed down until he'd realized that the room was dark, and there was no beam of light shining through his windows.

In the morning he'd rearranged the entire living room, transforming part of it into a workshop with several storage bins for wood, shelves for finished pieces, and a long trestle table covering the spot where the aquarium used to sit on its wrought-iron stand.

Mabel had been right about how eager the tourists were to buy his carvings, and he was busier – and happier – than he'd ever been in his life. It even made up for having to occasionally play the psychic voodoo witch doctor, though he'd never admit he was beginning to enjoy the role.

All in all, it was the best job he'd ever had.

Coming from Filidh Publishing in fall 2013.

Phineas Marshal returns in:

Voodoo

Mystery Tour

Turn the page for a sneak peek….

ONE

Morning mist curled and rolled over the glassy surface of Cricket Lake. It blurred and softened the spiky tree line on the far shore.

Phineas Marshal sat on the bench that ran the length of his porch, staring out over the water. The house faced the lake so he could keep an eye on it while he drank his morning coffee.

His hands were starting that third-cup jitter but he'd needed that extra jolt to keep him alert. He'd been up for hours – another nightmare. He'd leaped out of bed and had run out onto the porch to stare out at the lake, his eyes aching until they'd adjusted to the darkness and he could see that there was nothing there. No green glow. No glow of any kind – as usual. He'd then repeated out loud the four words that had become a mantra:

"I drowned the bogeyman." It hadn't sounded as funny as it usually did, but then again it was easier to laugh at monsters in the light of day.

Phin took a sip of his coffee and grimaced. It had cooled. He drank the rest in one gulp and got up to start another pot. Before stepping through the door and into the kitchen he glanced over his shoulder at the calm lake. The mist was dissipating quickly, tearing itself into tendrils that drifted upward and dissolved in the first rays of the sun.

He shuddered and turned on the light, squinting in the harsh glow of the overhead fluorescents. The kitchen was utilitarian and spare. Shiny aluminum appliances along one wall, a simple wooden table and two chairs, and the minimum amount of dishes he had been able to get away with.

The fresh coffee was finishing its last drip when he heard a quiet knock. He glowered at the door, annoyed at the early intrusion, then smelled the distinctive odor of pipe smoke wafting through the open window.

Tobias Reef.

The older man had moved into one of the four cabins next to Phin's house two weeks ago to write his memoirs. Phin had rolled his eyes when he'd heard, imagining ridiculous prose and exaggerated exploits, but Mabel claimed she remembered his face from an old news program – a journalist caught in the middle of civil war, and four years in a cell the size of a closet.

Phin liked Tobias and was glad he'd put on a fresh pot. "Hope you like your coffee black," he said as he opened the door. "The cream is at that chunky stage that doesn't look pretty in something you plan to drink."

"Black is fine. Cream doesn't do my innards any favours."

"You sound like Mabel."

"If you're referring to the diminutive woman's charm and humour, then I accept that as a compliment."

They carried their mugs outside and sipped their coffee in companionable silence, watching swallows skim the lake's surface for their breakfasts.

"Is it true you were a prisoner of war?"

"Is it true you're a fortune teller and can call forth ghosts?"

Phin scowled and gulped most of his coffee, gasping at the too-hot brew, much to Tobias' amusement.

"It would seem we've both got touchy issues." Tobias reached into a pocket and drew out a wrinkled pouch of fragrant leaves. He re-filled his pipe and tamped the tobacco down with a yellowed thumb.

"How do you like your cabin?"

"Oh, it'll do," Tobias said distractedly. He struck a wooden match and held the flame to the bowl of his pipe, drawing steadily until the packed tobacco glowed and spit orange sparks. He squinted against the smoke that curled up toward his eyes.

"A lot of people put a lot of work into building these cabins," Phin said, with what he hoped was a casual air of not caring either way.

"It's a cabin," Tobias countered. "I've rented dozens of them, and they've all been more or less the same." He slid a sidelong glance at Phin and the corner of his mouth twitched. "Four walls, smell of cedar – usually by a lake, or at least near enough to matter. No different than any other cabin I've ever been in." He clamped the pipe stem between his teeth and drew fragrant smoke into his mouth, savouring the taste before inhaling fully. "From what I hear, you slapped them together just in time for tourist season."

"There was a demand to be filled – at least that's what Mabel claimed." Phin glared into his empty mug. "She had this list of people who were waiting to rent by the week." He nodded at his neighbour's mug and Tobias drained it before handing it over.

Phin set the two mugs on the porch railing and ducked inside again. He snagged a cardboard baker's box from the counter and brought it out along with the coffee pot.

"And how do your innards like muffins?" He held out the box to Tobias, who grinned and helped himself to two.

About the Author

Monique Jacob has been writing stories and songs since her first

tortured-teen ramblings and she's never managed to outgrow the habit. She stares at the walls an awful lot and has yet to convince anyone that this is when she's working the hardest.

Born in Germany, Monique has moved 29 times in 9 cities and now makes her home on the West Coast, somewhere between Seattle and Vancouver – as the crow flies. Tye Dye Voodoo is her first novel, one of many. Follow Monique on Facebook and at moniquejacob.ca

Photo by Geoectomy Photography